# Mikhail's House

*House of Lustz, Book 1*

*Ciara St James*

# Copyright



ISBN: 978-1-955751-65-0

Printed in the United States of America
Editing by Mary Kern @ Ms. K Edits
Book cover by Kiwi Kreations

# Warning

This book is intended for adult readers. It explores the world of kink, and some topics may not be to everyone's taste. Subjects considered taboo by some will be explored. It contains foul language and adult situations and may even include things such as stalkers, assault, torture, and murder, which may trigger some readers. Sexual situations are graphic. If these themes aren't what you like to read or you find them upsetting, this book isn't for you. There is no cheating or cliffhangers, and it has a HEA.

# Dedication

There are so many people I want to thank for making this book, this series possible. To start, all the readers who have read my other books and encouraged me to continue to write and to expand the genres I write. They always encourage me to try new ones and support me when I do.

Then there is my husband, Trident. He was a driving force behind my ever putting words on paper, and he continues to support and encourage me every day. He's my assistant, driver, post office runner, the one I bounce ideas off of, and so much more. Thank you, and I love you!

Finally, I can't thank those who have helped me learn what I don't know about the world of kink enough. They have been invaluable in helping me. I continue to learn myself with every book. It is a fascinating and wonderful world. Thank you to the wonderful author, Elle Sparrow and to my loving friend, Brea.

Please note that any inaccuracies are unintended. I have done extensive research in the hopes of representing the fetish/kink lifestyle accurately and without judgment. Of course, this book is fiction, so some tiny liberties may be taken. I hope you enjoy it. I'm so excited and nervous to present to you, the House of Lustz!

xx,
Ciara

## House of Lustz:

Mikhail w/ Tajah
Hoss w/ TBD
Reuben w/ TBD

# Reading Order

**For Dublin Falls Archangel's Warriors MC (DFAW), Hunters Creek Archangel's Warriors MC (HCAW), Iron Punishers MC (IPMC), Dark Patriots (DP), & Pagan Souls of Cherokee MC (PSCMC),**

Terror's Temptress DFAW 1
Savage's Princess DFAW 2
Steel & Hammer's Hellcat DFAW 3
Menace's Siren DFAW 4
Ranger's Enchantress DFAW 5
Ghost's Beauty DFAW 6
Viper's Vixen DFAW 7
Devil Dog's Precious DFAW 8
Blaze's Spitfire DFAW 9
Smoke's Tigress DFAW 10
Hawk's Huntress DFAW 11
Bull's Duchess HCAW 1
Storm's Flame DFAW 12
Rebel's Firecracker HCAW 2
Ajax's Nymph HCAW 3
Razor's Wildcat DFAW 13
Capone's Wild Thing DFAW 14
Falcon's She-Devil DFAW 15
Demon's Hellion HCAW 4
Torch's Tornado DFAW 16
Voodoo's Sorceress DFAW 17

Reaper's Banshee IPMC 1
Bear's Beloved HCAW 5
Outlaw's Jewel HVAW 6
Undertaker's Resurrection DP 1
Agony's Medicine Woman PSCMC 1
Ink's Whirlwind IP 2
Payne's Goddess HCAW 7
Maverick's Kitten HCAW 8
Tiger & Thorn's Tempest DFAW 18
Dare's Doll PSC 2
Maniac's Imp IP 3
Tank's Treasure HCAW 9
Blade's Boo DFAW 19
Law's Valkyrie DFAW 20
Gabriel's Retaliation DP 2
Knight's Bright Eyes PSC 3
Joker's Queen HCAW 10
Bandit & Coyote's Passion DFAW 21
Sniper's Dynamo & Gunner's Diamond DFAW 22
Slash's Dove HCAW 11
Lash's Hurricane IP 4
Spawn's She-Wolf IP 5
Griffin's Revelation DP 3

**For Ares Infidels MC**

Sin's Enticement AIMC 1
Executioner's Enthrallment AIMC 2
Pitbull's Enslavement AIMC 3
Omen's Entrapment AIMC 4
Cuffs' Enchainment AIMC 5
Rampage's Enchantment AIMC 6
Wrecker's Ensnarement AIMC 7
Trident's Enjoyment AIMC 8

Fang's Enlightenment AIMC 9
Talon's Enamorment AIMC 10
Ares Infidels in NY AIMC 11
Phantom's Emblazonment AIMC 12
Saint's Enrapturement AIMC 13
Phalanx & Bullet's Entwinement AIMC 14
Torpedo's Entrancement AIMC 15
Boomer's Embroilment AIMC 16

**For O'Sheerans Mafia**

Darragh's Dilemma
Cian's Complication
Aidan's Ardor

**House of Lustz**

Mikhail's Playhouse

Please follow Ciara on Facebook. For information on new releases & to catch up with Ciara, go to www.ciara-st-james.com or www.facebook.com/ciara.stjames.1 or https://www.facebook.com/groups/342893626927134 (Ciara St James Angels) or https://www.facebook.com/groups/923322252903958 (House of Lustz by Ciara St James) or https://www.facebook.com/groups/140489416021085 1 (O'Sheeran Mafia by Ciara St James)

# Mikhail: Prologue-
# Five Weeks Ago

Walking away from everything that made me who I was, everything that gave me satisfaction, happiness, and purpose, was damn hard. I almost didn't do it, but I knew I had to. It wasn't like it was forever. I just needed a break so I could regain my former enjoyment and excitement for all I'd built. I knew I didn't want to turn my back on it permanently, but I wondered how long it would take for me to get back to being the old me.

Staring at the sand and the waves washing up on the beach, I had to chuckle. This was the last place anyone who knew me would ever expect to find me. Maybe that was the point. Something had changed. It had been coming for a while, but I resisted acknowledging it. I worked even more. I played harder, but eventually, I knew none of it was helping. If anything, those things felt like they were making it worse.

Reuben, my friend and assistant manager, had sat me down and told me I had to take this break before I broke. He could see it, even though I thought I'd been successful at hiding my discontentment. I was no longer loving my life's work, the House of Lustz, or the life I led.

The House of Lustz had been my brainchild years ago. I wanted to bring people like me to a safe place where they could explore and express themselves sexually, but within the confines of absolute consent. There was nothing more important than consent unless it was communication, trust, and respect. I had been tired of the reaction I received when people found out what I wanted when it came to sex, or I should say, what I needed. For a long time, I thought I was in the minority and there was something wrong with me. I tried to suppress my needs and urges, but eventually, I had to let them out. I did my research and found those who would explain this life and mentor me. It was due to them that I made the decision not to hide who I was and to create my very own club.

Some called it a sex club, others a kink or fetish club. I called it home in a lot of ways. It was a house of freedom for me and many other like-minded individuals. To say Nashville, Tennessee, didn't quite know what to make of it when I began the process of getting it established was putting it mildly. The city tried to prevent me from opening the club, but they couldn't get the backing to stop me. I guess there were more people out there who were either into the various things I wanted to promote or they wanted to be.

After getting the place renovated and then opened, I found out it was a healthy combination of both. Some who came were at various stages in their discovery of the lifestyle and all it entailed. Others were at the beginning and wondering if their urges and thoughts could be given life at my club. I listened and made sure to offer them a safe place to explore and engage in the many forms of play, although I didn't ever tolerate anything that was borderline lethal, illegal, or actually non-consensual. Anyone coming in and found not to follow the rules was thrown out and not allowed to return.

To help ensure the least amount of problems, because you couldn't weed out every problem person ahead of time no matter how thorough you were, I had them undergo an extensive background check and an online training session before allowing them through the doors. It took me several tries before I found someone who could do what I wanted when it came to those background checks. It was the weirdest thing when one of my patrons, a biker no less, became friendly with me. He underwent the process himself and then asked who I used to conduct those checks.

I told him, and he gave me more ideas for things to delve into. The next time I saw him, he offered one of his biker brothers to be my investigator. Apparently, his brother did the same thing and more for his club. Payne had done me a huge favor that day. I've paid Outlaw ever since. I was fine with him fitting them in when he could between his other duties to the Hunters Creek Archangel's Warriors. They would always come first, and I understood why.

It was kinda weird to have Outlaw know so much about my patrons, yet he wasn't one himself. He said he'd leave it to Payne, although he did come once to watch what went on. He hadn't been judgmental. It just wasn't his thing, even though I had no problem seeing him being a Dom. Now, Payne enjoyed his time at Lustz immensely. Well, he had until he met Jayla. All it took was one look at her, and he fell hard.

Of course, it hadn't been easy for him to win her heart. His own stupidity almost ruined his chances with her but, luckily, she was a forgiving person, and she gave him a second chance. They were now married and had a son, Storm. I laughed when he told me the name they gave him. It was so appropriate for his son. I had no doubt when he got older, he'd be like a storm. God help them.

They'd been together for just over a year and a half. They gave every indication they were damn happy. They rarely came to Lustz, and when they did, they only played together and it was always in private. Payne was too possessive to let others see Jayla. Before her, he never cared who watched him and his partners, but he claimed it made a difference when the woman was yours and you loved her. Or at least it did for him. I personally didn't know. I'd never had a woman in my life who I felt that way about.

Sure, I'd played with several over extended periods of time, but it had never been exclusive for me, and I played with others at the same time. The thought that I would find someone and turn into a possessive man made me snort. It would never happen, just like it would never happen that I'd settle down with one woman. There were too many out there not to enjoy them. I wouldn't call myself a manwhore. It wasn't like I was with a different one every night of the week. I was selective, but I did enjoy women, and my house gave me ample ones who were more than willing to play the games I enjoyed. That wasn't to say I wasn't happy for Payne. I was, and he deserved it.

The chatter of excited voices and shrill screams roused me from my thoughts. I glanced around and saw a crowd of beachgoers coming toward me. They had a bunch of kids in their group—time for me to go. I was here to relax, not to hear a bunch of noisy kids. I stood to gather my things. I didn't dislike children. I just wasn't in the mood to be around them right now.

I thought I was going to escape unscathed, but I was wrong. Just as I started to walk away from my spot, a woman detached herself from the group and came toward me. I knew that look. She was on the prowl and thought she'd found a likely candidate to give her a good time. Now, typically, I might be willing to give her a chance to show me if she could handle me, but for some reason, she stirred nothing in me. Zilch.

It wasn't because she wasn't attractive, because she was. She was showing her body off in a barely there bikini. It hardly covered the vital parts. Rather than appreciating it, my first thought was, *What the hell was she doing dressed like that when she was with a bunch of kids, and a few of them were teenage boys?* They were drooling over her. I wanted to tell her to cover up. Her path wouldn't let me bypass her, and I refused to divert my course. I ran from no one, so I steeled myself to hear what she had to say and to send her off nicely to find another victim.

She gave me a flirty look as she came to stand in front of me, blocking my way, although I could walk around her. I didn't encourage her by smiling back.

I wasn't looking for company. I didn't say anything. I waited for her to say something. I bet it would be original, not.

"Hi, my name is Tammy. You shouldn't hurry off yet. It's a beautiful day. Why don't you join me? We can go further down the beach, which is more private if the kids are too much. I bet we could have a great afternoon. Who knows? We might just become friends," she said as she ran her gaze up and down my body.

I was dressed for the beach, which meant all I had on at the moment was a pair of swimming trunks and sandals. My towel, book, and a large container of water were in one hand, and my phone was in my trunk pocket. I knew what she saw. I wasn't vain or anything, but I knew I was pleasing to the eye for most women.

I might be in my mid-forties, but I'd kept myself in shape. It wasn't just a matter of looking good but more about staying healthy. I enjoyed life and wanted to live as long as I could but still be able to have a quality of life. I ran five days a week, minimum, worked out with weights, and did other exercises three to four days a week. In addition, I had some tattoos, and those always seemed to fascinate women and some men.

"Thanks for the invitation, but I've had enough of the beach for the day. I have plans and need to get back to my place to get ready. Enjoy the water and sun, though," I told her politely.

She frowned a tiny bit, then smiled again. She stepped closer. Damn, she was gonna be one of those—one who wouldn't want to take no for an answer. I could see in her eyes she wasn't used to being turned down. I didn't mind a woman knowing what she wanted and going after it, but I hated it when one got pushy. The Dom in me would discipline them if they were with me or mine, but since she wasn't and wouldn't be, I reined in my automatic tendency to issue an order. Besides, that only worked after a lot of communication and agreements on boundaries. Again, not happening today or with her.

"Oh, come on. Surely, you can skip whatever it is to stay with me. You look like you're on vacation, which means you shouldn't have anything urgent to do. If you do, it'll negate your relaxation. I say go with the flow. I have no doubt we can help each other relax and enjoy our time even more. After all, vacations are meant to let go and have fun." Her expression became more predatory as she blatantly licked her bottom lip and batted her lashes at me. I wanted to laugh. She wasn't winning me with those moves, and she looked ridiculous.

She was on the beach, yet her hair was perfectly styled and she had on a full face of makeup along with fake lashes. Jesus, talk about a turnoff. Don't get me wrong, I didn't mind a woman wearing makeup as long as it was tasteful, but she should also be comfortable enough to go bare-faced and show her natural beauty. This one was made up like she was about to go out on the town for the night at a club.

"I said I have plans, and no, they can't be changed. I can see to my own relaxation, thank you. Now, excuse me." This time, I did step a couple of paces to the side and moved to pass her. I was hungry, and I needed a shower. After that, I'd decide what I would do next. I didn't actually have anything planned.

As I passed her, she grabbed onto my arm. I halted and stared down at her and her hand. She didn't take the hint. God, was she stupid? I let my predator side peek out a tiny bit as I barked at her. "Let go of my arm. Now!"

Her eyes widened, and she gasped, letting go of me as if she'd been burned. Then she stepped away from me. "I-I'm sorry. I didn't mean to upset you. I'd just like to get to know you, that's all. What's your name?"

"I don't want to get to know you. Someone should've taught you not to touch unless you've been invited to, and you weren't. I'm not looking for a plaything," I told her gruffly before walking away. This time, she didn't try to stop me.

As I got to my car, I chided myself. What the hell was wrong with me? I hadn't been with a woman in more weeks than I could count. I was on vacation. I should be having fun. No one knew me here. There were no expectations of me. It was a golden opportunity, but I had zero desire to play. I had already been here a week, and I was no closer to resolving this melancholy, or maybe it was a midlife crisis. Hell, I didn't know. If I didn't know the cause, how the hell could I fix it? I refused to go back home until I got my answers. I prayed it wouldn't take me forever to do it.

# Tajah: Prologue-Three Weeks Ago

I was so nervous my hands were sweating, and so were my armpits. Good thing I had put on extra deodorant. On top of sweating, my heart raced, and I was weak in the knees. Wouldn't it be humiliating if I passed out? As I stared at the building I was about to enter, I gave myself another pep talk. I think this was the tenth one today. I wouldn't chicken out. This was an opportunity I might never get again. Carver had gone to a lot of trouble to get me in, and it had taken me weeks of begging before he'd do it. If I backed out now, I'd never get him to help me again, and I'd probably never hear the end of it from him.

Taking a deep breath, I stiffened my spine and pasted a pleasant smile on my face as I followed him to the entrance. There was a doorman who was big and intimidating. The sight of him made me want to run in the opposite direction. He nodded to Carver while he eyed me.

"Hey, Tuck, it's good to see ya, man. This is Tajah. She should be on the list. Reuben was supposed to add her," Carver told him.

Tuck pulled out a tablet and scrolled through it

for several moments before nodding his head. "Here she is. Have a good time, and welcome to the House of Lustz, Tajah," he told me with a smile.

I was surprised it was a friendly one. Lesson one, his fierce persona, hid a nice side, and not everyone would automatically leer at me like I was a piece of meat. Carver had done his best to prepare me for what I was about to see and experience, but he also said I had to see most of it to understand.

"Thank you, Tuck, I plan to," I said back automatically.

Carver reached back and took my hand to lead me inside. He gripped it tightly. Just inside the door, we stopped at a small alcove where there was a woman sitting. She had a variety of colored beads and lengths of silver wire to make bracelets on the table. She smiled and nodded to Carver. He'd explained those to me. Each color indicated what you were willing to do. He had his own already.

He told her I was there to observe only and wouldn't be participating in anything. She gave me one with a single, orange-colored bead on it, and I was told to wear it on my right wrist. She cautioned me to keep it on that one at all times. Otherwise, it would be seen as me being available for anything, anytime. I hurried to put it on the right side. Carver, the asshole, laughed at me. I gave him the finger, which made the woman giggle.

He kept grinning as he led me through another door, and we were finally inside the actual House of

Lustz. I gazed around, trying not to gape, but it was hard. I had tried to imagine what it would be like, but it was nothing like I pictured.

I realized I was guilty of thinking it would be pitch dark and look sleazy and dirty, kinda like the strip clubs I'd seen. Not that I spent a lot of time in those, but I'd been in a few. While the lights were low, it wasn't dark. This first floor was set up like a very nice high-end bar. The actual bar ran an impressive length of one wall. There was seating all along it. Plus, there were a variety of other seating options, tables scattered in another section, and a large dance floor. A DJ was playing music. People were talking, drinking, laughing, and even dancing. It was like most of the nightclubs I'd been to.

Carter turned to me. "Do you want a drink to help you relax, or would you like to go on a tour first? We'll be meeting with Reuben later to have him go over some things."

"You mean there's more than the online orientation I did?"

"Yep. Nothing to worry about, Taj. If you've changed your mind, just tell me. I'll take you home." He sounded like he was hopeful I'd say yes.

"No, I want to stay."

He sighed, then waited for my answer to his offer of a drink. It was a bit too soon to start doing that, and I wanted to keep all my wits about me, so I shook my head and told him, "No, I don't want anything, but you can if you want."

"Nah, I can wait. Tour it is." He took my hand again and began to weave us through the people. As he did, he had to yell to be heard as he pointed out various things to me. I worked to absorb it all. I didn't want to forget a single detail.

After he finished showing me the highlights of the first floor and explained how it was more for relaxation than viewing or playing, we went up a flight of stairs to the second floor. This was where the real stuff happened, according to him. You could observe like I was about to do, or you could participate. It was dimly lit, too, but there were areas that were brighter. There were raised stages, for lack of a better word. I saw people on most of them and they were doing a variety of things. It was much harder not to stare or show astonishment up here. I knew enough not to react in a way that would come across as kink-shaming someone. Whatever got people off was their business. As long as all parties consented and it didn't involve underage kids, then go for it.

As we wandered, Carver pointed out a variety of doors. "Those are the fantasy rooms. Each has a different theme, I guess you call it. The theme is on the door. For example, this one is set up for impact play. Some aren't comfortable performing in front of others, so they go in those for privacy. You can open the privacy screen on the windows and let people watch, too. There are a few you'll find that don't have windows at all."

I wanted to read all the signs to find out precisely what themes there were. Before I could, he tugged on my hand and took me over to a couple of leather chairs.

There were numerous leather chairs and couches scattered everywhere. Some had people sitting and talking, but others engaged in more amorous pursuits. I didn't know where to look.

He reached out to lightly grip my chin, so I had to look at him. "Hey, you're doing fine. You're allowed to watch, Taj. If they didn't want you to, they wouldn't be doing it out in the open. As long as you remember what I told you, no one will get upset or offended. I'm gonna send Reuben a text to let him know where we are."

"Okay."

As he typed out a quick text, I watched a couple across the way. They were in a passionate embrace, and it appeared they'd be moving into a much more passionate one soon. When Carver was done, he talked to me more about the club. It wasn't long, though, until Reuben approached us. He wasn't wearing a suit, which surprised me. He smiled and held out his hand to Carver, and they shook. He then smiled at me.

"Hi, Tajah, it's good to see you again. Are you ready?"

I nodded. He held out a crooked arm. I placed my hand on it. *Here went nothing. Let the real adventure begin.* At least I'd met him before. I had to come in and be interviewed by him before he would even consider letting me go through the process to gain entry. I had to explain to him what I was expecting to get out of the experience and why. When I was done that day, he seemed to be all for it, which made my life much easier. I think Carver had hoped he'd say no.

As Reuben and Carver showed me around, I began to relax just a tiny bit. It was still nerve-racking, but I thought I could get used to it. All I had to do was remember why I was here and the end goal I was trying to achieve was.

# Mikhail: Chapter 1

My six-week hiatus was at an end. I wished I could say I'd figured out my problem and corrected it, but I hadn't, at least not entirely. What I did figure out, I was hesitant to say aloud even to myself, let alone tell anyone else. I didn't want to believe it, so I was ignoring it a while longer. Not the best course of action, but I'd run with it until I couldn't suppress it any longer.

A few good things I did walk away with from my vacation were I had a great tan, I'd read a ton of books on my to-be-read list, I ate a bunch of great seafood, and I now had an appreciation for the beach and the ocean that I never had before.

Reuben had picked me up from the airport on Saturday. He told me I looked like a beach bum with my tan, in my casual clothes, and that my hair had grown out a bit. I hadn't bothered to keep it trimmed while I was gone. I told him to kiss my ass. The bastard just laughed at me and said he didn't swing that way, so stop propositioning him. Asshole. I wondered how we were even friends. Well, not really. We were both assholes, so that was probably why.

We hung out for a good chunk of the day and had dinner together before he went to work. While we did, he asked me if I'd discovered what was wrong with me. I avoided giving him a clear answer. I waved it off and told him it had been exhaustion and a slight case of burnout, but I was over it now. I hadn't taken a real vacation in years. I wasn't sure if he believed me. He'd given me a probing look but didn't outright call me a liar. I didn't delude myself into thinking this meant he was satisfied. He'd hit me with it again.

On Sunday, I got ready to go back to work, which meant I got my hair trimmed first. My barber usually didn't work on Sundays, but he made an exception for certain customers, and I was one of them. I always made sure to tip him well for doing it. After he had me back to looking like myself, I had groceries delivered, and I made sure my suits for the week were ready to go. Sandra had picked up the ones I had at the dry cleaners and delivered them to my place while I was gone. Thank God I had her to clean and run errands for me. I could keep the surfaces clean and picked up, but I hated to do the more in-depth cleaning, so I hired her to do it. If I'd told her what I wanted, she would've had the groceries ordered, too, but I hadn't known what I was in the mood for.

As I made my way to work Monday evening, I didn't have far to go. Open to the public were the first two floors of the House of Lustz. The third floor was my private domain. Not only was my private office up there, but so was my home. I had a kick-ass apartment. Some might think it would be too noisy, but I'd made sure it was well soundproofed. I didn't hear anything from below, and they couldn't hear me from above. There was way more square footage than one guy needed, but I loved it. The extra bedrooms and bathrooms were there if they were needed. There was only one area I was disappointed with because it didn't get used. It was my personal playroom.

I had many of my favorite things in it, but I'd never felt right about bringing a woman up here to play. It sounded ridiculous, but it was the truth. What I was waiting for, I didn't know. Every time I thought about doing it, my gut told me no, so I didn't. Maybe I should ignore my gut next time and go for it.

When I played, it was always down in the club. We either did scenes in front of others or occasionally in a private room if we weren't feeling it. My last partner and I had parted ways three months ago. I wasn't meeting her needs, and she wasn't meeting mine. There were no hard feelings, but the thought of finding someone else filled me with dread.

Sure, if all I wanted was sex, there were plenty of women and men who were willing to oblige me. It had become a challenge for some to see if they could get the owner of Lustz to be with them even once. I wasn't interested in that game. The idea of starting over again and trying to find someone to start the process with made me cringe. Not wanting to think about it, I pushed the thought to the back of my mind right before the elevator opened and I walked out. It was only accessible to the third floor via a fingerprint scanner, so there was no worry about anyone accidentally or on purpose wandering into my private space.

It was a Monday night, but that didn't mean the place was quiet or empty. Yes, Thursday through Saturday were our peak nights, but there were always people coming when they could, so the other nights of the week did more than a decent amount of business. I was anxious to see how everything was going. I wanted to see my baby, which was what I called Lustz. I was starting on the first floor, and then I'd work my way to the second. First stop was the front door.

People greeted me as I passed them. I smiled and nodded or called back a word of greeting, but I didn't stop. There would be time for talking later. I stopped at the table in the alcove where our greeter sat. The greeter was there to welcome people who got past the security doorman, to answer any questions, and to issue the color-coded bracelets. Tonight, it was Laura. She'd been with me for a couple of years now. She was my full-time greeter.

She smiled at me. "Hey, you're back. How was your vacation?"

"Yeah, I'm back. It was a much-needed break. It's good to see you, Laura. How's it going tonight? Any problems tonight or while I was gone?"

She kept smiling, but rolled her eyes at me. "Come on, Mikhail, you know, if there had been while you were gone, Reuben would've handled it and told you all about it already. As for tonight, it's been quiet. I'm good."

"Damn, I guess that means I'm not needed. If you all did fine without me and Reuben handled everything great, I'm obsolete," I grumbled, only half-jokingly.

"You know that's not true. Just because Reuben is more than competent doesn't mean you're not needed. If you left, so would others, especially some of the patrons. They come here to see the scary Russian who runs this place. They think you're in the mob, you know," she teased me.

I grinned at her, but I didn't say anything or deny it. What could I say? They weren't off in their assumptions in a way. No, I wasn't part of any mob, especially the Russian mob, the Bratva, the brotherhood, but I had connections to it which only a few people knew. My cousins on my dad's side were all in the brotherhood. My dad had been the oddball who hadn't followed them into that life. I was thankful as hell he hadn't.

That didn't mean I had no contact with the ones who were, just that they knew not to involve me in their business. It didn't change the fact they were family, and I treated them as such as long as they didn't mess with me. They learned a long time ago, my life and work, my club, were off fucking limits. Anyone trying to mess with me or it would find out how bloody I could get. Fortunately, they listened and, so far, other mobsters thinking to muscle in on my thing had stayed away when they found out I had the connection. As long as they did, I was happy.

I made sure to laugh at what she said and shake my head. "I know. Just because I have a Russian name, they assume the worst. You would think people would know better. Oh well, that's their problem. If it brings people into the club who behave, I'm fine with it. Let one of us know if you have any trouble. I hate to run, but I've got a ton to check on. I'll see you later."

"You know where to find me," she said with a wink.

Chuckling, I nodded, then went out the door to the outside. Tonight, Hoss was working as the doorman slash security guy. He lived up to his nickname. The guy was built like a damn Mack truck. I wasn't a small man by anyone's standards, but he put me to shame. He looked me up and down when he saw me. His stern expression didn't budge, but I didn't expect it to, nor did I take it as an affront. He was always a very stoic guy. I raised a brow at him. I was waiting to see what he'd say. I didn't have to wait long.

"Hmm, it looks like you survived in one piece. Great tan. Did you get yourself straightened out?"

I hadn't told him anything about my issues before I left. However, the fact he knew told me how intuitive he was. I knew Reuben wouldn't have said anything to him. Anyone thinking Hoss was just a dumb musclehead was in for a shock. The guy was Mensa-level smart. He did this as a way to de-stress from his job as a freaking owner and CEO of a highly successful company. Yeah, not what you'd expect. I decided not to insult him by lying.

"I did survive, and I relaxed, but I can't say I've solved my dilemma yet. But I might be onto something. I need more time to figure it out. How've you been? Keeping people straight while I was gone? Did you have to get rough with anyone?"

"Hell no, it was boring as hell. I mean, would it kill for at least one dumbass to come along and make my day? I think we've scared them too much, boss. Our reputations precede us."

I grinned at him, which made him crack a slight grin. "Well, sorry to fuck up your enjoyment. I'll see what I can do to make you happy. I can't afford to lose you."

He shook his head. "You're not going to lose me. I just like something every once in a while to break up the monotony. You know. You're the same way, so don't pretend you're not. As for your dilemma, I hope you find your answers soon. It's not good to see you like you have been. Well, I hate to run you off, but people are coming, which means I have to get back to work before the boss fires me," he said with a bigger grin and a wink.

I slapped him on the shoulder and muttered softly to him, "As if you have to worry about that. Have a good one. Call if you need me." He nodded as he turned to give a stern eye to those coming up to the door. He had his tree-trunk arms folded, which made them look even more prominent—the bastard.

I went back inside, and as I passed Laura, I warned her she had incoming. Then, I re-entered the main part of the first floor. The area was dimly lit, but you could still see well enough. The bar was the brightest-lit part, and there were a decent number of people at it, either sitting on stools or standing to place their drink orders.

Scanning the area as I leisurely walked through it, I noted the people sitting at the tables and those already on the dance floor dancing to the music the DJ was pumping out. I wasn't looking for anyone in particular but rather for anything out of place or signs of trouble either happening or brewing. I could usually spot the troublemakers before they got started. If that happened, a friendly word was dropped in their ears. If they ignored it and did something anyway, they'd been warned, and they would be put out. If things got a bit rough, oh well, they should've listened.

I didn't see anything untoward, so I kept going. I checked in with the bartenders, the waitstaff, and the floor manager. Each floor had one, and they reported to Reuben and me if they had issues or concerns. In addition were the tour guides who helped orient newbies to the club along with our attendants. The attendants were there for questions, to help find things, get something fixed, and wipe down the equipment in between people. You know, all the unglamorous parts. We also had roving security.

I wanted people to have fun and to enjoy themselves but it had to be within the rules. This had to be a safe environment for everyone. Anyone breaking those rules, depending on the infraction, might get a second chance, but others could be gone on the first offense. We worked to handle the issues ourselves, but sometimes, we had to get the local police involved. We tried to avoid it so we didn't get a reputation for trouble, although some cops felt just by the fact it was a kink club, we were automatically trouble. Tolerance wasn't universal.

Once I said hello to all the staff on the first floor, I went up to the second. Here was where the real action was. I was proud of the entertainment we provide our patrons. In addition to them being able to do scenes in front of others or to have private sessions, we offered tutorials, or maybe demonstrations was a better word, and shows.

Those who were considered "experts" in different types of kinks were allowed, with permission, to demonstrate for the crowds and answer questions. Payne was one of those experts. Another reason I was sad to see him no longer here. He'd brought in the crowds when he demonstrated. I wasn't bragging when I said I did the same.

At other times, not every night, we had "shows" where we had people who worked for us doing erotic displays or dances. They didn't engage in sex, just in titillation. They were in demand from many of the patrons. The patrons came here not only for those and the freedom but also for the knowledge we would do our absolute best to protect them and their privacy.

I should've known things were going too well, and it was about to go wrong. I groaned softly and had to fight not to turn and go the other way. I wasn't a man who ran from much and I could stand up to the biggest and most badass guy even if I knew I was gonna get my ass whipped, but the person coming toward me made me want to hide. I had to steel myself to stand there and face the train coming at me head-on.

Sylvia came slithering up to me. God, why couldn't she stop? I wasn't now nor ever going to have her as my submissive or anything else in my life. Not happening. When she first approached me about it, I'd been polite and pretended not to pick up on her hints. When she progressed to asking me outright, I told her I had someone and wasn't looking to add anyone else, which at the time was true. Once Tessa and I parted ways a few months ago, Sylvia had become relentless. I hadn't missed her bullshit for the past six weeks.

She was dressed to be seen. She wasn't a bad-looking woman, and she showed off her body in the skintight, sexy outfits she liked to wear. Tonight, she was dressed in a black leather catsuit. It was so tight, I wasn't sure how she could move or breathe. The stilettos she had on were so tall, she pranced like a newborn giraffe. I wondered how soon she'd fall on her ass. She couldn't walk worth a shit in them. I smothered my laugh.

"Master M, darling, I'm so happy you're back. It's been terrible here without you. Please, tell me you're doing a demo tonight. I can be your partner. You know I've been waiting forever for us to do them together," she purred as she came to a stop about a foot in front of me. Her hand came out to rest on my chest. I pushed it away before she made contact. She knew the rules.

"Sylvia, I know I haven't been gone so long that you've forgotten the rules for me and everyone else. No touching unless you've been invited to do so. I don't recall you asking or me saying yes."

She pouted out her bottom lip and looked up at me through her lashes. "Oh, come on, don't be like that. Surely you don't expect friends and lovers to abide by that rule?"

"Friends and lovers, it depends, but you're neither. Was there something you needed? If so, one of the Lustz Disciples can help you." Lustz Disciples was the fancy name we gave the attendants.

"Master, when are you going to give me a chance to show you I can be the submissive you need and deserve? I know you haven't replaced Tessa and there's no reason for you to look anywhere but to me. I'll do anything you want. You can take control of me. I want to please you. Don't make me beg," she whined.

That right there was one of the biggest reasons she and I would never scene, let alone do more together. She didn't understand the whole premise of this lifestyle at all. As a Dom, it wasn't about me exerting my control over her to satisfy me. It was about her trusting me enough to gift me with her control temporarily. When that happened, the submissive was the one in control and it was an exchange of power. When it was done correctly, we both got pleasure and our needs met. In her mind, it was all about conquering, which wasn't the case at all. And as much as people tried to educate some, it never stuck.

"The answer is no, just like all the times you've asked before, and it will remain no. You don't understand at all what this life truly means. I'm not being an asshole, just telling the truth. You and I would never fit. Now, this is my first night back and I need to finish checking with my staff and meet with Reuben. Have fun."

I didn't hang around for more of her blathering. I walked off. Usually I wouldn't be that rude to someone who was a patron but, in her case, I had no patience left for her. If she took exception and didn't return, I wouldn't be upset. I ambled off leisurely, although I wanted to run. I saw one of the Disciples so I headed toward him. He was as good of a person to talk to as anyone as I waited to find Reuben.

## Tajah:

Even after three weeks of coming here on and off, I still couldn't get over my awe, surprise, and sometimes my shock, over the things I saw and heard at the House of Lustz. My first night here with Carver had been so much more than I expected. I thought I'd prepared myself with my research and what he shared with me in advance, but I was so wrong. That night opened up a whole new world to me, one I thought I had a basic knowledge of.

Of course, Carver tried all night to get me to change my mind and let him take me home. I refused every time he offered. At one point, I told him if he wanted to leave to do it. He refused to do so and got outraged when I suggested it. After that night, I came a couple more times with him then I told him I was good to go solo. He was stifling me. He'd grumbled and complained but I stuck to my guns so in the end, he did it, but only after making me promise to let Reuben know if I had any trouble or worries while there. It was a promise I gave him.

My biggest problem was that there was so much to see and remember. Luckily for me, I was allowed to take notes. No phones or anything that could record were allowed. This was to ensure everyone's privacy. I know if it was me, I wouldn't want someone recording what I said or taking pictures of what I was doing. We all had to sign nondisclosure agreements as part of our admission process. An NDA was nothing you wanted to fool with.

Being a Monday, it wasn't wall-to-wall people which I found nice. I always felt like I was missing stuff when it was super crowded. It was an occupational hazard to want to see and hear everything. I headed upstairs after getting a soda from the main bar. I wasn't comfortable drinking alcohol while here, especially alone. Others seemed not to have my hang-up. Good for them. I prayed they'd never have reason to regret it. I knew too much about the evil which lurked in the world to forget that rule. It was second nature for me to never accept a drink from someone or leave mine unattended. Hell, I watched the bartenders like a hawk while they made my drinks. I never let a waiter take my order either.

If I didn't do those things, then my dad would roll over in his grave and come back to haunt me. As a career policeman, he'd raised me on the warnings of the awful things that could happen to you, in particular if you were a woman or child. Thinking of him made a wave of nostalgia sweep through me. It had been five years since I lost him and I still miss him so much. He'd been my rock in this sometimes crazy world.

Finding an open seat which was back out of the way but still let me watch a large section of the room, I got comfortable. I liked to start out my night with just people watching and getting a feel for the vibes. Later, I'd walk around and take closer looks at what was happening. Sometimes, I had enough courage to speak to people and ask them questions if they were inclined to talk. I never pushed myself on anyone and I backed off immediately if they said no or gave me any indication, verbal or non-verbal, that they weren't interested. Placing my glass on the nearby table for a minute, I took out my notebook and pen.

I was about a half hour into it when I spotted someone I wanted to avoid at all costs. I winced when I saw him. Damn, why tonight? His club name was Dominus, and I'd meet him my second week here. Most people used a club name, but some didn't. According to him, if it was true, he was a longtime patron of the club. He bragged about how he was friends with the owner and was one of the top Doms here. He also told me his actual name, which was Duncan.

He approached me the first time to ask me to do a scene with him. I showed him my bracelet, which still had only an orange bead on it and declined his offer. I figured he hadn't seen it. It didn't take me long to realize he didn't care what beads I had or didn't have. He was on the prowl. I talked to him for a few minutes then politely excused myself. I thought that would be the end of it. I was wrong.

He kept watching me throughout the night. On subsequent visits when he'd been here, too, he always made a point to come over and talk to me. He continued to hint at, then blatantly spoke about me and him hooking up. He offered to show me the ropes and be my guide. I kept turning him down, but I was tired of him. Everyone else who might ask, despite my bracelet, wasn't pushy about it and would back off as soon as I said no.

I knew if I went to one of the consent monitors or even Reuben, they'd have a word with him, and if he still didn't stop, they'd likely suspend or even ban him. The reason I didn't was I didn't want to make waves and have them think I was more of a problem than I was worth, and I ended up the one to get kicked out. I knew I wasn't their typical patron. My inclusion had been an exception, but I had heard so much about the House of Lustz. I knew I didn't want to experience this life anywhere else, even if I could find a club like them nearby.

He hadn't seen me yet, so I hurried to stand, grabbed my drink and stuff, and moved off to the opposite side of the room. I kept to the shadows and placed people between me and him whenever I could. I breathed a big sigh of relief when I got to a new spot, and he was nowhere in sight. I found another place to sit and got back to why I was there.

It wasn't long before a scene caught my attention, and I got lost watching it. Well, it wasn't really a scene between patrons, as much as it was a show between two of the workers who did them here. I loved discovering they did these at times. This one was two women who were up on a raised platform, dancing to sexy music. They were dressed in provocative costumes with eye masks on. It made them appear sexier and more mysterious. They had great bodies, and they were able to really dance. Watching them caused an idea to pop into my head, so I scribbled it down so I wouldn't forget it later.

It was while I was finishing my scribbling I

discovered I made a mistake. I'd gotten so caught up in watching them I forgot to watch my surroundings for Dominus. His voice from behind me made me shudder. I closed my eyes for a second and silently cursed myself. *Way to go, Tajah. You had to get caught up, and now the goddamn creeper caught you. Idiot.*

"Hello, beautiful. I'm so glad to see you're here tonight. Let's get a drink and then go somewhere we can talk," his oily voice crooned.

Why I bothered to paste a polite smile on my face before swinging around to look at him, I didn't know. Being raised to be polite by a Southern mom was my only excuse. The next time I talked to her, I was telling her so. I got to my feet and put my notebook and pen in my purse. I left my now empty glass on the table. I gave him a vague nod as I faced him. He'd crept up along the wall to get to me.

"Hello, Dominus. I'm sorry, but I'm meeting someone, and they should be here any second. I hope you have a good evening. There are a lot of people here tonight. I know you should be able to find someone to have a drink with. Excuse me, but I've gotta go."

I made sure to step wide when I passed him. He was staring intently at me, and I didn't like the look in his eyes. He was getting less and less patient with my evasions. I knew I'd have to either get blunt and shitty with him soon or swallow my pride and fear of being kicked out and tell someone. I thought I was safe when he didn't respond as I hurried away. I made it maybe five feet before I was grabbed by the shoulders and propelled around and backward. My back hit the wall, and I started up in surprise at him.

He no longer looked pleasant. He was pissed off. His grip was tight and hurt my shoulders. Now he'd done it. Polite Tajah was gone. It was time for him to meet my other side. I might be what some thought as submissive, which was what he saw, but I had another side to me—one which wouldn't take someone laying hands on me. This side came out in defense of others, too. If he'd acted the way he had with me with someone else, and I saw it, I would've been all over him.

"Let go of me right this minute or else," I hissed at him. I jerked my upper body for emphasis, but he held on.

"No, not until you agree to come with me and talk. We need privacy. You've been avoiding me and leading me on a chase for weeks. It's time to stop it. I know you women like the chase and to have a man panting after you, but I'm done. I don't let my subs lead me around by my nose or my cock. You do as I say. It's time you learned how this whole relationship thing goes here."

His audacity made me speechless for a few moments, which gave my temper a chance to rise more. What an absolute fucktard! The way he said it and the look on his face told me he believed the words coming out of his mouth. I might not be an expert on this world, but even I knew enough to know this wasn't what a genuine Dom/sub relationship was, nor did you approach someone you wanted to be your sub or even to do a scene with them in this way. Who in their right mind would ever agree? Only an idiot, and I was no idiot.

I yanked harder, and his grip slipped. I got one arm free as I snapped at him. "Dominus, let me make this crystal clear so even someone as dense as you can understand me. I will never, not in a hundred years, ever have a drink or private conversation with you. I will never agree to do a scene with you, and I most certainly won't ever be in a relationship with you. You have no clue what a dominant and submissive relationship means. I suggest you go educate yourself and make changes to how you approach women or stop coming here. For someone who brags he's so knowledgeable, I don't know why you haven't been kicked out on your ass!" I snapped.

His annoyance turned to rage like a flip of a switch. His face reddened, and a vein in his temple pulsed. God, why didn't I keep my mouth shut until I was away from him? Instead, I let my anger get the better of me, and I had to mouth off while he still had me trapped against the wall. I could scream, but with the noise in here, would anyone hear me, or would they care? He automatically pressed against me, cutting off my ability to knee him in the groin, which was probably why he did it. My arms couldn't raise enough to throw an effective punch, either.

"If you don't let me go, I'll scream this place down," I threatened.

His free hand came up again, and he grabbed my upper arms and shook me. The back of my head bounced off the wall a couple of times. I opened my mouth to scream, but he cut me off by kissing me.

His mouth ground my lips against my teeth painfully. I struggled, but I wasn't getting away. I latched onto his bottom lip with my teeth. He jerked back and swore.

"You goddamn bitch! I'll teach you to—" his words were cut off as he was torn away from me. I cried out as his fingers bit into my arms harder before letting go. The next thing I knew, he was slammed against the wall next to me. A huge guy had a hold of him by the throat. I shakily stumbled to a nearby chair and sank on it. I could hear what my rescuer was saying to him despite the noise.

"You never touch someone in here without their consent," the stranger snarled.

"She's just playing around," Duncan sputtered hoarsely since the scary man still had him by the neck.

The man shook him like he was a rag doll then leaned even closer to him. "Like hell she was playing. I saw the fear on her face and that kiss wasn't returned. You had your hands on her. You fucking assaulted her, Dominus. You know the goddamn rules," my rescuer hissed.

"You need some help over here, boss?" a man asked, surprising me. I recognized him as one of the consent monitors, but I couldn't recall his name at the moment. He wore a worried expression as he examined Dominus, the mystery man, and then me. I needed to get out of here. I stumbled to my feet.

"I-I need to leave," I muttered. I felt sick to my stomach. Before I could get more than a step or two, I was halted by my rescuer's voice and his words.

"Leon, take her up to my office. You stay with her until I get there. Don't you leave her alone for a second. I'll be up as soon as I take care of this one." His tone hardened as he said the last part.

"There's no need for you to take me anywhere. I just want to leave. I didn't mean to cause trouble," I assured them. This would be the last time I was allowed in here, for sure. Damn it. I had no doubt this guy wanted to talk to me so he could kick me out. People were gathered and staring avidly at the scene. I wanted to sink into the floor and disappear. Carver was going to kill me. He warned me not to cause trouble or it would come back on him since he sponsored me. I had to warn him.

My rescuer, "boss", as Leon had called him, turned his head to look at me. He looked me up and down before he said anything. "You're not going anywhere until we talk. Go with Leon. No one will harm you. He's there to protect you. I'll be up as soon as I can. Get her something to drink. Make her comfortable."

His tone told me he wasn't taking no for an answer. Deciding I might as well get my open invitation revoked now, I gave in. I nodded dejectedly, then walked over to Leon. He placed his hand on my back.

"There's no need to touch her!" his boss snapped at him, making me jump.

He sounded angry. Leon's hand fell away immediately. He wasn't doing it to be inappropriate, not like Dominus had. Although, after what just happened, the boss was probably worried about what I would do. It wasn't the club's fault Dominus was an arrogant douchebag. I wasn't planning to cause trouble for them. I'd have to tell my rescuer that when he got to me.

"Come on, we'll take the elevator. It's faster and more private," Leon said kindly. He was frowning as he glanced at me. I gave him a timid smile.

"Okay, lead the way."

As he indicated for me to go ahead of him, I wondered what I did to warrant Dominus to refuse to take no for an answer. Had I inadvertently done or said something to make him think I could be steamrolled into doing what he wanted? I didn't think so, but I was running through all our prior encounters to see if I had. This kept me busy in the elevator. Leon wasn't talking. The ride didn't take long, and before I knew it, I was on another floor of the club. He led me into a vast office and closed the door. I was busy checking out the beautiful space. I could live here and be happy was my inane thought. Had I died and gone to heaven?

# Mikhail: Chapter 2

I was so pissed I could barely see straight or through the red haze my vision seemed to be tinged with. I watched as Leon took the woman with him. I pushed part of my thoughts away as I resumed staring hard at the fucker in my grip. I still had him pinned to the wall by his throat and I wanted to squeeze harder. Fury pumped through my veins.

When I saw him with his hands on her and how he had her pressed against the wall, I knew immediately it wasn't a game they were playing. She didn't want anything to do with him. It was plain as day by the way she was struggling and the frightened way she looked. I couldn't see his face but I recognized his profile. I was rushing to get to them when he kissed her, which only made me angrier. When I saw her bite him, I thought, *Good for her*.

I shook him and made his head bang off the wall the way he had hers. "What the fuck were you thinking, Dominus? You know better than to touch anyone without consent! You've been coming here long enough. I told you what would happen if I got another complaint about you. You don't learn."

I was upset with myself as well as him. I'd given him a second chance after there was a complaint a while back from a woman. She said he was harassing her and wouldn't accept her declining his suggestions that they do scenes together. I'd talked to him immediately, and he'd acted remorseful and swore he would never do it again. Since then, he'd been on his best behavior. What the hell happened?

"Please, Mikhail, I swear it wasn't what it appeared to be. She's been teasing me for weeks. She flirts with me then acts all cold. Tonight, she finally admitted she wanted to do a scene with me, that it was all pretend, and she wanted to role-play. I admit, I got caught up in it and made it too real. We were doing a CNC scene."

CNC stood for consensual non-consent which was when individuals agreed one would become the aggressor and the other was forced to engage in non-consensual behaviors such as a fantasy of being forced to do things, including having sex or being kidnapped. It was all about role-playing. There were several patrons who liked that form of play and dominance and it was allowed as long as all parties agreed. If he was telling me the truth and this was all a game, she was the best actress I ever saw.

"Really? So when I go up to my office and talk to her, will she verify this?"

Uncertainty flickered in his eyes for a moment but he nodded. "Yeah, she should. If not, then it means she's still playing the game. She's been acting like an innocent but she's only acting. It gets her off to do it. She admitted it to me when she asked me to do this. I should've told someone what we were up to so it wouldn't be taken the wrong way. Mikhail, there's no way I'd break the rules. I don't want to get kicked out. You know that."

I'd eased my hand on his neck so he could talk. Now, I slowly lifted it away. I was disinclined to believe him, but until I heard both sides, I had to reserve judgment. Tonight, though, I didn't want to see him again. I was still angry and I wanted to pound on someone. The best course of action was to have him leave, and I'd talk to her then have him come in tomorrow after I calmed down. I moved away from him. He gave me a relieved glance.

"Get the hell out of here. I don't want to see you until I call you. We're going to talk about this, but later. Right now, I have to talk to her."

"Let me talk to her first so she understands it's important she tells you the truth and not continue to play."

"No, you'll stay away from her. Go. If you don't, I'll take it to mean your membership here is at an end," I warned him.

"No! No, that's not necessary. I'll go but please remember, I've been here for a long time and she's not even been here a month."

I didn't say a word back. I just glared at him. He took the hint and scurried toward the stairs. Not taking any chances he might not leave, I followed him. People were watching us with avid interest. Fuck, what a way to welcome me back. I thought tonight would be a chill one and I could enjoy the club. He practically ran down the stairs and to the exit. When he got outside, I watched him hurry to his car. Hoss was watching him, too.

"What happened?" he asked me.

"He and a woman were in an altercation. He claims it was CNC but I don't think it was. Until I talk to her and clear it up, he's banned. Make sure to let everyone know."

"Not a problem. Consider it done. You know, I've never liked his ass. Go talk to the woman and find out if we can kick him to the curb. If we can, I wanna be there when you tell him," Hoss said with an evil grin on his face. I chuckled and gave him a chin lift.

"Deal. Now let me handle this so I can get back to the rest of my work. Has Reuben come in yet?"

"Nope, I think he said it would be after ten. Why? Do you need him? I can give him a call."

Glancing at my watch, I saw it was after nine already. I shook my head no. "Nah, that's fine. I'll talk to him after he gets here. Tell him to come to my office, will ya?"

"I will."

I fist-bumped him, then went back inside. I ignored the whispers and stares as I went to the elevator. I got on and let it take me to my office. As it did, I leaned back and let the other thoughts I'd pushed away earlier surface. They pertained to the woman but in a whole different way. They had to do with the way I'd reacted to her.

Yes, I was enraged to see her pinned to the wall, but along with it was another sensation I had. It was like being punched in the gut. She caught my eye for a whole different reason, too. It was an instant awareness. One I'd never experienced, not this intense. There shouldn't have been any reason she hit me like she did. She wasn't dressed provocatively. In fact, most of her skin was covered unlike a lot of the women in here. Her hair was up in a bun on the top of her head. By the looks of it, she had a good bit of it. I was unable to see her eyes or hair color in the dim light. Her face was delicate and attractive, but then so were a lot of women.

When I walked into my office, I was still trying to decide what it was about her that grabbed my attention so hard. Leon was standing right inside as if guarding the door. I wasn't sure if it was to prevent anyone from getting in or her from leaving. She was pacing on the other end of the room. She whipped around when she heard me. She had her hands clasped together, and they were white with tension.

Leon snapped to attention. I wanted to know where he was tonight and why it took him so long to get to her, but first, I needed to talk to her. "You can go. I'll catch up with you later," I told him.

I heard a soft sigh leave him. He knew what I'd be asking. He gave me a curt nod, then he grabbed the door handle and opened it. I closed it when I entered out of habit. He was out, and the door closed in seconds. Once he was gone, I glanced back at her. She was watching me like a hawk. I needed to put her at ease, but it was hard to think about doing it or anything else because she was affecting me again. Now that I could see her better, it only made me want to get closer to her and to study her more. I cleared my throat.

"Did Leon get you a drink?" I asked as I went to the wet bar I had in my office. I needed one.

"No, he offered, but I don't need one," was her quiet response.

"Are you sure? I'm having one. Please, sit, relax. There's no need to be tense."

"Do you have any bottled water?"

"I do."

I grabbed a bottle out of the fridge under the bar, and then I poured myself a shot of whiskey. Maybe it would settle me down. As I did, I was glad to see her take a seat out of the corner of my vision. I carried the bottle to her. Before handing it over, I set down my glass so I could twist off the cap for her. I noticed she watched me do it. Hmm, she was cautious. Not a bad way to be. I handed it to her and then sat.

"Thank you. May I ask who you are and what happened to Duncan, I mean, Dominus?"

Her first question took me by surprise. Hadn't Leon explained who I was? Hell, why hadn't I done it myself downstairs? No wonder she was so leery. I gave her what I hoped was a soothing smile.

"How rude of me. I assumed Leon told you. I'm Mikhail Ivanova. I'm the owner of this club. As for Dominus, I told him to leave so we could talk. May I ask your name? I've never seen you here before. I assume you're new."

"Oh, now I'm the one being rude. I'm Delilah, oh, if you mean my real name, it's Tajah Michaelson, sorry. Yes, I'm new. I joined just over three weeks ago. It's nice to meet you although this isn't the way I would've chosen to do it."

"I bet not. Do you mind telling me what went on tonight with Dominus?"

"What did he tell you?" was her immediate comeback.

"I want to hear what you have to say before we talk about what he said. Just start at the beginning. Did you and he arrange to meet here tonight, or was it by accident?"

"No, we didn't arrange to meet. I would never agree to do that with him," she responded, wrinkling her nose in distaste.

"Why not?"

"Because he's pushy and gives me the creeps."

"Tell me what happened," I coaxed.

She took a drink of water before answering me. She shifted as if she was uncomfortable. Hmm, something about it made her reluctant to tell me. Maybe Duncan had been telling the truth. Disappointment filled me. Deep down, I didn't want her to be someone who would play games with him.

"I came in and I was sitting down observing

others. I saw him so I got up and moved to a different area. I had hoped he wouldn't see me. I was watching one of the floor shows and wasn't paying attention. He snuck up on me. When I went to leave, he grabbed me and next thing I knew, I was against the wall. He was too close for me to be able to punch him or knee him in the groin. He was holding my arms and hurting me."

"Why were you trying to avoid him?"

What she'd told me so far could either be part of the CNC game or someone trying to avoid someone else. I needed to know if it was the latter and why.

"He's been overly pushy. Ever since I started coming here, he's kept pushing for me to do scenes with him, to be his submissive. I told him I was only here to watch." She held up her wrist and I saw she had an orange bead. She continued after she showed me. "He didn't seem to care and kept doing it. So when I saw him, I took a chance that I could avoid him tonight. I was wrong."

"Did you tell any of the consent monitors, security people, or my floor managers what he was doing?" If she had and they hadn't taken care of him, heads would roll.

"No, I didn't. I thought if I told him enough times he'd stop." She shifted her gaze away as she spoke. She was lying. Knowing she was lying flared my anger again. I leaned forward in my chair. I put my glass down on the table hard. She jumped and her startled eyes met mine.

"Don't lie to me! Tell me the real reason, or you

can get out and not come back," I snapped.

"It's not a lie, just not the whole reason. There's no need to bark at me," she snapped back.

Having her argue excited me. The urge to see how much she'd fight back rose within me. I had to fight it back. This wasn't the time or place for it. "If it's the only way to make you tell the truth, then I will."

She stiffened and some fire came into her gaze. Fuck, there it was. I wanted to groan in pleasure. "You might own this place, Mr. Ivanova, but you don't own me nor are you the boss of me. I don't have to tell you anything else. Why does it matter why I didn't? What did Dominus say happened?"

"I'm not telling you until you tell me the rest."

We got into a staring contest. I scared grown men twice her size with one of my looks, and here she was, giving me an attitude back. I couldn't stop myself from growing hard. She was so close to triggering me. If that happened, she would most likely run out of here screaming. Images of what that would do to me and how she'd look flashed one after the other through my mind.

After a good two or three minutes, she rolled her eyes. "Fine, if you must know, I didn't want to take the chance I'd be the one kicked out. He told me he's been a member for a long time, that he's one of the lead Doms here, and he's friends with you. Who would you be more likely to believe, him or me? I need this club. That's why I didn't say anything."

I wanted to praise her for doing as I asked but I didn't. "Dominus has been coming here for a few years, that's true. The bit about him being one of the lead Doms, that's not. It's not automatic that he'd be believed. And he sure as hell isn't my friend. You said you need the club. Why? Surely when you were approved, you were oriented to our rules and such. Who's your sponsor? Did you meet with Reuben?"

If he hadn't done it, I'd be having words with him. He knew I always insisted on meeting all new patrons. If I could, I met them when they were merely prospective ones. He'd done it in my place more than a few times so he knew the process.

"Yes, the rules were covered with me. I met with Reuben for several hours. He was great. He explained everything again and answered a ton of questions for me." She smiled when she spoke his name. My gut tightened.

"He did? What did you talk about? And you still haven't told me who your sponsor is."

"He did. I had a lot of questions about what goes on here. My sponsor also told me the rules and how to handle myself. You can't blame him or Reuben for this," she almost pleaded.

"Name," was all I said. I was reserving judgment. I raised my brow.

"You're nothing like Reuben," she muttered before she answered me. "Carver Anderson is my sponsor."

I knew him, of course. I was kinda surprised he'd brought a woman here. He was one who played, but it was always with someone here. This was the first time he brought someone in. Again, my gut tightened. I detested the thought of either Carver or Reuben meaning something to her and vice versa. While it wasn't forbidden for Reuben to get involved with a patron, it had to be only when he wasn't working. On top of those feelings, I was upset that Carver allowed her to come alone and to be harassed. If she was his, then why wasn't he here with her? Protecting her?

"Why isn't Carver here with you?"

"Because I don't need a babysitter. No one said it was required that my sponsor come with me every time. It's not convenient for him to do it, nor do I want him around. It makes us both uncomfortable."

"Having the man you're involved with here with you makes you uncomfortable? What the hell? As your Dom, it's his duty unless you're not in a monogamous relationship," I blurted out.

Her mouth fell open and she gave me a stunned look. It lasted for several seconds then she began to laugh. She fell back in her chair and laughed hard, holding her stomach. I scowled. What was up with that? I waited for her to get a hold of herself. When she quieted down, she gave me the information I wanted but never expected.

"Carver isn't my lover, Dom, or anything like that. Yuck, he's like a brother to me. That's gross. He feels the same way about me. I'm a little sister to him. I had to beg and threaten him for weeks to get him to do it. Oh my God, wait until I tell him."

"If you two aren't involved, why sponsor you? If he was reluctant, why did he do it?"

"So I could do my research. He was afraid I'd find a less savory place to go if he didn't. He told me this was the best club for miles and miles. He explained how it worked. Also, I think Cady worked on him too."

"Who's Cady and what kind of research?" Everything she told me only made me ask more questions. I was going down a rabbit hole I might never get out of.

"Cady, Cadence, is his little sister and my best friend. As for what kind of research, I'm writing a series of books and I need to have real-life experience and answers."

"What kind of books?" I asked in dread.

More than a few times, people tried to do interviews or write about the club and the lifestyle. At first, I'd allowed it, but after they all turned into bashing sessions that vilified the lifestyle and didn't show it in a positive light, I refused to allow more. Those articles almost destroyed my club in the early days. What people did outside the club was their business if they wanted to talk to people about their lifestyles.

"I'm a romance author and I wanted to write a series unlike any other I've done. The BDSM lifestyle intrigues me, so I chose to put in the work to find out what it entails so I can write the books."

Son of a bitch, she was a romance author. Fuck, this wasn't good. Lord knows how she'd portray the club and the people here. There was no way I could allow it. What was Reuben thinking to allow her access to the club and my patrons? I got to my feet, shaking my head as I did.

"Nope, sorry, but there's no way you can use my club for research. I don't know what Reuben was thinking when he said yes or Carver for bringing you here in the first place, but you're done. Now, if you'll come with me, I'll escort you out. Don't try to return, Ms. Michaelson. You won't be admitted. I'll refund your money. And if you know what's good for you, you won't print anything about this club or my patrons. If you do, I'll know and I'll sue you."

"Wait, please. You can't do this. Listen and let me explain," she cried out.

I ignored how my chest was aching. Any secret fantasies I might've been having about her went up in smoke. No way she and I could ever be anything to each other. I tuned her out. As she kept trying to talk, I opened the door and waved for her to leave. If I didn't, I was in danger of listening and letting myself buy into the idea she would be different. It would only end up coming back to haunt me. When I wouldn't listen, her shoulders slumped, and she got up and walked past me. She wouldn't even meet my eyes.

We were silent in the elevator on the way to the first floor and the exit. She marched to the door and then out into the open area, where patrons were greeted, without stopping or saying a word. When she got there, she turned to face me. I was standing outside next to a curious Hoss.

"I'm sorry you're such a distrustful person and that you won't even let me explain. I was never here to cause trouble or to harm anyone or your club. But I see you've made up your mind without knowing my side. Don't worry, I won't mention your club, Mr. Ivanova," she said haughtily before she turned on her heel and stomped off. I watched her until she drove away.

After she left, Hoss whistled. "Goddamn, what happened?"

I wasn't in the mood to talk about it, or at least not with him. "Later. Did Reuben come in yet?"

"He arrived about five minutes before you came out with the lady. I told him you wanted to see him. He said he'd go right up as soon as he checked on something. He didn't say what."

"Thanks."

I didn't waste time getting inside and back to my office. When I didn't find him there, I sent him a text.

***Me: Get your ass to my office, now!***

It only took him maybe fifteen seconds to respond.

***Reuben: On my way. WTF?***

I didn't bother to answer. I continued seething the longer I waited. When he came through the door with a puzzled look on his face, I wanted to punch him.

How could he do that? He knew the history of this club with reporters. Was he crazy?

"Mikhail, what's going on?"

"Have a seat. We have shit to discuss."

He sank into a chair. I sat in the one across from him. "Mind telling me why you look like you want to kill me? What did I do?" he asked.

"Why don't you begin by telling me what you were thinking?"

"Thinking? About what?"

"About allowing a writer into my club! You know what they're like and you did it anyway. Not only did you open us up to scrutiny and God knows what else, but you put someone clearly out of her depth out on the floor alone. She was assaulted tonight." I was practically yelling at him.

His face flushed from red to white. "What do you mean she was assaulted? Is she okay? Where is she?"

He wasn't bothering to defend his decision. All he cared about was her. Jesus, I was right. He wanted her for himself. The way she had spoken his name earlier told me she liked him. "Apparently, she's been being hassled by Dominus. She didn't report it, and tonight, he got physical. He had her up against the wall. He not only shook her but he forcefully kissed her. I had to throw his ass out. He tried to tell me it was all a misunderstanding and they were doing CNC."

"There's no way she'd do that. He's lying. Did you

tell him not to come back? Is she still here?" He went to stand up.

"Sit. No, I sent her home. As for him, I told him I'd call him later and we'd talk. I told her she's no longer welcome here. We'll refund her money, and if she writes anything about the club or the patrons, I'll sue her. How could you be so stupid?"

"I wasn't stupid, and you have her all wrong. She's not here to write bad things about the club or the people. She's a romance author. She's writing a series. Didn't she tell you that?"

"She did tell me she writes romances. That doesn't change the fact she's an outsider, and we can't risk it."

"She's not a risk. She explained her idea to me and what she wanted to get out of being here. She's doing it the right way, Mikhail. She did this so she would accurately portray our lifestyle. She didn't want to offend people or give out false information. We talked for a really long time before I agreed. And there's nothing in her background to cause alarm. Outlaw investigated her thoroughly. I'll show you the report. I can't believe you just kicked her out without talking to me first," he said disgruntledly.

"Why didn't you tell me you did this? She's been here for weeks," I countered.

"I didn't tell you because I planned to tell you tonight. Plus, you were taking a much-deserved break. It wasn't an emergency you needed to know about. You've always trusted my judgment. I had no reason to think it would be different this time."

I sighed and rubbed my forehead. He sounded hurt. "I do trust you. I just can't wrap my head around you doing something like this. Even if what you say is true, after what Dominus did, I can't see her sticking to portraying anything here in a good light. We need to do damage control. I need to talk to Carver."

"I don't think she'll do anything to hurt the club. I swear. As for talking to Carver, it's late, and he'll have to work tomorrow. It's too late to call him tonight. I'll do it first thing in the morning and see when we can meet him. In the meantime, I think you should listen to what she pitched to me."

I waved my hand. "I can't right now. I need to mull it over. Call him first thing and get him here tomorrow as soon as possible. Alright, let's talk about what else has been happening."

"Not a lot, but before we talk about the rest, I need you to tell me what we're going to do with Dominus. He had a warning months ago. I thought he had learned his lesson but I guess not. You're not allowing him back, are you?"

"I need to question him more and see what else he says. He lied to me and I want to see how big of a hole he digs for himself."

He slowly began to grin. The tension between us eased. "And then once he's dug it nice and deep, we bury him."

I smiled and nodded. "And then we bury his ass.

Good riddance."

He laughed. "Give me a drink then we'll talk."

"Get it yourself and while you do, grab me one," I told him.

He chuckled again then stood up. I hated being at odds with him. He was my best friend. For tonight, I'd put all thoughts of Tajah out of my mind. I had a feeling it would take a lot to purge her completely. As I worked to do it, her image kept popping in and out of my head. Damn it.

# Mikhail: Chapter 3

It was a confident Dominus who came strolling into my office the next day around lunchtime. When I got up this morning, I'd placed a call to him to insist he meet with me as soon as possible. I told him it had to be today when he attempted to put me off. He hadn't been happy about it, but he agreed. Reuben called Carver, and he said he couldn't get away until after work, but he promised to come right here. When he asked what it was about, all Reuben told him was that I was back and wanted his thoughts on something.

Reuben and Hoss came in behind Dominus and closed the door. He swung around when he heard it. I guess he had no idea our bouncer was around. Hoss had been waiting for my text to tell him Dominus was here. Hoss waited just down the hall in my apartment for my text to join us. Dominus's smile faltered for a moment or two, and then it was back in place. He came over and offered me his hand. I didn't take it. He let it drop. I pointed out a chair at the table which was to one side in my office. He took the hint and sat in it. We took three of the others which put us across from him.

"Afternoon, guys. Sorry I couldn't come earlier, but you know how it is. When you run your own business, the work is never done, and you have to stay on top of everything and everyone. What can I do for you?" He was trying to maintain a cool, confident demeanor, but I saw the tension around his mouth and eyes.

"You know what this is about, Duncan. I'm not in the mood for games. We need to talk about what happened here last night with Delilah. You grabbed, shook, and kissed her without her permission. You had her pinned to the wall. I had to yank you away from her," I said with a snap. I was done using his alternate name, although I was careful to use her club name that she told me.

"I told you it was all a misunderstanding. We were role-playing. What did she say happened? Just a warning, I found she's very committed to sticking to her role once the game starts. She refuses to break her character."

"She said you've been bugging her for weeks to do scenes and to be your sub. She's turned you down every time, and then last night, you got rough. She didn't consent to any kind of role-playing. You touched her violently without her consent. You know the penalty for that. I gave you a second chance, and you blew it," I told him gruffly. I wanted nothing more than to lay my hands on him again. I clenched my fists in my lap.

"No! Please, you have to believe me. I didn't do anything she didn't want. She's playing you. I thought she was someone I could have fun with. I had no idea she'd do something like this to get someone else kicked out. You can't allow her to get away with it. I'll do anything you want. You can't suspend me or ban me." His voice got higher and higher as he pleaded. It wasn't going to do him any good. I let him run out of steam and spew more lies, and then I informed him of his fate.

"Save it. You're done. I can't have people like you in my club. End of story. I gave you the benefit of the doubt months ago. You pretended to change, but you haven't. That's all I have to say. We'll escort you out. Don't try to come back, Duncan. The staff will be told not to let you in, and so will the other patrons."

He kept protesting the whole time we rode the elevator down and walked him out the door. It was early, and the club wasn't officially open yet, so there was no one here. Hoss was crowding him as we marched him out there. He glared at all of us after we stepped outside. "You'll regret not believing me. She's a lying bitch."

"I stand by my decision. You've never kept to the rules and skated by. It was a mistake to give you a second chance. It was only a matter of time before you fucked up. Goodbye," I told him coldly.

We stood there watching him until we could no longer see him after he drove off. He gave us the finger when he pulled out. Not a surprise. Reuben smacked me on the back. "Let's go inside and forget his stupid ass. We have some stuff to do before Carver gets here. Do you know what you're planning to say to him?"

"I do. I want to be clear why she's no longer welcome and although he sponsored her, as long as he doesn't try to get her reinstated, there are no hard feelings."

"Mikhail, I—" he cut whatever he was about to say

off. I knew it was because Hoss was with us. He wouldn't criticize me in front of staff, patrons, or other friends. We had agreed long ago to only voice those kinds of things in private. We also vowed to always be honest with each other no matter what. I knew he was going to keep vouching for her and I had to find a way to get him to see he was wrong.

"Thanks for inviting me to watch him get his ass kicked out. I wish he would've fought a little. I've wanted to beat his ass for a long time," Hoss grumbled.

I laughed. "Sorry to disappoint you and I agree. I kinda wanted him to do it too, but I don't think you would've gotten to be the one to beat his ass. I had the urge too."

"Me three," Reuben added. We all laughed.

"You're free to go. I know you left work to come do this. Thanks. I'll see you Thursday night," I told Hoss. He wasn't on until then. Last night hadn't been one of his regular nights. He covered for one of the others. His schedule was to work our peak nights of Thursday through Saturday. It worked best with his main work schedule.

"It was worth it. It's one of the perks of being the boss. I'll see you later. Oh, and Mikhail, I know I don't have any say, but I think you should reconsider letting the little lady come back. She didn't strike me as someone to cause trouble. Just saying," he informed me, before nodding to Reuben and walking off to get into his sports car.

Reuben and I went back inside. I was mulling over

what Hoss said. That was two of my closest companions telling me I was wrong. Hoss was not only an employee but a friend. Was I wrong about her? Should I give her a chance? In the end, I decided to postpone deciding until I talked to Carver. Maybe he would help me. Needing to catch up on work, I told Reub I'd see him later after Carver got here. He agreed and went off to his office to get some work done.

It was hard for me to concentrate on what I was doing. I couldn't stop thinking about how she affected me. The awareness, the excitement when she fought back, the physical draw to her. When she was in the light of the office, I saw her so much better. Her hair was a light blondish-brown color with lighter golden streaks in it. It looked natural, not from a bottle. Her skin was ivory and so damn smooth looking. I wanted to see if it was soft and if the rest of her body was the same.

Her eyes were an unusual, gorgeous, amber color, surrounded with long, thick lashes. She'd played them up with a small amount of eyeshadow and mascara, and her mouth was a pale pink color. God, that mouth made me think of all the things she could do with it. Her lips were plump, and the glossy lip stuff she wore only made them look more delectable.

Her clothing was nice and casual but covered too much of her for me. They weren't skintight, but even without that, I knew she had a good body. She was curvy with a tucked-in waist, nice round hips, and a large rack. When she walked away from me, I zeroed in on her ass. It was pert and plump. I itched to squeeze those cheeks. I was an ass and leg man, but I would never turn down a good rack, either. She appeared to have it all. I wanted to see them for myself.

*Jesus, stop it. You can't get involved with an author. She's essentially a reporter. You know how that ends,* I chided myself.

Early on, when I first allowed reporters to interview me and the patrons who were willing to talk, as well as give tours of the club, I'd made the mistake of giving one woman who was doing a story a big taste of what it was that we did here. She'd been one hundred percent on board with it and seemed excited to experience the life. We had extensive discussions, and she went through all the orientation and signed the NDA.

I didn't do anything too extreme. It was an impact play scene. She insisted she wanted to be restrained. I did it even though I thought she should ease into it. During the scene, she didn't complain, use her safe words, or anything. When it was over, I thought she was fine. She and I even ended up in bed that night.

So imagine my surprise when, a week later, her article came out, and she only said scathing things about the kink lifestyle, the club, and me. I learned my lesson, and that was the last time I allowed anyone to knowingly come into the club who could write about it. If it was discovered a potential patron had ties to anything like a blog, newspaper, magazine, or any kind of writing or reporting, they were denied. The club had taken a hit, and I'd worried my dream would come crashing down. Luckily, we were able to keep it going and overcome what she wrote.

It was a struggle to keep pushing thoughts of Tajah out of my head so I could work but by the time Carver arrived, I'd gotten some of it done. Not as much as I wanted, but it was better than nothing. Besides, Reuben had been good about keeping up on my work and his in my absence. There wasn't a ton waiting for me, but I was going through things to get back on top of what was happening in the club. I prided myself on always being in the know. I wasn't a hands-off owner.

It was almost six o'clock when I was informed by Reuben that Carver was here. He said he was bringing him up to my office. I was up waiting to greet him when he came through the door. I saw Carver was a tad uneasy, but he didn't seem upset or alarmed. Had she told him what happened last night? If she did, surely he'd be more upset. I met him halfway and held out my hand. He shook it.

"Hey, Carver, I'm glad you could make it. Sorry to drag you in but I need some information. Can I get you something to drink? I have water, a variety of alcohol and a few different sodas." I led him to the leather couches and chairs in my office. I had more than one area set up to talk with people. If they weren't invited to the comfy couches, then we sat at a small conference table like we had with Duncan or in a couple of chairs in front of my desk. Reuben went to the wet bar and waited for his answer.

"Uh, yeah, sure, a soda would be nice. Anything you've got as long as it isn't diet," he grimaced as he said diet.

I chuckled. "You don't need to worry about that here. I hate the shit. If you want one of those, we'll have to get it from the bar downstairs. Reub, I'll have water, please."

I wanted Carver to be at ease. Reuben and I talked beforehand, and we decided to let him be more in the background until it came time for him to get involved if it was required. I'd held him back from pleading for her case this afternoon. I knew he wasn't happy about it and we'd be talking after this meeting.

Once we all had a drink and were seated, Carver was the one to get the conversation started. "It's good to see you back, Mikhail. Reuben did a fantastic job, but you were definitely missed. Now, as much as I want to think this is just a chat to catch up, I know it's not. What happened? He said you wanted to talk about something. Did I do something wrong?"

I heard the unease and worry in his voice. "Not exactly wrong, but I do want to talk to you about something I feel has put the club at risk."

He frowned. "And what exactly is it, and why tell me if I didn't do anything wrong? Do you need legal advice?" Carver was a lawyer so it made sense he'd ask that.

"I hope not. It seems you and Reuben let someone in while I was gone, who I would've never agreed to admit."

He stiffened. "This is about Tajah. What did she do? I swear, I would've never sponsored her if I thought for a second she'd cause issues. Is she here? Can I see her? Is she alright?" The questions flowed out of him, and he became anxious.

I held up my hand to stop him which worked. "She's not hurt, or at least not anything serious. She's not here. As for what she did, last night there was an incident. I'm trying to determine if she was totally innocent in it or if she had some culpability in what happened. Before we talk about that, I want to know what you were thinking in proposing her membership. Surely you can see how allowing someone who wants to write about the club and the lifestyle is inviting trouble. I've never had anyone who hasn't twisted it and portrayed us as a bunch of deviants who are a perversion needing to be stamped out." I planned to remain calm and let him lead but my feelings on the matter came out.

A look of dismay spread across his face. He shook his head. "Mikhail, I swear, if I for a moment thought Tajah would do something like that, there's no way I would've gotten her in here. I don't know what happened, but whatever it was, there's no way she did anything malicious or would attack the club or anyone in her books. She's a romance author. She wants to ensure realism in her new series. That's all. She knows about the life from me, but I'm not an expert by any means, and there are a lot of kinks I don't know much about. She wants a broad understanding, so she asked me to sponsor her. I tried for a long time to dissuade her, but in the end, I had to say yes."

"Why did you have to say yes?" I was curious to hear his answer. He didn't appear to be a weak man who would just give in.

"Because she was looking into going to one of the less desirable clubs. You know which ones I mean. There's no way in hell I would allow it. For one, she wouldn't be safe there alone, and secondly, I couldn't go with her to ensure she was."

That was true. There were other clubs, but they didn't take the safety of their patrons as seriously as we did. I'd heard more than a few stories about what went on at them. I was shocked they hadn't been shut down by now. No way I'd allow anyone I knew and cared about to go to one of them. I couldn't blame him.

"Okay, I can understand why you don't want her to go to one of those but still, why not wait until I get back and talk to me to be sure I was alright with it?"

"It wasn't planned because of you being away. She's ready to start writing her first book, and she had worked on me for so long the time was now. That's all. Knowing she was going to do it whether I helped her or not, I did what would make her safe and allow me to help her. Now, you said there was an incident, and she wasn't seriously hurt. Tell me what happened," he pleaded.

The way he was acting, I couldn't tell if it was all concern for someone he considered a sister like she'd said, or if he had other feelings for her, ones she might not be aware of. I exchanged a look with Reuben. He raised a brow and shrugged. He knew what I was thinking. He was frowning. Was it because he was interested in her too, and didn't want a rival? Shit, since when did I give a shit if two men wanted the same woman. They could share her if she were inclined to it. However, the thought of her with either or both of them sent a jolt of dismay through me.

"Has she said anything to you about someone bothering her to do scenes with him and to be his sub?" I asked.

He vehemently shook his head no. "No, absolutely not. Is that what happened last night? Who? How bad was she hurt?"

"He probably bruised her arms. I caught him when he had her pinned to a wall downstairs, and he shook her and then kissed her. She said she couldn't fight back because he was plastered against her. She did bite him, though," I recalled with a smile.

"Motherfucker! Who did it? I want his name. He's lucky she was pinned or she would've done more than bite him," he said darkly. His fists were clenched.

"Why do you say that?" Reuben asked suddenly.

"Because she knows how to handle herself. Yeah, I didn't want her going to those other clubs because no matter how skilled you are, if enough people come at you all at once, there's no guarantee. And she's my sister's best friend. If anything happened to her and it was because I didn't help her, Cady would tear my balls off. She's tiny but evil." He shuddered.

It was kinda comical to see a big man like him wary of a woman, especially if she was tiny like he said. However, Cady wasn't the issue here. Tajah was. "The culprit said they were playing a CNC scene and she was all for it." Carver opened his mouth to interject as soon as I said it, but I cut him off. "I sent him home and I talked to her. She denied it and that's when I found out he'd been bugging her almost since she came and she hadn't told anyone. I spoke to the man earlier today and his membership has been revoked, but I can't have her here, Carver. I won't risk my club on what she might write about it and our lifestyles."

"His name," he demanded through gritted teeth.

"It was Dominus," I confessed.

"I fucking knew it!" he shouted as he hit his thigh with a fist. "I saw him checking her out. I made sure before I stopped coming with her to warn him she was off-limits and not to bother her. That son of a bitch, I'm gonna beat him black and blue."

"If you knew he was interested in her, why didn't you warn her or, better yet, talk to Reuben and the staff so they would keep an eye on him?" I snapped.

"I did warn her but I didn't say a particular name. I told her if she had any trouble to go immediately to someone who works here. I didn't think she'd hide it. Goddamn it. As for why I never told anyone, I didn't want to cause trouble for someone if all he was doing was looking."

"Well, he wasn't just looking, and he had been warned before not to push if a woman says no. You know the rules. You get a second chance if the incident warrants it. Strike two and you're gone."

"I didn't know he'd been warned or I would've said something. Jesus, this is a mess. I want to clear up one thing first. I want to address your concerns about her research. Tajah may write romances and most people think those aren't real writing. They are and she's very dedicated and serious about it. She does her research because she doesn't want to misrepresent something or cause offense. That's why she was so eager to come here. Kink-shaming isn't in her wheelhouse, Mikhail. It's just not. I hope you reconsider letting her come back. It would be a shame for her to get something wrong due to not being able to ask someone. I don't know it all but I'll do my best to help her. Now, I need to see her to make sure she doesn't go to one of these other clubs and she's alright. I hate to run but is that all? Or do you want to talk about something else?"

His anxiety was causing me to feel it, too. Surely she wouldn't run out tonight or even later to one of the other clubs after what happened? But what if she felt she had to? The thought of her going to one of them and getting hurt much worse than here made me feel sick. I wanted to run out the door with Carver to go see her. His assertion she would never paint the club or lifestyle in a negative light made me waver in my conviction that banning her was the right thing to do.

"No, go, we can talk more later. Please make her see it's not safe to go to any of those clubs. No one wants her to get hurt, and there's no guarantee she'll get accurate information there."

He got up, nodding. "I will. Thanks for letting me know, and I'm sorry this caused you an issue. It was never our intention. Hate to run, but I gotta go." He quickly shook our hands then hurried out of the room. Once he was gone, Reuben sat down and looked at me.

"You know what you have to do," he said.

"And what is that?"

"You have to talk to her, apologize, and bring her back. If you're so damn concerned about what she'll write, make sure she knows the truth from an expert."

"And who do you suggest I pair her with to learn the truth? You?" I challenged him.

He smirked. "Well, if you want, I won't say no. Tajah is a sexy, beautiful woman, and any man would be lucky to have her scene with him or even have her become his sub. Although if she was a man's sub, I don't see him sharing her or letting her go. She's a remarkable woman from what I've learned so far. So yeah, I'll do it."

Instant denial roared through me. Before I could stop it, the words burst out of me. "No! Like hell, you will."

The bastard laughed and sat back in his chair. "I knew it. I fucking knew it. She caught your eye, didn't she? That's what's really bothering you. You kicked her out because of past issues with that bitch reporter and others, but you didn't want to because you want her."

I could try to deny it, but he'd known me too long. I knew he wouldn't believe me, so I sighed. "Fuck, what the hell am I thinking, Reub? Talk me outta this. It's gonna come back and bite me hard if I let her back in. I know it. My life will never be the same if I do."

"Nope, I won't do it. I do think your life will never be the same, but in a good way, a great way. I know your extended vacation wasn't just because you were exhausted, Mikhail. You're not enjoying life anymore. There has to be more to life than work. Hell, you've stopped playing ever since you and Tessa called it quits. I haven't seen you look at a single woman with a bit of desire. Even before you and Tessa parted ways, your heart wasn't in it for a long time. I need my best friend to be happy."

He wasn't wrong. I hadn't been feeling it for a while. Tessa and I parting was inevitable. Tajah was the first woman to catch my interest, and it was so much more powerful than anything I could recall. The thing I'd come to realize on my vacation was the idea of settling down and having domesticity didn't sound horrible anymore. I thought I was having a midlife crisis, and I was determined to forget it when I returned until I saw her.

"Maybe you're right, but you deserve to be happy too. I don't see you trying to pick a woman and settle down," I reminded him.

"I would if I ever met the right one. Could Tajah be the one, maybe, but something tells me it's a definite if you're the guy. Do you want to take the chance she's the one for you, and you let her go over something like this? The fact she's not already taken boggles the mind. Don't wait until someone else sees her and recognizes what a catch she is. Regrets suck."

"I need to think. Get outta here. We'll talk later."

He didn't take offense to my abruptness. He knew me. He got up and headed for the door. Before he left, he turned back to say, "I'm here if you need to talk. Think hard on what I said. I don't see you regretting taking a chance on her being different. I know deep down she's what she appears to be."

As the door closed, I sank deep into my chair. I had a lot of soul-searching to do. I needed to think about what everyone said, what I felt when I met her, and to read through what Outlaw had found on her. I'd resisted reading it all day, but it was time. Time for me to see if I would take a drastic step that could alter my whole life.

# Tajah: Chapter 4

I couldn't concentrate on writing today. I tried, and I did get some words down, but it wasn't flowing like it usually did. I hated it when this happened. The only times I struggled this way was when I was upset or there was a lot of outside stuff going on. To say the altercation last night with Dominus the Douche had been a jolt was true, but there was a bigger issue that had me feeling off-kilter and scattered. It was my meeting with Mikhail Ivanova and how that not only went but how he impacted me.

In my preliminary research into the House of Lustz, I hadn't thought to dig into the man behind it all at the beginning. I knew his name from Carver. I admit that when I found out he wasn't around when I joined, I was disappointed. I wanted to meet the man behind it all and see if he would be willing to let me question him about his motive for starting the club. Well, I guess that was never happening. The man didn't want me in his club, and he was too arrogant or maybe just too rude to listen to me so I could explain what I wanted to do and why. Once he heard what I did for a living, he dismissed me like I was nothing.

Being treated that way pissed me off, but it also hurt. I'd been treated like that before, and it had been one of the worst times in my life. I never wanted to experience it again, although there was no way to prevent it. I wouldn't have taken it so personally if I hadn't been stunned by him. When he came to my rescue, I'd been too caught up in Dominus to pay much attention other than to be thankful someone had helped me get away. I vaguely knew he was attractive, but so what.

However, when he entered his office later and dismissed Leon, I was calmer and his aura, his whole presence, struck me. He was a large, imposing man who stood several inches over six feet. His shoulders and chest were wide and he filled out the suit he'd been wearing to perfection. I knew he had to have them custom made to fit his frame. He was deeply tanned and had dark hair, which had a sprinkling of silver mixed in. A thick five-o'clock shadow covered his square jaw. In contrast to all that and the dark brows and lashes, he had light gray eyes that stood out against his skin and hair. He was a devastatingly sexy and handsome man. One who made me want to beg him to touch me, which was crazy. I wasn't there to find a man, and I certainly didn't go around having an instant desire for someone. However, his attitude had cooled my ardor. I wish it had killed it, but no such luck.

When I got home last night, I had to vent to someone, so I called Cady. Thank God she kept late hours. She answered and let me vent and then I listened to her rant. She was all for me going back and giving Mr. Ivanova a piece of my mind. When I said no, she said she'd go. I had to talk her off the ledge. I made her promise not to do it and not to say anything to Carver. I needed to be the one to tell him but I had to figure out what I would say. After all the begging I did to get him to sponsor me, I was embarrassed I'd been kicked out. I hoped it didn't come back on him. That was my worst fear.

As for Dominus the Douche, I prayed they would see him for what he was and kick his ass out, but I wasn't holding my breath. In my experience, most men stuck together even if they knew one of them was wrong. Carver was one of the rare exceptions. Why I couldn't fall for him, I didn't know. The thought made me queasy. We'd grown up as siblings. I could never imagine us together. In the past, when others suggested it, we laughed ourselves silly and told them not in a million years, just as I did last night with Mikhail Ivanova.

*Jesus, get out of my head, why don't you?* I yelled at his mental image. Yeah, I was nuts. Authors tended to have full-blown conversations in their heads. Most of the time, it was with our characters or between characters. I liked to equate it to having multiple personality disorder where I could get rid of a personality by writing his or her story, but they kept being replaced with new voices. It was an unending cycle.

I needed to get up off this couch and call Carver before he was called into Lustz. I should've done it first thing this morning, but I didn't want to disturb his work. Or at least that's the excuse I made. In reality, I was avoiding the tongue-lashing that I knew was coming. Plus, I'd been trying to figure out where to turn to get answers for my research. Ugh. I thought I was set and now this.

A knock at the front door made me jump. It was loud. I uncurled my legs to get up, but I didn't make it off the couch before there was another one and it was followed by a loud voice. "Taj, I know you're in there. Open the damn door. We need to talk," Carver called gruffly.

Oh shit, he knew. I could tell by his tone. I scurried to the door and undid the locks. When I opened it, he was standing there with his arms crossed and an upset look on his face. I didn't say anything. All I did was move back so he could step inside, and then I locked the door. He stomped over to the couch and plopped down. He watched me through narrowed eyes. I hated when he did that.

"Hello, Carver, make yourself comfortable," I said with a touch of sarcasm.

"Don't give me any crap, Taj. Tell me why the hell I had to find out there was a problem at Lustz last night and you were not only accosted but banned? Why didn't you call me right away?" he barked.

"Because I knew how you'd react. I was just about to call you when you pounded on my door and shouted so my neighbors could hear you. Jeez, give a girl a damn break. It hasn't even been twenty-four hours."

"Why wait? I bet you came home and called Cady right away, didn't you?"

Since I was guilty as charged, I didn't answer him.

"I knew it. Neither of you thought I should know this? I vouched for you. I could've been banned along with you for something that wasn't my fault."

"I'm sorry, but I told him you had nothing to do with it and not to hold it against you. I know you vouched for me, and I appreciate it so much, but I didn't do anything wrong. That man wouldn't take no for an answer."

"You did do wrong. You didn't tell anyone he'd been harassing you. Why? This could've been prevented."

"You don't know that. I didn't say anything because I didn't want to cause trouble and have them decide to kick me out. He said he had been a member for a long time, was a lead Dom, and he was friends with the owner. I was trying to fly under the radar," I snapped back.

"Well, that didn't happen, did it? Fuck, I had to go see Mikhail, and I walked in having no idea what happened. I looked like a goddamn idiot!" he shouted.

"Oh, now we get to the real issue. You don't give a shit if Dominus scared or hurt me, just that your precious reputation wasn't smeared by associating with me. You don't want High and Mighty Ivanova to think less of you. Well, you both can kiss my ass! I'm done with Lustz, so problem solved. Now that you've gotten that off your chest, you can leave." I stood up and marched back to my door. This was my home. I didn't have to put up with being yelled at.

"Goddamn it, come back and sit down! We aren't done talking."

"Yes, we are. This is my home, and I don't have to put up with you yelling at me. Don't worry. I won't ask you for any more help. I'll find my answers some other way."

He got up and stomped to the door. He was shaking his head. "I'm sorry for yelling. Please, we need to talk. I need to be sure you won't go to any of those other clubs. You know they're not safe and have questionable practices. Promise me you won't go." I heard the worry in his tone.

I was hesitant to go to any of the others, but I could only do so much research online, and I'd asked him a ton of questions already. He gave me a good overview and could talk about his kinks, although he had been hesitant to tell me. I promised him I wouldn't tell anyone, not even Cady. There was so much more he didn't know, and the whole reason I went to Lustz in the first place. He'd warned me about the other clubs. However, the one thing I wouldn't do was lie to him.

"Carver, I can't promise that. I need to find sources somewhere, and those are the logical places. I can promise you I'll be super careful, and if anyone even looks at me weird, I'll go straight to their floor managers or security. I know the thing with Dominus makes it seem like I can't take care of myself, but you know I can."

He sighed and gripped my elbows gently. He stared hard into my eyes. "I know you can, but even you can be outnumbered. Don't go. If you decide you must, then you have to take me. I'll find a way to get us in, although I did ask Mikhail to reconsider banning you.

He might change his mind. Just wait and see if he does."

I snorted. "Yeah, when hell freezes over. I don't see that man changing his mind. Forget it. Lustz is a dead end."

"I don't think it is, but we'll see. And another thing, I do care about you and not just my reputation. Did Dominus hurt you? Mikhail said you might have been hurt. Let me see." His voice had gentled.

He ran his hands down to my wrists. I had a loose sweater on since the air conditioning had made me cold. He tried to push up my sleeves, but I grabbed his hand. I didn't want to set him off again after he'd begun to settle. If he saw the bruises, he'd be livid. He gave me a stern frown.

"Taj, show me. I'm not leaving until you do. I can stay here all night."

Knowing he could be stubborn, I rolled my eyes then I shrugged off my sweater. I tossed it on the table by the door then I rolled up the quarter sleeves I had on. Dark bruises, five of them on each shoulder, stood out on my pale skin. You couldn't mistake what caused them. They were fingerprints and they looked worse than they were. Sure, there was tenderness, but against my skin, they appeared horrible. He inhaled loudly and a hiss came out of him.

"He fucking did that? I'm gonna kill him. Let me take pictures."

"You're not killing him. You can't. You'll go to jail and jail for a lawyer is *no bueno*. You'll be disbarred or killed or both. It looks worse than it is. There's no need to take pictures. Why would you need them?"

"You let me worry about why. Stand still."

I didn't have a choice. He whipped out his phone before I could move and snapped several shots. When he was done, he gave me a hug. "I'm sorry I wasn't there, honey. You know I'll never let anyone hurt you."

I hugged him back. "I know, but I'm a big girl. I can take care of myself. Now, promise me you won't go after him."

"I promise I won't go after him," he said quickly, which stunned me.

"Good. Tell me, did you have dinner yet?"

"Nope. I went straight to Lustz after work then here. Why? Are you offering to cook?" he asked with a grin.

"I have leftovers if you're not too good for them."

"Lead me to the food. If you made it, I know it has to be good, no matter what it is."

That's how our fight changed to us having dinner and laughing. Like a family, we fought but then we made up. We hugged each other tightly before he left. He had work in the morning and I was struck with inspiration. I needed to get it down before I forgot.

# Mikhail:

After a restless night of going over and over what Reuben had said, along with Carver and even Hoss, I wasn't in the mood for a whole lot of bullshit today. However, I had work to do, so I locked myself in my office and got to it. The good thing was a lot of the time I worked variable hours. I liked to be available on the floor as much as I could at night, but there were still things I had to do, which required me to be awake and working at least part of the time during the day.

Today, a big shipment of alcohol was coming in. Sure, the managers and Reuben could handle it, but I wanted to see what they sent. The last couple of times before I left, they had shorted us. While I was away, they did it once again with Reuben. He'd called them and issued the final threat if it happened again, without them calling to tell us why, then we were changing vendors. They'd assured him it wouldn't happen again.

I suspected they had some people with sticky fingers who thought no one would bother reporting one or two missing bottles. I doubted they were doing it for personal use. Most were expensive bottles, which would fetch a good price if they sold them. Well, they were wrong. I cared. I was working in the back when Reuben came in. He had a concerned expression on his face. I straightened up from what I was doing, which was counting bottles against the order. “What’s wrong?”

“You’re needed out here. Carver is here and he’s upset. He wants to show you something.”

An uneasy feeling crept into my stomach. I put down my tablet and went out to see what was wrong. It was early, so we hadn’t opened for the day yet. There were only a few staff members working. I got into the main bar area and saw him standing at the bar with a thunderous look on his face. When he saw me, he came marching over. He stopped a couple of feet in front of me. He didn’t say hello or anything. All he did was hold out his hand with his phone in it.

“Carver, I’m surprised to see you here at this time of day. What’s this?” I asked, not taking his phone.

“You need to look at those pictures,” he muttered darkly.

Taking his phone, I lit up the screen and glanced at the picture he had pulled up. I admit I was curious what kind of pictures he wanted me to see. I hissed as I saw the dark bruises on ivory skin. I knew without him saying a word it was Tajah’s skin. I flipped to the next one and saw the same thing, except they were on the opposite shoulder. I raised my eyes to him.

“He fucking marked her,” I growled. Reuben stood behind me, looking over my shoulder and saw the same thing I did. I could feel his anger coming at me in waves.

It was one thing to mark a woman’s skin as part of consensual play, but this way wasn’t to be tolerated. They had to hurt and not in a good way. He’d marked her and it offended me to see his prints on her. Or at least marks I hadn't placed there while ensuring her pleasure. The thought of him infuriated me and thoughts of me with her aroused me. I was fucked in the head but I didn't care. In the wee hours of this morning, I'd come to a few conclusions. I hadn't said anything to Reuben or made a move, but this changed things.

"Why did you show me those?" I wanted to be sure we were on the same page.

"I did it because she made me promise not to beat his ass. She's worried it'll get me disbarred or thrown in jail and killed. I don't give a damn, but she does."

"And you think I'll go handle him?"

"If not you, then someone you trust. I've heard the rumors about you. I don't know if they're true or not, but if they are, I want him to know he'd better never come near her again. I have no doubt he's probably already gone to one or more of the other clubs. If she runs into him at any of them, I want him to walk away."

"Other clubs? You've got to be kidding! Those aren't the places for her. Why didn't you stop her?" I almost shouted.

"I tried! She said she couldn't promise not to go, but if she did, she wouldn't go alone. I told her I'd go somehow. She's determined to do this series right and that means research. I can't stop her, so I'll make her as safe as I can. Scaring the hell out of this bastard helps with that."

"You let me worry about Dominus. I'll take care

of him. I need these," I muttered as I fiddled with his phone, then sent them to mine. Once I had them, I handed him his back. "There's no goddamn way she's ever going to one of those places. You tell her... never mind. I'll tell her. She's reinstated here, but with a few caveats she has to agree to."

"Mind if I ask what those are? Not that I'm not glad you reconsidered banning her, but I'd like to know."

"The rules are between her and me. If she chooses to share them, that's on her. Don't worry, they're nothing harmful. And I'll take care of this situation, but it's gonna take time. Bear with me. It's my fault for giving the bastard a second chance that she has these. I'll make it right. You have my word." I held out my hand. He took it and gave it a hard squeeze.

"I'm trusting you to do this. If you don't, I'll do it myself, even if I do break my promise. She'll hate it. One thing she detests is promises not being kept. She's had too many broken to her in her past."

His remark made me curious but I didn't ask. I wanted to find out more about her, but from the source. I knew from the report I read from Outlaw that she was thirty-three and she was divorced. She had no kids and her marriage ended eight years ago. I was dying to know why. What was her ex-husband like and why had they parted ways?

"I won't let this go. I knew he might've bruised her, but seeing those, nope, he's not walking without repercussions. Being banned isn't enough. Consider it taken care of."

"Thank you. I hate passing this along."

"No worries. Is there anything else I can do?"

He shook his head no. "Not that I can think of. When do you think you'll talk to her about coming back here? Should I tell her you'll be calling her?"

"I prefer to talk to her myself and without her knowing I'm gonna do it. It's for a reason. I won't delay, I promise. I don't want her going to any of those other clubs, either."

We ended our talk not long afterward. Reuben had unashamedly stood there the whole time listening. I raised my brow at him after Carver left. "Well, wanna weigh in, Mr. Nibshit?"

He chuckled. "Nibshit, am I? How else can I keep you straight? So, did I hear you right? You're gonna tell her she can come back? I'd like to know what the caveats are," he said with a grin.

"All you need to know is they involve her and mentoring."

"Oh, you're letting me be her mentor! Thanks, man," he said with a smirk.

I couldn't hold back my growl. He heard it and smiled bigger as he practically ran out of the room. I heard his laughter come up the hallway a few seconds later. I swear, if he wasn't my best friend, I'd probably kill him. But he wasn't my concern right now. I'd planned to call her later and ask her to drop by so we could talk. After seeing those bruises, I couldn't wait and I wanted us to talk somewhere she would be more comfortable. Her home would do. I hoped she was there. Dropping in unannounced wasn't good manners, but I didn't want to chance her putting me off. I was afraid she'd be so upset about what happened and she wouldn't return. I couldn't let that happen. Ready or not, Tajah Michaelson, here I come.

⁂

Two hours later, I was standing at her apartment door. I'd gotten her address from the application she'd filled out for Lustz. After checking the wine had all been delivered, which it was, I'd gone to shower and change. I was caught on my way out the door by one of the floor managers, Freddy. He wanted to talk about ordering new chairs for the bar. Some were showing wear and tear. He could've asked Reuben, but since he saw me first, he asked me. After I told him to write it up and submit the whole proposal, I left.

The drive to her apartment wasn't too far. Without traffic, it only took me twenty minutes. During the busy time of day, it would take more than a half hour. She lived on the first floor of a three-story complex. I didn't like it as soon as I saw it. A first-floor apartment meant anyone could enter easily through her windows. At least on the second or third floor, they'd have to put a bit of effort into it.

I had no idea if she was home, but I knocked anyway. I was about to knock again when I heard the sound of locks being undone. She had an apprehensive look on her face when the door swung open. I felt tongue-tied for a couple of seconds, as I saw her in a pair of shorts and a tank top. They hugged her body, and it was even better than I imagined. What loosened my tongue was seeing the fingerprints on her shoulders. My anger came back full force.

"Mr. Ivanova, what in the world are you doing here?" she asked in surprise.

"Please, call me Mikhail. I came to talk to you. I hope that's alright. I took a chance you'd be home since you work from here, I presume. Or do writers have office spaces? I'm not sure now that I think about it," I told her with a smile, hoping she'd relax and I could chill my anger. The urge to reach out and run a finger over her bruises and take care of her was almost overwhelming.

She smiled. "No, most of us don't have separate offices, and working from home is a major perk of my job. Won't you come in? I don't think my neighbors should hear our conversation." She stepped back and held the door open for me.

Walking in, I took in her space. It wasn't huge, but it was done up to be comfortable and pretty, without being overly feminine. It was very tidy, too. The only thing I saw out was a laptop and a glass on the coffee table. She gestured to the couch.

"Won't you have a seat? Can I get you something to drink?"

"Thank you, but I'm fine," I said, going through the niceties as I took a seat. I hoped she'd sit next to me. When I passed her, the smell of her hair had wafted up and it made me want to bury my nose in it and sniff her. Less than five minutes in her presence, and she was teasing my beast. *Not now,* I ordered myself. She did join me, but she sat as far away as she could. She clasped her hands in her lap.

I started the conversation. I prayed it went well. "Tajah, is it alright to call you that or do you prefer Ms. Michaelson?"

"Tajah is fine. Forgive my bluntness, but I can't imagine why you're here, Mikhail. I believe we said all we needed to the other night at the club. Unless there's something I need to do to withdraw. If so, a phone call would have sufficed."

"No, there's no paperwork, but I believe I owe you an apology. I didn't let you explain what your idea was for the research you want to do at Lustz. Also, I wanted to let you know, Dominus is no longer there. He's been banned."

"Ah, okay, I'm glad to know, but why would you come all this way to tell me that?" She appeared puzzled.

"Because you won't have to worry about running into him or having him harass you again when you're there."

"When I'm there?" she asked slowly.

"Yes, when you come back. Although, there are a few stipulations to that. I'm here to tell you the ban on you can be lifted. It's that and the stipulations I came here to talk to you about, but first I have something else to ask you."

"Okay, go for it."

"How badly do those hurt?" I pointed to her bruises. I had to resist touching her skin. I wanted to wipe them away with a touch, after kissing them better first. God, she was driving me crazy.

She got a startled look on her face as she glanced down at herself. I realized she'd forgotten they were exposed. She automatically put her hands up to cover them. I moved closer and grabbed her hands to prevent it, breaking one of my main rules of no contact without consent.

"Don't. I'm so sorry I didn't get there before he had a chance to do this to you. I brought you something, which will help with pain and make the bruises go away faster."

"How?"

I reluctantly let go of her hands and reached into my pocket. I wasn't dressed in a suit today. I wore jeans, a collared-shirt, and a blazer. I took out the tube and handed it to her. "This is arnica cream. It comes in gel form, too. It's often used for bruises and soreness. It increases blood flow and stimulates the body to heal itself. You'll be interested in this for your research for your books. It's often used in our lifestyle for those liking hard impact play and other things, which can leave bruises or other marks."

"Wow, thank you. I didn't know that. I'll put some on later. That's actually fascinating."

She went to take it, but I held onto it. Before she could ask why, I twisted off the cap and squeezed a small amount on my fingers. “Here, you’d better put some on now. Those are damn dark. Let me do it.” My voice dropped to a low murmur.

I had to touch her, and I had to care for her. It was an impulse I couldn’t ignore. The Dom in me needed to give her aftercare, even though I hadn’t caused these and she wasn’t my sub. I waited a second or two to see if she’d say no. When she didn’t, I reached the rest of the way and touched her skin. I felt her shudder. I rubbed gently. Jesus Christ, I was right. Her skin was like silk and so warm. I made sure to thoroughly rub it into her first shoulder as slowly as I could. As I did, I talked to her.

“Do you want to hear what the stipulations are?”

“I do, but first why did you change your mind? You seemed adamant you didn’t want me there.”

“I was and then I listened to what Reuben and Carver told me, and I thought about what I witnessed that night. I had to reconsider my stance. You hadn’t caused any trouble. Dominus was out of line. It should’ve never gotten to that point, so I decided to give you a chance to prove to me all writers aren’t the same.”

“All writers? What does that mean?”

I switched over to the other shoulder. “I’ve had past experience with writers, reporters, and such who claimed to want to write about the club and our lifestyle. Every one of them ended up writing stories, which essentially vilified us and our choices. We’ve been called deviants and a whole lot worse. Early on, it almost destroyed my club. Different doesn’t mean wrong. We may not like the same things as what the mainstream does, but we have as much right to do what makes us happy within reason. I don't tell those couples how to live or what they should or shouldn't do in the bedroom, so why should they be allowed to do it to me?"

"Mikhail, I don't disagree with you. It's my desire to portray things accurately, which led me to want to join your club. Everyone I asked, who would know the answer about which was the best place to explore kink, said the House of Lustz. I admit, there's a sense of the taboo and mystery about your world, but it also intrigues people or at least it does me. That's what led me to want to write about it. I don't think anyone is deviant. Well, I take that back. Rapists and child molesters I'll never understand or condone their behaviors. The people who go to Lustz won't be kink-shamed by me. If I don't understand their attraction to certain things, so be it. I'll either not portray those things in my books, or I'll make sure to have someone more knowledgeable in it proofread what I write."

"I totally agree with you about those two kinds of people. I hope you mean the rest because if you write or say anything I consider libel or slander, I won't hesitate to make you regret it," I warned her.

She leaned back so my hand fell from her shoulder. A feeling of bereft hit me. "You don't need to threaten me."

"It's a promise, not a threat. And to make sure you get the full picture, and the proofreading you mentioned, I have stipulations."

"Fine, hit me with them."

"One, you will never observe anyone in an enclosed room, at least not alone. You must be where you can be watched over. It's for your protection. Two, you may ask anyone questions as long as they agree to participate. Three, you will only get your mentoring on the various forms of kink and the intricacies of the life from one person, your mentor. Four, do not come to the club if your mentor isn't there. Five, when you write, your mentor will read what you wrote to ensure it is depicted appropriately."

"And who assigns my mentor and what is this person's qualifications? How did you decide who will do it? What if he or she can't be there when I can?"

"I chose your mentor and there won't be problems aligning schedules. His qualifications are that he's been in the life for two decades. He's considered a master in being a Dom. He often gives demonstrations and answers questions about most aspects of our lifestyle. If he doesn't know it, he'll find you the answer. Finally, he'll ensure not only do you get a thorough education, but he'll keep you safe from any kind of unwanted attention. No one will act the way Dominus did."

"Well, he sounds like he's too good to be true. Who is this expert and when can I meet him? Are you even sure he'll want to do this? It'll mean a lot of his time."

"He's eagerly waiting to start. Time is of no consequence. He can start right away. And his name is…" I paused before telling her, "Mikhail. I look forward to our partnership."

Her mouth fell open and astonishment spread across her face. I tried not to smirk. Yeah, when I was done with her, I hoped not only would she be in love with the life, but she'd be sharing my bed. I was committed to making her mine. A one eighty from where I was even a couple of days ago, but sometimes, I was learning, that was the way it went.

# Tajah: Chapter 5

I had to have heard him wrong. There's no way Mikhail freaking Ivanova not only lifted my ban but volunteered to be my BDSM mentor. I must've hit my head and didn't realize it. Or I was asleep and this was a dream. Yeah, that was it, and since it was a dream or a hallucination, I laughed.

His brow furrowed. "What's so funny?"

"The fact I imagined this whole conversation and in it you just told me you want to be my mentor for your club. I need to wake up and write this down before I forget it," I mused. I turned my back on him and reached for my laptop. I picked it up and woke it up. I opened one of the documents where I kept notes and started to type. I stopped when the couch shifted. I glanced up to find him still here.

"Tajah, you're not dreaming. I did tell you that I'll be your mentor at Lustz. It's the only way I can be sure you don't get into trouble and my club and patrons aren't hurt."

I stopped typing. "How would that even work? You're the owner. I know you have to be extremely busy. You don't have time to follow me around or to sit and answer all my questions. I have a ton. If you insist I need a mentor, why not Reuben or someone else you trust?"

He scowled at me. "Let me worry about how I do it. Either you agree with me or no deal."

I could see he was dead serious, so I hurried to answer him. "Agreed. So when do we get started?"

We spent a few more minutes setting up my schedule for the rest of the week. We exchanged phone numbers, and he instructed me on how often to use the arnica cream. I was still stunned when he left. I had so much to think about and plan.

☘ ☘ ☘

I was nervous as I approached the door to the House of Lustz. I didn't know what to expect from Mikhail. Would he become impatient with all my questions? Would he change his mind and have another person mentor me? Or worse, would he decide his first decision was the right one after all and ban me again?

I'd dressed with care tonight. I wanted to look like what I wanted to project. A confident, successful, attractive woman. During my past visits, I'd dressed nicely, no ratty sweats and a t-shirt, but I'd kept things low-key. Tonight, I wasn't dressed in a leather catsuit nor were most of my goodies hanging out for the world to see, but I was wearing different clothes than I'd ever worn here. Cady had picked it out for me and insisted I wear it.

It was a black jumpsuit, but it hugged my boobs and was low cut so you could see my cleavage. The top was held up by thin straps. On the front where my lower ribs and upper stomach were, there were slits in it to expose small sections of skin. I paired it with three-inch heels and a short leather jacket. My hair, I left down long, and I'd gone to the trouble of applying a little more makeup than I typically wore. It was like what I would do if Cady and I were going out dancing or to a regular club.

Hoss was at the door, which was expected. It was Thursday night. He and I had talked a few times, and he'd told me which nights he worked. He was a huge guy who could crush me with one hand, but I found once you got to know him, he was sweet, as long as you didn't step out of line. I smiled at him as I got to the door. "Hi, Hoss, how's tricks?" I asked him with a wink. It was an inside joke.

He whistled. "Goddamn, woman, are you trying to cause a riot going in there dressed like that? Fuck, that's hot. Bossman is gonna lose his mind when he sees you."

"Why? What's wrong with it? Too dressy? Do I look wrong?" I asked, my anxiety rising. Why did I listen to Cady?

"Whoa, calm down. You don't look bad and it's sexy, but still dressy. I've never seen you in anything like this or with your hair down. Damn, woman, you have a ton of hair."

"You're sure? I mean, I know a lot of the women in there dress much more revealing than this. I was trying to boost my confidence. Why would Mikhail lose his mind if I don't look bad?"

"Why the hell would you need a confidence boost?" he asked, frowning.

“Come on, you see some of them. They’re so sexy and gorgeous. It’s kinda demoralizing to the rest of us. I didn’t want to embarrass Mikhail when people see us together. Maybe I should go home and change.”

I turned to walk back to my car, but I was halted when he gently latched onto my arm and tugged me back toward him. I stumbled, as I lost my balance in my heels. I thought I’d fall, but Hoss caught me. Damn, he was like a brick wall. I looked up at him. It was a long way up, too. He was taller than Mikhail.

“There’s no need to go home and change. You could never embarrass anyone, especially Bossman. You’re gorgeous and sexy,” he told me with a smile.

I was about to thank him, when a deep gruff almost growling voice stopped the words in my throat. They came from behind Hoss. “Mind telling me what the fuck is going on out here? Why do you have Tajah in your arms, talking about how gorgeous and sexy she is?”

Hoss turned sideways, which let me see Mikhail. He looked pissed. Hoss let go of me and stepped away from me. “Hey, Mikhail, it’s not what it looks like. Tajah was worried about how she’s dressed. I was assuring her she looked good. She stumbled, so I caught her to keep her from falling. As for the sexy and gorgeous part, she was comparing herself to the other women here, and I was telling her she had nothing to worry about in that department. Look at her. Doesn’t she look amazing?”

I flushed as Mikhail dragged his gaze from my face to my toes and back again. He took his time, too. It was all I could do not to squirm. When he made it back to my face, I swore I saw desire in his eyes, but it had to be a trick of the fading light.

"You have nothing to worry about. There's no comparison. You look beautiful. Come with me so Hoss can do his job. We can't have him distracted, can we?"

I hesitated only for a moment, then I took the hand Mikhail had extended to me. As I took it, I swear a zap or something went up my arm. I gasped and tried to pull away, but he held on tight. He tucked my hand over his arm and escorted me inside. He was greeted by the lady at the bead table as I called it. She gave me a curious look. It took a second to remember her name was Laura. I smiled at her. "Hello, Laura," I said.

She nodded and said it back before addressing Mikhail. "Have you gotten caught up on your work, Mikhail? It's so good to have you back. It's not the same without you."

There was an undertone to her voice, which made me think she was being more than innocently friendly. If I wasn't wrong, she liked him. Glancing at him, I don't think he'd picked up on it. He was smiling politely.

"I got a lot of it done. Reuben did an excellent job doing most of it while I was gone. Hopefully, tonight will be a busy one. If you have any problems, let Hoss or one of the others know. If you'll excuse us, we have some business to conduct." As he led me away, she stared hard at us. Or I should say me. Yep, she was into him.

"Business? What business?" I asked him.

"We need to talk in my office," he muttered. He took me to the elevator. However, when we got on, he put his hand on a shiny panel. I knew from last time it was taking us to the third floor even if he hadn't told me. No one could just get on the elevator and go to that floor. I didn't blame him for protecting his office.

When we stopped and the door opened, we only had to walk straight out and across the hall to his office. He used his palm again to get in. Inside, he led me to the leather couches. I sank down and he sat beside me. I tried to ignore how close he was, how handsome he looked, and the scent filling my lungs. He smelled so good. I subtly squeezed my thighs tight. He was making my body tingle and crave things I had no business craving, at least not from him. I was becoming slick and my nipples were hard. Thankfully, I had a strapless bra on and it kept them from showing through my jumpsuit.

I blamed it on my long dry spell. People assumed since I wrote romances and they were steamy, that I must have wild sex all the time. They'd laugh their ass off if they knew the truth. It had been so long since I'd been with a man, I forgot what it felt like. Well, okay, maybe not that, but it was hazy. It had been three years, almost four. My only fun was the battery-operated kind. At least it was always hard, available, and faithful.

I shoved those thoughts away. I wasn't here to lament over my boring life. I was here to learn and to come up with some wonderful ideas for my new series. I was nervous, but also excited about writing a whole new subgenre and different tropes. I broke the awkward silence.

"What business do you want to discuss? Are there some additional forms I have to sign?"

He shook his head. "No, no forms. I wanted to talk to you about this outfit and the rules for tonight, Hell, the rules for every night. Why did you wear this? It's nothing like what you had on the night I met you."

"Why are you and Hoss making a big deal out of it? If it looks that bad, just tell me. I'll go home and change. In fact, I'll be back. It shouldn't take me more than an hour. It's still early. Or if you can't wait, I'll come back tomorrow night."

"Tajah, don't you dare leave. There's nothing wrong with your outfit, other than I'll be fighting off guys and even some gals all night. I was already prepared for it, but not to the level this will cause. I'm not sure how much observing or talking we'll get done." He sounded put out.

"Mikhail, you don't have to do this. I can wander around and observe like I did before, and if I have a question, I'll ask Reuben or someone." I offered him an out. I ignored his assumption about people needing to be fought off. I had no worries about that. Dominus was gone, after all. Maybe he was regretting offering to be my mentor.

"No way. It's me and you. You look stunning. Now, here's what I want us to do. We'll go down to the floor for a bit and walk around. You can tell me what things interest you. Maybe we'll find some scenes that catch your attention. After we get our fill of those, we'll come up here. That way you can have privacy to ask me anything, which you might not want to ask where others might hear you. But first, I thought we could do private people watching." He stood and went to a far wall. He opened a hidden panel and pushed a button. The wall slid back, and it became a wall filled with screens. They showed the first and second floors.

I got up to get closer. The bulk of them showed the second floor, which made sense to me. It was the one that was most likely to have issues. Seeing the different views, I thought of something. "Is this how you knew what Dominus was doing to me that night?"

He shook his head. "No, I was down on the floor and I happened to glance your way and I saw him. I tried to get to you as fast as I could, but there were too many people in my way. I'm sorry I didn't."

"You don't need to apologize. As much as you try, there's no way you can eliminate all problems or bad apples here. This is so cool. What if you're not here to monitor these? I can't see you doing this every night, all night."

He laughed. "I don't. There's a security office on the second floor. Reuben has an office there too. They're tucked away. There are people in there who monitor camera feeds very much like this. It's their job to see stuff. They didn't catch you and Dominus because you were in a blind spot. We fixed that oversight, by the way."

You could see all the platforms where scenes happened on some of the screens. The private rooms weren't on them. As I ran my eyes over them, I had to ask. "Mikhail, is it permissible to ask you personal questions or is that too much?"

"What personal things do you want to know?" His voice deepened.

"Seeing all these, I wondered if they were for more than security. Are you a voyeur? If you don't want to answer, I understand."

"Before I answer, let me explain something. Let's sit again," he suggested. I quickly followed him back and we sat on the couch together.

"Most people in our community aren't just attracted to one kind of kink. We can have several of them, although we usually have a predominant one or two and then lesser ones. Over time, you can become interested in new ones. Some may become less important as time goes by. We're always growing and changing like everyone else." He paused as he studied me. I nodded so he knew I understood what he was saying. Then he answered my question.

"Yes, voyeurism is one of my kinks, although not my main one."

"May I ask what you get out of it?"

"First, let me say I'm not into the type of voyeurism they call criminal voyeurism. That type is when one has sexual desire or behaviors, which come from someone's distress, injury, or death. No way does someone unwilling or unable to give legal consent do a thing for me. Mine is purely the consensual kind. I get turned on by seeing provocative things such as undressing, nakedness, and sex. Everyone who decides to perform outside of the private rooms knows they'll be watched. They want that because they're an exhibitionist to some degree. Therefore, consent is given by the mere fact they do it out in the open."

He showed no embarrassment in sharing this with me. I'd gotten out my notebook and was jotting down a few points. As I did, he asked me a question. "Now, it's your turn. Are you into it? Do you like the things you've seen so far down there? Does it turn you on? Do you like porn? That's voyeurism at its simplest."

I nibbled on my lower lip. I didn't know if I should share mine, but as I thought about it, I knew it wasn't fair to ask him or anyone else to bare their souls to me, and then have me tell them nothing. "I never actually thought about it as voyeurism, but yes, I enjoyed watching the different demos and the encounters down there and I do like watching porn."

"And what about exhibitionism? Do you like that, too? Do you want people to watch you tied up, maybe being spanked, or having a man strip you naked and doing things to you as he makes you scream for more?" His tone turned guttural. My breathing picked up as what he said triggered so many images in my mind. He leaned close and whispered the next part.

"There's so much you don't know about this world, and I can help you explore it all. What I need is for you to be open to it, and to communicate with me. Communication is the first lesson you must learn. Without it, this whole thing falls apart. You can't be embarrassed to ask questions, or to tell me what you want to know. Shame, embarrassment, and preconceived notions belong in the outside world, not here, just like judgment doesn't. Can you do that for me, Tajah?"

God, I wanted to do that, and be free to explore to my heart's content. My issue was, I didn't know if I could. There were things that were holding me back. However, he said communication was key, so I had to tell the truth.

"I want to, Mikhail. You have no idea how badly I do, but there are things, history, which make me hesitate to do it. Being open with someone the way you want makes you vulnerable. My past experiences say being vulnerable ends up hurting you more. People rarely are what they seem."

"We can work on that. It's not about getting there all in one night. Sometimes, it can take a lifetime. How about I make you this promise? I won't push you beyond what I think you can handle, and I'll be just as honest and open with you as you are with me. We'll be vulnerable together. We'll protect each other, together."

My heart seemed to skip a beat at his offer. Staring at him, I noticed he was patiently waiting for my answer. It took me a minute or so to make my decision. When I did, I prayed I wouldn't regret it. Something told me, if he betrayed me, it would hurt a thousand times worse than anything from my past.

"I must be crazy, but my answer is yes. I will if you will. God, I hope you know what you're proposing,

Mikhail. This could go very wrong."

"It could, but it won't. I promise. Now, let's go see what we can find downstairs. I want you to stick close to me. No wandering off on your own." He stood up and held out his hand to help me up, as he issued this demand. His tone told me it was a demand, not a suggestion. I chose to not push back unless it became a problem.

"Are you worried someone will do what Dominus did?" I asked worriedly. I thought it was supposed to be safe here.

"It's very unlikely. I'm more worried they'll follow you around like a pack of slobbering dogs. I don't want to have to kill anyone tonight. This is a new suit and bloodstains are a bitch to get out," he said with a grin. I couldn't help but laugh as I took his hand. My gut told me tonight would change my life. Was it for the better? Only time would tell.

An hour later, I had to concede that Mikhail might've been right. There seemed to be a lot more attention on me, but I wasn't so sure it had anything to do with the way I was dressed. I think it had more to do with who I was with. Having him standing beside me, holding my hand most of the time, and him never leaving my side, caught a lot of people's attention. They were curious in some instances, and outright jealous in others. I could tell by the hateful looks I got from a ton of women and even some men. They'd give or do anything to be in my place.

When someone would ask if we were together,

rather than telling them he was mentoring me, Mikhail would smile and not answer them. Whenever I tried to clear it up, he'd run a finger across my mouth, which effectively shut me up because my brain went haywire. If I didn't know better, I'd think he was seriously into me. However, that couldn't be the case. It had to be because he didn't want them to know about our deal, so he wouldn't be inundated with requests to be others' tutor. He'd never have a moment's rest. Once I realized that, I stopped trying to tell them the truth. He was doing me a huge favor, and I wouldn't repay him by making things hard for him.

It was a whole different experience watching the various demos and scenes happening on the second floor with him. He was constantly pointing out things and filling me in on so much I had no idea about. I tried to scribble fast to take notes but it was impossible. After the first few times, he took my notebook away. I protested.

"Mikhail, I need that! There's no way in the world I can remember everything."

"There'll be plenty of time later for you to get all the notes you possibly can need. We'll go over this again where it's quiet and we can take our time. Right now, I just want you to watch, listen, and feel. If you have questions, ask. Let me guide you. You're in safe hands." That reassured me. I put it back in my bag.

Currently, we were watching a couple having an impact play scene. Her ass was really red, and she cried out every time the man with her landed a smack with the strap he had. I knew it had to hurt, but her cries were a mix of pain with pleasure. The expression on her face showed the same.

"How can that be pleasurable?" I asked without thinking.

Mikhail gave me a searching glance. "Haven't you ever been spanked?"

"Only as a child and it wasn't something I liked."

He laughed. "Most of us didn't like it either. This is different from that. Spanking in this context can do many beneficial things. It can release you from feeling responsibility or stress. Some do it to explore power roles and others use it to work through trauma or negative emotions. It can be soothing and relaxing for many. There are even psychological benefits to spanking, such as decreased mental activity, meaning it slows down racing thoughts, or the inability to shut down your brain, and can increase your concentration."

"So when I can't sleep due to my mind not shutting off or I need to concentrate on writing and can't seem to do it, all I need is a good spanking?"

"Maybe. You'd have to experiment and see if you like it and get the benefits you desire," he softly responded.

I didn't bother to reply, but I watched the woman even closer. I felt hot and my clothes were feeling tighter. I was having trouble not picturing myself as the woman up there. And the man with me was none other than Mikhail. God, I had to stop this. I couldn't be having fantasies about him! He was here to teach me, not let me practice with him.

The whole reason I decided to write about the kink world wasn't because it was the "in" thing to write. It was due to my own inner desire to know more about it. I'd read and heard just enough to intrigue me, and some of my secret thoughts and feelings had led me to this. They were secret because I'd never had the guts to tell anyone about them, for fear they'd think there was something wrong with me. As I did more research for the series, I discovered many people felt this way at first, but it wasn't about what a lot of people thought it was. His remarks about being deviants had resonated with me.

Not that I'd had anyone to do it with anyway. My luck with men hadn't been good. Case in point, take a look at my ex-husband and my two boyfriends after him. Sex and intimacy had never been satisfying with them. I knew sex wasn't the only thing important in a relationship. Intimacy and a host of other things played a part. When you didn't have any of those and the sex wasn't anything to rave about, how could it work? Sure, I guess you might stay together for the sake of children. Thank God, I'd never had any with those three. I wanted kids, but not with them. As each year took me closer and closer to forty, I knew my chances were slimmer and slimmer it would happen. Yes, women could have children now into their forties, but the risks were higher, too.

Now wasn't the time for a trip down memory lane. I needed to pay attention and not waste this opportunity. It was this thought which got me out of my past and back into the present. When we were done watching them, we ambled around to see if anything else caught our attention. Mikhail headed for the bar. As soon as the bartender saw him, he was over to us in a flash. I guess being the boss did have perks. There were people waiting, but the bartender left them without a qualm.

"Master M, what can I get you and the lady?"

"Jack, I'll have my scotch. Delilah, what would you like?" He'd been careful to use my club name tonight. I worked to remember to call him by his.

"Can I have a virgin mojito, please?"

"Of course, you can. A virgin mojito for the lady coming right up," Jack said with a smile before he walked off.

I heard Mikhail make a faint grunting sound. When I looked up at him, his face had a bland expression on it. I guess it was someone else. He smiled down at me when he saw I was looking. "Don't you drink alcohol? Not that it matters. I'm just curious."

"I do, but not often and never when I'm out alone. You can't be too careful. My dad would haunt me if I did something that risky."

"It's a smart habit to have, but I can assure you, if you want to drink when I'm with you, go ahead. I'll make sure nothing happens to you and you'll get home safely. I see you're watching Jack closely. Have you had an incident with someone trying to dose your drinks? Where?" There was a growling quality to his voice when he asked. He appeared to be upset.

Before I could answer, Jack was back with our drinks. I took it with a nod. I was pleasantly surprised to see Mikhail hand him a nice tip. It went without saying, as the owner, he wasn't paying for the drinks. He took my elbow and led me to a couple of chairs out of the main traffic area. When we sat down, I replied to his questions. He was still frowning.

"No, I haven't been dosed, thank goodness, but I know it happens. My dad was a cop. He was always harping on me to be aware of my surroundings, to never accept a drink from anyone, not even the bartender, unless I watched him or her pour it. Drink bottles should only be drunk if you are the one who opens them. Things like that."

The tension eased from him. "Good. You can't be too careful, but with me, you're safe just in case you change your mind. You said he'd haunt you, so he's gone?"

"He is. I lost him five years ago to cancer. I'm lucky. I still have my mom. What about you? Do you have family and do they live close?"

I saw a slight tightening of his jaw. Oops, maybe I should keep my questions to those only pertaining to the club and the life. "You don't need to answer me, Mikhail… I mean, Master M. Sorry. I know it's personal."

"I have no issue with you asking me. And as for calling me Mikhail, everyone knows me here. I don't hide my true name. I only insist on Master M being used during play or specific moments though a lot of patrons and staff use it. I asked you about your family. It's only to be expected that you ask me about mine. I was trying to decide how to answer you.

"The truth is, I have family but they're not always around and we don't spend much time together due to their work and mine. I know if I need them, they'll be here for me, but I've been careful not to need them much. I grew up differently from them, and I naturally went a different path than they did. My parents are gone. I lost them many years ago. I never had any brothers or sisters, but I do have several cousins. You said you still have your mom. Tell me about her and do you have siblings? A lot of cousins?"

"My mom is very much a free spirit. She's always been someone who loves to try new things. It used to drive my dad crazy sometimes. He never knew what he might come home to find her involved in. It made it fun though as a kid, not so much as a teenager. You know how it is when you hit those years. Everything your parents do seems to be embarrassing. Anyway, I grew out of that. After she lost my dad, she was depressed for a few years and rarely left the house. As different as they were, they fit. She's out living again, which is great. I have two brothers, both younger than me, but they don't approve of what I do for a living, plus other things, so we're not close. As for cousins, yes, I have several of those, although many of my aunts and uncles are gone like my dad."

"Sorry about those lost, but your brothers, it's their loss not yours. You're a fascinating and intriguing woman. How about a toast? Here's to a grand adventure." He held up his glass. I lightly tapped mine against his before we both took a drink. Grand adventure wasn't the half of it, I thought.

# Mikhail: Chapter 6

I was close to losing my mind, and I didn't have a clue what to do about it. And the reason for it was due here any time. Jesus Christ, she was driving me insane, but I couldn't stay away from her. She was like a drug. I had to be close to her and it was getting worse. I thought after a few sessions with her, my fascination and desire might decrease or even go away. It had always petered off over time with a woman. And since she and I weren't doing scenes or having sex together, there was no reason for her to hold my interest.

Or that's what I told myself and found I was a damn liar. Everything about her captivated me. All she had to do was come to mind and I was hard. I spent so much time dreaming and fantasizing about her, I was almost raw from jacking off. Only those times weren't ever satisfying enough. I was left wanting more.

You might think since I owned a kink club, it was easy to be satisfied. I had countless women I could have sex with to get relief. Even if all I wanted was to masturbate, I had several scenes to watch to do it to. Well, you'd be wrong. I couldn't watch other people having sex or playing and think of her. It felt wrong, dirty, and like I was cheating on her, which was ridiculous. She and I weren't in any kind of relationship. It shouldn't matter. And I sure as hell couldn't go have sex with another woman. The thought of it made my skin crawl.

The past month since we began our tutoring had been hell mixed with heaven. I got to spend several nights with her, but not all of them. I resented the nights she didn't come to the club. I would wander around feeling lost. My temper was more prevalent and people noticed. I would wonder what she was doing and if she was alright. When she was here, my desire for her increased tenfold. It was a fight not to drag her upstairs to my place and ravish her. To show her all the things I could do to and for her. The things she'd found the most intriguing, I wanted to do with her.

It wasn't just about sex and playing, though. It was so much more and deeper. I was falling for her, which I'd never done with a woman. My heart had never been in danger before, but it was now. Hell, who was I kidding? I wasn't falling, I'd already fallen.

Years ago, when I first started to explore my sexuality and the kink world, I had a teacher I guess you'd call her. She was an older woman who had been in the lifestyle for a while. I was young and I thought I was in love with her. We'd been together for two years, and I was all ready to propose to her, when I found out she only saw me as a playmate and I wasn't the only one. Whereas I'd only been with her, she had been with many others behind my back. I thought my heart was broken when I gave her the ultimatum, me or the others, and she chose the others.

A few years later, I realized I hadn't been in love with her. By then, I'd grown in my dominance and I found I could have many partners, whether I had sex with them or not. A few I'd stuck to for longer periods of time over the years, but it was never with the understanding I would be exclusive. Although, as my sub, I demanded they were, which was probably shitty of me, but I didn't share. Some men were all for it and I had no problem with them doing it. Just not me. The women weren't special other than they attracted me, but they were mine.

The desire to be with others was one of the reasons Tessa and I parted ways. I wasn't giving her the attention she needed, and I hadn't cared to try. Our encounters had grown less and less satisfying for us both. We'd parted ways when she brought it up to me and it was a mutual decision. I had no hard feelings and wished her luck. She still came to Lustz, although not as often. I had no idea if she'd found a dedicated Dom or not. When she was here, she seemed to play with different ones.

When I thought of Tajah being with anyone else, I wanted to tear shit up and kill the imaginary men. I saw her interest and desire growing the more she learned, and I didn't want her to explore any desires with anyone but me. I wanted to be her Dom and not just at the club. I wanted her to be mine. Mine to satisfy, protect, and grow with. Dare I say, I wanted to be the one to love her and have her love me, which blew my mind.

I knew coming back from my vacation that I had to possibly think about finding someone to spend my life with. It seemed to be what I determined my dissatisfaction stemmed from, although I couldn't be sure. Even though I'd come to that conclusion, I hadn't thought it would necessarily entail love, more like mutual respect and desire. Meeting Tajah had changed that notion. I wouldn't settle for anything less than desire, respect, and love, and my gut told me I could have it all with her. I just had to get her to see it.

I knew she desired me. I saw the way she looked at me, and I knew her body reacted even though she tried to hide it. Those were all encouraging signs, but they weren't enough. I wanted all of her, not just her body. Her heart and soul had to come with it. Everything I saw told me she was a submissive but not in life. I wasn't looking for someone I could tell what to do twenty-four seven. That kind of relationship held no appeal for me. I needed that in my sex life a lot of the time, but not the rest of my life. Any other time, I found I respected a woman who was independent and able to make her own decisions.

This didn't mean she couldn't lean on me in her regular life or ask for help. Absolutely she could and I wanted that, too. I just didn't want it constantly. I was coming to recognize I needed to be able to do the same with her. I was so used to being in control and making all the decisions. Even when I might be uncertain, I rarely talked about it, even with Reuben. I forged ahead. A knock at my office door startled me out of my thoughts.

"Come in," I hollered.

Instead of Tajah walking in, Reuben did. I tried not to show my disappointment. She no longer had to wait for me to come get her downstairs when she arrived. I'd put her prints into the elevator, so she could come right up. Something I'd never done with a woman, not even Tessa. He had a serious expression on his face as he closed the door and moved over to me. I was standing in front of the monitors on the wall, although I hadn't been seeing them.

"What's that look on your face for? Is something wrong?" I asked him.

"Relax, everything is fine downstairs. That's not why I'm here. You and I need to talk." He sat on the couch, so I moved to sit across from him in one of the chairs.

"Okay, if everything's fine downstairs, what is it we need to talk about? Are you alright?"

"I'm fine. It's you we need to talk about."

"What about me? There's nothing wrong with me."

"Like hell, there's not. Mikhail, we've been friends for a long time. You've been struggling long before you went away. When you came back, I had hoped it would get better, but I think it's only getting worse. When you agreed to mentor Tajah, I was surprised but hopeful. I thought at least you're getting back to yourself, but you haven't. You're not playing with her or anyone else. You spend all your time either showing her around, or up here locked in your office or apartment. When was the last time you got laid or had fun?"

"Since when are you my babysitter? When and who I play with or have sex with isn't for you to worry about. I've been taking a break. There's nothing to worry about."

I didn't want to share with him what I was feeling for Tajah before I even had a chance to discuss it with her. I knew if I came out and told her I'd fallen for her, she'd most likely run. I'd gotten the feeling she hadn't had the best experience with men in her past. The last thing I wanted was to move too fast and scare her away. Once I had her convinced, then I'd tell him.

"Come on, it's me, Mikhail," he argued.

We went back and forth for several minutes before he threw up his hands and said he gave up. I assured him again that I was fine before he walked out. Checking the time, I pulled out my phone to text her, to see if she was almost here. I was growing concerned and my mind automatically turned to things like she'd been in an accident.

Before I could text anything, there was a quick rap on the door, then it opened again. I sighed as I opened my mouth to tell him to stop, only it wasn't Reuben. It was Tessa. To say I was surprised, was an understatement. As it registered she was here, it hit me that Reuben had to have brought her up here and let her into the office. Goddamn his interfering ass. When I got done with her, I was tracking him down and making sure he never did shit like this again.

She was smiling as she came straight toward me. "Mikhail, it's so good to see you alone. I've been wanting to talk to you. You're a hard man to get by yourself."

She stepped into my personal space and raised up on her tiptoes to kiss me. I turned my head so her lips landed on my cheek instead of my mouth like she intended. When she drew back, she was frowning. I didn't bother to reprimand her for the kiss.

"Tessa, what're you doing up here? You know this area is off-limits to patrons. Why the hell did Reuben bring you up here?" I stepped away from her. Her perfume was cloying and made me want to choke. I hadn't ever noticed that before.

"Mikhail, I'm not just a patron. We're old friends and he brought me up because he knew we needed to talk. I can't wait any longer."

I knew just kicking her out would probably do no good. She'd keep trying to talk to me until she got her way, so I pointed for her to sit. She did but gave me an annoyed look when I chose to sit across from her rather than next to her. "You've got five minutes," I informed her.

"I've missed you, and I know we agreed our parting was mutually beneficial for both of us, but I've had time to think about it. I overreacted and was hasty. I should've never done it. I miss you. I want us to get back together. I know we can make it work, and it'll be even better than it was when we first started."

I shook my head. "No, it wouldn't. Our parting was the right thing to do, and we should've done it long before we did. It wasn't working, and nothing we did would've made it work. You need to move on. I've seen you with different men here. Not one of them makes you want more?"

"They're not you. None of them come close to

making me feel like you do. And I know no one can make you feel like I did. Not even that woman you've been hanging around with the past few weeks." Her lip curled up as she said the word woman.

"She's none of your business. Delilah and I aren't something I'm willing to discuss with you."

"Delilah, what a name. Come on, you can't tell me she does it for you. I've seen her. She's nothing special. All she does is watch. You need a woman who's able to explore and let you release your inner self. That will never be her in a million years."

I didn't want to have her focus more on Tajah, so I decided to divert her attention by telling her a partial truth. I wasn't in the mood to explain and argue with her. "Delilah isn't the kind of woman I would ever set up to play games with. She's nothing like you."

A smile spread across her face. "I know she's not. I knew you'd never go for someone as vanilla as her. That's why we need to get back together. We're perfect for each other."

I'd heard enough. I wanted her out of my sight. I got up. "It's time to leave. The answer is still no and it'll remain no. We're through, and I don't want to hear you say anything about it again. You need to leave."

She protested and begged all the way to the door. I hated it, but I escorted her down to the first floor, so she would leave my safe haven zone. As soon as she was there, I went looking for Reuben. I had to make sure he never did anything like that again with her or anyone else. He'd never done it before. What was he thinking?

I scanned the first floor. Not seeing him, I went to the second to do the same. When I didn't see him there either, I headed to his office in the back. I was lucky. He was there with his door open. I walked in without knocking, then slammed it shut. He sat up straight when I did.

"I know you're pissed. I can tell, but let me explain," he said in a hurry.

"Go ahead, then you're gonna listen to me," I snapped. I didn't have time for this. I needed to find Tajah. My anxiety over where she was had grown. She was usually here by now, although we never had a set time.

"You need to get your mojo back or whatever you call it. Tessa and you were good together at one point. I thought it could be again now that you both took a break. I think it's significant you haven't been with anyone since her. Even if you two don't get back together, you can blow off steam with her."

"Tessa and I weren't good for a long time before we called it quits and you know it. There's no going back to how it was in the beginning, either. As for me not being with anyone since, there's a reason for it."

"What!? What aren't you telling me? I thought we were best friends and we're here for each other," he said loudly.

"We are, but I didn't want to say anything until I knew for sure and then I had to do something first," I snarled back at him. He was going to make me tell him before I spoke to Tajah. I knew he'd never drop it now until I confessed, the bastard.

He slammed his fist down on his desk as he came to his feet. "Sure of what? Do what? I'm fucking worried about you, Mikhail. Goddamn it!"

"That I was really wanting something more than just a Dom/sub relationship. I'm ready to have someone special in my life, who I can hopefully grow fucking old with and maybe have a damn family!"

His mouth dropped open, and he dropped down in his chair. I saw I'd floored him. I walked to his desk and sat down in front of it. We stayed silent, studying each other for a good minute or two before he spoke again.

"Shit, I don't know what to say. You never even hinted at wanting something like that. In fact, you've always said you didn't see yourself settling down. What changed?"

I sighed. "Honestly, I didn't think I did want it. I never saw it, but my dissatisfaction kept growing. When I spent all those weeks away, I had a lot of time to think about why. I went through my life. Overall, everything is the best it's ever been. Business is booming. I've got great people in my life, like you. I can have anything I desire, pretty much. I should be perfectly content, but I'm not. No one was capturing my attention, not even for a simple round of playing. The more I examined why and thought about it, I came to the same conclusion over and over. What the hell good is it to have money and all this, if I have no one to share it with or to leave it to when I die? I'm forty-five years old and just now mature enough to handle a monogamous relationship. However, not just anyone will do. I thought liking would be enough, but it won't be. I have to love her and she has to love me back."

He rubbed his hand down his jaw. "Christ, I can't believe I'm hearing this out of you, of all people. I don't know what to say other than, are you sure? This isn't some midlife crisis shit, is it? What if you change your mind in a couple months? How can you be sure?"

"Because I've met the woman I want to spend the rest of my life with. I just have to make sure she's on the same page."

"Who? When? Where did you meet her? The only person you've been around that I know of is Tajah," he exclaimed.

I raised my brow and said nothing. It took several heartbeats before it registered. When it did, he practically yelled. "You're fucking kidding! Tajah? The woman you wanted to kick out of here? The one who knows nothing about this life? She's not your type."

"What does that mean, she's not my type?" I growled.

"You know, an experienced sub who knows the lifestyle and who can satisfy your desires. She's barely a neophyte. What if she doesn't want to do those things? It's one thing to write about them, but another to do them. How do you know you can love her?"

"Yeah, in the past I stuck to women who knew the

role and lifestyle, but it doesn't matter to me when it comes to her. I want to teach her everything she wants to explore. The thought of another man doing that with her makes me crazy. And I know she wants to do more than write about it. I've seen her response to what we talk about and she sees. She's shy about voicing those desires, but she's loosening up more and more. She has the sub nature underneath her independence. I know I can love her because I'm already more than halfway in love with her. I just need to make sure she can love me."

"Well, fuck me sideways. You're serious. How can you know it's love, though? It's been only a month. It takes months, if not years, for people to fall in love, Mikhail. Lust can happen in days or weeks but not love," he said dismissively.

"Have you ever been in love?"

"Well, no, but still, everyone I know who has said they were in love took longer to fall."

"Maybe they did, but not everyone is like that. Look at Payne? He was someone we'd never see falling for a woman or being monogamous. He saw Jayla and that was it. He was gone, even if it took him a little bit to accept it and get her. No one seeing those two can doubt they adore and love each other. From what he's said, everyone in his club who has settled down was the same way. He told me when you know, you know. I think I can make Tajah fall in love with me. I just have to take my time and not scare her off."

My phone buzzed, interrupting us. Not knowing if it was something important with the club or if it was her, I took it out and looked. It was Leon. He said there was an issue he needed me to come see.

"Damn it, Leon needs me. Listen, we can continue this talk later, but you need to realize, I'm not changing my mind. This isn't a passing fancy or midlife crisis. I want this, so no more sending Tessa or anyone else up to my office."

"I'm sorry, you're right. I should've never done it. I promise it won't happen again. Come on, I'll go with you in case we need to knock some heads together. It's been too long since we've had that kinda fun," he said with a big grin as he got up. I chuckled and nodded as we headed out to the main floor. It was where Leon said he was. He was near the private rooms according to his text.

There was a crowd there when we got there. We had to tell people to move to get through, although when they saw us, they were quick to do it. I found him and Freddy facing off with two men. I wondered why they called me until I saw Tessa standing near them. What the hell?

"What seems to be the trouble here, Leon? Freddy?" I asked.

"Sorry to bother you, Master M, but Tessa demanded we get you. It seems these two gentlemen are having a dispute about who she'll be doing a scene with tonight. She said neither, that you and she are, but they don't like her answer. Knowing your history, I decided to call you," Leon told us.

"Our history is just that, history. As for these

two, if they can't behave, they can leave. If she said no, then that means no. The same as with anyone else here. Tessa, don't tell any of my staff to call me for shit like this. And don't lie and say we're doing anything together. You know that's not happening."

"Sorry, boss, I thought… Well, never mind that. Got it. Sorry for disturbing you. We'll take care of this," Leon apologized. I could tell he was afraid of the dressing down I'd give him later.

I slapped him lightly on the shoulder. "It's fine. Now you know. Pass the word to the rest and I'll do the same. The only one who I want to be called for, unless you can't handle it yourselves, is for Delilah."

"Got it."

Tessa sputtered as I walked off. I had no time for her and her dramatics. If she thought I would get jealous or come to her rescue when she lied, she was mistaken. Reuben excused himself to make rounds. As he walked off, I took out my phone and sent Tajah a text message.

***Me: Where are you? I'm worried. You're usually here by now. Are you okay?***

I waited impatiently for her to answer. When five minutes went by and there was nothing, I headed toward the door. I was going to go check on her. I hit the door just as a text came in. I stopped half-in and half-out of the doorway. It was her.

***Tajah: I'm not coming tonight. Something came up. Sorry. You're free to enjoy yourself.***

***Me: Enjoy myself? What came up? Talk to me. This isn't like you.***

"Everything alright, boss?" Hoss asked.

"I don't know. Delilah was supposed to meet me here tonight, but she didn't show up. Now, she says she's not coming and for me to enjoy myself," I muttered, only half-paying attention to him.

"What do you mean, she didn't show? She was here. I let her in myself, then not long afterward, she came back out. I asked where she was going and she said you needed the night off. I thought it was weird, but she didn't stick around for me to ask her more."

This got my attention. "She was here? When?"

He glanced at his watch. "She left about a half hour ago. She came in maybe ten or less minutes before that. Damn it, I knew something didn't seem right. First, you'd never make her come all this way and then send her home. Secondly, she wasn't acting like herself. She usually talks to me for a few minutes at least, and this time, she didn't, nor did she make eye contact."

Unease filled me. "I've gotta go. Thanks. I didn't send her away, so I'm not sure what happened, but I'm gonna find out. I just need to talk to Reuben for a minute. Send one of the guys to get my car, will ya?" I handed him my keys. We had valet parking for those who didn't want to bother with finding their own parking spots. My car was in the private garage, but they'd get it for me.

"Sure will."

I hurried back inside. Thankfully, I found Reuben quickly. I hauled him to a quieter spot against one of the walls. He gave me a concerned look. "What's wrong?"

"I need to leave. Can you cover for the rest of tonight?"

"Sure. I thought you were waiting on Tajah to get here?"

"I was, but then I got a weird text and found out she was here and left. I need to find out why. She claims she can't come tonight. That something came up."

"Do you think she couldn't find you because you were with me and she left?"

"I don't think so, but I'll find out. She needs to know she can always text or call me if she can't find me. I gotta go. Later and thanks." I didn't hang around to hear him say more. I bolted. When I got to the front, my car was waiting for me. I got in and brought up her address in my navigation system to remind me where I was headed. As I sped off, I couldn't help but worry. I had a sick feeling about this. I prayed I was overreacting.

# Tajah: Chapter 7

I wiped the tears out of my eyes again. It wasn't smart to be driving when you could barely see the road because of them. I needed to pull over until I got control of myself. The last thing I needed was to wreck or hurt someone. I glanced around for a safe place to stop. I was still a ways away from my apartment. Seeing a fast-food place on the right, I pulled off there. I parked toward the back of the lot, but still close to one of the lighted lamp posts. I dug in my purse for a tissue after I stopped. Finding a crumpled one in the bottom, I wiped my eyes. I knew I had to look like a raccoon by now, but I didn't care. It wasn't like anyone would be seeing me.

I tried to block out the hurt, so I could calm down, but it wasn't working very well. Every time I thought I had myself under control, I'd recall what caused me to break down in the first place, then I'd tear up again. Damn it, why did I let myself hope? I knew better. I should've listened to my head when it tried to warn me. I was an idiot. The words kept running through my head repeatedly. I never imagined when I went up to Mikhail's office I'd overhear what I did, although it was a good thing I did. Better to know now, rather than later when it would hurt even worse.

*"Delilah, what a name. Come on, you can't tell me she does it for you. I've seen her. She's nothing special. All*

*she does is watch. You need a woman who's able to explore and let you release your inner self. That will never be her in a million years," a woman's voice said condescendingly. I froze just outside the office door. It was cracked open.*

*"Delilah isn't the kind of woman I would ever set up to play games with. She's nothing like you," I heard Mikhail immediately say back to her. My stomach clenched.*

*"I know she's not. I knew you'd never go for someone as vanilla as her. That's why we need to get back together. We're perfect for each other," she said huskily.*

*I didn't need to hear any more of this. I turned around and rushed to the elevator. The last thing I wanted was for them to realize I was outside the room. I shoved people out of my way so I could get to the door and escape once I got to the main floor. I vaguely muttered something to Hoss before I went to find my car.*

God, what the hell was I going to do? There was no way I could go back to Lustz and face him. His true feelings shouldn't have bothered me, and if I hadn't been letting myself hope he was coming to see me as more than a patron and a business arrangement, I wouldn't be. I thought all the time we'd been spending together and some of the looks he gave me meant he saw me as someone he might be able to have something with. The more I learned about his lifestyle, the more I wanted to know, but more than that, I wanted to experience it firsthand. There were so many things I wanted to try, but only if he was my Dom.

What a pathetic fool I was. All I could hope for now was he had no idea I'd been thinking anything of the sort. If he knew I was, I'd probably die of mortification. One thing was for certain. Mikhail Ivanova had seen the last of me. I had enough information to continue my research on my own.

Blowing my nose, I rummaged for another tissue. While I did, my phone scared me into yelping as it buzzed loudly. I didn't get it out of my purse at first. I didn't want to talk to anyone, not even in a text. However, after a few minutes, I couldn't resist checking to see who'd sent it. My heart skipped a beat when I saw it was from Mikhail. I tried not to read it, but I had to. Reading his casual words and his statement that he was worried made me want to scream. I had to take a few deep breaths before I responded. I kept it simple and short. I couldn't keep from adding the part about him being free to enjoy himself. Why was he texting me anyway? Shouldn't he be relieved to be free tonight? He and the mystery woman are probably getting ready to do a scene together? Or had he made arrangements to do it after I left, before he found out I wasn't coming?

He responded to my text asking what I was talking about and he wanted to know what came up. I didn't bother to answer him. I kept thinking about them. I didn't stay until closing every night I was there. For all I knew, he'd been seeing her or others the whole time, which made sense. A man like him wouldn't be going without sex just because of me. The thought of it made me sick. Another reason to berate myself for being a fool.

I wasn't ready to go home. With my tears finally dried up, I put my car back into drive. A long drive was what I needed to clear my head and get myself back on track. This wasn't the first time life didn't go as planned and it wouldn't be the last. The story of my life when it came to anything personal. I didn't know how long I'd driven before my phone chimed again. As much as I wanted to ignore it, I couldn't. I quickly glanced at it, even though I shouldn't while driving.

***Mikhail: WTF? Where are you? Call me. We need to talk.***

I resisted answering him. He'd get the message and stop soon. I was wrong. Over the next several minutes, I got text after text.

***Mikhail: Tajah, please answer me. Why did you come to the club then leave without seeing me?***

***Mikhail: I need to see you.***

***Mikhail: Where did you go? You're not home.***

The last one got my attention. I shot off a quick text back to that one.

***Me: How do you know where I am? It's none of your business where I am.***

***Mikhail: I'm at your apartment. It's my business when you were supposed to be with me.***

***Me: I told you. Something came up. Go back to the club. I won't be home tonight.***

There were more texts, each one getting more and more demanding. Finally, I turned off my phone. He was pissing me off. Why did he care where I was? I was nothing but a damn obligation, a job to him. One I had no doubt he was getting tired of and wished he'd never agreed to allow me back or to educate me. He should be celebrating his freedom from the vanilla woman who'd stolen a month from him.

It was eleven o'clock but I decided not to go home. I'd just sit and brood anyway. Besides, I didn't want to chance him coming to my place. After driving a while longer, I stopped at a hotel. I'd stay tonight and go home in the morning. That way there would be no chance he'd still be there.

I got a weird look from the front desk lady when I checked in without any luggage, but I didn't care. She didn't know me. As soon as I got into my room, I stripped and went to take a long hot shower. All the crying had exhausted me. I hoped I could sleep. I desperately needed it. Twenty minutes later, I slipped into bed, naked. I shut off the light and closed my eyes. To keep my brain from thinking about Mikhail, I concentrated on working out scenes for one of my books. It wasn't the first one in my BDSM series. I didn't want to think about it.

I didn't sleep worth a damn last night. As hard as I tried, I couldn't stop my mind from dwelling on Mikhail and the conversation I overheard and how it made me feel. That's why I was up and headed home by seven this morning. I was dragging when I walked into my apartment. However, I had things to do and I couldn't afford to go to bed no matter how badly I wanted to. Life and work went on no matter what else was happening.

I had a ten o'clock meeting with a new editor who happened to live nearby in Franklin. We decided to meet at the coffee shop there to discuss possibly working together. My current editor had decided to retire soon, so I had to find a new one quickly. Once I got back from that, I had not only writing I wanted to do, but several other things.

A lot of people thought all authors did all day was sit and write. I wish. Most weeks, I was lucky if I spent forty percent of my time actually writing. And I didn't work a couple hours a day then I was done, either. It was eight hours or more. Hell, there have been days I did twelve or more and I rarely took a day off. Something I was trying to break the habit of doing and at least taking one day a week for just me. It was a work in progress.

Today, I had editing to do, then get the book formatted so I could upload it. Also, I had a cover to design, pimping to do, which is what we called promoting. I had to do it online in groups geared toward readers to get my name out there. On top of that, I had readers to acknowledge because I truly appreciated them, and more on social media and a video to make to upload to another social media site. And this was a lighter day. I got in the shower right after I walked in, so I would get out the door on time to get to Franklin.

At nine o'clock, I was ready and had gotten my emails answered and responded to posts. Grabbing my purse and car keys, I headed out the door. At this time of day, I should get there with time to spare, but you never knew, so I liked to leave early. I turned on my phone right before I got on the road. The dinging as things registered was insane. Surely, I hadn't missed that many messages. I quickly checked to be sure nothing was from the lady I was going to meet or from Cady. I should've warned her that I was turning off my phone. I had none from the editor or Cady, thank goodness, but I had text after text and several voice messages from Mikhail. I wasn't ready to deal with those so I ignored them. I needed my head in the right space for work. I turned it off again.

Three hours later and I was almost home. My meeting with the editor lasted longer than expected, but I was glad it did. We seemed to hit it off and found out we had a lot in common. I promised her I'd send her a small excerpt for her to edit and send back to see if what she did would meet my needs. She'd given me several people to talk to, who she'd done work for either in the past or still worked with currently. I had my fingers crossed she would be as good professionally as she was personally. Suddenly remembering I still had my phone off, I dug for it then turned it on. There was a flurry of dings, but I couldn't check them while driving. I'd do it as soon as I got home.

I was less than ten minutes from home when it rang, scaring the bejeezus out of me. I yelped. My handsfree system showed who was calling on my dash screen. It came up showing it was Carver. Wondering what he was calling for, I quickly answered it.

"Hi, Carver, is everything alright? You don't usually call me."

"You tell me," he said gruffly.

"What do you mean?" I was puzzled. He sounded upset.

"I mean, I've had Mikhail Ivanova blowing up my damn phone, demanding to know where you are and if you're alright. He's losing his shit. He said you were supposed to meet him last night at Lustz and you came. Then you left without talking to him and never came home last night. What the fuck?"

"He did what? I can't fucking believe him. Ignore him. If he calls or texts you again, tell him I'm not his concern. I'm sorry. I had no idea he'd do that. I'll reach out and tell him to stop. It's ridiculous."

"I want to know why you won't answer him. That's not like you. The last I heard, he was helping you with your research. What changed? Are you alright?"

"He was helping me and now it's run its course. End of story. I went for a long drive last night and ended up getting tired, so I stayed in a hotel rather than driving when I wasn't safe. I had my phone off so I could rest. I've been out and about busy this morning." I gave him enough of the truth that I hoped it would satisfy him.

"You never turn off your phone, Taj. Talk to me." I heard the worry in his voice.

"Carv, I'm fine, really. Just tired and super busy. I promise I'll talk to Mikhail today. Now, I hate to run but I'm almost home. I'll talk to you later."

There was a long pause before he answered me back. "Okay, I can take a hint, but if you need to talk, call me. I'll see you maybe next weekend."

"Next weekend. Bye, love ya."

"Love you too. Bye."

I sighed in relief once he hung up. A few minutes later, I was parking my car at home. I didn't waste time getting to my apartment. I fixed a quick protein drink as I scrolled through my phone. I still wasn't ready to deal with Mikhail, so I skipped his texts and voicemails. I saw I had one from my cover artist. She wanted me to check out what she sent. Sitting down at my laptop, I opened her email. After reviewing it and sending her my feedback on one minor change, I read the others I'd gotten in my work email account. I looked at work emails several times a day compared to my personal one which I did a daily check of and cleared out the junk.

I finished those, and I was about to open my document for my book when there was a loud knock at my door. Wondering who it could be, I got up and went to answer it. It was probably one of my neighbors. Most knew I worked from home and they'd come by to chat or borrow things. I had to pretend sometimes not to be here to get any work done.

Luckily, I looked out the peephole first. I gasped when I saw Mikhail standing there with an angry look on his face. Without thinking, I jumped back, like I thought he could see me. *What a moron*, I thought. What should I do? I wasn't ready to face him, but if I didn't, how long would he keep calling and texting me? As much as I hated to do it now, I needed to put on my big girl panties and do it.

There was another knock then he called out, "I know you're home, Tajah. Open the door."

To prove a point if only to myself, I waited a good thirty seconds, maybe more, before I unlocked the door and threw it open. I made sure my expression was calm and disinterested. I placed my body, so I was blocking the opening. I leaned against the doorframe in what I hoped was a casual pose.

"Mikhail, is there a reason you're pounding on my door in the middle of the day? I'm working and I don't have time to talk. I need to concentrate."

"Really? You wanna play games with me?"

I crossed my arms so I wouldn't punch him. "I'm not playing games. I'm working and I have a lot to do. As a business owner, you should understand that. Can this wait?"

"No, it can't goddamn wait! I've waited all night and half of the day. I'm not leaving until we talk. Now, we can do it with me on your doorstep, where God and everyone can hear us, or you can let me in so we can have privacy. Which will it be? I don't give a damn, personally," he snapped.

I didn't want my neighbors to know my business, especially since so many knew I was an author and I tried hard to keep my personal life separate from my business one. Slowly, I moved out of his way and waved for him to come inside. I might as well get this over with. As he crossed the threshold, I told him, "You have ten minutes then you have to leave. I've got a conference call in a bit and I need to prepare for it," I fibbed, before closing the door and turning to face him.

I wasn't expecting him to crowd into me, which made me step back. My back hit the door. He caged me in with his arms on either side of me and gazed down at me. I fought not to flinch, but I did prepare to defend myself if I had to. I would've never thought he was a man to put his hands on a woman, particularly after the way he reacted to Dominus doing it, but I could be wrong. Better safe than sorry. Why did I let him inside?

"If you don't back off in the next ten seconds, this conversation is over and I'll make you move. Lay a hand on me and I'll have you thrown in jail for assault," I told him softly.

Shock flashed across his face then he moved back. He ran a hand through his hair as he glanced around my small living room. I moved so I had more room between us. He knew what I was doing by the way he frowned. His next words confirmed it.

"Jesus, Tajah, surely you know I'd never lay a hand on you in anger, and I sure as hell wouldn't hurt you. What the hell? Tell me what's gotten into you. I've been going crazy all night and this morning, trying to figure out where you were and if you're alright. I even called Carver to see if he had heard from you or knew where you were."

"I know you called him. He told me, which wasn't your place. You had no reason or right to call him and make him worry. Leave him alone. As you can see, I'm perfectly healthy. As for knowing you wouldn't lay a hand on me or hurt me, I don't know you. We've barely known each other casually and only for a few weeks. I'd be stupid to assume that or anything else."

"Are you for real?"

"Very much so. You've wasted three minutes already. Mind getting to the point of why you've been blowing up my phone and bothering my friends?" I went over and sat in my favorite chair. He followed but he didn't sit down. He paced.

"I've been trying to find out what happened last night. You said you couldn't make it, but Hoss told me you were there then you left. Why didn't you stay? I was talking to Reuben in his office, but if you couldn't find me, why didn't you text me or ask someone to find me? And why leave then act like you couldn't come? You're freezing me out. I want to know why."

"I'm not freezing you out. As for why I left, it's simple. I got there and realized I shouldn't have come. I've learned a ton from you. I thank you for giving up all your precious time, but I have enough now that I can do the rest on my own. There's no need to continue our lessons. I was going to call you and tell you this once I was done working today."

"So you think after a month you know all there is about the House of Lustz and the life? I hate to tell you, but we've barely scratched the surface. How do you propose to learn more, ask Carver?" he asked with a bite to his tone.

"Carver and you aren't the only Doms in this town, in case you forgot. I doubt I'll have trouble finding one or several to help me," I said without stopping to consider how it might be construed, but I wouldn't have ever guessed how he'd react to my words.

He let out a growl, then in a flash, he was standing over me with his hands on the arms of my chair. He had his face close to mine. I lashed out instantly to defend myself. I threw a punch, only he grabbed my hand and kept it trapped in his. I tried to lift a leg to kick him, but he'd placed his legs to trap mine against the chair. Panic filled me. How could I be so stupid?

"I told you. I'd never hurt you and I mean it. Don't look at me like that. There's no reason to fight me. I'm sorry I scared you, but you can't say shit like that and not expect me to react, Tajah."

"I'd be stupid not to fear you, and why should you react like this? All I did was say the truth."

"If you think for a second I'll let you go to another man to have him teach you about my lifestyle, you don't know me at all."

"Come on, surely you're not that egotistical to think once a woman comes to you, she can't and won't go on to others. I doubt there haven't been plenty of women you've had fun with who did it. Do you forbid all of them from doing it? And it doesn't apply in our situation even if you did do that with them. I'm not your sub. I'm an author you were helping professionally. It was consulting. Nothing else. You should be happy about me moving on."

"And why exactly should I be happy about it?"

"Move back, please. I don't like you crowding me like this."

"I will once you answer the question. Why should I be happy that you want to move on?"

"I would think it's obvious. Now you don't need to waste precious time teaching me and you can get back to what you've had to either postpone or do only when you've had a break from me. You can go back to sharing your expertise for real with the women at Lustz. I bet they'll be happy to see you've stopped wasting your time on me. Thank you for your sacrifice. I'm sure there'll be plenty of people who will love what you've taught me."

"It hasn't been a goddamn sacrifice to be with you, and if you think I'll let another man touch you, you're wrong," he snapped. As I gasped at his audacity, he shocked me even more by letting go of my fist, which I'd forgotten he still held.

"I'm gonna kiss you, so if you don't want that, tell me now," he muttered.

I was so stunned by his comment, I couldn't say a word. My brain seemed to be frozen by the vision of him doing it, how much I wanted it, and what his mouth on mine would feel like. Because I didn't say no, his hand came up to grip the back of my neck and pulled me closer. His mouth landed on mine and his tongue swept into my mouth as his lips hungrily took mine. I didn't know what to do, so I kissed him back. My whole freaking body burst into flames. *God, I'd gone and done it now.*

# Mikhail: Chapter 8

Her taste burst on my tongue, as I thrust it into her mouth and let my mouth take hers the way I'd been dreaming of doing for weeks. I knew vaguely I should slow down, but I couldn't. The thought of her letting another man teach her anything, to kiss her, and take her body, made me insane. I wanted to kill, while at the same time, I wanted to drag her off to my private cave and hide her. To spend hours, days, even weeks, taking her in every way I could and while I did it, I'd make sure she'd never want anyone but me. I'd mark not only her body but her mind, heart, and soul as mine. And while I did those things, I'd plant my baby inside of her. Yeah, that's right. I now had a brand-new kink—a breeding one.

And while I did all that, I wouldn't be sharing any part of me with anyone else. My heart, mind, soul, and body would be only hers. My cock would only ever need or want her. I'd gone from an uncommitted, non-monogamous man to a totally committed and absolutely monogamous man. She was mine and I was hers. I'd do everything I had to in order to make her see it, accept it, and to fall for me like I'd already fallen for her.

A whimper came from her. It wasn't one of distress, though. It was one of desire. I was experienced enough to know the difference. I groaned when her hands threaded into the hair on the back of my head. The slight bite of her nails in my scalp made my cock grow harder. Sliding my hands from her neck, I worked them behind her shoulders and lower back. When I had a good hold, I lifted her, spun us around then sat down, bringing her down to straddle my lap. As she did, she writhed on me, which ground her groin into mine. She cried out in my mouth and pressed down on my aching cock harder.

As we kept kissing, I ran a hand up to cup her tit through her thin t-shirt. I squeezed. I wasn't able to feel as much as I wanted, though. I needed bare skin. Letting go, I moved my hand down, then underneath the hem of her shirt to push it up. This time, I pushed her bra cup out of the way before I enclosed her firmness in my palm. Her taut nipple dug into the center of my palm. I squeezed, then plucked it hard between my forefinger and thumb. She tore her mouth away from mine to cry out and throw back her head.

I groaned. "Fuck, Tajah, I need this off. I need to see and taste you."

Her eyes were closed. She didn't answer me, but she did nod her head yes. I didn't wait for more. I worked off her shirt then her bra. As the last piece fell to the floor, I took in the beautiful sight in front of me. Her ivory skin against my very tan hand was mesmerizing. Her pale pink nipple was so hard and begged for my mouth. I gripped both of her mounds in my hands, kneading them, then I leaned forward to suck a nipple into my mouth. I lashed it hard with my tongue.

"Oh God," she murmured hoarsely.

I already knew from the kiss and this, that she was super responsive and would submit beautifully to me. However, this wasn't about playing. That would come later. This was about pure need. I didn't neglect her other tit as I sucked on the first one. Wanting to gauge her response to pain just a tiny bit, I bit down on her nipple and tugged. I made it hard enough to be somewhat painful, but not agonizingly bad. It had to stay more in the pleasure zone than the pain zone.

She moaned loud and long and pushed herself deeper into my mouth. I wanted to shout for joy, but I didn't want to stop or let go, so I merely growled. Not wanting her to get sore, I switched sides. She moaned and rubbed her sweet, luscious body against me. Her short-clad groin was grinding hard on my zipper. I had a monster of an erection happening in my pants. And that monster wanted out to play. It needed her anyway it could get her, even if it was just her hand. I felt like I might explode any second, and I didn't want to do it in my jeans or without her touching me. Would she do it?

I had to let go to ask her. As crazy as she was making me, I still held on to enough reason to know I had to ask her. I had to have her permission. Even if we weren't fully into a scene or anything, I had to start with the basic tenant I lived by.

"Tajah, my Dove, I need you."

"H-how do you need me?" she panted.

"Anyway you'll let me. I want nothing more than

to strip you bare and feast on your body until we both come to completion, in whatever form you allow it to take, but I don't want to push you into something you're not ready for. God it's hard not to try. You've got me so damn close. I don't know what to do. It's never been like this since I was a damn teenager," I admitted.

Instead of her saying something, she answered me with her actions. She reached down and rubbed her palm over my bulge, causing zaps of pure, painful pleasure to streak up my cock and into my low belly. I groaned and pressed up, so I was tighter against her hand. I guess I was coming in my pants after all.

Suddenly, her fingers were fumbling around, then I felt her tug on my zipper. Jesus, was she doing what I thought she was? What I hoped she would? Her hard tug lowered my zipper. Even though I was still in my pants, there was a bit of relief. Or there was until she snaked her hand under my underwear and grasped me in her palm. I growled loudly. She stroked me. Her eyes were staring into mine. They were filled with heat, passion, and more.

I may have only known her a month, but I knew she felt something more than lust for me. She wasn't the kind of woman to have sex with a man, not even the mild stuff we were doing, unless she felt something. I prayed it meant she was at least partially falling in love with me. There was no way I could have her then let her walk away. I needed to slow this down and make sure she understood this.

"Baby, wait. We need to talk."

"No, we don't. I don't want to stop," she pleaded.

"I don't either, believe me, but we have to. Look at me and listen, please. This is important."

She reluctantly did as I asked, but her hand stayed wrapped around my cock. I left my hand on her tit. "Okay, I'm listening, but hurry."

I chuckled. "You have no idea how happy that makes me to hear you say that. I need to be sure you understand what it means if you give yourself to me. Okay? It means you're mine. No one else will touch you, instruct you, and they sure as fuck won't have anything to do with bringing you pleasure. I'll be your Dom and we'll work on what it means to be my sub. Exclusivity is the game. I don't share."

I saw a look of doubt come over her. She eased her grip. I wanted to tell her not to. I let go of her. "What's wrong? I thought you wanted this. Wanted me."

"I do, but why're you doing this? I know what you think of me. I'm not your type. I'm too vanilla. You say you don't share, but I'd be expected to share you. I'm sorry. I wasn't thinking. I can't do this," she said brokenly, as she tried to stand up so she could move off me. I quickly moved my hands so I could grab her hips and hold her still against me.

"My Sweet Dove, what the hell are you talking about? You're not my type? Vanilla? What're you talking about? I don't think that about you. As for sharing myself with others, I never said that."

"Yes, you did. Don't lie. I heard you and that

woman talking. The one who wants you back. She said I couldn't satisfy you and I wasn't your type. You agreed with her, Mikhail. I heard you," she accused.

My confusion instantly cleared up, then another realization came to me. This had to be why she left last night without seeing me, and why she had been refusing to talk to or see me. She'd overheard what Tessa said in my office. I hated that she had and it caused her pain, but I was relieved it was something I could easily explain. I nodded my head.

"You're right. I did say you aren't the kind of woman I'd play games with and you're nothing like her." She stiffened in my hands. I continued. I could see her shutting down on me.

"However, you misunderstood what I meant. Tessa is my former sub partner. We broke up four or so months ago. It was never more than a transaction, I guess you'd call it, between us. She needed a Dom to play with and I needed a submissive. It was a mutual parting of ways. Last night, Reuben let her into my office, thinking I needed to let loose and she was the ideal person to do it with. She did say things about you not being the woman for me, but you didn't stay long enough to hear me tell her to leave and there would be nothing between us again."

"Even if you did, what she said is true. I'm nothing special. I don't know anything about your lifestyle other than the theory of what you've told me. How can you want to be with me when you can have her or plenty of other women who know how to be your sub? You said you don't want me to play games with."

"Not the kind of games where we're performing like it's a transaction, only for mutual gratification and nothing else. I don't want that with you. I want it to mean much more than casual. It's got to be more than exploring and sex between us, Tajah. I'm looking for long term here."

She stared at me in disbelief. What did I have to say or do to get her to believe me? I was beginning to panic. What if I couldn't? The thought of her walking away filled me with terror. Finally, she said something. "Long term? What does that mean? Wait, it doesn't matter. You said you won't share, well, neither will I. That's non-negotiable for me, so you should take Tessa up on her offer."

She tried to jerk her hips out of my grasp, but I held onto her and jerked her, until she fell against my chest. I wrapped my arms around her to hug her tightly to me. "I don't fucking want Tessa. I want you. I never said I wanted you to be only mine, but I would continue to be with other women. This would be a two-way street in that regard. Do you know how long it's been since I did a scene or had sex with a woman?"

"No, and I don't want to know. I don't want to know who you've been playing with this past month. The fact you have been shows me you're not ready for something monogamous."

"I haven't touched anyone this past month! How can I when all I can think about is you, and you're the only woman I want? I've been walking around in so much need, it's a wonder I can walk. My cock is raw from all the hand jobs I've given myself to thoughts of you. I haven't been with a woman since Tessa and I broke up. No one interested me until I met you. You've got me on fire, woman. My inner beast wants out so badly. He goes crazy whenever you're near."

Her mouth dropped open in surprise. She closed and opened it a couple of times before she could speak. "Are you serious? No one in months? I don't understand what you see in me. And what do you mean by your inner beast?"

It was time to confess a big part of me. We'd spoken in general about various kinks over the weeks, and I'd confessed I was a voyeur, but I hadn't told her any of my other ones. Here went everything.

"Yes, I'm serious. What I see in you is an intelligent, independent woman who has an underlying submissive hiding inside her. One who will be mine to guide and please if you give me your control. I'm not looking for someone I can command twenty-four seven. I need someone who has the qualities you have. As for my beast, it's my major kink. Remember when we talked about primal hunters?"

Her eyes widened as it registered what I was telling her. She slowly nodded her head. "Yeah, I remember. They like to focus on raw feelings and actions that are part of their natural impulses and urges, right?"

"Yes, that's right. I'm a primal hunter. I need to hunt, baby, but never to harm. Please know that. As a primal, I have to prove I'm worthy to have my sub. We use the term prey but not in a negative way. You control the experience, just like you would in all other types of play. As my prey, I need you to trust me to meet all your needs and that you have nothing to worry or think about. You can let go. We display animalistic behaviors, like wrestling and hair pulling. We can growl, scratch, sniff, lick, chase, and even take down our submissive. We love it when you resist us, fight back, or even run. Using your hair, nails, teeth, and skin are a must. The one thing it will never include is actually harming you. There will be scratches, bruises, and even bite marks, but nothing severe enough to truly harm you. Remember those bruises Dominus put on you?"

She nodded.

"I wasn't just angry that he forced himself on you and manhandled you against your will. It pissed me off he did it and left marks, when the only marks on you should be the ones I give you during our play. Ones you want. The arnica cream I gave you and I insisted you let me apply the first time was me giving you aftercare."

I'd explained aftercare to her the first week, too. It had to coexist with power and aggression, like we experienced in the kink world. If a Dom didn't do it, then he or she wasn't upholding part of their responsibilities. It was crucial before, during, and after sex. It was the time and attention we gave each other to wrap up our play and make sure the other was safe and comfortable. By allowing me to give it to her, she was fulfilling my needs, too. I had a need to be a caregiver. There would be times I'd want care from her in return.

"It was? But you didn't even know me, Mikhail."

"I know. And I never had such a strong urge to take care of someone, not even someone who was my sub. That need was what made me start to think you were what I've spent my life waiting for, even though I didn't know it."

"I want to be sure we're talking about the same things here. When you say monogamy and long-term, what does that mean to you?" she asked.

"Tell me first, what does it mean to you?"

"Monogamy is kinda obvious. Neither of us would play or have sex with anyone but each other. Flirting isn't allowed or watching someone with sexual interest in my definition. You can cheat in more ways than just by having sex. Pointing out someone else's attractiveness and comparing your partner to them in a negative way is a no. Long term is hard to define. The hope is always you'll go into a relationship and it'll turn out to last a lifetime, but it rarely does. I know this first hand. So I guess it's a relationship we see ourselves, hopefully, in for months, if not years to come."

"We'll go back and talk about a couple of the things you mentioned, but let me tell you what it all means to me. I agree with every point you made about monogamy. And you need to know, I would never flirt or show interest in another woman in thought or behavior. As for long term, I've never used that term until now. For me, it means I want this to last forever, and we'd have every aspect of that kind of relationship in the traditional sense."

"Every aspect? Traditional?"

"Yeah, a formal Dom/sub relationship, along with marriage and kids, if you want them. We'd share every part of our lives in and out of the bedroom."

"Wow, I don't know what to say. You've surprised me. Maybe I should get dressed, so we can talk about this more. I don't want us to make a mistake, and we jumped into getting hot and heavy without talking first."

The last thing I wanted to do was stop, but I understood the need, so I nodded. I watched as she got up and found her bra and top, then put them on. While she did, I adjusted myself and zipped up, while I tried to think boring thoughts, so my erection would go away. I knew watching her get dressed wasn't helping matters, but I couldn't seem to look away. Once she was clothed, I gestured for her to come back to me. When she did, I gently pulled her down on my lap. I cuddled her close. I needed physical contact with her, even if it wasn't sex. She placed her head on my chest.

I rubbed my hand up and down her arm. "Talk to me. What else do you want to clear up?"

"For one, how can you be so sure you want this with me? Secondly, how do you see our Dom/sub relationship being defined? Would we have a contract? How much say would I have in the terms? If it isn't working for either or both of us, can we renegotiate it or once we commit, that's it? What other kinds of kinks are you into? What if there are things I don't want to do but you do?"

I could hear an edge of panic in her voice. I knew

I had to tread carefully yet be totally honest with her. Telling her lies or evading answers would only blow up in our faces later. Communication was key and along with it respect, which would help lead to trust.

"I can't tell you one hundred percent how I know I want this with you and no one else. I told you how you affect me, and that I've never truly thought along the lines of permanent and monogamous ever before. That's part of it, but there's also this deep-in-my-gut feeling, telling me this is meant to be. I guess you might call it faith. I'm willing to put in every effort to make sure it works between us, and I want the same commitment from you. As for how our relationship will be defined, we negotiate it together and put it in an actual written contract we agree to and sign. It's not legally binding, but it is still binding to us. If we find something isn't working, either of us can ask to renegotiate. It's not set in stone or one-sided.

"As for what kind of kinks am I into and what if you don't want some of it and I do? Let me answer the second part of that first. We'll discuss hard and soft limits and safe words. If it's a hard no, then we don't do it. Soft ones we'll stop, discuss for as long as it's needed, before deciding whether to do it or not. Now, let's talk about my kinks. You know about the main one, my primal one and that I'm a voyeur. Obviously, I'm a Dom. The other main things I enjoy are impact play, bondage, anal, role-playing, and orgasm control. Others I've tried and either don't need or I'm willing to discuss. Do any of those scare you outright that you think they're a hard no? I want you to be honest with me."

"Most of the ones you mentioned I'll admit, they

make me nervous. I've never really done most of them which makes me lame, I bet, however it doesn't mean I'm not curious. It was my curiosity about them, which led me to wanting to write my series and to bug Carver to get me into the House of Lustz. I just have no idea if I'll enjoy them or not. I'm worried you'll get bored teaching me, even if I discover I like them. And how can I know if something is a hard limit if I've never done it? I mean, some are no-brainers for me. No cutting or burning me, things like that."

"I suggest we start with the things you know you'll like or are willing to do, then move on to those that are a maybe and find out. If we start something and you change your mind, all you have to do is say your safe words. I won't force you to endure something, Tajah. Doing that kills trust and neither of us will be happy or satisfied. The scarier ones, we can decide if you want to try over time, as you get comfortable with us.

"As for your worry I'll get bored teaching you, that's not possible. I've been finding myself fantasizing about teaching you so much, which is new for me. I've always been someone who stuck to experienced subs and women who know firsthand, at least, some about the lifestyle. In your case, I don't care if you only have the theory as you call it. It just means you're all mine, which I love the thought of." I couldn't help but let a low rumbling growl loose at the thought. I began to get hard again, just thinking about it.

The way she blushed and darted her eyes up to mine told me she felt it. I grinned as I adjusted her around to press against her ass more. "Mikhail, stop it!"

"I can't help it. You do this to me and I can't control when or what does it. Fuck, at the club the other night, the smell of your damn shampoo had me imagining holding fistfuls of your hair, as I fed you my cock. I had to hide behind you until it went away."

She moaned softly. I couldn't resist licking up her neck to her ear where I nibbled softly. I blew a puff of air along the wet trail I left behind. She shivered. "I want to lick, bite, suck, touch, scratch, and so much more, every square inch of you. I want to chase you and have you fight me until you submit. Being primal can be rough, but it doesn't always have to be. There are parts of it which aren't. And afterward, I'll pamper you so good. I want to feel you come on my tongue, my hands, and my cock. Toys will be a part of our love life, too. Please say yes. Tell me you'll come on this journey with me. Even though I'm experienced, I have no doubt I'll learn many things, too."

The ideas running through my head were making me almost sweat, and I was fully hard. She wiggled herself to face me more, which made me moan. She gave me a sexy smile. I opened my mouth when she nipped my bottom lip with her teeth. She slipped her tongue inside, and it parried with mine until she withdrew it. I tried to chase it but she shook her head.

"Do we have to wait until we make our contract and all that before we can do more of this? Or take care of that?" She wiggled her ass on my straining erection as she asked.

I let out a snarling sound which made her eyes

widen. I stood with her clutched to my chest. That was the last straw. I had to have her naked in my arms. If she only wanted to taste each other, I'd take it. She could jack me off or suck me dry. I didn't care, but I'd make damn sure she came more than once.

"Where's your bedroom?"

"Last door on the right," she said breathlessly.

I didn't waste time striding down there. I kicked the door shut then carried her to the bed where I laid her down. She was breathing hard, just like me. I didn't waste time taking off my shirt, shoes, and socks.

# Tajah: Chapter 9

I could barely breathe when I saw his naked chest. I knew he was muscular. You could tell by the way his clothes fit him and the way he carried himself. However, even they didn't do him enough justice in my opinion. He was ripped and dark hair covered his chest and ran in a tantalizing line down to his waistband where it disappeared. I needed to see the rest of him soon.

Our discussion and the images it evoked in my mind, had me turned on, but the feel of him pressing into my bottom and recalling how it felt earlier when his hands and mouth were on my tits had made me wet. I was afraid I'd soaked through my panties and shorts to leave a wet trail on his jeans. I was relieved to see I hadn't. That might've been embarrassing. Not wanting to be fully dressed and him to be completely naked, I sat up to take off my shirt and bra. He stepped closer to the bed and shook his head no. I froze. What did he mean? Had he changed his mind already?

"I want to undress you. First lesson in being my submissive. I want to be the one to undress you unless I say otherwise. Although, if we're alone either here or at my place, that may not be often since I'll prefer you to be naked."

"And does being naked include you too or just me?"

"Oh, I'll be the same. I hate clothes and go without them as much as I can," he said with a wink.

"Well, it might take me a little while to get used to it, but as long as I'm not alone. I think I can."

"There will be times when you're the only one, but I promise it'll be for a reason and in the end you'll enjoy it. Right now, I want to even us up a bit. Raise your arms for me."

I did. A small thrill went through me, especially when he reached out and lifted up the bottom of my top. He didn't hastily take it off. Instead, he took his time inching it up past my tits then over my head. He watched as each of those inches of skin were revealed, as if he didn't want to miss anything, even though he'd seen me topless not very long ago.

Before he moved onto my bra, he ran his fingers over the upper part of my boobs, down each arm, and across my ribs. His touch was so light it tickled and made me squirm. He smiled. "Ah, so you're ticklish, I see. Good to know. I can't wait to find out where all the spots are."

"I'll warn you, if you touch my feet, you'll more than likely get kicked. I can't help it. Ask the ladies who do my pedicures. I warn them every time," I warned him.

"I'll take my chances. God, your skin is so soft and pale. I love the contrast between yours and mine," he said softly.

"And I'd love to be able to tan like you. I've always been one to burn. I tried as a teenager to get a tan and stopped after a couple of nasty burns."

"I'm glad you stopped trying to ruin this perfect skin. There's something else perfect I want to admire." He followed saying that, by running his hands behind my back. My bra came loose. He slid it down my arms and laid it on my nightstand. His gaze hungrily looked at both tits before he traced his fingers down the slope of each one, over the nipple, and then to the undersides. My nipples hardened even more into tight buds. Just a simple touch made them ache.

When he ran his hands up to my shoulders, he pressed on them. I lay back so he could look his fill. I hoped he'd do a lot more touching, too. He didn't disappoint. He stretched out beside me then raised up on his elbow. I moaned when he sucked one of my breasts into his mouth, He made long draws on it, while his hand teased and kneaded the opposite one. Every so often, he'd thrash the hard nubs with his tongue or pluck with his fingers. He also switched from side to side. Not to be outdone, I used my fingers to play with his nipples. I wasn't only about receiving. I wanted to give pleasure, too.

After I didn't know how long, I knew I needed more. I was unsure if he'd want me to take the lead or not, but I gave it a try. I slid my hands to his stomach and rested them on the button above his zipper. I paused to see if he'dd say something. He lifted his head and smiled at me.

"Are you trying to tell me something, Tajah?"

I gave him what I hoped was an innocent look. "Maybe. What do you think I'm saying?"

"That you're trying to get my pants off. Shame on you. What a minx you are. Hmm, should I make you wait, or should I take your bottoms off first? Choices, choices," he said in a teasing tone.

I couldn't hold back my giggle. Just those couple of sentences told me he could be fun in bed. Something I'd never had with a guy ever. When this came to mind, I pushed it away. I refused to think about anyone other than him at a time like this, and I prayed he was doing the same.

I played along. I ran a finger back and forth just under the waistband of his jeans. "Hmm, let me think. Do I want to see what you have hidden, or maybe we should take a nap? I'm kinda tired," I said before I pretended to yawn.

He released a low growl deep in his throat before he pounced. He attacked my neck with his teeth and lips, while he used one hand to capture both of my hands and pin them to the bed on my pillow. The other quickly undid the four buttons holding my jean shorts closed. Recalling what he said about being a primal hunter, I struggled mockingly, like I was trying to get loose and away from him. He lifted his head and the flare of increased desire in his eyes told me I'd done the right thing.

"Are you trying to tempt the beast, Sweetest

Dove? If so, keep it up and I'll show you more of him. Remember, if you get scared, tell me."

"I will."

"I need both hands. Keep your hands up here. No touching or moving," he demanded.

I was willing to do it, at least for the moment, but I didn't tell him that. My heart sped up from more than just being turned on. I was excited to see more of his hunter side, even if I was nervous, too. Like with my top and bra, he took his time getting my shorts off. As he did, he caressed, kissed, nibbled, and licked all over my lower stomach, thighs, and lower legs. He did heed my warning about my feet. All he did to them was kiss the top of each one.

I was even wetter than before by the time he came back to my panties. He got up on his knees and hooked two fingers under the lace band of my dark purple bikini panties. They matched the bra he removed. I liked pretty under things. They made me feel feminine and pretty no matter what I might be wearing on the outside. He held my eyes for a couple of heartbeats, then slowly and torturously worked them down. I barely had enough brain cells not occupied with feeling to remember to help him, by lifting my ass off the mattress, by pressing my heels into it.

By the time he had them completely off and my legs spread apart, I was almost whimpering with my need. I let out an undignified whine when he got off the bed. I reached out to him. He shook his head and frowned.

"If you want me to take off my pants, you've got to keep your hands on the pillow. No touching me yet. Soon."

I snapped them back in place, which made him chuckle. I watched him without blinking, as he undid his button then lowered his zipper. I saw his black underwear peek out. He didn't glance away as he pushed them to his knees, then to his ankles. Once he had them off, I could admire his legs. He had thick, muscular thighs covered in dark hair. His underwear was tented by a big bulge. I licked my lips in anticipation of not only seeing his cock, but hopefully of tasting it.

"Lick your lips again," he muttered.

I slowly circled them a couple of times. He groaned, then his underwear disappeared onto the floor in a flash. He straightened and stood next to the bed, gripping the base of his cock. He was more than average-sized. He was long and thick and I saw prominent veins running his length and shininess on the head. He gave it a couple of strokes and a twist around the head before he climbed back onto my bed.

He pushed my legs apart even wider, then lay between them on his belly. I wanted to protest him hiding such a gorgeous sight, but I bit my tongue. It was a tossup between what I wanted more, him to touch and taste my pussy, or for me to do the same to his cock. I was the one making hard choices now.

He ran his nose over my lower stomach, just above my pubic area. I swore I heard him sniff before he let out a low groan. He nuzzled into my short-trimmed hair, then he placed kisses over my mound and my inner thighs. In between the kisses, he began to talk.

"Tajah, my Sweetest Dove, you smell so goddamn good and I love that you keep yourself natural. I need a taste. I've been patient long enough."

"Please," was all I got out before he circled my hard distended clit with his tongue twice, then he swiped it slowly down my slit to my entrance. He paused there to flutter the tip of his tongue just inside me, then he ran it back up to suck hard on my clit. I cried out and bucked my hips off the bed. He growled, clamped an arm over my hips, and pressed them down.

As he made pass after pass up and down my folds and around both my clit and entrance, he got faster and worked me harder. His fingers and teeth were in on the action, too. I tried to lie still, but I couldn't do it for long. I broke. My hands lowered to clutch the back of his head. I figured he'd order me to put them back up, but to my surprise he didn't.

"Mikhail, God, that feels so good. I don't know what I want more, though. To come on your tongue or to have my hands and mouth on you. I want to taste you," I pleaded. I wanted to cry when he stopped long enough to answer me.

"I want your touch on me, too, but not until I get at least one orgasm out of you. Come for me. I need more of your sweet honey. You taste sweet and salty. Two of my favorite flavors."

As soon as he stopped talking, he fluttered his tongue along the entire length of my slit, then thrust a finger inside me, while sucking on my clit, and with his other hand, tugging on my short pubic hairs. The slight bite of that, along with the motion of his finger inside me and his tongue pushed me fast toward a climax. It only took him maybe a minute or so to push me over the edge. I couldn't have held in my cry, even if I wanted to.

I came hard. It seemed to last longer than I recall any past orgasms ever had. By the time I went limp, I felt so good, like I was half-floating. Jesus, if he could make me feel like this from going down on me, what would it be like when he actually fucked me? I might die. As I lay there dazed, I knew I had to rouse myself. After making me come like that, the man deserved a blowjob. I was going to put my all into it, too. I caressed the back of his head and neck. He was resting his chin on my mound watching me. He had a self-satisfied smirk on his face.

I tugged on a tuft of his hair. "You're proud of yourself, aren't you?"

His smirk grew bigger. "I am. I think you enjoyed it more than a little, the way you came and yelled. I wonder if your neighbors heard you? Although, if you think it needs to get better, I'm more than willing and able to up my game."

I moaned as I shook my head. "Lord, don't say that. I still can't totally feel my legs. I do believe you deserve a reward for doing such a stellar job, though. Why don't you let me see if I can get you off? I want to taste you, Mikhail."

"Misha. I want you to call me Misha."

"Misha? Shouldn't it be Master M like at the club?"

"Usually it would, but I don't like the idea of you calling me anything others have. You're special. I'll have to think on what to have you call me when we play."

"What if I call you Master Misha? Would you like that?"

"Mm, I think I like it. Yes, that'll work," he said with a note of satisfaction.

"Okay, Master Misha, may I touch and taste you now?"

He nipped my lower belly, making me yelp, then he sat up and back on his heels. I swear his cock looked bigger than before, and it was even redder and precum was halfway down his length. He cupped his balls and squeezed them, then moved his hand to grasp the base.

"You may."

He maneuvered himself until he was sitting with his back to the headboard and his legs were splayed wide in front of him. As much as I wanted to start tasting him, I wanted to return some of the teasing, like he had done to me. The light touches, bites, licks, and other things he'd done to me had increased my ultimate pleasure, and he deserved the same. I might not be as knowledgeable in all the different kinks, but I'd always been one who worked to make my partner enjoy himself. He curled his finger up a couple of times to beckon me. I wiggled myself up to straddle him. He raised his left brow at me, but he didn't say anything.

I began with kisses and light nibbles on his lips. Before he could take over the kiss, which I thought he was about to do after about a minute, I left his tempting mouth and moved to his jaw. The prickle of his stubble on my lips felt good. As I worked my way down his neck, I put my hands to work, outlining his muscles and teasing his nipples.

I was concentrating on his nipples with my mouth in no time, while my hands kept going lower to scratch and pet his ribs and stomach. He had a delicious six-pack stomach. I was jealous. No matter if I worked out or not, I always had a slightly rounded belly. His cock was a mere inch or so from my lower body. I wanted to rub myself against him, but I resisted.

"Tajah, if you don't want me to take control, you'd better put your sweet fucking mouth on my cock."

I fluttered my eyelashes at him and smiled. He growled, then I was airborne. He rolled me onto my back and then he was straddling my chest. He fisted his cock and held it above my mouth. He tapped my lips with the head, which left a smear of precum across them. I wasn't able to stop myself from licking my lips to taste him. I moaned.

Suddenly, he was pressing the head insistently against the seam of my mouth. "Open and take a proper taste," he demanded.

I didn't know what made me do it, but I barely cracked them open far enough to stick out my tongue. Apparently, he was waiting for it, because he thrust harder. I opened wider since I didn't want to have him take his cock away or to hurt him with my teeth. With his whole head now inside my mouth, his taste burst on my tongue and made me moan. The vibrations must've felt good because he groaned and thrust deeper. I didn't want him doing all the work, so I gripped the base and used it to control his slide. I sucked hard and lashed the sides with my tongue. Using my other hand, I massaged his sac.

"Fuck, that's it. Harder. Squeeze my balls. Give me teeth," he uttered hoarsely.

I gave him what he demanded. The sounds he made, along with the way he was thrusting deeper and harder, told me he was enjoying what I was doing. When his fingers sank into my hair and bit into my scalp, making it sting a bit, I groaned. He hissed. "Again. I wanna see how far you can take me, Sweetest Dove. You've got me close already."

Working him deeper, I gagged when he hit the back of my throat. I thought he would pull back, only he didn't. He hummed in appreciation and spoke again. "I want you to try and swallow it. Take a deep breath."

I barely had time to do it, before he was pressing deeper. As I gagged, he kept going. I'd never taken a guy this far. I tried not to keep gagging, but it was impossible. As he blocked my airway, I felt panic welling up. He held it for a couple of seconds then pulled back.

He soothingly petted my hair. "Such a good girl. Thank you for doing that. Let's try again. I promise I won't let you suffocate, even though it might feel like you are. You have no idea how good it feels, or how happy you're making me, baby."

His praise made me want to do better. I slid down.

This time I gagged a little less, and it wasn't as startling when he slipped deeper. I still felt panic, but not as bad. This set up a pattern over the next few minutes. As I got more and more into what I was doing and following his directions, I began to hold him longer in my throat. Occasionally, I'd hum, which made him groan louder. His balls tightened, and I knew he was close to coming. I sucked tighter and sank my nails into his inner thighs. If he liked his balls squeezed hard, what were the odds he might like other slightly painful touches?

"Shit, I'm gonna come. You decide. Swallow or not," he muttered hastily.

It was an easy choice. I'd never seen the sense in expecting a man to go down on me, then refuse to let him come in my mouth. Cum wasn't terrible tasting in my experience. I kept up the suction. Seconds later he jerked, and the first spray of cum filled my mouth. I swallowed over and over. He growled like an animal as he came. I made sure to keep up my ministrations until he stopped coming, then I gently cleaned him with my tongue before I let go. He ran his thumb across the corner of my mouth then pressed the tip inside. I sucked it clean.

"Christ, that was amazing, Tajah. Give me time to regain my senses, and then I'll show you what else I can do. I hope you weren't planning to do much this afternoon."

I whimpered. "Mikhail, I mean Misha, I'll gladly let you lead me to playing hooky. Although, if you make it better, I might not be able to stand it."

"Challenge accepted," he said with a grin.

I opened my mouth to accept his offer when a phone rang. It was coming from over on the floor. My cell was out in the living room, so I knew it was his. He swore, then eased off me to roll over and reach down. He came back up with his phone in his hand. He was frowning as he answered it.

"This better be life or death, Reub," he barked.

I could hear distant muffled words, but not well enough to understand them. His frown worsened, then he swore. "What the fuck? You've got to be kidding me. Yeah, I get it. Thanks for calling. I'll be there as soon as I can. Keep him busy."

He didn't bother saying goodbye before disconnecting it. He looked over at me. "Babe, I'm sorry, but I've gotta go. There's a fire inspector at the club. Some bullshit about receiving a complaint. I need to go see what the hell it's about."

He got up and started to put his clothes back on. Feeling too bare when he was getting dressed, I flipped the comforter over me.

"You don't need to apologize. It's work and you should be there. Hopefully, it'll turn out to be nothing." I told him.

He nodded as he finished getting dressed. As soon as he was, he leaned over and kissed me. It was a slow and intense one. When he lifted away, I wanted to follow him. "I'll get done as soon as I can. I'm not finished with you. Why don't you come to the club later? We can relax upstairs. I have something to show you."

I didn't have to think long about his offer. I'd take any opportunity to spend more time with him. I wanted more of what we just did. "I'd like that. Why don't you call me when you're ready for me? That way I'll have time to get ready and maybe do some more work."

"Good. See you later. Damn it, give me one more for the road," he muttered before he kissed me again. "Stay here. I'll lock the door behind me. Drive safe when you come."

"You drive safe, too."

I hated to see him walk out of the room. I lay there a few minutes after I heard the front door close before I made myself get up. I needed to shower and make myself presentable, then I could work until I received his call. I wondered what it was he wanted to show me.

☘ ☘ ☘

I spent the next several hours getting myself situated to go when he contacted me. I was surprised it was close to six o'clock before I got his text. I swear I could feel his anger through his typed words, but I knew it wasn't anger at me.

***Mikhail: Goddamn asshole finally left. Please say you can get here within the hour? I'm dying and I need you to distract me.***

***Me: I can be there in less than an hour. See you soon. Do you want me to come to your office?***

***Mikhail: No, text and I'll come get you. Bring a bag***

***with you.***

***Me: A bag?***

***Mikhail: Yes, you can't think I'll be done with you until very late or even morning. I need you. Stay tonight.***

Suffice to say I was surprised he'd ask me to do it this soon. He struck me as a man who guarded his privacy. Maybe I was wrong.

***Me: OK, I'll bring one.***

***Mikhail: TY. Remember, drive safe.*** I replied with a thumbs-up emoji.

It didn't take me long to pack a bag. Out of habit, I included my laptop, then I locked up and went out to my car. It didn't take me more than a half hour to get there. It took that long mainly due to it being the last part of rush hour. The parking lot wasn't totally full yet and somehow I lucked out and found a spot not too far from the entrance. It was Saturday night, so I knew it would soon be full. I sent off a quick text to Mikhail then got out.

Hoss was at the door when I got there. He smiled at me as he opened it. "It's good to see you, Delilah. I guess this means you and the boss are speaking again."

"Who said we weren't?"

"The way he reacted last night and tore out of here, I knew something was wrong. Now, you're here and it looks like you're staying." He gestured to the oversized bag I had slung over my shoulder. "Go in. Do you want me to text him you're here?"

"No, I already did, but thanks. Try to stay out of trouble tonight."

He laughed. I grinned at him before stepping inside. At the front table was Laura. I swear she was here all the time. I smiled at her. She gave me a stiff nod then lowered her gaze. I ignored her rudeness and went through the second door into the actual club. I saw Mikhail coming toward me. I met him part way. I admit, I didn't expect what he did when he got to me.

Rather than saying hello to me and taking my arm the way he usually did, he swept me into his arms and laid a kiss on me that made my brain go fuzzy. The chatter of all the voices around us faded away. When he let go, I would've fallen if he wasn't holding onto me. He smiled down at me.

"I needed that. Come on, let's get out of this crowd and upstairs."

"I'm good with that plan," I told him.

As we made our way to the elevator, I saw numerous sets of eyes on us. Along with surprise and curiosity, I saw several less than happy looks. I knew he was the object of many women's desires. I'd have to be blind and stupid not to know it after this long. They wanted to be the one he was kissing. It made me feel warm inside to be the one he was with. When we got in the elevator, we weren't the only ones to get on it. He spoke to the couple who did. They chatted with him about nothing specific. When they got off on the second floor, he put his handprint on the screen, so we could continue to the third floor.

Getting off it, instead of him taking me directly across the hall to his office, he led me down the hallway. I knew from something he said before, this was the way to his apartment. I hadn't thought about it when he said to bring a bag, that we wouldn't be staying in his office. Duh. I grew excited to see his personal space. I was looking forward to seeing and learning more of the personal side of him. A person's home told a lot about them.

# Mikhail: Chapter 10

Holding onto Tajah's hand as I took her toward my inner sanctuary, my personal retreat, I took one last opportunity to think about what I was doing. Other than Reuben and a select few others, no one had been in my home. Certainly, no women I'd had sex with or just played with. I hadn't wanted them to leave any memories of them here. Maybe that made me an asshole, but it was just the way I was wired.

Did I want her in my space and to leave her imprint there? And possibly, or more like definitely leaving things here, which would mix with mine? I thought about it as we rode up the elevator with the chatty couple, I knew it was the right thing to do. No matter how little time I'd known her, I was never more certain she was to be mine. In order for it to happen, I had to let her in all the way, like she would have to do the same with me. Secrets led to mistrust and the inability to communicate, which would kill everything. She had to know all of me to love me. I had to know all of her to do the same. And make no mistake, having her love was crucial to me, which shocked me as much as it had Reuben.

After the very frustrating time with the fire marshal, I pulled Reub aside to tell him I was having Tajah come to the club, and I needed him to keep an eye on things, since I would be behind closed doors with her in my apartment. The look of astonishment on his face when he heard it was comical. He literally did a double take.

*"Mikhail, did I hear you right? I swear you just said Tajah will be in your apartment."*

*"Yeah, you heard me right. We have unfinished business, the fire inspector interrupted earlier. I want to focus on her and not the club."*

*"I get you wanting to spend time with her, but isn't it a bit soon to invite her into your home? You've never had a woman up there. Maybe you should slow things down some. I know what you said about her, but still."*

*"I'm not slowing anything down. She's the one, I know it. And I know it sounds crazy to you, but it's true. I want her to share herself with me in every way. She's going to have to learn how to live in my world. In order to do it and make it work, there can't be pieces held back."*

He'd tried to convince me to wait, but I refused to consider it. Now that she was here, I did one final internal check to be sure I was totally at peace with it. As we got to the door of my home, I knew I was. There was only excitement inside of me, no worry or unease. Like my office door and the access on the elevator to this floor, it took a handprint to get into my apartment. Keys could be lost or stolen. Yeah, someone could hack my scanner too, but it was much less likely. Plus, I loved tech stuff. I pressed my hand to it and the screen lit up green, so I could open it. I held onto her hand, as I brought her inside my sanctum. I wanted to see her reactions to it.

The lights were on one of those automatic deals, so they came on at the lowest setting. The entire space was three thousand square feet. Most of it, with the exception of the bedrooms, bathrooms, my office, and one other room was open into each other. The ceiling had metal rafters and beams, giving it a rather industrial feel. I liked metal and colors like black and red. There were splashes of gray too. So it wouldn't be too dark in here, I kept the walls white but the furniture and artwork on the walls were filled with color. I went for things that not only looked good but were comfortable and would be able to hold up to a big guy like me. No tiny chairs you had to fear sitting on, or that felt like a slab of concrete.

There was an electric fireplace in the living room and the master bedroom. A large fully equipped chef's kitchen, with a big island separated the living room from the kitchen area. Off to the side was the dining nook. She was looking around with curiosity on her face.

"Let me give you the tour. We'll start over here."

I led her to the kitchen. As we worked our way around it, then the other open spaces, she asked me questions about how I came up with the design and the colors. After we were done with those, it was onto my office and the guest rooms and baths. I had three of them with two bathrooms. She paused in my office when I took her there after the bedrooms.

"Misha, you have that gorgeous office down the

hall and this one, too. You're a very lucky man. Either space is to die for to work in. These make my tiny closet of a room look pathetic. I have office envy," she said with a laugh.

"I'm incredibly lucky, I know. I do most of my work in the main office, but sometimes when I'm home and something comes up, I don't want to go to it, so I work from this one. I can work in the nude if I stay here," I said with a grin.

She laughed again. "I guess you don't want to chance just anyone walking in and finding you like that, although you said not a lot of people have access to up here. You must be worried you'll scandalize Reuben."

"It would take more than that to scandalize Reub, believe me. It's not as if he hasn't seen me naked."

"I guess not. It amazes me you can be so casual about so many people seeing you that way. I'm not sure I could do it."

I heard the worry in her voice. I hurried to clarify something. It was a good place to start. I took both of her hands and led her to a chair. I sat then had her sit on my lap. She gave me a puzzled look.

"Dove, yes, I've been naked in front of plenty of people. It has never bothered me. Nor has it bothered me to have those same people see the person I was playing with." She stiffened hearing this, but I held her so she wouldn't move away.

"Wait and let me finish. They didn't bother me. Now, you, I can't see myself letting anyone see you naked, Tajah. The thought makes the beast side of me want to rip heads off. That's new for me, so you never have to worry about me insisting on us doing that. If we want to play downstairs, we'll go to a private room, but I don't think we'll have to do it often."

"Why not? Don't you want to play anymore?"

"Oh, I do and we will, but we have other options. Come on, let's finish the tour."

I let her go, so we could stand. Taking her next door, I showed her my bedroom and bathroom. Both were big and had every comfort. The bathroom had a high-tech multiple heads shower system and a separate soaking tub along with double sinks. She gasped when she saw them, but she got even more excited when she saw the walk-in closet.

"That's it, I'm stealing your closet. I have no idea how I'll get it in my tiny apartment, but I'll figure it out. No wonder you don't bring many people up here. They'd want to kill you for this place."

I hugged her against me. "Do you want to kill me for it?"

"No, but if I could sneak this out, and come over once in a while to soak up everything else, I'd be happy."

I had to bite my tongue to keep from telling her she could have it every damn day if she moved in with me. That was going way too fast, so I held it in. Instead, I told her, "You're welcome to come over as often as you like. Okay, there's two more things I want to show you."

I led her to the opposite end of my apartment. I

had two rooms there. One was a small gym. She was impressed with the equipment. "Misha, I see the secret of your body now. You're a gym rat. I wish I was. Then I'd have a six-pack and be a size six," she said with a sad sigh.

"I work out a lot, but I don't want you to do anything to change your body. It's perfect the way it is. I don't want a woman who feels like a man. I like soft. A size six would make you even more breakable. I love the way you are now," I told her sternly.

She surprised me by giving me a kiss. I was about to take it further when she broke away. "That right there might just get you laid tonight, Mr. Ivanova. What a sweet talker."

"Babe, I am getting laid tonight, and it wasn't sweet talk. It was the damn truth. Now, before we get distracted again, I have one more room to show you."

Taking her out in the hall and over to the last door, I placed my hand on a scanner next to it. When it was unlocked, I didn't open the door immediately. She frowned. "What is it, another office? Don't you have enough of those? Or is this where you keep your valuables?"

I shook my head. "Nope, it's neither of those. This is a very private place to me and you're the only woman to ever see it."

I pushed the door open and took her inside. The lights came on and she gasped. This was my inner playroom. One I'd designed to have all the equipment and things I loved the most. The dream was to one day be able to bring someone up here to play with me. Until her, I'd never been tempted. I was glad I never did it. This would be our space. I had so many things I wanted to explore with her in this room, and in my other personal space. It was fine to do things downstairs, but this was all ours.

She slowly walked the room looking at everything. She didn't say anything. I watched her stop and study some things, while she picked up other items. I let her look her fill. I knew she'd have questions soon. I was ready to answer them. The idea of teaching a neophyte had never interested me, but doing it with her, I was all in.

It was a good twenty minutes or more before she stopped and looked up at me. I saw wonder, a little worry, and excitement all on her face. "Misha, I don't know what to say. This is incredible. I can't believe you've never brought anyone here. If you have this, why play downstairs? Is it because you wanted to be watched? You admitted you're a voyeur and if you didn't mind being seen playing, you're an exhibitionist. Is that why? But still, surely sometimes you wouldn't mind playing in private?"

"I didn't always have to be watched. The reason I never brought anyone up here is it's special, and I didn't want to just have anyone in it. I always hoped I might one day get to use it, but after more than a decade and nothing, I gave up hoping. And then this romance author wormed her way into my club and knocked me for a loop. When that happened, I knew it had been waiting for you, for us. This is our place to play. Well, it's the one here anyway."

She was staring at me with her mouth open. I could see I'd shocked her. Unable to resist, I tugged her to me and lowered my head to kiss her. She wasn't a passive participant, and within moments we were hungrily devouring each other. I lifted her and walked her over to the leather chaise I had in the corner. I lay her on it, then straddled her so I wouldn't squash her.

My temperature was going through the roof. I planned to have dinner with her and then let the rest of the evening progress. It was remembering that and the fact I'd ordered dinner after I texted her, which made me reluctantly move off her. She sat up and gave me a concerned look. "What's wrong, Misha?"

God, I loved her calling me that. It was a nickname from my youth, which I rarely heard. It reminded me of people who loved me. Earlier it had hit me. I wanted her to call me that, not that I didn't like my actual name, I did, but Misha was more personal.

"Nothing's wrong. I forgot. I ordered us dinner, and it should be here any minute. Damn it, I don't want to stop, believe me, but we'll need our energy so food is a must."

Her concerned look turned to a smile. I saw amusement. "Oh really, you think I'll need energy, do ya? That's a lot to live up to. Are you sure you can do it? Maybe we should eat and watch movies."

She shrieked when I stood and snatched her up. I attacked her neck. I bit her lightly as I pressed her to the wall beside the chaise. The tease wrapped her legs around me and ground her pussy against my growing hard-on.

"Misha," she gasped out so prettily.

"Does this feel like I can't live up to it? There won't be any movies tonight. Now, behave and stop tempting me. I only have so much self-control. Let's go back to the living room and I'll get you a drink."

She sighed but nodded. I slowly let her slide down until her feet touched the floor. She rubbed against me so sensually, I was tempted to say fuck the food, but I didn't. She had to be hungry, I knew I was. Plus, it was her favorite. Over the weeks we'd been talking, we hadn't just talked about kink. We had shared personal things, like our favorite foods and what we liked to do to relax. Which movies and television shows we enjoyed. It was from one of those discussions I got the idea for dinner.

She loved Thai food and it was a favorite of mine. When we talked about places to get it, she had never heard of the one I went to religiously. She said she had to try it. As of a couple of days ago, I knew she hadn't gotten a chance yet. Well, tonight she would.

Closing the playroom's door, we went back to the main area. She came into the kitchen and checked out the drink selection. It wasn't a surprise to me that she stuck to a non-alcoholic choice—a bottle of green tea which she was partial to. I'd paid attention to what she drank downstairs and what she told me, too. She gave me an appreciative look when she saw I had it. I winked at her. She would find out this was all part of my inner need to take care of her. It wouldn't just be after sex and playing. I would need to take care of her in everyday ways, too.

Since the food was to be here any time, we sat at the island. I was drinking a beer. When I worked downstairs, I rarely drank alcohol, but here in my home, I could relax. We were only a couple of sips into our drinks when my phone buzzed. I knew what it meant, but I checked it to be sure and saw I was right. The delivery person wouldn't be brought to the third floor, so I had to go get it. Some might see that as a pain, but I didn't. I got up.

"The food is here. I'll be right back. I have to go grab it downstairs."

"Do you want me to come with you?"

"No, you stay here and relax. It won't take me long."

Before I walked out, I couldn't leave without giving her a quick kiss. God, she was becoming a drug I needed constantly. I dragged myself away and hustled to get the food. The ride down to the first floor was quick. It had been Laura who texted me, so I went to the front table to get it. She was sitting there with a tense look on her face. I almost asked her what was wrong but didn't. I was off tonight. If she had a problem, she could let Reuben handle it. The days of me constantly being on and available were over. I wanted alone time with Tajah. All the staff had been informed not to disturb me tonight.

"Thanks for texting me. I'll get this out of your way."

"Is everything alright, Mikhail?"

"Yeah, why wouldn't it be?"

"Well, we were told not to disturb you tonight and to go to Reuben. That's not like you. You're not sick, are you?"

"No, Laura, I'm not sick. I just need private time tonight. Thanks. I'll see you later," I told her as I picked up the bag. Her hand on my wrist stopped me from walking off. I stepped away. I didn't let people freely touch me. "Was there something else?" I asked.

"I wondered if you wanted company later. I'm only working half a night. I wanted to relax, and if you're doing the same, maybe we could do it together."

To say I was stunned would be an understatement. Did I know she had a fascination with me, yes, but I never gave her encouragement, and she had never gone past admiring glances and very mild flirting. To have her suggest this was new and unwanted. I hurried to shut her down as nicely as possible.

"I have company, but even if I didn't, I'd never get involved with an employee, Laura. You know that. Why are you suggesting this?"

She got a cross expression on her face. "You mean you've got that patron, that Delilah up there? You don't let people in your personal spaces, Mikhail. Why her? She's nothing special, just another person curious to see what we do here. Why pick her? I've been waiting for you to decide it's time to choose another sub. I think we can be good together."

Shit, this was worse than I'd thought. "Laura, I don't mean to be mean, but I've never seen you that way. You're a great employee, however, that's as far as our relationship will ever go. As for Delilah, she and I aren't up for discussion. All you or anyone needs to know is she's in my life, and she's here to stay."

She gave me a look which was partly upset and partly disbelieving. I decided not to waste any more time talking about it. There was nothing she could say or do to change my mind. My woman was waiting for me. I needed to see to her needs. I walked off without another word. The ride back up to my place gave me time to push Laura out of my mind. She'd get over it. If she didn't, then I guess we'd have to find a new greeter. As long as she stayed in line, she could stay.

Tajah was where I left her. When I came in, she jumped up to help me. I set down the bags and began to take out all the various containers. I'd gone a little overboard, but who didn't love Thai food and it warmed up to make great leftovers. Plus, I found a lot of Asian food seemed to burn off fast and you'd be hungry again in a few hours.

As I got plates, bowls, and utensils out, she opened one of the containers. I heard her inhale then moan. Hearing her make that sound made my cock stiffen. *Get your mind out of the gutter. You need to feed her*, I lectured my inner self.

"Oh God, Misha, this smells so good. I've died and gone to heaven. Is this from that place you told me about?"

"It is and no, you're not dead. There's lots to choose from. I got fried rice as well as steamed. There's hot and sour soup, Laab meat salad, stir-fry with pork, basil and green beans, a red curry with chicken, and for dessert mango sticky rice. Here, do you want a fork or chopsticks?" I set our plates and bowls on the island. She reached to take a plate, but I shook my head no.

"I'll serve you. Tell me what you want. First, chopsticks or fork?"

"Chopsticks. I'm not used to anyone waiting on me. I can do it myself, you know?"

"I know, but this is part of me taking care of you. Tell me what you want." She'd find I was driven to take care of her in many ways.

"I want to try everything, so a little of each please."

I quickly dipped her a bowl of soup and passed it to her with a spoon, before I loaded the rest on a plate and gave it to her with the chopsticks. "Go ahead and start."

"I'd rather wait for you," she said.

While I didn't mind her starting, it did make me feel good she wanted to wait on me. This relationship thing was opening a bunch of new things up to me and triggering characteristics I didn't even know I had. This need to care for a woman outside of a scene never happened in the past. When I had mine, I took a seat next to her and we dug in. There were a lot of satisfied moans coming not just from her. I'd forgotten how good this place was. It didn't take us long to inhale it and then sit back full and happy.

"Do you want another tea? We can go outside on the terrace." Outside, there was a third story terrace on the backside of the building. Sure, it overlooked other buildings around us, but it was nice sometimes to just be out in the air.

"Sure, but first, we should clean this up and I'm helping."

I let her get away this time with demanding, but not always. Nodding, so she knew I agreed. We quickly cleaned up and put the dirty dishes in the dishwasher, then got our drinks and went outside. I had a large lounger out there as well as a patio set. I took her to the lounger and situated us, so she was reclining back against my chest with her between my legs. For a summer night, it was surprisingly nice out. Summer could be very hot and humid in Tennessee.

This section of Nashville was called The Gulch. It was south of downtown, so we weren't in the middle of all that. It had once been an industrial area, which had been abandoned so there were lots of empty warehouses. I'd been lucky enough to get one of those, and be a part of the remodeling, which happened to a lot of those warehouses. It now had some of the best real estate in the city, and I shared it with restaurants, clubs, and upscale hotels along with cafés, boutiques, and other small businesses.

"It's surprisingly nice out here," she said.

"It can be. It's not as nice as being out of town. We'll do that soon."

"We will? Where do you want to go?"

"It's a surprise. Just know it's private and exceptionally beautiful, or I think it is."

"Sounds fun. I love being out in nature. If I could afford it, I'd buy a place out in the country. I don't mind people, but I'd rather be somewhere more secluded."

"Then I think you'll love the place I'll take you for sure. I like this location for the club, and the different businesses around here help to bring in more people. If I need anything, most are within walking distance, but as a true primal, I need the outdoors, too."

The next hour sped by as we talked about anything and everything. It was just more getting to know each other, but all of it told me we were going to be more than compatible. It was dark and the outside noise had grown due to the nightlife, so I suggested we go inside. I was finding it harder and harder to resist starting something and if I did, I didn't want to do it out where someone in a building across from us would see us. I wanted her all to myself.

Inside, I took our glasses to the kitchen then I held out my hand. "Let's go to my room."

She gave me a small smile. "I'd like that." As we walked by the couch, I grabbed the bag she brought in with her. Once we were in my room, I put it on the bench at the foot of the bed. "Why don't you use my bathroom? You can shower or take a bath. I'll use one of the others."

"I'd love a bath in that tub, although the shower is tempting, too. But why do you have to go to another bathroom? Why don't you join me? There's more than enough room in there."

"I'd like nothing more. I just thought you might want to be alone. You know, so you could perform secret female rituals we men aren't supposed to know about," I teased her. Even when I was involved with my mentoring kink lover, we hadn't lived together. She always wanted her space. Another reason I should've been suspicious.

She laughed at me. "Sure, I swear there's nothing that mysterious. I promise I don't need to shave my legs or underarms. I did that earlier. It's all unexciting, just bathing and brushing teeth. See, boring. You'll probably fall asleep."

I smacked her ass. She jerked and gave me a wide-eyed look, but the flush that came over her cheeks told me she enjoyed it. "Smart ass. Grab what you need and let's go. I'll try not to fall asleep."

She couldn't wipe the smirk off her face, as I left her to get her things. I went ahead and started running water in the tub. Not knowing how hot she liked it, I called out to her. "Sweetest Dove, how hot do you like your water?"

She came striding in. "I like it as hot as you can get it. I need to be a nice shade of red when I get out. Anything less, and it's not worth a soak in my opinion."

"Good, we agree. I'm the same way. If that's the case, would you mind company in this tub?"

"I'd love company."

Letting the water run, I straightened and went to her. I was happy to see she wasn't trying to undress herself. She remembered. That was something I'd noticed about her. Once she heard something, she recalled it. I wondered how much she'd remember and comply, and how much she'd resist. Earlier today had shown me she might just have some brat in her. I was fine with that. I could be a brat handler and enjoy the process, although I was far from an expert unlike some I knew. One in particular came to mind.

"We need to get rid of these pesky clothes. I've endured them covering up this sexy body long enough," I told her as I grasped the bottom of her tank and slowly lifted it.

She'd worn a tank paired with a long flowy skirt and sandals. Her shoes were by the front door. I didn't wear outdoor shoes around the house. I was barefoot and dressed in a pair of cargo pants and a t-shirt. Her hair was up in a bun on the top of her head, so no worries about it in the tub. After we were done, I'd take it down. I wanted to feel her hair against my skin and in my hands.

I groaned when I removed her tank. It had a built-in section, so underneath there was no bra for me to remove. I cupped her tits and gave them each a squeeze, before placing a kiss on each nipple, after swirling my tongue around them. She whimpered and pressed them into my lips. Raising up, I hooked my fingers into either side of the waist of her skirt and pushed it down. When I got it down to her hips, I saw the other thing she was missing. She had no panties on. Jesus, she was trying to kill me.

I kissed right above her mound then kept pushing it down until she could step out of it. Not wasting time, I shrugged out of my shirt and then took my pants off. Like her, I was commando. She watched my every move. I took all of our clothes and tossed them in the nearby hamper. I walked around her to take in all of her. Earlier, I hadn't done this. She was so damn perfect. Her lush ass caught my attention. I had to pause and squeeze both globes of her ass, before continuing to circle her. When I got back to the front, I held up a finger. She stayed there while I got under the sink on the right. It would be hers.

Underneath I'd put a bottle of bath salts. Normally I didn't use any unless it was one for a medicinal muscle soak, but she always smelled so good. I'd asked her one time what it was she used, and she said it was a combination of several flowers. I'd paid attention and found one with those same ones in it. For tonight, I wouldn't mind smelling like flowers, if I could be in the tub with her. I poured some in the water then put it back.

"Misha, where did you get that? It smells like..." she paused.

"It smells like you. I found them at a specialty shop not far from here. I went in and told the sales lady what I wanted and she told me this was the one. I hope you like it. Let's try it."

I held out my hand. She took it and I led her to the edge. There were steps so it was easier to get into the tall tub. I held onto her so she wouldn't slip. She gave me a grateful smile, as she sank into the water and sighed in bliss. I didn't waste time joining her. I slid in behind her, so she was between my legs. She leaned back against my chest. With us in it, the tub was almost at max capacity, so I used my foot to turn off the water.

"When did you have time to go get those bath salts with the whole fire inspector deal?"

"I didn't get them today. I got them a few days ago. See, I was planning to make my move soon, but the whole misunderstanding about Tessa made me realize I didn't want to delay a second longer. You'll have to make me a list of the other things you use and like, so I can get them stocked for you."

"Misha, you don't need to do that. If you want me here overnight, I can bring a few things with me or even bring some from home."

"I'll want you either here with me or me with you at your place. It makes sense to have stuff here and I'll get them. Now, relax and let me wash you. When we're done soaking, I have plans to get you dirty again. We'll get to use that shower tonight before we're done."

She laughed. We spent the next fifteen or so minutes soaking and she let me wash her, which I loved doing. It was my first time bathing a woman. It was going on my list of caring. Sure, I'd done aftercare with a woman before, but not to this extent. Holding, getting her something to eat or drink, playing soothing music, and talking had been the extent of it.

When she was clean and we were both relaxed, I helped her out of the water and took down her hair. It was time to make love to her. Tonight, we wouldn't go full force into the whole Dom/sub dynamic, but I would be making demands of her, and I'd see how she complied.

# Tajah: Chapter 11

My heart was pounding hard as I lay on the bed. Mikhail had ordered me to do so, while he went to his closet. I had no idea what he was doing, but I was filled equally with excitement and nerves. The way he'd cared for me all night so far had been beautiful and surprising. I'd never had a man do anything close to that before, not even my ex-husband.

I was torn from the unpleasant thought of my ex by Mikhail's return. There was no reason to taint us with thoughts of Sam. He was long past, even though he'd left emotional scars I still struggled with. I knew I'd have to at some point tell Mikhail about him. He knew I'd been married, but that was it.

In his hands, was a dildo and in the other a tube of lube. He put them on the stand near the bed. He got on the bed and slowly came crawling toward me. His movement reminded me of an animal stalking its prey. What did he want? Did he want me to wait for him to give me commands, or should I start fighting and trying to get away from him?

I'd researched a lot about various kinks over the past month, even more than I had before coming to Lustz. After finding out Mikhail was primarily a primal hunter, I'd done even more research after he left this afternoon. I knew for him, it was all about the fight to subdue his prey, me. He didn't want me merely to submit, although I was the submissive in our relationship. I admit, I got a secret thrilled sensation at the thought of having to fight back. Right before he got to me, I made my decision. I rolled off the bed and scrambled to my feet. I took off running for the hallway.

His growl was loud and scary. I heard his feet hitting the floor as he raced after me. I ran faster. I had no idea where exactly I was headed, but I was running. I didn't make it beyond the bedroom door before I was captured. As his strong beefy arms came around me, trapping my arms at my sides, I kicked back with one leg, while throwing back my head. It didn't reach his face, but it hit his chest hard. He lifted me off the floor, With both feet dangling, I could kick back with both at the same time.

"That's it, fight, little Dove, but you won't get away. You're mine," he growled in my ear, then he nipped it with his teeth.

Squirming as much as I could, I flung myself forward. It didn't get me out of his arms, but it did make him pitch forward a little and his arms loosened a tiny bit. I took advantage and jammed my elbow into his ribs then lowered my head to his arm. Hoping I wasn't going too far, especially our first time together, I bit his arm. I didn't break the skin, but it left teeth marks.

He hissed, but I was helpless as he carried me back to the bed. He dropped me on it. I shot off the opposite side. He was grinning like a predator at me, as I kept the bed between us. I tried not to be distracted by his raging hard cock. He was definitely liking this, and I'd known that when I was struggling with him, only then I couldn't see it. However, it had been noticeable, and I'd started to get wet just thinking of what he'd do with it. I wanted to feel him inside of me so badly.

"You keep staring at my cock like that, and this'll be over too soon. Give me what I want and I promise, I'll make you scream over and over. I'll eat your pussy and fuck you until you can't walk or scream. Come on my Dove. Make me work for it."

I gave him a taunting smile, then I rolled across the bed. As I reached his side, I swept out both legs to catch him. It was a self-defense move my dad had shown me. I caught him by surprise and he stumbled. I came to my feet and kicked out at him. He grabbed my ankle and I went down. I caught myself with my hands, so I didn't hit the floor too hard.

As he jerked me toward him. I kicked back and tried to scramble to get loose. His grip tightened, and then he was over top of me, pinning me face down on the floor. He was panting in my ear. His cock was thrusting between my ass cheeks, as he bit my shoulder then licked my skin.

"Yeah, what's my Dove gonna do now? Huh? I could take you like this. Just slip my cock inside of your pussy and fuck you like this. Or I could have you suck me off. Is that what you want?"

What he said all sounded good to me at the moment, but I wasn't ready to submit, so I decided to get verbal. "No! Get off me!" I yelled.

He chuckled and thrust himself harder against me. I knew he had to feel how slick I was. Throwing back my head, I caught his chin. He went "oomph" and his weight eased. I flipped over and took my nails down his chest. He captured my wrists and jerked them above my head. God, I was loving this. I raised my head and did the only thing I could. I bit his bottom lip. I did it a bit too hard and tasted blood. That sent him over the edge.

He transferred both of my wrists to one of his hands and used the other to grab my hair and hold my head still. It hurt. His eyes were practically gleaming, as he lowered his head. He started at my chest where he bit and licked all over my aching tits. He sucked my nipples hard then bit down. I was making mewling sounds. There was no other word for it. His stubble scratched my skin so deliciously. When he wasn't biting or rubbing his facial hair on my skin, he was licking and kissing it. I continued to try to get away and struggle as much as I could, but it was hard to do. He worked his way to my mouth. I cried out when he bit my lip and drew blood. Then he licked it gently, before placing a tender kiss on my mouth.

"Jesus Christ, I want to play so much longer, but I can't. Not this time. Baby, please tell me you're ready for me. I swear next time I'll give you a couple of orgasms before the main event, but you've got me so fucking wound up, I can't wait. Let me inside of you."

"Yes, take me," I pleaded. I was half crazy. My inner thighs were soaked. He let out a loud growl then he was up and I was airborne. He tossed me on the bed. I barely had time to take a breath before he flipped me onto my stomach and tugged me up onto my knees. He came up over me and pressed my upper body to the mattress. I felt the head of his cock probe my entrance for a moment, then he was thrusting inside. I screamed. It not only felt good, but he was stretching me so much it stung a bit, too.

"Do I need to slow down?" he panted out hoarsely.

"No," I whimpered.

He kept going, and even despite the burn I wanted more. I thrust back against him. He grunted then gave one final thrust and buried his cock to the root. I was shaking. He lifted off my back and his fingers bit into my hips, as he grabbed them and pulled back so only the tip was still inside of me. He didn't wait to thrust back inside with a hard long stroke. He used his hands to work me on and off his cock. He was slamming it deep and I couldn't stop it. After only a few thrusts, I came. I felt myself soak the bed. He let out a howling sound and sped up. I was barely able to think as he kept fucking me through my orgasm. It had barely finished, and I was starting to work toward another.

As he kept going, he was back to talking. "Fuck, you're incredible, Tajah. I've never felt anything this tight or wet. This pussy is mine. You hear me? MINE. I'm gonna live inside of you," he snarled.

I curled my nails in the sheet and whimpered. "Please, oh God, please no. I'm gonna come again. It's too much."

"No, it's not. Come for me, Dove. I wanna feel you soak me again. Squeeze my cock with that beautiful pussy. Make me come. You can do it."

Even though I could barely stay on my knees, I pushed my hips back to meet his next thrust. He pounded into me harder and faster. A few minutes later, I'd come two more times. I soaked him like he wanted and I swear I saw dark spots in front of my eyes as they blurred. I was sobbing into the pillow and waiting to die when he started to grunt. Then he buried himself all the way inside me and froze. He let out a roar like a lion, as his cock began to jerk and I felt him come. The warmth of his cum filled me. I was mindless and just lay there as he kept jerking and giving me load after load.

When he was done, he dropped and rolled onto the bed. Somehow he kept us connected, and I ended up cuddled in his arms, with him spooning me from behind. We were both panting like we'd run a marathon. I jumped when his teeth nipped my shoulder then he kissed it. His hand came up to gently grasp my chin then he turned my head enough for him to reach my mouth. He kissed me ravenously and didn't stop until I was about to pass out. As he did, he smiled lovingly at me.

"Tajah, you're absolutely without a doubt the best thing to ever happen to me. I never expected this, not our first time at least. Jesus, woman, you made me see stars when I came."

"Misha, I saw dark spots you had me so close to passing out. I can't even describe what that felt like. You're a menace."

He laughed, before giving me a peck on the nose. He lay his head back down. I stayed there floating as he caressed my skin and scattered light kisses all over my back and neck. I wasn't sure how long we stayed that way before I felt him soften and start to slip out. When he muttered darkly, then pulled the rest of the way out, I regained my senses. What caused it was I could feel his cum leaking out of me. I gasped as I sat up. I whipped around to stare at him. He gave me a questioning look.

"What's wrong, baby?"

"You didn't wear a condom?" I half shouted.

"No, I didn't. We should've talked about it before we got too far gone. I meant to and then you started to fight me and I lost my mind. Let me guess, You're not on birth control."

He said it so calmly, like it wasn't a big deal. It would serve him right if I said no. However, I didn't do it, though I did tell him I should've. "I should tell you no, just to see you sweat."

"I wouldn't sweat it at all. If you weren't and you got pregnant, I wouldn't give a damn."

My mouth fell open in shock. Had I heard him right? "Misha, are you crazy? Do you go around having unprotected sex with women and not caring if they get knocked up or not?" How many kids did he have running around? The thought of him having them made my stomach drop.

He sat up and leaned over me, so he was staring hard into my eyes. I was now on my back. "No, I do not. I always wrap up, and I still make sure to get checked often. I'm clean. However, those women in my past weren't you. I wasn't planning to be with them for the rest of my life. You, I am. And the thought of getting you pregnant speaks to the animal in me. I want to fill you with my seed over and over until I breed you," he said in a deep, growling tone.

"Breed me?" I squeaked. Of course I knew what he meant from my research, but it was still a shock to actually hear it said.

"Yes, breed you. Make sure you carry my baby. So threatening me with the possibility of you not being on birth control doesn't bother me a damn bit. However, I take it that I'm not that lucky."

"Lucky he says. You know, most men would be jumping for joy to know I am on birth control."

"I'm not most men. So what's the problem? I'm clean. I assume you are too."

"I am."

"Then we're good."

"What if we weren't clean? It wasn't very responsible of us. You make me crazy. I can't believe I did that," I complained.

He pulled me into his arms. "Dove, you and I don't usually do this. Hell, you're the first woman I've ever been with that I haven't worn a condom. That should tell you a lot."

"It does, but I can't believe I forgot. I've always double protected myself except with you and my..." I paused. In bed with him wasn't where I wanted to have a discussion about my ex-husband.

"Your ex-husband. I hate the thought that any man ever touched you before me, but I know it's not reasonable to be that way. Right now isn't the time, but soon, I want you to tell me about him. I want to know everything about you—good, bad, and ugly. But at this moment, why don't we go get cleaned up and then we can come back here and work on round two?" he grinned at me.

I moaned, which only made him laugh before hauling me off the bed, then into the shower. I hoped I'd live to see the sunrise, but it was doubtful. I guess there were way worse ways to go. *Goodbye world, I died happy.*

⁂

Lying on the couch with Mikhail late the next night, after hours of incredible sex, we were just chilling and talking. We were working on getting to know each other more than on a sexual level. Both of us knew this was key to a relationship just as much, if not more, than the physical. At the moment, we were talking about why he had to leave so abruptly yesterday.

"What did the fire inspector have to say? You said when you left my place there had been a complaint?" I reminded him.

He scowled. "It was a bunch of bullshit. I wish I knew who did it. I'd tear them a new asshole. He wouldn't say who made the complaint. All he said was they'd received one, stating we weren't following all the safety codes, and that lives were in danger, and they should come do a surprise inspection to ensure no one got hurt."

"Who would do something like that? I mean honestly, only a fool would knowingly endanger people's lives. And who is this anonymous person to be an expert on such things? If they noticed something, why not come to you, and tell you their worry?"

"I don't know, but I do know one thing. Whoever it is, they have to be a patron, an employee, or a vendor. Those are the only ones who've been inside the club. Oh, and if someone brought a guest, which does happen sometimes. He did slip up though and say whoever it was had suggested the club be shut down until a thorough inspection was done. Someone is trying to fuck with my livelihood and life's work. Whoever it is better prepare themselves. I won't rest until I know who and why."

"I have no doubt you'll figure it out. How did he leave it?"

"He did his inspection and wasn't able to find anything. He seemed upset when he left that he didn't. I don't know. There's just something totally off about it and the inspector makes me uneasy, too. Why would he care that there weren't any issues? He should be happy. It's not like he's out any money if nothing is found. Wouldn't he be glad people are safe?"

"That doesn't make sense, you're right. I wish there was something I could do to help, but I have no clue how to address this," I told him as I rubbed his arm. I could tell it was really bothering him.

He smiled at me. "Sweetest Dove, it helps just to

hear you say you want to help. Having you here does, too. Thank you," he gave me a tender kiss.

When he ended it, I had to mentally shake myself to stay with our current sharing session. The man had turned me into a nymphomaniac. I was sore and still wanted more. "Is there any way you can find out the information, if the inspector won't tell you?"

"There might be. I'm holding off trying, but if it doesn't become clear soon, I'll have to consider going that route. You know what, let's not talk about him anymore. He's gone and I want to talk more about us. Hit me with your next question."

"I have one and it's a simple one, but I've been wondering. Why do you call me Dove?"

"It's for a lot of reasons. When I met you and we cleared the air about why you were here, and I agreed to let you come back, I started right away to see so many things about you. You're gentle and devoted to your work and others. You're beautiful and give me a sense of peacefulness. And there's a purity about you. All of those in an animal form to a primal like me equates to a dove, so in my head I've come to call you that sometimes."

"Misha, I don't see myself as all of those things but I'm flattered you do. I never thought of equating you to an animal. I'll have to think about it but thank you. I do love the name and I love it even more now that I know why you use it." This time I was the one to give him a kiss.

He groaned when I stopped. "Damn, I want to get

lost in your kisses but I won't. Not yet. So back to my animal form, I figured you would just say I'm a grumpy, mean, snarly bear."

I giggled. "Don't get me wrong, you can be but you're nothing as simple as one ordinary animal. You're a hybrid of some kind, maybe. I see a bear and a lion for sure, but there's more. Okay, your turn, what do you want to know next."

His smile faded a bit which made my heart jump. Before I could freak the hell out, he asked. "I want to know about your ex-husband. You don't have to tell me every little detail, but who he was and maybe why he's your ex. I'd like to know, so I don't fuck up like he did. I have no intention of losing you, Tajah. I don't want to make the mistakes he did, which cost him you. Or the mistakes any man has made to do that."

My throat became clogged with emotion. Not only at the thought of telling him those personal details about a painful time in my life, but because he was so sincere about not making a mistake with me. If I was honest, although he hadn't been in a serious relationship, I needed to understand why, so I wouldn't mess us up either. It took me a minute to gather my thoughts then clear my throat so I could tell him.

"My ex-husband is named Sam. We met when I was in college during my sophomore year. I was the quiet, nerdy girl who guys didn't seem to notice. He was the popular guy everyone liked and wanted to be friends with. He was a senior. I was studying English, and he was moving onto law school at the end of that year. I still really don't know why he ever spoke to me one day in the student quad area. He just came over and struck up a conversation. From that day forward, he kept talking to me and things progressed from there."

As I paused, he made a statement and asked me a question. "He came up to you because you're beautiful and you draw people to you with more than that. It's an aura or whatever you wanna call it. This vibe you give off. Even when I was telling you never to come back, I was noticing it and it scared me, I'll be honest. I gotta ask, was he your first serious boyfriend?"

"He was my first boyfriend period. The guys in high school didn't notice me anymore than the guys in college. Eventually, after several dates, he asked me to be his girlfriend and brought me into his circle of friends. I knew they didn't get what he saw in me, but they acted nice enough. I was so happy for a while, thinking I'd finally found the one who would love me no matter what and that I had friends."

"How did it go wrong? I mean, it had to be good for you to marry him. You know we do background checks on prospective patrons, so I know you divorced him when you were twenty-five. I didn't dig into why."

I wasn't offended that he knew. I figured it had to come up in any background done on me. I was glad he hadn't looked at the divorce decree to see why. He needed to hear the story from me. There was more than met the eye. "It was at first. We continued to date until I graduated with my bachelor's degree. By then, he was finishing law school. He asked me to marry him the week after I graduated. I was in a daze planning our wedding and our future, while starting work in my field. I was lucky enough to get an editing job at a small company. We got married six months after he asked.

"With both of us in school and he was at a different university for law school, we had to find time to be together. We'd go days without seeing each other, but we would text and call all the time. I thought we were solid. I found out how wrong I was after we got married and started to live together."

I paused again. He jumped in. "If this is too much right now, we can table it. I don't want to make you relive memories that are obviously hurting you. I only wanted to know what I shouldn't do."

"I know that and I want to tell you. It's not raw anymore. I've accepted it. I just hate that I was such a fool, a blind one. I'm usually a rather smart person, I think. Anyway, after we were married and in the same home, he was always distracted. He had graduated by then and started working at a law firm. I knew he was busy getting his career off the ground, so I chalked it up to that. He spent hours and hours away and was rarely home. When he was, he was always busy on his phone. This went on and on. I thought after the first year at his job it would ease up, but it didn't.

"We'd been married a year and a half when it all came to a head. He was distant. His friends who I thought were my friends were acting weird. My work was going well and on all accounts so was his. I was at work one day and I was feeling lousy. My boss told me to go home and rest, so I did. I didn't bother to tell Sam because I didn't want him to worry, and I didn't know if he was in the middle of something really important.

I didn't need him to take care of me, so I decided I'd tell him when he got home."

"Fuck, please tell me you didn't catch him in your bed with some other woman," he growled.

"No, not that, but in some ways it was worse. I came into the apartment and I must've been too quiet because he was there and didn't hear me. I have no idea to this day why he was even home. I was walking to our bedroom when I heard him talking. I was about to call out when what he was saying registered. He was telling someone he loved them and how much he couldn't wait to see them, and living this lie with me was killing him. I felt like my heart was ripped out. I wanted to scream and curl up in a ball and die in the middle of the hallway."

"What did you do?" he snarled.

"I stood there getting myself under control, and then I marched into our room and let him see me. God, the look on his face. He went so pale I thought he'd pass out. He hurried to hang up and tried to act like nothing was wrong. That I had imagined shit. We got into a screaming match. After a while, I'd had enough. I'm not proud of it, but I hit him and shoved him. When he fell, I grabbed his phone and took it into the bathroom and locked the door. I never got into his phone or him into mine ever, but I'd seen him enter his code and I knew what it was. I unlocked it. I found months' worth of texts and calls between someone only identified as Z. The texts made it clear that they'd been in a sexual relationship for a long time and were in love with each other."

"What did you do?"

"I read as much as I could, then I walked out to him, flung his phone at his head, and told him to get out. He pleaded with me but I couldn't stand to hear it. Finally, he packed some clothes and left, after telling me we'd talk after I wasn't so emotional. Like I was being unreasonable for being upset. I took the rest of that day to settle down then I called my parents. My dad came to get me and I went to stay with them. I had a hard time keeping Dad from killing Sam, but I told him a police chief in prison wouldn't be good and I needed him.

"Sam kept calling and texting me, begging me to talk to him. I ignored him until Dad called him and told him if he didn't stop, he'd make him stop. He knew Dad would, so he did. The following week I went to a lawyer and filed for divorce. I found out later, all his close friends knew he was seeing someone behind my back. That hurt even more. But that wasn't the worst thing to come out during the divorce. Because I filed it due to infidelity, and I was smart enough, even if he wasn't, to go into our phone account and have the carrier send me the text messages. Since I was on the account as a joint owner, I had proof. He had to come out and reveal his lover if he didn't want me to take him to the cleaners. And in the end, I got my revenge, I guess you could call it."

"How?"

"His lover, the mysterious Z, was a man named Zach, who he worked with. They'd actually met in law school and had been seeing each other even before we got married. Sam had been hiding he was really gay for years before he met me. I guess I was just a convenient cover for him. His parents were hugely religious and believed homosexuality was a sin. They had money and paid for his schooling. He was afraid of them finding out and disowning him, which they did in the end. Since I'd never had a lover before, I didn't know what to expect in the sex department, so I thought all the things you read about in romance books were make believe after I started to sleep with him."

"When did you find out it wasn't?"

"Later when I got enough nerve to try to have a boyfriend again. It took me a couple of years to get my confidence as a woman back. It took me some therapy to do it, too. Sam made me feel like I was undesirable. I had two boyfriends after my husband and though they did show me there was more to sex than what I knew, they had other issues we couldn't resolve. It was because of them and my whole history, that I ended up becoming a romance writer. It was due to my desire to think there was more out there and that you could have a happily ever after full of love and passion. And I was lucky enough since I worked in the profession I did, I had people show me the ropes. It was due to that ongoing desire we met. I was still searching for more than myths when it came to sex. That women can have multiple orgasms and there's more than missionary position. That sex is important too in a relationship, even if it's not the only thing. I was curious and wanted to learn more."

"Baby, I'm so fucking sorry he hurt you like that. You didn't deserve it and it had nothing to do with your desirability as a woman. You slay me and I've seen how others look at you. Never think that for a moment. However, don't take this wrong, but I am glad it did happen because if it hadn't and the other two morons had been enough for you, I would've never met you. For that alone, I thank them and won't track them down and kill them."

His serious look and what he said made me not only feel wonderful but amused. I had to laugh. "Oh my God, you'd really do that? Go after them? You're crazy, Misha."

"I'm crazy about you, and I'll do anything I have to, to protect you. How about we put more talking on hold, and we go to the bedroom, and see what we can do to give you more material for your books? I'm here to be your muse in any way you desire," he said with a low rumble. I nodded my head yes which made him get up, lift me in his arms, and carry me off to his room.

# Mikhail: Chapter 12

I'd waited long enough to set into motion a plan to ensure Duncan or Dominus as he was known around the club, would never bother Tajah again. I'd put him way on the backburner then forgot him. I might've let it slide altogether since he had been totally silent, if he had stayed the hell away from the club and her, but he didn't. All these weeks and not a peep out of him until a couple of days ago, when he raised his head like a worm and made his mistake. And he did it in the worst way. He went after her.

He didn't come to the club and try to get back in or attack her there. No, he did it out on the street when she was going about her day. She had no idea he was anywhere around until he literally ambushed her on the street in the middle of a busy section of town. In fact, she was in The Gulch shopping, while I was busy at the club. She'd wanted to explore some of the boutiques and shops there.

*I'd sent her off with a kiss and we arranged for her to come back to the club and stay with me for the night when she was done. I had no idea anything was wrong until I got her call and I answered. Her shaky voice instantly put me on alert.*

*"Hey, Sweetest Dove, how's the shopping? Are you*

*exhausted yet? Do you need me to bring more money?" I teased.*

*There was a pause before I heard a ragged breath. "M-Misha, I need you. I don't know what to do." Her shaky voice came over the phone.*

*"What's wrong? Where are you?" I asked urgently. I was up and headed toward my office door even as I asked.*

*"I'm over on Twelfth Avenue. I'm in my car. I can't seem to stop shaking. I was coming out of one of the shops and I was accosted on the street."*

*"Are you hurt? Do you need an ambulance?" My head was about to explode as worry for her and fury filled me. Whoever dared to hurt her was dead.*

*"No, physically I'm fine. God, I shouldn't be bothering you with this. It's stupid. I'll see you in a bit once I calm down enough to drive," she said in a hurry.*

*Before she could hang up, I jumped in. "Tajah, don't hang up. You're not bothering me, and if you're upset, then you should always call me. Tell me which store you're outside of, then wait there until I come get you. Hear me? Don't move," I ordered.*

*She whispered the name of the store. I knew exactly where it was. After promising I'd be there soon, I hung up. I was riding down the elevator, seething by then. Whatever happened, I'd take care of it. She better not be harmed. As I stepped off the elevator on the first floor, I saw Reuben. I waved him over. He came rushing to me. He could tell by my face I was pissed.*

*"What's wrong, Mikhail?"*

*"I need you to take me to get Tajah. She's shopping over on Twelfth. She called me. She's shaky, upset, and in her car. I need to get her and bring her back here."*

*"Shit, let's go. Did she say if she's hurt?" he asked worriedly.*

*As we hurried to the front, I shook my head no. "She said she wasn't physically hurt, but she's upset. Something about being accosted. No way do I want her alone or driving back here in that condition."*

*"Of course not. I just stopped in to grab something, so my car is out front. You have perfect timing."*

*I felt a tiny relief. I wasn't in the mood to wait for my car to be brought up, or to even go get it myself. My skin was itching to get to her. I had to see with my own eyes that she wasn't hurt. No matter what upset her, I'd make it right. We jumped in his car, and he shot out of the parking lot and onto the street. It wasn't more than five minutes or more before I spotted her car outside the store she named. I pointed to it. "There she is. Drop me off and then you can go. Thanks, man."*

*"You're welcome, but I'll stick here and follow you back. I want to know if we need to hurt someone," he said, frowning.*

*I nodded. I knew he was becoming really fond of Tajah. We'd spent the other night watching movies and having dinner with him. I hadn't laughed that much in ages. After he left, the following day he told me not to fuck it up. He acknowledged she was perfect for me. I agreed.*

*By some miracle, there was an empty parking spot*

*right behind her. He quickly parked, then I jumped out and ran up to her. She was out of the car by the time I got to it. I moved her off the street and to the sidewalk where I hugged the hell out of her. She was shaking a little. I gave her a hard kiss before I reared back to look her over. I didn't see any sign of injury.*

*"Baby, tell me what happened. Why're you so upset?"*

*"Can we go home? I don't want to talk here," she said hoarsely. As she said it, I saw her glancing around uneasily. Warning bells went off in my head and my hackles went up. I scanned the area, trying to see if anyone was paying undue attention to her. I didn't notice anyone, but she was stiff. Reuben came striding up to us.*

*"Is everything okay? Tajah, honey, what's wrong?"*

*"Reuben, thank you for bringing Mikhail. I don't want to talk about it here. I want to go home."*

*"Fine, we'll go home," I told her, as I moved her toward the passenger side of her car. I opened the door and helped her inside.*

*As I did, Reub softly said, "I'll follow you. We need to find out what the fuck happened. She looks spooked."*

*I nodded. I didn't mind if he wanted to come. And he was right, she did look spooked. He headed back to his car. I got her situated then I got behind the wheel after I knocked the hell out of my knees getting in to move the seat back. Being just shy of a foot taller than her made a lot of difference in legroom requirements.*

*It took about the same amount of time to get back as it did to get there. This time we went around the building to my private garage. It had its own access. I'd been so consumed with getting to her, I hadn't been thinking, so I didn't go straight down the elevator to the basement level. You could access it from the elevator with the same palm scanner used to access the third floor. It worked out though because it allowed me to find Reuben.*

*She was quiet the whole time. I didn't push her. All I wanted to do was get her to my place and make her feel safe, then we could talk. Reuben and I parked. and I got her out of the car. She clung to my arm. I wrapped her securely underneath my shoulder, then we got on the elevator. I made sure to set it so it was on bypass, which meant no one could stop it on the other floors, and it would go immediately to the third. When we got there, I bundled her down the long hall then into my apartment. I took her straight to the loveseat where I sat her down.*

*"I'll get us something to drink," Reuben said as he went to the fridge in the kitchen. I sat next to her and hugged her close. She laid her head on my chest. I kissed her hair and rubbed up and down her arm. I was bursting to ask my questions, but I didn't want to rush her. It didn't take him more than a minute to be back with bottles of water and even a green tea for her if she didn't want the water.*

*"Which one do you want, baby?" I asked her.*

*"The tea, please."*

*I opened it then handed it to her before opening my drink. She took a long sip then sat it on the coffee table. "Dove, I don't want to push you, but I'm dying here. I need to know what happened. Whatever it was, you're still upset."*

*She let out a ragged sigh. "I'm sorry, I know you do. I'm acting like a baby. I just wasn't expecting it, so it shook me up. It was so jarring."*

*"Being upset doesn't make you a baby. Tell me. What was jarring?"*

*"Okay, I was shopping. I was coming out of a store down the street from my car. I was fumbling in my purse to get my sunglasses and I bumped into someone. Or I thought I bumped into them. I looked up to apologize, and that's when I saw who it was. I was surprised, but didn't really think too much about it, other than to wish it was anyone else."*

*She paused a moment before continuing. "It was Duncan. I mean, Dominus. He was standing there smirking at me. God, he makes me sick. I said excuse me, then I went to walk around him. He didn't let me."*

*"What do you mean, he didn't let you?" I asked softly.*

*"He grabbed my arm and asked me where I was going in such a hurry. I told him I needed to head home. He suggested we go have a coffee and talk. I told him there was nothing we had to talk about and to let go of me."*

*"Did he do it?" Reuben asked.*

*"No, he held on, and said there was something we did need to talk about. I was trying not to make a scene, while I figured out a way to get away from him without doing that. I asked him what he thought we should talk about. He said how I was going to get him back into Lustz, since it was all my fault he got kicked out. I told him it wasn't my fault. He*

*broke the rules and touched me.*

*"Dominus said it was because I'd been acting like I was all sweet and innocent, when he knew I wasn't. He accused me of playing games with him all along, and when I saw I got you to stand up for me, I used it as my opportunity to get your notice. I told him it wasn't true. He laughed and said all women are the same. We're nothing but whores who'll do anything to get a man to take care of us, and if a richer one comes along, we always go after him. He accused me of using sex and lies to turn you against him. He said no slut was going to deny him his place here."*

*Fury bloomed inside of me. I gritted my teeth to stop from swearing. If I wasn't holding her, I'd punch something. It took me a couple of deep breaths before I could say anything. "What did you say to that? How did you get away from him?"*

*"I told him he was wrong, and I hadn't been acting with him, nor had I lied or anything else to get you to throw him out. You made that choice and I knew nothing about it until after you did it. He then went on to say he knew I was spending time with you, and that you wouldn't be wasting your time on a beginner, so he knew I wasn't one and had been lying. He said if I didn't get you to allow him back in, I'd regret it.*

*"I asked him what he meant by that, and all he would say was I'd find out. He was loud and it attracted people's attention. He still had a hold of my arm. I yelled at him to let go of me again. When he didn't, I decided the hell with it, and I kicked him in the shin then punched him in the stomach. He let go and I took off. I thought for sure he'd come after me, but a group of people who'd seen our*

*altercation got between us. They were threatening to call the cops, so he took off. I ran to the car, and that's when I called you. I was too shaken to drive. I didn't know what to do."*

*I couldn't contain my growl of fury any longer. She jumped when she heard it. I sucked it back in as fast as I could. I didn't want her to be scared of me. "Babe, I'm sorry. I didn't mean to scare you. I'm not upset with you. I'm happy you called me. I always want you to do that no matter what. I'm furious with that cocksucker. He did the last thing he should've ever done. I promise you, he won't come near you again."*

*"How can you promise that?"*

*"Because I'll make sure of it."*

*"What're you gonna do, Misha?" she asked fearfully.*

*"You let me worry about that. All I want is for you to stay here and not go to your place. If he's seen us together, he might've followed you home. Until I take care of this, I don't want you to be there, not even during the day."*

She tried to get me to tell her what I planned to do, but I didn't. The less she knew the better. After she calmed all the way down, I took her to her place to get more things. She'd been with me ever since. It took two days for me to get what I needed in place, and to track him down. It was time for Dominus to pay for ever touching or scaring her. I berated myself for not taking care of him sooner.

I'd contacted my family. I hated to ask for any favors, but I knew they'd have what I needed. If it wasn't

Nashville, I would've asked Payne if his club had a place nearby I could use, but I doubted they did. I knew my family would, or if they didn't have one, they knew someone who did. I needed a secluded spot where no one could disturb me or call the law.

My second cousin Matvey was the *Pakhan*, the boss of the Bratva in this area of the US. He and my father had been close growing up, and he had a soft spot for me. When I called him and told him what I needed, he hadn't hesitated to say he'd be happy to help. He even offered to throw in a couple of his men. I told him I didn't want them to mete out the lesson. I would do it. When he offered to have them at least pick Dominus up once he was located, I agreed. He was thrilled to hear I'd found someone, and insisted I bring her to meet the family. I promised I would soon. I knew I'd have to tell her about my family first. I prayed she'd understand that I had no control over them, and had nothing to do with their businesses, but I did still have some association with them.

It took them until today to call me to say they had located his ass, and he would be at the address they would send me. I didn't waste time heading out. I shouldn't have been shocked to find it was a warehouse along the Cumberland River in the Heron Walk area of the city. Heron Walk was one of the most crime ridden sections of Nashville, so no one would be quick to report shit to the cops. Before heading there, I made sure I was armed, and picked up a vehicle which wouldn't garner attention like my usual ones would. Again, Matvey was able to help me with that, too. It was a beat up junker no one would look twice at.

I didn't tell Tajah where I was going, only that I had to go out for a while and I'd be back. She was busy working in my home office on her writing. She sent me off with a kiss. Reuben had wanted to come along, so I let him, but only after I made sure Freddy was at the club and Tajah knew if she needed anything to let him know.

Reuben whistled when we pulled up to the derelict warehouse. "Damn, your cousin sure knows how to pick 'em, doesn't he? How did he know of this place? I swear I saw two drug deals on the main street. That doesn't include what I'm sure was gangbangers and prostitutes."

"You're right. It's one of the most dangerous areas of the city. I have no idea how he knows of this place and I didn't ask. It's better if we don't. Forget you ever saw this place when we leave. Now, Matvey said he left Duncan with a couple of his guys. Let me do the talking. When I'm done with him, they'll take him where he needs to go."

"And where is that? Home, the hospital, or the morgue?"

"This time, it might be the hospital. If he messes with her again, then he'll disappear. No one's gonna terrorize my Dove."

"Do you think he'll be that stupid?"

"When it comes to Dominus, who the fuck knows. Alright, they said to pull up to the big doors and honk twice then three times. Once the door opens, drive inside."

We drove around the building until I saw the doors. I did as instructed. It opened right away. As we drove inside and parked, the door closed behind us. That's when I saw a man standing there. He was dressed in an expensive suit, but anyone looking at him could tell he wasn't a businessman. His whole vibe screamed muscle. He was holding a gun. Several paces behind and to the left of him was another man dressed identical and armed, too. They had grim looks on their faces.

"Remember, let me do the talking and keep your hands where they can see them. These guys can be jumpy."

"I believe you. Shit."

We both got out, and I made sure to keep my hands away from my body. They scanned me then him. I'd told Matvey I was bringing a friend. I assured him he was trustworthy. They didn't say a word. I was starting to get impatient when I heard a familiar voice call out my name. I turned to find Matvey coming out of the back. He had a big smile on his face. If you overlooked the tattoos on his hands, he'd look like a middle-aged businessman as long as you didn't look into his eyes. They could be the coldest things you ever saw.

He came striding over to us with his arms wide. "*Kusen*, cousin, it's been too long. You need to come and see your family more often." He grabbed my upper arms and kissed me on both cheeks. I returned the same.

"Matvey, it's good to see you. I know, I will, I promise. You look good. Life must be treating you well."

"It is, it is. And who's your friend?" He was eyeing Reuben.

"This is my friend, Reuben. He's my right-hand man at Lustz. Reub, this is my cousin Matvey."

Reuben stepped forward to shake his hand. Matvey took it and gave him a firm shake. "Ah, yes, Misha has mentioned you before. It's nice to finally meet you. I wish it were under different circumstances, but that's life."

"It's nice to meet you, too. I agree life isn't always the way we want it," Reuben said in return.

"Where's he at?" I asked.

"The whiny *svoloch'*, bastard, is in the back. Honest to *Bog*, God, I'd hoped he'd be at least half of a man, but he's a pussy."

Both Reub and I chuckled. "Sorry to disappoint," I told Matvey.

"Ah, it can't be helped. They don't make men like they used to. I can't stay, although I wish I could, but Isaak and Rurik will. When you're done, let them know where you want him taken. If it was me, I'd cut his balls off and bury his ass, but whatever. Don't forget to bring your lady to meet the family. Victoria is missing you, and she's excited to meet her."

"I will and thank you."

He waved off my thanks then he walked over to his car. That's when I noticed there were two men sitting in it. One got out and opened the door for him.

Those were his personal bodyguards. I waited until he left before I gestured for the remaining two to show us the way. Isaak took the lead. We fell in behind him and Rurik brought up the rear. I could tell they made Reuben nervous. As for me, I'd been around this life enough to know they wouldn't dare touch the cousin of the *Pakhan,* unless I was a threat to him then I was fair game.

The room in the back they took us into was dank and smelled of piss and other horrible things. It was obvious it had been used before to torture people. There were dark stains on the floor. I was pretty sure it was blood. Sitting in the middle of it, tied to a chair, was Duncan. He looked a little worse for wear with what I saw was the beginning of a black eye and a split bottom lip. He was gagged. When he saw us, he began to try to yell through his gag. He jerked in his chair, not that it did him any good. His eyes bugged out. I gave him a cold smile.

I'd come dressed for the task ahead. I wore jeans, boots, and a dark t-shirt. Reuben was similarly dressed. No use ruining a good suit. Plus, they would be easy to get rid of if need be, and I had a spare set in the car. Reaching into my back pocket, I took out a pair of leather gloves and slipped them on. I'd told Reub what to bring so he did the same.

"Do you know why you're here?" I asked Duncan, just to fuck with him. He shook his head no, but I caught the slight hesitation before he did. "You don't? Are you sure?" I taunted him. I'd prolong it anyway I could, even if by only seconds. He shook his head again. His eyes were already half wild.

I glanced at Rurik. “Would you mind taking off his gag? If I want it back on, I’ll let you know.”

He gave me a chin lift, then went over and yanked the gag off. Immediately, Duncan began to plead. “Mikhail, thank God. What’s the meaning of this? These thugs came out of nowhere and jumped me, then tied me up and brought me here. Wherever here is. Please, you’ve got to get me out of here.”

“I don’t have to do any such thing. And I highly doubt you have no idea why you’re here. Think. What did you do recently that I might want to talk to you about? And these thugs, as you call them, did me a favor. Do you know who they work for?”

“No, I don’t know who they work for. Listen, whatever Delilah told you, it’s a lie. I admit. I saw her a few days ago. I guess that’s why I’m here. She obviously lied and told you I did something. All I did was talk to her. She’s been lying to you since day one. I told her she needed to come clean to you about it, and to tell you we were enacting a CNC scene that night at the club.”

“Like hell that was what was going on, and I know what you said to her on Wednesday, and that you put your hands on her again. No one touches her and walks scot-free. You should’ve walked away and left well enough alone. Your expulsion was never gonna be rescinded.”

“She had no right telling you shit and getting you to kick me out of the club! I’ve been there for years. You don’t know her!” he yelled.

"You're right. You have been there for years, and I should've kicked your ass out the first time you got out of line. That's on me. However, Delilah isn't a liar and I'll believe her over you any day."

"She's a lying bitch!" he snapped.

I didn't say another word. I was standing right in front of him by then. I lashed out and hit him in the mouth. The cut he already had split open and he began to bleed. I threw another punch, taking him in the nose. A sickening crunch was heard. He howled in pain as his eyes watered. I smiled. Reuben and the other two snickered.

*"Kakoy tupitsa,"* Isaak said laughing. Rurik laughed and nodded in agreement.

"What did you say?" Duncan mumbled to them.

"They said 'what a dumbass'. They don't even know you and they know that much. Only a dumbass would call my woman a bitch, when he was tied up in front of me. You're not very smart, are you?"

His eyes widened. I saw him gulp. "Y-your woman? Since when? You've taken her on as your new sub?"

"Ah, I see your spies who have been feeding you information or your surveillance didn't tell you everything. She's much more than a sub. She's mine. The woman I intend to spend the rest of my life with. I'm gonna marry and have a family with her. You really picked the wrong woman to accost and tell lies about."

He opened his mouth, but I cut him off before he could say anything. "Don't. I don't wanna hear any more of your lies. I know the truth. You need to listen to me. You will never get back into Lustz. If I catch you hanging around it, this will be made to look like a playdate. If you see her on the street, you better turn and run the other fucking way. I don't even want you to pass her on the opposite side of the street. If you ever come near her again, I won't have you brought here to be taught a lesson. I'll end your miserable life. If you think I can't do it, think again. Take a good look at these men. I'll ask you again, do you have any idea who they are?"

I raised a brow at him as I waited for him to answer me. "No," he mumbled weakly. I'd barely touched him and he was done for. He was a pussy.

"They're part of the Bratva, the Russian mob. I bet you've heard the rumors about them haven't you?"

He started to shake. I could see the whites of his eyes, he was so scared. "Y-your part of the Bratva?" he whispered hoarsely.

"The man you saw earlier who left. He's the boss and he's my kin. There's nothing he wouldn't do for family, which includes helping me to make sure you disappear. Now, here's the deal. I'm going to teach you a valuable lesson. One I hope you take to heart and never forget. If you don't do that, then the next time we meet there will be a different outcome. One where you'll never be seen or heard from again. Understand?"

"Yes, yes! I understand. Please, you don't need to do anything else. I'll leave you and her alone. I won't ever go near the club again, either. I'll do anything you want," he begged. He looked pitiful. Too bad for him, I felt zero pity.

I shook my head at him. "Duncan, I can't let you walk with just a few bruises and a busted nose. I have a reputation to uphold. Besides, I haven't taught you anything yet."

If I was a better man, I might've let him go, but I never claimed to be that good of one, although I did do one thing. I gave him a chance to defend himself, which was more than he deserved. I walked around and took out a knife and cut his arms free. As he rubbed them, I let him have a couple of minutes to get sensation back. The whole time he kept talking away, trying to get me to let him go without a beating. I stood it as long as I could, then I got to work to shut him up. He was grating on my last nerve. The sight of him infuriated me to no end.

"Get up," I snarled at him. Blood was pumping through me. I was ready to give him the ass beating of his life. I not only worked out to build muscle, but I knew more than one form of martial arts as well as boxing.

He stumbled to his feet. He held up his hands. I knocked them out of the way then threw a punch. If he didn't try to defend himself, that was his problem. It smashed into his jaw. From that point on, I pounded him over and over. He was pathetic in his feeble attempts to defend himself, and the few times he threw a punch back, it came nowhere close to touching me. It was clear he didn't know how to fight. A man like him with his mouth and attitude should've spent time learning. Knowing what Reuben wanted, after a while I stepped back and waved to Duncan with a flourish.

"Go ahead," I told Reuben, smiling.

His smile was huge as he landed some punches of his own. By the time he was done, Duncan was on the floor curled in a fetal position, sobbing, and shaking. He'd be feeling those for days, if not weeks. I was sure a few ribs were at a minimum cracked, if not broken. He was quickly turning black and blue all over his face. His body had to be the same. Giving him one last disgusted look, I turned to Isaak and Rurik.

"Take him home and dump his ass. Oh, and Duncan, if you go to the cops and say a word about any of this, you're a dead man. My family can find you anywhere, anytime. There's nowhere you can hide."

He remained there sobbing, but he did nod weakly to acknowledge he heard me. We shook Isaak and Rurik's hands and I thanked them, then we went back to the car. We took time to change into clean clothes. They offered to get rid of our clothes that had blood on them. Taking them up on the offer, we handed them over then we got in the car and were soon on our way back to Lustz. I needed to see my woman.

# Tajah: Chapter 13

Mikhail had been gone for hours with Reuben. I had no idea where they went. All he told me was they'd be back later, and if I needed anything to ask Freddy. I didn't think anything about it when they first left. I assumed it had something to do with Lustz, but as time passed. I began to wonder. For one thing, they hadn't been dressed in their usual suits or even dress clothes when they went. They were both in jeans and t-shirts. What kind of business would they conduct dressed like that? I knew Mikhail was a stickler for projecting the right image for his business. He was always dressed in a suit or at least dress clothes.

I didn't want to interrupt him by calling or texting to ask where he was, so I tried to see if I could get the information out of Freddy. I called the number for him. He answered swiftly. "Hello Tajah, how can I help you?" The main staff knew my real name by now.

"I hope I'm not disturbing you, Freddy, but I'm wondering if you know when Mikhail will be back? I want to make dinner, and I need him to stop to pick up something at the store. Is he close by? I don't want him to go out of his way."

"He didn't say where he was going, or when he'd return. I can have someone run out and grab what you need though."

"No, no that's okay. I'll text him and ask. I just thought you might know. I didn't want to disturb him. Thank you."

"Is there anything else I can do for you?"

"Not that I can think of. I'll let you get back to work."

"Okay, call if you do," he said before he hung up.

Damn, no luck there. I paced the office for twenty minutes or so, before I broke down and texted him.

***Me: Hello honey, hope I'm not bothering you. Do you know when you might be home? I want to make dinner and I don't want it to get cold.***

It only took him a minute to answer me.

***Mikhail: I should be home within the hour, maybe sooner. Just finishing up. Don't start until I get there, so I can help you fix it.***

***Me: That's great. Is your meeting here in The Gulch?***

***Mikhail: No, why?***

***Me: Just wondering. If you were, I wanted to see if you'd stop at the bakery down the street to get one of their desserts. No biggie. I can go get it.***

***Mikhail: I'll stop on the way home. Anything else you need?***

***Me: No. Is your business going well?***

***Mikhail: It went as planned. Be home soon.***

***Me: See you then.***

That didn't get me any closer either. The more I thought about it, the more I was certain he wasn't telling me something, but what could it be? He had no reason to hide anything. I wasn't concerned he was out seeing another woman behind my back. I'd learned my lesson about jumping to conclusions after the whole fiasco with Tessa. *You're being ridiculous. What's wrong with you? Why would Mikhail lie?* I scolded myself.

I thought about sitting down to write more, but my mind couldn't concentrate. I saved my document then went to make sure I had all the ingredients for what I wanted to make for dinner. Seeing that I did, I tried to occupy myself by reading a book. I couldn't concentrate on the words. I tossed my e-reader aside with a huff. Staying in the apartment was making me feel antsy, so I decided to go downstairs and see what the staff was doing. The club wouldn't start to get busy for a little bit, but with it being a Friday, I knew it would be packed later.

I changed out of my shorts and tank, and I slipped into a nice, although not fancy, dress and a pair of sandals. My hair I pulled up in a bun. Once I was changed, I went to the second floor. This was my chance to check out some of the rooms more closely. Mikhail had shown me several of them, but it was hard to explore them thoroughly when people wanted to use them.

I got off the elevator and headed to the first one on my list. There were several I was curious about, but there were two I wanted to see the most. One was the forest room and the other was the jungle. The reasons were obvious. My man was a primal first and foremost. These had to be the ones which called to him the most.

I had to admit the jungle one made you feel like you were in the middle of an actual Tarzan movie. There were even loin clothes and itty-bitty outfits for people to dress in. They had the air in there more humid, too. There were a bunch of different props or whatever you wanted to call them to use during your play. I spent a good fifteen minutes exploring, before I had to get out. I was sweating, and it felt like I was breathing water into my lungs. I thought the South was humid, but whew this was worse. I hoped Mikhail preferred the forest room.

As I walked out to go to it, I saw Freddy. His eyes widened when he caught sight of me. I wanted to giggle as he came scurrying over to me with a slightly panicked expression on his face. "Tajah, what're you doing down here? How can I help you?"

"I'm fine. I just thought I'd look around while it was quiet. I don't need anything. Don't mind me. I know you're all busy getting ready to open."

He swallowed nervously. "I don't think the boss would like it if we left you alone. If you want to explore, I'll have someone stay with you."

"Freddy, what kind of trouble can I get into? Surely, no one in here right now would harm me."

"No, I don't believe they would, but I'd still feel better if you had someone with you. If you needed anything or had questions, they could assist. Please, let me do that."

I didn't want to make him lose focus on his work, but I also didn't want a babysitter. Finally, I gave in. "Okay, how about this? If it wouldn't be too much trouble, I'd like to see how you do things around here. I want to be able to help Mikhail with his work if he ever needs it. Do you mind if I shadow you? I promise not to drive you crazy with a lot of questions, although it might kill me as an author not to ask them," I said with a grin.

This eased the tension in his face and he laughed. "I can do that. Don't worry about asking too many questions. I love talking about this place. Besides, if you hurt yourself holding them in, the boss will kick my ass."

I shook my head as I moved next to him. "I swear, he wouldn't."

"Oh, yes he would. We all know how he feels about you. We've never seen him like he is with you. It's a good thing. He deserves someone who loves only him and that he can love. He's been alone too long, even if he won't admit it. Honestly, I was beginning to worry it would never happen."

I was happy to hear this. And he was right. I did love Mikhail, only it was too soon to tell him that. I hoped he was falling in love with me. "How long have you worked for him?"

"Ten years. He gave me a chance without any real experience and I started out as a Disciple then worked my way up to this. He runs a tight ship, but as long as you stick to his rules, he treats you well."

"Do you ever..." I cut off my question. It was probably too personal. My author's mind and mouth at work. I had to learn to control it.

"Do I ever play here? No, I don't. My wife and I are more private about things, but that's not to say I haven't learned things to take home. She apparently likes them. We're expecting our fourth kid in a couple of months," he said with a wink and chuckle.

I couldn't help but laugh. "Well, I guess not. So tell me about your wife and your kids. What are their names and ages? Which one or ones act like you?"

As he went about his work, he not only shared details about his family, but he talked about the various things he did as the floor manager. There were a lot of moving parts to it, and he was busy the whole time the club was open. All the other staff brought their issues and concerns to the floor manager and only if he or she couldn't handle it, did they go to Reuben or Mikhail. Or if they thought it was something Mikhail and Reuben would want to know, even if the floor manager did handle it, such as the whole Dominus thing with me. If Freddy had been the one to kick him out, he would've told them what happened right away.

I saw the other staff giving us curious glances. I smiled and greeted them. Those who I didn't know by name and there were some, he introduced me to. Every time he did, I got a warm sensation in my chest because he told them I was Mikhail's woman. He didn't call me the boss's sub, although technically I was. I enjoyed learning so many things about the club's inner workings. I never intended to stop writing, but I had no problem helping Mikhail if he needed me to. I wanted us to be partners in more than just the bedroom and our personal lives.

We'd been at it for about a half hour when I was surprised by the return of Mikhail and Reuben. I found out he was back when I heard his voice behind us. "What are you doing down here?"

I jumped, then swung around to face him. He was frowning. Reuben was behind him with a quizzical look on his face. "Freddy is showing me around and explaining what he does. He was sweet enough to take pity on me and help to relieve my boredom. I couldn't focus on writing or reading. How did your business go?"

He opened his arms so I walked into them. He gave me a hug and a passionate kiss. However, as I went into his arms, I saw the way Reuben grimaced. He wasn't comfortable with my question. Damn it. Where did they go? As Mikhail kissed me, I resolved to ask him about it, but not here in front of the others. This was a private matter.

When he got done, he nodded to Freddy. "Sorry about that. I was surprised to see her down here, that's all. Thanks for doing it, although babe you could've asked me to take you around."

"I know, but I liked hearing it from the perspective of the person who does it every day. No disrespect as the boss, but there are things you wouldn't think of or know to tell me I bet. I want to include those in my books as well. Besides, Freddy refused to let me explore the rooms alone. I gave the poor man a heart attack when he saw me come out of the jungle room."

"What!?" Mihail asked, doing a double take. I laughed while Freddy let out a soft groan.

"He had no idea I came down until then. I wanted to explore a bit while the club was closed. I know you showed them to me, but it was busy and they're in demand when you're open."

"Babe, if you want to explore them when the club is closed, all you have to do is tell me. I'll be more than glad to explore them with you," he wiggled his eyebrows at me and smirked, which made me blush. Reuben and Freddy laughed.

"Hey, none of that. If you piss me off, you'll become characters in my books, and I won't write you as the sweet guys you are." I warned them jokingly.

"Hey! No fair. And cut out the sweet talk. I have a reputation to uphold," Reuben grumbled, even though he winked at me. Freddy rolled his eyes.

I stood there as they checked to be sure Freddy was all set for the night then we excused ourselves to go upstairs. I made sure to thank Freddy.

"Thank you and I look forward to seeing pics of the new baby."

"It was my pleasure, Tajah. Anytime."

When we got to the elevator, I asked Reuben if he

was planning to join us for dinner.

"I'd love to, if you're both sure you wouldn't rather be alone."

"I don't mind," Mikhail told him.

"I wouldn't have offered it if I did. I always cook more than enough."

"What are we having and what time? I'll go get some stuff done until then if you don't mind."

"It's tortellini carbonara with garlic toast. Does that sound good to you guys? I need about a half hour to make it. If I was at home and had my pasta maker attachments, it would take longer, since I'd make the tortellini myself. Although, the frozen ones in the freezer are good quality ones. Did you bring dessert? If not, then add another half hour or so and I can whip up something for after dinner."

"Damn, you can make pasta from scratch? And yes, we grabbed dessert," Reuben said in what sounded like awe.

"Of course I can make pasta. It's not that hard, especially if you have the assorted attachments to make the different types of pasta. My mom would disown me if I couldn't. How does six-thirty sound? I know you both have to work tonight. Is that too late?"

"It's perfect. You know, I think you should reconsider making Mikhail your man. After all, I saw you first. If you make homemade meals, I'll be your devoted slave," Reuben said with a smirk.

Mikhail let out a growl. "If you'd like to remain in the land of the living, friend, I suggest you take that back. She's mine and I'm not giving her up."

Reuben grinned then sighed. "Well shit, then I guess I'd better back off, but if you change your mind," he laughed as he took off running when my man tried to grab him. "Later Tajah. Kisses," he yelled back. Those around us all smiled.

"I swear, if he makes a real move on you, he's a dead man," Mikhail muttered.

"You know he won't. He's just messing with you. Do you need to work on things before dinner? If so, I understand."

We got on the elevator. He shook his head. "No, I wanna spend time with you, and you can tell me what things to get so we can make pasta here. I promised to help and I meant it. I enjoy time with you no matter what we do."

"Well then, you'll be my sous chef and I enjoy spending time with you too, no matter what."

Once we were back in the apartment, I got out the ingredients and explained what we'd be doing. I purposefully didn't ask him anything else about his day or what he did. I didn't want to ruin dinner or get into a drawn-out discussion before he had to work. The time went by fast and before I knew it, we were making it and laughing. The dessert he picked up would go perfect with an Italian dinner, tiramisu. It was like he knew what I would fix.

Reuben came wandering in around six-fifteen with a bottle of wine. As we chatted and worked, he set the table. "I have zero kitchen skills, so setting the table and fetching is the extent of my contributions."

I gave him a mournful look. "Then there's no way you could be my man. Sorry. I'm sticking to Mikhail."

While he pouted and my man gloated, I laughed. Even if he proclaimed to have no skills, I still had him watch. We had it done and on the table with five minutes to spare. Sitting down with our food and wine, we dug in. I stared at the portions they scooped up, but only after Mikhail fixed my plate first. It was one of his things. I did have to tell him to stop before he loaded it up.

We had an enjoyable time eating and talking about just things in general. Most of it was about growing up. I knew Mikhail had no siblings. It seemed Reuben had three brothers and three sisters all younger than him. He was forty. His family was a close-knit Hispanic family, but the women were traditional, and didn't believe a man should be in the kitchen, hence his lack of skills.

"Boy, my brothers would've loved that. My mom isn't traditional. She's more of a free spirit and even though Dad worked a lot, when he was home he did help her. My brothers always bitched and complained it was a woman's job to cook, clean, and take care of kids. That is until Dad smacked them on the back of the head a few times, then they stopped saying it where he could hear them. I pity their poor wives. They let them get away with it."

"Are they older or younger? Are you close?" Reuben asked.

"Both are younger. One is a year younger than me and the other is two years younger than him. I'm not close to them, unfortunately. They don't approve of my writing, and they don't know why I didn't hang on to my husband. According to them, if I'd been more like their wives, I would've been able to save my marriage."

"How the fuck can they think that?" Mikhail exclaimed.

"I guess he would've changed from being secretly gay to straight if I'd been a more subservient wife."

Reuben choked on his drink. We waited for him to stop coughing. Once he did, he asked in a strangled tone, "He was what?"

I guess Mikhail did keep that between us. I didn't announce it to just anyone, but I didn't mind if Reuben knew. "Yeah, my ex apparently had been gay all his life, and married me to hide it from his religious family, so they wouldn't disown him. Too bad for him I found out and blew it up in his face. He got his lover, which he had before we ever got married by the way, but he lost his parents and his inheritance. I definitely think I made out on the deal." I informed him with a smile then a laugh.

"Jesus Christ, how could he do that to you, to anyone? Fuck, does he live around here? I wanna pay the fucker a visit," Reuben snapped. It made me feel warm to have him take my side.

"If I can't beat his ass and kill him, then you can't," Mikhail told him.

"Come on. We could even make it a road trip if we have to. It would be fun," Reuben pleaded.

I couldn't stop from laughing even more. "God, I'd love to see his face if you two rolled up. I'd never do it, but still, I can dream about it."

"Do you know where he lives?" Mikhail asked casually.

"No, and I never cared to keep track. As soon as the divorce was final, we had zero contact. I took back my maiden name. Luckily, I write under a pen name, so he has no idea what I do now. I assume wherever he is, he's still practicing law. Enough about Sam, who's ready for dessert?"

"You sit. I'll get it," Mikhail said. I mouthed *thank you* to him. He gave me a kiss then went to get it from the fridge. Thankfully, it had been soft already before he brought it home. I was discovering taking care of me was a big part of his love language. There were four main ones I'd discovered over the years. They tell how you express and receive love. They were quality time, physical touch, acts of service and receiving gifts. No one was one hundred percent one of them. For me, I knew acts of service and physical touch were my two biggest ones. I was working to find what his was, so I would be able to meet those needs for him.

Dessert was consumed in a flurry with lots of

moaning about how good it was, then Reuben had to get downstairs to work. He thanked me again for dinner after the guys did cleanup for me, while I relaxed with another glass of wine. Lucky for him, he'd changed into his nice clothes before coming to dinner, which meant he could go straight to work. Once he left, I indicated to Mikhail. "I know you'll wanna go see how things are tonight. Whenever you're ready, go."

"Do you want to come with me or stay here? I won't be on the floors the whole time. I do have work to do in the office, too. Or do you have plans to write tonight?"

"I'm not sure. I'd like to try to see if I can write, but I was distracted today. I might not be able to do it."

"Tell you what. Why don't you try and if you get bored or can't concentrate and you want to join me, let me know? I love spending time with you, even if we're nothing more than together in the same room. I won't spend all night down there. I just like to be seen."

I wrapped my arms around him and gave him a kiss. He eagerly returned it. It was becoming more heated when he stopped it. "You can distract me so damn easily, Dove. I hate to stop but if I don't, there won't be any work done tonight by either of us. I'm going to change and get ready. Can I get you anything before I do?"

"No, I'm good. You need to leave so you can get back here. I'll come down if things don't go as planned."

He kissed the tip of my nose then slapped my ass before he headed to the bedroom. I sat on the couch and waited until he returned. One more kiss and I saw him out the door, then I went to his office.

I tried for close to an hour to concentrate and get significant words on the page. When I was no closer than I was before I started, less than a few hundred words, I gave up and decided to hell with it. I would go spend time with my man, even if all I did was watch him work or follow him around. I hurried to the bedroom to change into something nicer and to fix my hair and put on a little makeup. After all, I had to project an image to compliment his image. When I thought I looked good enough, I grabbed my phone and left. My first stop was his main office down the hall. I found it was empty.

I didn't linger. Instead, I went to the first floor. I wasn't sure which one he'd be on and I knew if I texted him, he'd tell me, but if he was in the middle of something, I didn't want to interrupt. I could look around for him and ask the staff if they knew.

As I wandered the first floor, I didn't see him. The place was busy as usual. There were people talking, dancing, and drinking all over. After I realized he wasn't there, I went to the second floor. I'd been here enough that I was no longer taken by surprise by the various things people were involved in. I made sure to have my bracelet on. The orange bead had been changed out. It was now a black and red striped one worn on the right wrist, which indicated I was taken, in a committed relationship, and not available. I hadn't added any others to it. Mikhail said it was up to me if I wanted to do it or not. He had changed out his beads, too. The various ones he had before were gone and he had the same one as me.

I was making my way through the crowd. I was about to ask one of the staff if they knew where he was when I saw him. He was standing by a couple of chairs. There was a woman with him. They were talking animatedly. I hesitated. If it was business, I didn't want to disturb them, although her outfit hardly screamed she was here on business, unless it was kinky business. My resolution to stay away flew out the window when she suddenly grabbed his hand and tried to place it on her chest. Oh, hell no, she didn't! As I started toward them, I saw him jerk his hand away and scowl at her. He was shaking his head and pointing toward the exit.

I came up behind him and placed my hand on his back. He swung around. When he saw me, I saw consternation on his face then he smiled. His hand snaked out to take mine, and he drew me up next to him where he put his arm around me. He dropped a kiss on my mouth. It didn't last long enough for me, but it was filled with passion. When we parted, I glanced at the woman. She was still standing there and she was glaring at me. I could see she wished I was anywhere but here. Too bad. He was mine and no way would I let her make moves on my man. The no touching rules applied to him as well.

"Who's this? A new member?" I asked just to be sure.

"No, I'm not," she spat out.

"Oh, well, then you know the rules then don't you? No touching unless you're invited to do it, and I know he didn't invite you. Mind telling me why you had your hands on him? People get thrown out for that."

"I've known Master M for a long time. It's not your place to tell me what I can and can't do," she said snidely.

"Really? I think this says differently." I held up my wrist with the bracelet on it, then I reached over and lifted up his arm. I glanced up to find him with an amused look on his face. "Don't you think so, babe?" I asked him.

"It sure does. Tessa knows the rules and no matter how long she's been here, or how we know each other, those still apply. Tessa, this is Delilah. She's mine. Like I told you, I'm not in need of a sub. Not now or ever again."

"Master M, why her? Why commit to her? I was your sub for two years and you never gave me that bead," she said in outrage. So this was what Tessa looked like. Her voice sounded familiar now that I thought about it. Meeting his prior sub face-to-face didn't thrill me.

"You're right. I didn't because you were nothing but a sub and not my only one, Tessa. You know I was never only with you. It was a mutually beneficial arrangement, period. Delilah is mine in every way, and she'll remain as such. This is the last time I'll tell you to stop approaching me to take you back and not to touch me. If you do it again, your membership will be revoked."

"So you'll kick me out like you did Dominus all because of her! She's a nobody. When she fails to give you what you need, I expect an apology," she spat out, before turning on her heel and stomping off.

"Well, isn't she just a ray of sunshine? Maybe I should've punched her in the mouth to get your point across. She appears hardheaded." I told him, as I glared at her retreating back. Her long hair would make a good handle to swing her around by.

He chuckled as he shook his head. "Settle down there, tiger. No need to get physical. I think she's finally gotten the message. And if she hasn't, she'll be gone. I thought you were gonna text if you wanted to join me?"

"I thought about it, but then I didn't want to interrupt you if you were in the middle of something important, like fighting off a pawing kitten. I hope she knows a tiger beats a kitten every time."

"Fuck, stop with the animal analogies before I let my beast out to play," he growled. I saw his expression growing heated by the second.

"May I touch you, Master Misha?" I purred.

"Abso-fucking-lutely."

I ran my hands up his chest. Over the past week we'd negotiated an actual contract between us. Sex between us didn't always have to be that of a Dom with his sub, but if I wanted to play, I had to address him as such and wait for him to give permission. The contract didn't just say what I would or wouldn't do, but also what he, as my Dom, would and wouldn't do for me and what his expectations were.

His hands came down to grip my ass to tug me hard against him. He took my mouth in a ravenous kiss.

I moaned. I heard him make those delicious growling sounds he liked to make. My nipples were hardening and the crotch of my panties were beginning to get damp. He was excited too if the erection growing and pressing into my body was any indication. I shifted from side to side to rub against it.

He tore his mouth away. "That's it. You've done it. You've teased the beast, and he has to come out to play. Upstairs. Tonight, you and I are gonna explore our private room."

It might not sound dignified, but I let out a squeal and clapped my hands together. He laughed at me. "Get going crazy woman," he said as he slapped me on the ass.

As we made our way to the elevator, I thought of the things I'd been discovering about myself since not only I started coming here, but just in the past week with him. I had a lot of new desires I wanted to explore, and he had no objection to any of them. We were slowed a bit by people stopping to say hello to him or by them calling out. I felt the tension in his body, but he made sure to smile at each of them and acknowledge them.

By the time we made it onto the elevator, the door barely closed before he had me pinned to the wall, and had his hands underneath my top, toying with my tits. Not to be denied, I tugged his shirt free of his pants and slid my hands up his torso to pet his muscles and run my fingers through the hair on his chest. I sank my nails into him. His hiss then groan told me I was in for a pounding tonight. I was excited for the chase. Bring it on.

# Mikhail: Chapter 14

Everything flew out of my head except the driving need to have her. I'd always been a beast inside, and let him out to play in degrees, even if I couldn't fully release him. Hell, even with Tessa and other subs I'd never fully let them see how much of a primal I was. Only my initial mentor had seen me close to it, and what I felt for Tajah was so much greater than it ever was.

I'd kept myself from doing more since our first night together. She'd surprised the hell outta me when she fought back. For someone new to all of this, she'd played it perfectly. I'd done it to give her time to know me better. I wanted a contract in place. I never wanted to do anything that would hurt or scare her. We'd sat and went over the contract in detail, and it took us a couple of days of talking to get it right.

Seeing her stand up to Tessa had only made me hotter for her. Yes, I wanted a sub, but not a doormat. Seeing she could take care of herself and stand for what she wanted or didn't want, thrilled me. I'd been distracted even before she came down with thoughts of her and what I wanted to do when I was done making sure the club was in order. I'd never had someone distract me from work.

Filling my hands with her tits, as I pressed her to the wall of the elevator and devoured her sexy mouth, made me even more ravenous to have her. She made the most delicious sounds when we kissed and had sex. Actually, it was more than sex. No matter what we did, it was underlined with love. I was head over heels for her. I was just waiting for the best time to tell her. I prayed she was starting to feel the same. I was forty-five damn years old, and I'd never really been in love before. Lust, yes, but not in love until her. Thank God I listened and brought her back to the club after our disastrous first meeting.

I hissed when she sank her nails into my chest after feeling me up like I was her. I needed to see her and touch every delectable inch of her body. I leaned back far enough to grasp her top then I tore it. She gasped. If she loved it, I'd buy her a new one. I threw it on the floor then slid my hand behind her to undo her bra. It joined the remnants of her top.

"When the door opens, run," I growled. Fuck, I was so damn hard. I wanted to strip her and rut right here and now, but I didn't want it to be over too fast. She had a deep pink flush across her chest, and she was breathing hard. Her pupils were dilated. Oh yeah, she was feeling it.

The door opened and I stepped further back. She didn't say a word. She just bolted. I had to hold myself in check, so I wouldn't chase her immediately. I gave her a head start, but that was all the concessions she was getting. Tonight, I planned to show her even more of my beast, and take her to my special room. It will be christened tonight.

As I waited, I stripped off my clothes and shoes. I had barely enough civilized senses left to grab all of our clothes and take them with me when I exited the elevator. I rushed to the apartment. I slammed my hand on the scanner. As I entered, I dropped the clothing on the floor and shut the door. The only other one to have access to my apartment was Reuben. Although he would probably not just walk in, I didn't want to take chances, so I entered the code to lock it down. No one but me would see her in all her glory.

I'd seen plenty of women naked. Some might say too many. All of them were different and unique. I didn't have a type. I loved so many things about the female form, but for me, Tajah was perfection. Her tits were more than a handful. I loved that she was soft and not made up of hard muscles and angles. Her wider hips and lush ass made me think of her being ripe and fertile. Yeah, I was still thinking about breeding her. Images of her swollen with my baby made my cock jerk and more precum leak from the slit. I had to stroke myself a couple of times. I moaned. Now to find my prey.

I prowled the kitchen and living areas first, looking behind the island and furniture. I even opened the walk-in pantry. She wasn't there. I let out a growl, making it loud so she could hear me. Nothing. Good. She was playing this perfectly. I crept down the hall to where the bedrooms and office were. As each room came up empty, my excitement grew. I was literally dripping for her and the final catch. I called out to her.

"You can run and hide, my Dove, but I will find

you and when I do, I plan to eat you up…and out. I have so many delicious things I want to do to you."

I listened hard to see if I heard anything. Again nothing. I finished searching this end of the apartment and she wasn't there, which only left my home gym and my special room. My heart sped up thinking about it. So much care and thought had gone into creating it. Being finally able to share it with someone was heaven. I knew I had created it for us, even though at the time I didn't know her. I couldn't imagine sharing it with anyone but Tajah, my Sweetest Dove.

As I stalked down the other hallway, I saw a pile of discarded clothing. Bending down, I snatched up her panties and held them to my nose. I inhaled her intoxicating musk. Jesus, I loved her smell as well as her taste. I could taste her on my tongue. I groaned then wrapped her panties around my aching cock and stroked a few times. The silky sensation felt so good. As a primal, smells, tastes, and physical sensations were huge for me.

I had to stop before I came. Reluctantly I dropped her panties and entered my gym. Other than the closet, there was nowhere to hide. I crept over and opened it. Empty. God, that meant she was in the other room. My heart sped up even more. I no longer could contain myself. I tore out of the room and slapped my hand on the panel. I could hardly wait for it to accept my palm print and get the door open.

Inside there was equipment all over. Most weren't big enough to hide behind, but there was a bathroom off of the main room, as well as a few bigger cabinets and a closet. I decided to search the bathroom first. I stalked over and flipped on the light. The shower was empty. I opened the under-sink cabinet and the linen closet. Bare. Turning around, I ran my eyes over the room. They landed on the closet. The door was barely cracked. Not wanting to end it just yet, I went through the motions of checking the other cabinets. Finding them empty as expected, I made my final approach.

I was five feet away when the closet door came flying open and she darted out. She ran for the door to the hall. The beast inside of me broke loose and I gave chase. She was trying, but I got to her right as she got to it. Her scream thrilled me. I yanked her toward me, but she didn't come peacefully. She fought back.

She struggled, kicked, punched at me, and even tried to bite me. I subdued her by wrapping my arms tightly around her and picking her up off her feet. She kicked back, but I had my legs spread far enough so she didn't make contact. She gave a scream of frustration, and slammed her head back, only to hit my chest. I chuckled darkly.

"You can fight, but you won't get away. You're mine and I can do anything I want with you. And do you know what I want to do, little Dove?"

"What, Dragon? Do you intend to eat me?" she hissed.

My heart lurched at her nickname for me. She had never called me that before. I found I loved it. "Yes, Dove, this big bad dragon plans to eat you, lick you, touch every inch of you, and fuck you until you scream and scream and come in my mouth and all over my cock. When you're done, I'll do it again and again until you can't fight me or scream anymore. Only when you're tamed, and I'm sated will I let you rest. Prepare for a long night." I pushed my hard cock into her back. She moaned and sagged in my arms.

I eased up my hold and lowered my head to kiss the back of her neck. I was caught off guard when she jerked her head back, taking me in the face. It hurt and I loosened my hold more. She took advantage, and ran her nails down my forearm, while she bit my upper arm. I roared. She wiggled out of my arms and ran across the room to place herself on the other side of the sex bench.

She was breathing hard. So was I, but it was from all the lust racing through me. Having her continue to resist made me crazier. I couldn't stop myself from gripping my cock and tugging hard on it. Her eyes dropped to it and she licked her lips.

"Give in to me and I'll let you suck it, Dove. Don't you want to taste my cum in your mouth? God, I can feel you deep throating me now and my cum filling your mouth. Your dragon wants you to suck his cock."

"My dragon needs to make me take it. Show me you're my primal," she said aggressively.

Letting out a roar, I launched myself across the room. She squealed, but she wasn't fast enough. I grabbed her and took her to the floor. She tried to fight back but I used my superior size to trap her. She was wiggling, but unable to get away or hurt me. Her eyes were wild, but not in fear. No, it was all unbridled lust.

I lightly gripped her throat and squeezed. "Do you submit?" I growled.

We'd discussed this. I would only give her what she and I needed if she submitted. She had to say the words, or we'd keep going. As much as I loved what we were doing, I was in need of her more. I was fighting not to sink my cock into her and fuck her silly.

The minx shook her head no. Chuckling, I lowered my head to kiss her. The bite to my lip made me want to howl. I ignored it and kissed her, anyway, thrusting my tongue into her mouth. She resisted, but she also kissed me back and let her tongue play with mine. I kept a hold of her throat with one hand and used the other to fondle her tits. I kneaded them, then plucked the nipples hard before twisting them to give her a bite of pain. She whimpered and thrust her hips into me. I could feel she was soaking wet.

After getting my kiss, I switched my hand on her throat to grasp one wrist then the other and I pinned them to the floor. With her like this, I kissed, licked, and nibbled my way down to her tits, where I sucked and squeezed them. I bit down on her nipples hard enough to be able to hold them and tug them. She cried out, but she didn't give me any of her safe words. We'd negotiated those, too. If she said feather, it meant she needed us to slow down or talk about it. If she said trap, then I knew it was a no and to stop immediately.

I thrust my cock against her wet core. She squirmed, making me groan. She had to submit soon, or I was gonna blow and embarrass myself like some raw teenager with his first girl. I tugged harder on her nipple and ground my cock into her wet pussy. I made sure to bump her clit with the head. She whimpered and went limp.

I lifted my head and stared into her eyes. She looked dazed. "Submit," I snarled.

She didn't say anything for a couple of long moments, then she opened her mouth and gave me the answer I wanted to hear. "I submit, Dragon. Take me."

I couldn't help the growl her submission tore from me. I gave her a hard kiss then moved down her body. I continued the licking, sucking, and biting that I did to her tits, but this time to her ribs and stomach until I reached her pussy. Her musk was so damn noticeable. I roughly pushed her legs apart so I could feast.

I lapped at her like I was a dog and she was my meal. Her cream slid over my tongue making me crave more and more of her. I needed her to give me more and come on my tongue. I buried my head further between her thighs, and not only licked but sucked, bit, and fingered her. When I slipped my fingers inside of her, she cried my name, "Master Misha."

I worked to drive her up and over the edge, so she'd come and gift me with more of her essence. She was so damn wet, and the wet sounds coming from her made me even hotter. It didn't take long to push her to come and when she did, she moaned loud and long. I greedily lapped up her honey. When she stopped coming, I got up. She gave me a confused look.

I hunkered over her and picked her up. She yelped as I took her to the sex bench she'd used as a barricade earlier. I placed her on her back on the main part. It was at the perfect height which I'd set for a man my height. Gripping her hair in my fist. I used the other to grip the base of my aching cock. I rubbed the leaking head against her lips. "Suck," I ordered her.

She smirked up at me, giving me a tiny bit more resistance, which primed me even more. Fuck, this woman could make me blow just playing with her. I tightened my hold on her hair, which caused her to gasp in pain. When she did. I pushed the head inside her warm, wet mouth. She moaned, then began to suck on me like I was a lollipop. Her tongue swirled around the head and probed the slit. I groaned in pleasure.

Her hand came up and pushed mine away so she could grip me and control the feeding. She slowly sucked my cock deeper. I swear I saw stars as she did. She could give head better than any woman I'd ever been with. Along with the magic she was creating with her tongue, her other hand came up to tease and play with my balls. She'd go from being gentle to rough. The squeezing and tugging made me push closer and closer to coming. I had a fucking surprise for her.

"More. Harder," I said gutturally. She listened, thank God. In moments, she was gagging on it and I had to push deeper. I held myself there with a hand on her throat so I could feel her trying to swallow me. I moaned. "That's it. Choke on your dragon's big cock."

She hummed as she gazed up at me. I saw nothing

but joy on her face. I was more than happy I had a big cock to give her. When I was fully erect like I was now, I had a thick nine inches. I eased back to let her breath then thrust again. Each time I did, she took me a tiny bit deeper and I was able to hold it longer. She began to pinch me when she was in need of air. This was another safety signal we put in place for instances like this when she couldn't talk. It only took a couple of minutes for me to be at the precipice of my orgasm. I barely was able to mutter a warning.

"I'm coming, Dove."

She squeezed my cock harder and pumped the base, as she sucked harder and gagged. I exploded and shouted out my bliss, as I pumped my cum down her throat. She was moaning and humming the whole time. I'd never seen a woman so eager to take a man's cum either. When I stopped erupting, my cock was still hard. This was her surprise. When I was as excited as she had me, I could come twice without any down time. I pulled out.

Without saying a word, I lifted her and flipped her over, so she was on the bench face down. I quickly secured her arms and lower legs to the padded extensions made for them. She gasped and looked at me over her shoulder.

"Master Misha, what're you doing?"

"I'm putting my Dove where I want her, so I can fuck her. I need you to scream and come for me, my love," I snarled as I thrust into her in one hard, long stroke. She was spread out perfectly to allow me to do it. She screamed and moaned as I filled her. Sinking in until my balls were slapping off her, I then paused to give her a second or two to adjust before I began to take her like the beast I was.

I gripped her hips hard and stroked in and out. She was whimpering and moaning as I rutted her. I bent over her and placed bites and licks all over her sexy back. As I pumped in and out, I told her everything I was thinking.

"You're perfection, my Dove. No one can compare to you. I've never been this hard or desperate. Take it. Your dragon wants you to come on his cock and make him come until he gives you his seed. I want to breed you, Tajah. I want my baby planted in your womb now. The birth control needs to go soon. I fucking love you and I'll never stop," I practically screamed the last bit, as my balls tightened. I was feeling nothing but intense ecstasy.

Suddenly, she tightened down like a vise and started to orgasm. As she did, she screamed and her words made me pump faster. "Yes, yes, Dragon, I want your baby soon. Fuck me, my love. Fill me up with your seed. Breed me!" she screamed.

Her cream gushed out around my cock and ran down my balls as she squirted. That sent me tumbling over the edge into oblivion, as I came growling and grunting. Despite coming not long ago, I gave her another good load. As my balls drained, I became lightheaded and weak in the knees. I ended up lying on her twitching and jerking. I barely had enough brain cells left to use my shaky arms to hold some of my weight off her. I was weak, and so goddamn sated by the time I stopped coming.

I kept my eyes closed for several heartbeats, so I could enjoy it. I'd hit subspace. As a Dom, I knew all the science behind it. I'd seen partners obtain it, but until now, I'd never gotten there. It was unbelievable. The altered state of my intense sexual release triggered chemicals to flood my system. They were the "feel-good hormones" as some called them —oxytocin, adrenaline, and dopamine, which affected your experience of pain and pleasure. I was feeling euphoria from the dopamine. The oxytocin had me relaxed and strengthened the bond I felt toward her. I didn't have an ache in my body. My fight-or-flight hormone, adrenaline, gave me such an intense thrill. There were other hormones released too, but those three were the biggies. I felt fucking giddy and like I had no bones left in my body. I wanted to curl up with her and sleep.

I aroused myself enough to open my eyes and check on her. I couldn't forget her. As I did, my need to make sure she was cared for began to kick in. She had her eyes closed and wasn't saying a word. For a moment, it didn't even look like she was breathing. My heart jumped and I shot up straight. I pulled out even though I hated to do it. I moved so I could crouch by her head. I gently shook her shoulder.

"Tajah, baby, look at me. Are you alright?" I asked, as I felt for her pulse and leaned close to see if I could feel her breath on my face. She let out a soft moan and struggled to open her eyes. The confused, faraway look in them worried me. I quickly undid her restraints, then carefully lifted her until I could shift her over and into my arms like a bride. On shaky legs, I rushed her over to the chaise. I laid her down, then kneeled on the floor beside it. I ran my hand gently through her hair and caressed her cheek with my thumb.

"Did I hurt you? God, talk to me," I pleaded. This wasn't like me, but what if it hadn't been as good for her as it was me? I should've dialed it back. She was new to all this. My beast should've been kept under control. "Fuck! I should've waited to do this. It was too much. I'm sorry, baby." I kissed her cheek then her mouth softly.

"Misha," she said so softly I almost didn't hear her.

"Yes, baby. Tell me what you need."

"Did you mean it?"

"Mean what?" I was confused and still feeling panicked.

"You called me your love. Did you mean it? Do you love me or was it just in the heat of the moment?"

It wasn't how I planned or imagined telling her I loved her for the first time, but I'd meant it. Her question raised whether her declaration was in the heat of it all or real too. God, I hoped it was real. Love for her was consuming me especially after this.

"I absolutely meant it. I know it's fast and sounds unbelievable, but I love you Tajah with everything in me. What about you? You said it, too. If it was just because I did, you can tell me. Don't say yes just to spare my feelings."

She gave me a tender smile and her hand came up to caress my jaw. "Misha, how could I not be in love with you? You're the best man I've ever met. It's fast and crazy sounding, but I feel the exact same way. You own me and there was nothing, I mean nothing wrong with what we just did. I loved it and you made me bliss out. My dragon can come out to play any time he wants."

Relief and joy flooded me. I got up, so I could straddle her, and I captured her mouth with mine. Our kiss went on for a while before I got control. She needed aftercare and I needed to provide it. I let go. "Let me take care of you. It's time for a long soak in the tub, then we can talk about what we just did, and if there's anything we want to change. Stay here and rest. I'll get the water going."

She tried to hold on to me, but I slipped away. The bathroom attached to the playroom was decked out just like the master bath with every convenience. I'd even stocked it with her scents and products like our bath was. I got the water going, and as the tub filled, I poured in bath salts. When those were in, I lit candles so I could turn off the lights, and I pressed the buttons on the wall to start the music. I had surround sound throughout the apartment and there were controls in various places. This happened to be one of them. Soothing music filled the room. I got out the towels and placed them on the towel warming bar. Like I said, it and the master had every convenience and then some. With it all in place, I went to get my Dove. She needed this and I needed to hold and take care of her.

# Tajah: Chapter 15

It had been three days, and I was still in a daze or whatever it was, after the amazing, mind-altering sex with Mikhail. After he got me in the tub, he took care of me like I was a fragile flower or something. He washed every inch of me in between massaging my body. His words still rang in my ears and remembering them made me smile like a loon.

*The washcloth ran down my arm as he slowly and thoroughly washed me. I told him I could do it when he first started. When I did, he glared at me, so I shut up.*

*"Tajah, you're so goddamn incredible, baby. That was without a doubt the best sexual experience ever for me. I hit subspace, and that has never happened to me before."*

*"Is that what that utter feeling of being relaxed yet floating and elated at the same time was?"*

*He nodded as he smiled at me. I was twisted around enough, so I could see his face. "Lord, I've never felt that either. That was intense. The whole thing was so thrilling. While you were hunting me, I thought my heart was gonna jump outta my chest. I couldn't wait for you to find me."*

*He moved the cloth over to wash my upper chest and neck. It was the fluffiest and softest washcloth I'd ever felt in my life. As he washed me, his other hand trailed over my skin, causing goose bumps to come out.*

*"That's how it should be. I was afraid I went too far, too fast. If I ever do, you have to remember to tell me. Use your words. I don't ever want to hurt or truly scare you, my little Dove. I love you, and I don't want to destroy your love for me. I can't believe you love me, actually."*

*I twisted further around until I was straddling him. The tub was huge, more like a hot tub. I wrapped my arms around his neck and pulled his head down to mine. I stared into his eyes. "Misha, why would you not be able to believe it? You're so incredible. How could I not fall in love with you? The real question is, how did you fall for me?"*

*He gave me an incredulous look. He gripped my face between both hands. He gave me the tiniest shake. "How could I not love you? I can't put it into words all the things you make me feel and think. I'm fascinated with you, and I want to be with you, even if all we do is sit in silence. You soothe me as well as excite me. I never knew love felt like this. You're beautiful, smart, and talented. I know things didn't work out with your ex-husband, but to have two more men be fools and not snag you, or someone else coming along after them to do it blows my mind."*

*"Those others were threatened by my success and they couldn't cope when I would need time to do my thing. They wanted me to be available for everything in their lives, but they couldn't do the same. I was treated as an object, an afterthought unless they wanted sex or someone to hang on their arm. They didn't want to hear my thoughts on anything. It was kinda the whole 'be seen but not heard' thing. After the second guy did it, I decided I sucked at picking men, so I stopped dating or even trying to date."*

*"They were goddamn idiots, but I have to thank them. I don't know what I would've done if I met you and you were someone else's? I would like to say I would've been a moral man and left you alone, but I don't know if I could've. It's likely I would've tried my damndest to get you away from him. Something I never would've done until you. The thought of you not in my life makes me sick."*

That had led to us kissing which then led to us making love slowly in the tub. When we were done, both of us could barely make it to bed. I fell asleep with a smile on my face. I was still smiling three days later.

However, I was reminded I had a question for him minutes ago. He just got off the phone with someone. He'd been talking quietly in his home office. I walked in and he stopped talking after giving me a funny look. That made me think of Friday and his hours away with Reuben conducting business. I walked out but waited for him to come back to the living room. It was a good ten minutes before he did. He tried to appear relaxed, but I could feel the tension running through him from across the room.

"Can I get you something to drink, Dove?"

"No, I'm good. Come here and sit with me." I patted the couch beside me. I saw his gait falter the ever slightest, then he was across the room to me and he sat down. He picked up the remote to the television.

"Let's see if there's a movie on."

"I'm not really in the movie or TV mood. I'd rather talk." I told him. He reluctantly laid down the remote.

Or to me it seemed reluctant. Maybe I was creating something in my head which didn't exist. My writer's brain did that sometimes.

"We can do that. What do you want to talk about?"

"On Friday, you and Reuben said you had business to do away from here. I was wondering what it was and how it went? You usually talk about your business meetings and decisions, but not that one. Also, I saw you didn't go out dressed like you typically do, either."

He tried to hide it, but I caught the grimace before he smoothed it out. "It wasn't anything exciting. There wasn't a reason to dress up for it, so we went for comfort. We ended up deciding not to have a repeat meeting."

I eased away from him. "Mikhail, if you don't want to tell me for some reason, just say so. Hell, if you think it's none of my business, say that, but don't lie to me. That's one thing I can't stand. No, it's something I won't stand for." I went to get up, but he grabbed my arm and held me there. I tried to shake him loose, but he hung onto me. I was beginning to get really upset. I needed to walk away before I said something I shouldn't.

"Babe, please, don't."

"Don't what? Ask? Tell you I won't stand for it? What? Now I'm going crazy wondering what it is. I had one man who lied to me for years. I can't deal with it." I tried not to let tears fill my eyes, but I couldn't stop them. I closed my eyes instead. He groaned. The next thing I knew, I was folded in his arms and pressed to his chest.

He whispered in my ear. "I just don't want you to think badly of me, okay. It's not exactly something I go about broadcasting, and I sure don't brag about it."

"Tell me," I whispered back.

"We went to have a talk with Dominus about him accosting you on the street."

That wasn't bad in my opinion. "So? What's so bad about that?"

"When I say talk, I mean fists were involved. Your man isn't far from the trees or the cave, whatever you want to call it. Someone fucks with you, and I want to beat their asses. If they do more, I want to kill them, Tajah. He already laid hands on you and scared you once. He did it a second time. I should've talked to him and warned him away from you right after I kicked his ass out of Lustz. It's my fault he did that last week. I had to fix it so he hopefully never does it again."

I didn't say anything for a few moments as I digested what he said. As I thought about it, I realized a couple of things. One, I wasn't at all surprised he would get physical. As sophisticated as he was, he was a primal and this went along with it. Two, I didn't feel a bit sorry for Duncan if he got his ass beat. I pulled away from him, so I could see his face. He had an apprehensive expression.

"Misha, stop it. It's no surprise you would do that,

now that I think about it. As for being upset you did it, I am…" I paused when he jerked and groaned then I continued, "But only because I didn't get to see it. You took Reuben, but not me." I pouted out my bottom lip.

His eyes widened then he burst out laughing. He gave me a kiss then shook his head. "Only you would say that. I was afraid you'd be upset with me."

"My only worry is he'll go running to the cops. If he does, you'll be in trouble. I don't want that."

"Believe me, he's too scared to do it. He knows what'll happen if he does or if he bothers you again."

"How can you be sure?" I pointed out. He took a deep breath like he steeled himself. Oh great, what else didn't I know?

"I know you haven't been around here long, but did Carver ever mention anything when you were working to get in here about my background? My connections? Rumors about me?"

I quickly thought about it then shook my head. "Not that I recall, why?"

"It's been fairly common gossip for years that I'm part of the mob. I'm not, I swear, so no worries, but it's persisted as something those in business in Nashville talk about, and a lot of them believe. It's leaked out to others. I admit it's kept people overall from fucking with me. I don't say I am, they just assume."

"Why would they assume you are? Because you're successful?"

"Well, I'm not in the mob, but it doesn't mean I don't know anyone who is," he said slowly.

This surprised me. "Really? Who?"

"Well, my last name is Ivanova and many associate it with the Russian mob. You've heard of the Bratva, haven't you?"

"Of course, but that's silly just because you're Russian."

"I'd agree, except in my case, it's not totally wrong. My dad's family is Bratva, babe. Dad and I were never involved. Or at least he wasn't after he came of age. He didn't want anything to do with that life, and it so happened his family allowed him to go his own way, which is kinda unheard of. He moved here to the States as a young man, where he met and married my mom and they had me. However, the family also had members here, and they ensured he wasn't lost to the family, even if he was lost to the family business. I have cousins and such in it, and they and I still speak and on rare occasions I even visit them."

I knew my mouth was hanging open, but I couldn't help it. Mikhail was a strong, even scary man, but I never thought of him as being associated with criminal activities. Finding out his family was involved stunned me. I sat there saying nothing for several seconds. He was giving me worried looks. I knew I had to say something to reassure him, but what?

"Please, say something. I'm dying here, Dove. I don't want my associations to ruin what we have and are growing, but I can't help who my family is, just like you can't. The association I spoke of is an occasional dinner at one of their homes or out to celebrate something like a birthday or anniversary. Business is never discussed with me or around me. I don't want to know, but I have second cousins and their parents who I consider aunts and uncles who are part of it."

"Wow, I don't know quite what to say, Misha. I never expected you to tell me this. So Duncan knows this, and you scared him by telling him you have the connection."

"Well, not just telling him. He got a visual along with it," he admitted reluctantly.

"Tell me all of it. I can't make a decision on how I feel about this if I only know pieces. And dragging it out is making me anxious."

He wrapped his hands around mine, which were clenched together in my lap. He gently squeezed them. "Okay, so I needed to find Duncan. He wasn't at his home, and I wanted to get him somewhere that wasn't his turf, so we could have our talk. I didn't want witnesses or someone calling the cops. I did something I haven't done before, and I asked my family if they would locate him for me. My second cousin Matvey is the local *Pakhan*, the boss. He happily agreed and a couple of his men found him and brought Duncan to a place where we could talk undisturbed.

"Reuben knew what I was doing and he insisted on coming with me. You've really made an impression on him and he hates what Duncan did, almost as much as I do. We went to the location and had a talk. We reinforced it with a beating and warned him what would happen to him if he ever approached you again or went to the cops. I admit, I pointed out my connection to the Bratva to scare him into not doing either. I don't regret it, baby. I'd do almost anything to protect you."

"Misha, I, well shit, what can I say to that? I love you want to protect me, but I can do that myself, you know? I'm not some helpless damsel you have to rescue. I know my interactions with Duncan haven't shown that, and it's my fault. You said you'd do almost anything to protect me. I'm afraid to ask what you would and wouldn't do."

"I'd threaten, scare, beat, and even kill if I had to. The only thing I won't do is hurt someone innocent. There would be no going after an enemy's family unless they were as bad as my enemies. I've had people in the past I had to warn away. I've never used my family directly to do it. I don't see you as helpless, but I can't turn off my need to protect you, either. It's ingrained in me. Fuck, please tell me this isn't a game changer for you. I don't know what I'll do if you say it is."

He looked like he was in physical pain the way his brow was wrinkled up and the grimace on his face. I tugged my right hand free of his grip and touched his cheek. "Honey, I love your protective instincts, just know I can and will protect myself, too. I've not had anyone who wants to do that since my dad died. He was a big alpha male in a lot of ways. Although he wanted to protect me, he also equipped me to do it myself since he couldn't be with me all the time.

"I know self-defense and I know how to shoot. Cops' daughters and sons are usually taught this along with being cautious. I screwed up with Duncan when he kept bothering me. I knew better, and I promise it won't happen again. Also, I know you can protect yourself, but I feel the need to do the same with you. Don't do anything that could get you hurt or taken away from me. I couldn't handle that." I said the last as a whisper before I kissed him. He eagerly kissed me back.

As he let go of my other hand, I threaded it though the back of his hair and sank my fingers into his head. He groaned, and I moaned as our tongues fought with each other. Desire was quickly rising inside of me. My nipples were hardening and my tits were starting to ache. Further down, my pussy was becoming slick. The man wrecked my panties all the time. I swear, I shouldn't even bother with them, but then he'd be destroying my other clothes. I squeezed my thighs together to help combat the ache.

A distant annoying buzzing sound interrupted what I knew was about to be another intense sexual experience. He hissed as he drew away and fumbled in his pocket. When he took out his phone, it clicked what I'd been hearing. The man could befuddle me so easily. I eased back and waited. Hopefully, it wasn't anything urgent. He read the text then swore.

"Goddamn it! What the hell is going on?"

"What's wrong?"

"Reuben said there's an electrical inspector here from the Department of Commerce and Insurance.

Apparently, they received a complaint that we aren't in code for our electrical and he is demanding to do an inspection right now. Who the hell is doing this? It's ridiculous. They'd better hope I don't find out," he snapped.

I didn't blame him for being frustrated. It was a silly and immature thing to do like the fire inspection was. I didn't want to make it worse, but I had to ask. "Do you think it might be Duncan causing trouble?"

"If it is, he's a dumbass, especially after Friday. It might be but if not, who? I can't think of anyone I've pissed off with my business dealings lately."

"Maybe not, but it could be personal. Tessa is upset with you about me. Would she do it?"

He paused to think then shrugged. "I guess she could be the one."

"Is there a way for us to find out?" I asked as he texted back to Reuben. I knew he'd be heading down momentarily, and I planned to go with him. Even if there was nothing I could do, I wanted to be there to support him.

"Actually, yeah, there is. I'll need to make a call later. First, I have to get rid of this inspector. I gotta go."

"Let's go," I stood as he did.

"You don't need to come with me. I know you need to work."

"I need to support my man. No arguing. I'm coming."

I was happy to see my insistence put a smile on his face. He put his arm around me. "Well, then, what are we waiting for? Let's get this shit over with. Then we can get back to what was so rudely interrupted."

"I love that plan."

It took a scant couple of minutes to get to the first floor. We found Reuben and a woman I'd met once, Sheila. She was another floor manager like Freddy. With them was a portly man who I guessed to be in his late forties or early fifties. He was scowling and scanning the room. When he saw us, he puffed out his chest and drew himself up. It didn't help him. He was only a few inches taller than my five foot five.

"About time. I'm a very busy man. Mr. Ivanova, I presume?"

"I am Mr. Ivanova, and I'm a very busy man as well. I had to drop everything to come do this. A few minutes to do so shouldn't be a problem, especially since I didn't know you were coming. Your name is?"

The man's face turned slightly red and his mouth tightened. What was his problem? Did he just hate to wait, or was he that egotistical to think everything and everyone should fall all over themselves to do what he wanted? I immediately didn't like him or trust him.

"You can call me Inspector Thompson. Complaint inspections are always unannounced," he said snidely.

"Since I know everything is within code, I have no idea who would call in a complaint. Let me guess, it's anonymous," Mikhail said with a roll of his eyes.

"It is. We wouldn't want anyone to be targeted for doing something right."

"Whatever. Let's get this done. I need your business card with your complete information, including your license. Before we go forward, I need to ensure you are who you say you are, and that your credentials are current to do this inspection. You can't be too careful. People try to con business owners all the time to gain access to their premises and such." He held out his hand.

Inspector Thompson gave him an affronted look. "How dare you?"

"I dare a lot, inspector. Card." Mikhail wiggled his fingers impatiently at him.

Thompson seethed as he dug in his wallet to get one. He slapped it in Mikhail's hand. All my man did was smirk, then handed it to Reuben who smiled and said, "I'll be back as soon as I check him out. Hopefully, it won't take long. Sheila, why don't you come help me?"

I saw her look glad as she followed him. I figured it was just to get her free of the man in front of us. The more he talked and reacted, the more I thought of him as being an asshole. I knew he had a job to do, but you could still be courteous.

"While we wait, can I get you something to drink?" I offered. Even if he was a jerk, I could be nice.

"I don't drink alcohol on duty. Who are you? The bartender or are you one of the women who work here, doing those acts I've heard about?" he asked with a sneer.

"I wasn't offering alcohol, we do have water and sodas. And no, I don't work here."

"Then why are you hanging around? Leave." He waved his hand dismissively. I felt Mikhail go rigid. Oh no, here it comes. I tried to soothe him by placing my hand on his arm and patting it, but it was a no go.

He crowded Thompson, who went pale as he gazed up at him. Mikhail towered over him. "Listen, I might have to allow you to do an inspection if you check out, but I don't have to put up with your attitude, and I sure as hell won't put up with you talking like that to my woman. She has every right to be here, and she'll remain as long as she wants. The offer of a drink was her being polite. You might want to try it sometime."

"D-does she own the club too?" he stuttered. He stepped away from Mikhail, which was a smart idea.

"Soon. We're in the middle of making changes. Do you want a drink or not?"

"No, thank you."

"We should sit and get comfortable while we wait." he pointed to the closest table. Thomson scurried to it and sat on the opposite side of the table from us. Mikhail made a production of holding my hand on top of the table. I had to fight not to giggle. "You won't tell me who lodged the complaint, but can you say when and what the particulars of it were? I think that's more than acceptable to share."

I could see Thompson didn't even want to share

that much with him, but why? I studied him to see what I could pick up. A lot of the time I noticed things about people just from their non-verbal cues. He had a film of sweat on his forehead. It could be because he was scared of Mikhail, but thinking about it, I realized it was there when we came down. His eyes were bouncing around the room. His hands were in his lap, but I bet they were clenched. Mikhail kept staring at him. Finally, he broke.

"It came in last Wednesday. Like I said, it was done anonymously. The complaint was that you had exposed wiring and wires not up to code. Those are serious infractions."

"They are, but they're not true. I pay for a top-to-bottom inspection on the structure, electrical, and plumbing every year to be sure. I had a fire inspector in here barely a week ago on a trumped-up complaint. He found absolutely nothing, and you know he would see things like exposed wiring. Don't the different inspectors talk? It seems like a waste of funding to do the same work twice."

"We can't talk about every case and no offense to whoever did it, but he might've missed something. Surely you don't want your customers or employees hurt?"

"No, I don't. I'd be an idiot to risk my livelihood by not fixing things if they exist. I don't doubt you see shoddy work, and people trying to get away with stuff, but I don't work that way. I've had this club for close to fifteen years and no one has ever been hurt because of something like that."

"Things can change. If your focus becomes diverted to other things, there can be slipups." As Thompson said it, he glanced quickly at me then back. What the hell? How would he know we were in a new relationship? Warning bells began to sound in my head.

I leaned over and made sure to smile before I whispered in Mikhail's ear. "He's up to something. How does he know we're newly together? Someone put him up to this. He knows who made the complaint."

Mikhail kissed my cheek and whispered back. "I caught that, too. If he comes back as legit, believe me, he won't go anywhere alone. I have cameras everywhere, too. I usually keep them off if I'm here. I'll activate the ones in the apartment. Not all of them are obvious. I bet he'll want to inspect it."

I nodded and said, "Good."

I waited to see what Mikhail would say next, but we were interrupted by Reuben coming back. He had a bland look on his face. He nodded to Mikhail. "He's with the Department of Commerce and his license is up-to-date. I verified with the office a complaint was filed against us."

Mikhail got up. "Well, then let's get this started. We have work to do to get ready for tonight. Reub, I'll stick with him, so you can get your work done. Tajah, you can hang with me, or go back upstairs. It's up to you. I expect you'll get bored though."

"I'd like to watch at least for a while. You never know when I might decide to write about an electrician.

I can call it research."

"Write?" Thompson asked. He sounded nervous.

"Yes, I'm an author and I find inspiration everywhere. I never know when something will end up going into a book."

"You can't write anything about me! If you do, I'll sue you," he said in a panic.

"I would never use your name or anything that would identify you. However, you can't tell me I can't talk about an electrical inspector in one of them. Or use your attitude to inspire one. That's why I like to tell people beware how you act, you may one day find yourself in a book. I prefer if they do due to their wonderful attitudes, but sadly often they're because they were jerks or assholes," I said sweetly. My evil side was peeking out.

He had his mouth gaping open like a fish. Both Reuben and Mikhail outright laughed. I winked at them so Thompson couldn't see it.

"Let's go," Mikhail ordered.

As Thompson stumbled to get his documents out, Reuben came over to me. "You're evil. No wonder Mikhail loves you. Lucky bastard."

I patted his arm. "I'm the lucky one. I never expected to find someone like him to love."

My declaration of love for his friend made him smile harder. He gave me a kiss on the cheek. I heard Mikhail growl then he was there, crowding Reuben out of the way. "Lips off. She's mine."

"I know. We were just talking about that, and how lucky you are. Find me one like her, will ya?"

"I'll give it my best. Kisses on the cheek then are fine, but only occasionally," Mikhail conceded.

This made Reuben and I laugh. Thompson cleared his throat to get our attention. Reuben left to do whatever and we got to work. The intervening hours were boring, but I stuck it out for most of them. You could tell having us along made the inspector nervous, and we watched his every move. Mikhail pestered him with questions. Thompson tried several times to get us to leave him alone, but we refused. It wasn't until he moved upstairs to the apartment that I went to do something else. I went to the office to write out notes on him. He would make a great character the readers would love to hate. I saw books and e-readers possibly being thrown over him when I was done.

I was still chuckling under my breath when he came into the office. Mikhail raised his brow at me but didn't ask. I kept tapping away on my keyboard. Thompson didn't take long, but as he and Mikhail left, I heard the annoying inspector asking what was on the opposite end of the apartment. I had to see his reaction to our special room. He'd appeared disgusted downstairs. I popped out of my chair and rushed out to catch up to them. I grabbed Mikhail's hand as he followed him.

I could barely stand to wait for him to get done in the gym then he pointed to the scanner-protected door.

"What's in there? I have to see it, too."

"I'll open it. Give me a sec," was all my man said.

As he unlocked it and opened the door, I moved so I could see at least the side of the inspector's face. I saw his mouth drop open and the red invaded his cheeks. He turned to glance at us and his eyes were bugging out. Why the reaction when he saw many of the same things downstairs, I didn't know. Did he think Mikhail ran a kink club, but wasn't personally into it? He walked into the room like he expected something or someone to jump out and attack him.

"Just tell me what you want to see. If you wanna check that the various toys work okay, we can do that. They run on batteries except for a few. This fucking machine plugs into an outlet." Mikhail said ultra casually, as he hit the on switch and it started moving the dildo attached to it up and down.

I almost busted my gut holding in my laugh as Thompson squealed and ran across the room. As Thompson trained his eyes elsewhere, Mikhail kept casually talking about various toys and things in the room. The St. Andrew's cross seemed to fascinate and repel the inspector. By the time he was done looking, I was almost in tears. I stood there watching him stutter and tell Mikhail everything was up to code.

"When can I get a copy of the full, official report? I need it for my files."

"I-well, I'm not sure. I should have it done this week."

"It better be. I don't want you all coming in here every damn week on some nuisance complaint. Someone is doing this to be an asshole. I promise you, I will find out who and they better watch out when I do."

"Is that a threat?"

"No, it's a damn promise. Now, if you don't mind. I have actual work to do."

I left Mikhail to escort him off the premises, while I was back to thinking about who was doing it and how we could find out. When Mikhail returned, I asked him since I remembered what he said earlier about having a way.

"Thank goodness he's gone. What a weasel. Okay, you said you had a way to find out who is making these complaints. Who? And how? Is it your cousin Matvey you mentioned?"

He shook his head. "No, it's not Matvey. Just wait a minute. Reuben is on his way up. I'll explain then we can make the call together."

I pretended to pout, which earned me a swat on the ass and a kiss. If that was my punishment, I'd do it every day. I told him that, which made him laugh and whisper naughty suggestions in my ear of the other things he could do to me. I was getting wound up when I heard a beep and the door opened to the apartment. Mikhail had it set to warn you if someone was entering. When Reuben saw us, he shook his head.

"You two need to cut it out. No sexual tension while I'm here. It makes me jealous and horny."

"Oh my God, really? I can't believe you said that."

"Believe it. Now, what's your plan to find the asshole making those false reports?" He asked as he plopped down on the couch. I was in the big chair on Mikhail's lap.

"It's a simple one. I just need to make a call. Hang on." Mikhail said as he took out his phone. I watched as he opened his contacts and chose a name. I couldn't see who it was. He pressed the button. After a few seconds he spoke when the call was answered. "Hey Outlaw, I hope I didn't catch you at a bad time. I need to see if I can use your skills to help me with something. Is it alright if I put you on speaker? I have Reuben here and my lady, Tajah." He paused, then laughed. "Yeah, I finally got one and I'm an old, settled man like you. It's great."

He pushed a button then we could hear a man's voice on the other end. "I've been telling you that for a couple of years and so has Payne," Outlaw told him.

"Yeah, I know. Hey, you're on speaker now."

"Oh hey Reuben, you need to get a woman next, man. And Tajah, hello. We have to talk about your taste in men."

Reuben groaned at his remark and muttered, "Tell me about it."

All I could do was laugh before I answered him back. "Hello, Outlaw. I've heard good things about you from Mikhail. Good to at least get to chat with you. We'll talk later about my taste."

"There won't be any of that shit, Outlaw. You scare her off and I don't care if you have a big bad club and a bunch of others backing you, I'll come after your ass."

"Truce, truce, okay tell me what you need so I can save myself." Outlaw pretended to plead. I heard the laughter in his tone. He was holding it back.

"I've had a problem the past week or so. Someone is calling inspectors out on us with bogus complaints. First, it was the fire inspector. Today, an electrical inspector showed up. They say the complaints are anonymous and they can't tell me anything, but I'm not so sure about that. The one today gave off other vibes like he was here with an agenda not just doing his job, you know what I mean. He actually looked upset when he didn't find anything. Of course, I never left him alone, so if he planned to sabotage anything, he was prevented from doing it."

Outlaw whistled. "Damn, you do have a mess. Any clue who might be doing it? Have you pissed off anyone lately?"

"I have. My ex-sub has been bugging me about getting back together. She isn't happy I have Tajah. The other is an ex-patron who was kicked out because of what he did to Tajah. I had a 'come-to-Jesus' talk with him on Friday. The inspector today said the complaint came in last Wednesday, so it could be him. I think he's too scared to do it after Friday but this was already in motion. Those are the ones I can think of off the top of my head."

As he talked he was tapping out something on his phone. I found out what it was when Outlaw spoke again. "I got the names you sent. Thanks. I'll look into them. Either could be the culprit. A jealous woman scorned can get ugly. Of course, the guy could be bent, too. Tell me what he did to Tajah." I could hear him typing on his end. Mikhail filled him in on my two run-ins with Duncan and then what they did last week to him. That made Outlaw chuckle.

"Damn, are you sure you're not a biker? That sounds like us. Good for you. Fucker deserved it. Okay, I'll do some digging and see if I find anything. In the meantime, if you have any more inspections or think of anyone else, let me know. Hey, you should bring Reuben and Tajah to the club on our next family and friends' day. Tarin would introduce her to the other old ladies. We've kept trying to get you here forever. It's time."

"Let me know when and I'll see what I can do, but you can't try to steal her away for one of your single brothers. If that's your aim, fuck you."

"Hey, no stealing but if she ends up liking a biker over you, well that's not my fault," Outlaw teased.

"That's not happening," I told him.

"Good. Reuben, make his ass bring you. If he won't, then you come alone. Okay, I hate to run but it's my turn to watch my kid. Later. I'll let you know what I find."

"Thanks, man," Mikhail told him right before he hung up.

"Interesting guy," I said.

"You have no idea. I've heard enough to know they all are in one way or another. I've only really spoken to Payne and Outlaw. If you'd like to go, I'm game."

"I wouldn't mind. Who knows, maybe I'll write an MC series next."

He groaned as Reuben smirked. "You're in trouble now. Sure, why not? It might be fun. I hear they get wild at those parties."

"They can, but only after the kids are in bed. Alright, enough of that. Hopefully, he'll find something. Anything you need me to help with before we open?" he asked Reuben.

As they talked about this and that, I zoned out and tried to imagine myself meeting a real-life MC. Excitement began to grow and thoughts flashed through my brain. God, why did he do this to me? Now I was outlining another new series when I didn't even have this one launched yet.

# Mikhail: Chapter 16

I was hurrying to get my surprise for Tajah done before she came home. She'd taken the day to go shopping, and go to the spa while she spent time with her bestie Cady. I'd finally gotten to meet her when she stopped by to pick up Dove. She gave me the twice over and I knew she was weighing her thoughts on me. I hoped I left her with a good impression. I wondered what all Tajah and even her brother Carver had said about me. I walked them out to her waiting car and made sure to send my Dove off with a kiss and a reminder to call me if she had any problems. She promised she would.

When she left, she had no idea she had a shadow. Until I knew for sure Duncan would stay away from her, I'd asked Matvey if I could borrow one of his men. I only needed them when she left without me, which wasn't often. He agreed readily and sent Rurik. I saw him waiting in a discreet car out on the street. He gave me a subtle chin lift when the women weren't looking his way. I returned it.

Since she was gone, it gave me the perfect opportunity to get the stuff I'd ordered hauled into the apartment and put together in a few cases. There was lots of rearranging and some removal of things. I was excited to see what she would think. I hoped she would love it. It was just one way to show I wanted her fully incorporated into my life. She hadn't been back to her place to stay at all since that first time we had sex. I kept asking her to stay, and she kept agreeing without much cajoling. We had made stops to pick up more of her stuff and to get her mail every few days. I wanted to tell her to let her place go and just move in with me, but I wasn't sure if it was too fast. This surprise would tell me if I should do it now or later, I think.

Finally, I had the last finishing touches done and I was just waiting for her to return. She'd texted about a half an hour ago to tell me they were on their way. Reuben had helped me out. He took off when he heard she was returning and told me she'd love it. I wondered if Cady would come up with her or not. I kinda wished she wouldn't, so we could be alone, but if she did, I'd deal.

I was in the kitchen getting myself a drink and pouring her one when I heard the beep of the door. I hurried to it and greeted her as she walked in. She had a big smile on her face. Behind her I saw Hoss. He was carrying several bags.

"Babe, why didn't you call me? I would've come to carry them," I chided her.

"I thought about it but I thought I could do it, then Hoss caught me in the elevator and he insisted on carrying them. He thought I was too delicate to do it," she teased him.

He flexed one of his big arms as he walked in with her stuff and he grinned at her. "You bet you are. How else can I keep these guns primed? Hey boss, how's it going? I think she's bought out the stores here." He went over and set them on the island.

"Thanks Hoss, Yeah, it does. Where's Cady? Did she leave already?" I asked before I gave her a quick kiss. When I was done, she answered me.

"She did. She said she had dinner plans with Carver or she would've come up. She promised me next time she would and by the way, me, you, she, and Carver are gonna go out to dinner soon. She wants to question you."

I groaned. "Just what I need. She's not a lawyer like her brother, is she?"

"No, she's not. She's a veterinarian. She says she can deal with animals way better than jackass humans. I couldn't imagine her as a lawyer. God that's scary," she shuddered.

"I'd be her animal any day," Hoss muttered.

As she gaped at him I raised a brow to him. He shrugged. "What can I say? She's a sexy little thing. Although as small as she is, I'd probably break her, so maybe not. Damn, too bad."

He was right. She was tiny, especially compared to him. My guess was she was only about five foot one or two compared to his six foot seven.

Tajah snorted. "You are a big one, but I think you should worry about her breaking you, at least mentally. More than one guy has been destroyed by her. She takes no bullshit and she doesn't give two shits. You play games or try to fool her and she'll leave you bleeding. Carver says she's tiny but her evil makes up for it. Beware what you wish for, Hoss."

The smile that spread across his face made me groan. Shit. She did it now. He was intrigued. "Hot damn, you need to get her back here soon, so I can talk to her. She might just be the woman of my dreams."

"She plans to come by more since I seem to be here all the time is what she said. I'll see what I can do, but no crying if she decimates you."

"No crying. Deal. Alright, I gotta go and get to my post before the boss fires my ass. See you later, I hope," he said to me.

I shook his hand and nodded. "I'll check with you later. Thanks again." He waved it off then left. He was okay to get downstairs. You didn't need a print to get downstairs on it although his scan was in the elevator.

"I have something I want to show you. Come with me," I asked her.

I couldn't wait a minute longer. She gave me a puzzled look but she didn't argue. I took her hand and led her down the hallway to the office. I had the door closed. "Close your eyes and keep them that way until I tell you to open them."

"Misha, what are you up to?" she asked as she shut them. She had a tiny smile on her face. I opened the door and led her inside to the spot where I wanted her to stand. It would allow her to see most of the room at once. I stood beside her, so I could see her reaction.

"Open them."

They flew open. I saw them widen in shock and her mouth dropped open as she scanned the room. Her hands came up to cover her mouth. "What do you think?" I asked softly when she said nothing.

"Oh my God! It's gorgeous, but you didn't need to do this. I could've moved to the kitchen table so you can use your office."

"I didn't do it for that reason. I want you to feel like this is your place, too. I want to share everything with you, baby, even this office. If you want it arranged another way or something changed or even something added, just tell me."

I'd moved things and arranged it, so there were two complete office spaces in the room on opposite ends of it. While my end was very masculine and dark, hers was lighter with a more feminine though not girly vibe. I'd seen her office space at her apartment. It was tiny, but it gave me ideas and I ran with them.

Next thing I knew she flung herself at me. I barely had time to grab her before she latched onto my mouth with hers and her arms encircled my neck while her legs went around my waist. I gripped her ass in both hands to help hold her as I kissed her back. I guess I had my answer. She loved it.

As we continued to devour each other, I walked her over to her desk. I gently pushed the stuff on it to the far side with one hand then I sat her on it. I thrust my hips between her legs. I knew of a great way to christen her desk. My burgeoning cock was more than willing to do it. I couldn't stop myself from pressing hard into her core with it. She tore her mouth away from mine and moaned. Suddenly her fingers were frantically tearing at the snap and zipper of my jeans. "Help. Hurry. I need you, Misha. I need you inside of me right now," she whimpered. She didn't need to tell me twice.

This would be quick and hard, but something told me she wouldn't mind. She seemed frantic for me, and God knows I was always in need of her. I'd always had what I considered a healthy sexual appetite, but she ramped it up to an insane level. I found myself thinking of her all the time and walking around with a hard-on at the most inopportune times. I'd had to hide behind furniture and stuff more than a few times while working or talking to someone. When I could, I started to keep my shirts untucked from my pants, but that wasn't possible when I was wearing a suit or dress clothes.

As she undid my pants, I lifted her ass so I could get off her long skirt. With it I took her panties. She tugged down my zipper then shoved my jeans down to my thighs. I was too impatient now to take them all the way off. They'd do. I pushed up her top and popped her tits out of her bra cups. Her light pink nipples were hard nubs which beckoned me to taste them. I sucked one into my mouth as I ran a hand up her thigh to her core. Damn, she was more than wet. She was dripping. Her moan of pleasure made my cock jerk.

I thrust a couple of fingers in and out of her a few times, which made her moan louder and thrust her hips toward me. I curled them to rub against her G-spot.

Miraculously, she got wetter. Switching to her other tit, I kept finger-fucking her. It didn't take much to have her crying out and contracting hard around my digits as she came. I knew I couldn't wait any longer. As soon as she stopped coming, I withdrew my finger and lifted my head. She whimpered and gave me a pleading look.

"Turn around and lay across the desk. Show me that sexy ass," I growled.

Her pleading look changed to excitement as she got down and turned around. As she did, she paused to take off her top and askew bra. Her whole glorious naked body was spread before me. I yanked off my shirt but left on my jeans. She lay her cheek on the desk and looked back over her shoulder at me. The desire burning in her gaze made me hotter. I couldn't help but stroke myself a few times. The precum leaking from the head of my cock helped my strokes.

"Jesus, look at how beautiful and sexy my Dove is? Fuck, it's a wonder I get anything done. All I want to do is think about you and make love to you. Does this mean you like my surprise?" I teased her. I had to in order to calm down or I'd blow as soon as I got inside her. I paused my strokes too.

"Yes, I love it, Misha. I'm in the same boat as you. I think about you all the time and want you inside of me. Although, it does really help with my books," she said with a smirk as she wiggled her ass at me.

I slapped her ass, which made her jump. She moaned. "Again," she begged. I'd found my dove liked to be spanked. I hadn't tried using anything but my hand yet, but I would. I gave her several more smacks, altering the cheeks and how hard I placed them. Her ass began to flush pink. I could see her honey glistening on her folds peeking out. I wanted to see more.

"Grab and spread those cheeks for me, Dove."

"Yes, Master Misha," she said breathily.

I watched entranced as she did it. Her folds were soaked and I could see her tight entrance. I ached to slide my cock into it, but almost as equally wanted was her tiny dark hole above it. I wanted to sink my cock into her ass and fuck her until we both came. I hadn't gone there or even talked about it with her yet, but I wanted to. Deciding to test the waters, I swiped a finger through her copious cream, then I moved up to rim the outside of her asshole. She jumped and gave me a startled look.

"Have you ever had your ass played with, Tajah?"

She hesitated before answering me. "I've had fingers a few times, but nothing else."

"Did you like it?" I kept moving around and across her hole.

"Not really. It hurt a lot. Although to be fair, I think some lubrication would've helped along with some patience."

"They didn't even fucking lube it? Oh, hell no, you need something even if all it is, is your sweet honey. Can I try it and see if you like it better? Remember, you can always say no or trap."

She took a moment to decide then she gave me an

awkward nod. "Okay. Do you have lube?"

"I do in fact.," I said with a wink before I opened one of her desk drawers and took a tube out.

"Hmm, one would think you planned this."

"I didn't plan this part, but you never know and I keep lube in my desk drawers. I always want to be prepared for whatever we might do. I hoped to christen your desk though at some point."

She groaned. "God, Misha, what will I do with you?"

"Let me love you. Relax and just feel. If you push out as I push in, it'll help."

I got to work slicking up a couple of fingers. The longer I waited the more anxious she might become. Leaning over, I nipped her back then licked the bite. She shivered. I did more of those to distract her. As she relaxed into it, I moved my finger to the rim and ever so slowly eased the tip inside. She tensed.

"Breath and relax," I reminded her.

She worked to do it. As she did, I slipped it in more. Getting past her sphincters was the hardest part. I worked at moving in and out while not hurting her too much. As I did and I went deeper, she began to be less tense. A small moan slipped out of her when I had my finger buried.

"God, you should see what I see. That tight little hole taking my finger. Damn, I don't know if you'll ever let me do it, but if you ever let me truly fuck your ass,

I won't be able to last. I can feel how tight you are just on my finger. Fuck," I groaned as I sped up my thrusts. Images of my cock in her flashed through my mind.

Her moaning was growing. I knew she was now enjoying it and it made me even more eager to shoot my load. Hoping she could take it, I grabbed the base of my cock and lined it up with her entrance and in one long stroke, I thrust my cock into her pussy, while my finger was still in her ass. She cried out brokenly, but bucked her hips back at me, driving both deeper. I groaned. She was always tight, but the addition of even one finger made her even more snug. Shit, I wasn't gonna be able to hold back, but I refused to stop unless she told me to.

Her whimpers and moans continued and got louder. Oh yeah, my dove liked what I was doing. I snapped my hips back and forward, driving myself deep. She cried out and more honey coated me. Not wanting to come before her, but already feeling the tingle starting in my feet, I pulled her ass toward me, making room between the desk and her pelvis.

"Spread your legs," I ordered.

She did it. I slid a hand around to rub her distended clit. She muttered, "God."

I chuckled. "Not God, just your dragon. Come for me. Soak me with your honey and scream for me. Take your Master's cum, Dove," I snarled as my hips snapped hard and fast in and out of her while my finger worked her ass in sync with my cock. She began to tighten.

"That's it," I hissed.

I knew she was close. Suddenly, she began to talk. "Please, Master Misha, please, harder. I'm so close to strangling your cock. Do you like that? Fucking both of my holes at the same time?"

"Jesus Christ, yes. I love it."

"Me too. I wish you had two cocks so you could fuck both. God, it feels so good now. I've written about anal sex but never really knew what it felt like. Jesus, I'm gonna be able to do it now."

The thought of her being inspired by our sex lives made my cock swell. I rubbed harder on her nub as I thrust faster. She clenched her pussy and ass tighter around me and then raised her upper body off the desk as she screamed and came so goddamn hard. She gushed as she jerked and came for a long time. Seeing her like that and feeling it, I couldn't hold back and I gave one final thrust then threw back my head and howled as I came. She milked me so fucking good, I saw stars and my legs got weak as I flooded her with my seed. Feeling it, I recalled what she said the other night about breeding her. I needed her to mean it.

By the time we were both done coming, she was panting on the desk and I was mostly lying on top of her. I had enough sense left to ease my finger out, but I left my cock in there. I didn't want to move until I was too soft to stay. Except for the way I was staying hard, I might be ready for round two. I'd never been able to do that as much as I did with her.

I kissed her sweaty back and licked the salt from her skin. I hummed. She shivered. "Dove, thank you.

Thank you for trusting me. I take it you liked that."

She weakly giggled. "You could say that. That was something, Misha. Suffice to say, you can do that again."

"And what about taking it farther? Toys and maybe me?"

"I'm willing to explore it."

My heart jumped at her agreement. I slowly stroked out then back in again. She moaned. "You're still so hard."

"I am and I think I'm gonna stay that way until you do something about it. What do you say? Wanna go again, only I think this time, we should get more comfortable."

"Oh, I think you can persuade me," she said as she tightened around me. I groaned and closed my eyes. Yes, she was perfect in every way.

☘☘☘

Later as I was walking around Lustz checking to be sure everything was going well, I couldn't stop thinking about earlier and the intense love making sessions with Tajah. She'd wrung a second intense orgasm out of me, but not before I'd made her come a few more times. I'd left her napping so I could come do a bit of work. In all my excitement about showing her the office, I'd forgotten all about what Outlaw had told me earlier today. I was disappointed to say the least. When he called me I was so sure he had good news, only I was wrong.

*"Hey, sorry it took me so long to get back to you. I*

*had some shit come up here. I hate to say it, but I can't find anything to tie either of those two to the complaints happening to you, Mikhail. If they're doing it, they're being super careful about it. No calls on their cell phones or emails. As far as I can tell from camera feeds near those buildings, they haven't been seen going into them. It's possible they asked someone else to do it verbally, but I have no idea who. I wish I had better news."*

*"No need to apologize. I'm just glad you checked for me. I wish it had given us something but that's the breaks. Thanks for fitting it in. I hope everything is okay at the compound and with the club."*

*"Ah, you know how it is. We have something all the time. Nothing we're not used to or can't handle. Maybe whoever is doing it will stop now that they failed twice. I mean what do they want? To get you fined and be a nuisance or shut down?"*

*"I think both of those first ones but if they keep it up, I might get temporarily shut down for the inspectors to gang up. I mean as good as my people are, if you look hard enough you can find something no matter how minor. And if they're like the last one, I wouldn't put it past them to make an issue. I hate feeling like that, but I do."*

*"I get it. Listen, if you have any other problems or think of someone else you want me to check out, just let me know. And I'm holding you to your promise to bring Tajah and if he'll come, Reuben to the next family day. We should have one soon. Hang in there. Talk to you later, man."*

*"We'll plan on it and thanks. Later."*

I tried to rack my brain again to think of anyone

else who would do it, but I was coming up blank. There was no use worrying about it right now. I needed to concentrate on the club and ensure everyone was having a good time while behaving. I didn't want any more Duncans. Overall, I rarely had issues thankfully. In the beginning there were a lot more, but once patrons learned I meant what I said, those had significantly reduced. Reuben wasn't with me at first, so I was always working before he and I met and our friendship became one where I trusted him. Making him my assistant manager was one of the best decisions I ever made.

After making one more sweep of the first floor, I decided to check on how things were going with Hoss and Laura. When I got to the front area, I saw Laura was busy talking to a couple of patrons. I said hello to them and welcomed them but didn't linger. I'd catch her hopefully on my way back. Since her offer to be my sub, she'd acted like her old self. I was relieved to see it. Stepping outside I walked over to the corner of the small raised entry where Hoss was standing.

"Hey boss, did Tajah get all of her stuff unpacked?" he asked with a grin.

"No, she's sleeping right now."

"Ah, so you wore her out, did ya?" he asked with a slight smirk.

"Bastard, I didn't say that but if you must know, yes. If you tell her I told you that, you'll pay for it."

He laughed. "What? Are you gonna fire me?"

"Like that would hurt you other than you'd be

bored. I know the chump change I pay you doesn't compare to what you make at your business. It doesn't make a dent."

"Hey, it's not about the money. You're right, I'd go crazy. I need something to occupy my time and speaking of that. Do you think Tajah would give me her friend's number?" he asked slyly.

"Shit, Cady really got your attention. Honestly, I don't know, but I can ask her if you want. The worst she can say is no. If she does, I can try to steer it so Cady drops by when you're working or I can let you know. My only warning is, if you're looking to get off and done, don't go after my woman's friends. It'll leave hard feelings."

"If all I wanted was sex, I can get that every night of the week and twice on Sundays at this place. I'm getting tired of easy women, Mikhail. I'm thirty-nine freaking years old. I have everything else in my life in place. I always thought I'd settle down and have a couple of kids, but it hasn't happened. Truthfully, seeing you find Tajah has given my ass hope."

"I hear ya. I wasn't really thinking along those lines until I took my sabbatical. When I came back, I suspected what I wanted, but still wasn't sure until after I met her. I'm just thankful she came back after I kicked her ass to the curb."

"You were. You know, I'll ask her for her friend's number myself. And I promise, it's not just for a hookup." He held out his fist so I bumped it with mine.

"Anything I need to know about tonight?" I asked,

getting back to the real reason I came to see him.

"Nope, all good. Go finish your rounds then get back to your woman. We've got this."

Thanking him I went back inside. Laura was now alone so I stopped to touch base with her. She gave me a warm smile. "How's it going so far tonight, Laura?"

"It's been good. Where's Tajah?"

"She's upstairs napping."

"Oh, I thought she might be home. I'm so used to seeing you with her. Is she living here now?" I wasn't sure I wanted to have this conversation with her, but she seemed fine.

"Not officially, no, but if I have my way, she will be. Why?"

"No reason, just making conversation. How's things been work-wise? The club seems to be doing really well. I swear we have more people every week."

"True. It has been picking up nicely. Has the increase caused you any problems? Are you able to keep up issuing bracelets and being the greeter?"

"I have no problem keeping up. In fact, if you need me to help in other ways just let me know."

"I can't think of anything, but if I do, I'll let you know. Well, if you're good I'm gonna go find Reuben and finish my walk around. Hope you have a good night."

"I will, and thank you, Mikhail. I just want you to know that I love working here more than you know."

"I appreciate it. It's hard finding good workers like you. Thank you," I told her before I walked off.

I wanted to find Reuben and make sure everything was good so I could go back to Tajah. Maybe I'd get lucky, and she was still asleep and I could slip into bed with her. I was thinking about that when I got to the second floor. My good mood went flying out the window when I heard a ruckus. It was coming from one of the theme rooms. I hurried toward the raised voices. What the hell was going on? There was a wall of people standing around watching when I got to the right one. I had to bark at them and in some cases shove a bit to get through. When I broke through, I came to a screeching halt. I couldn't believe my eyes.

Standing there in a heated argument was one of my long-term patrons, Savage Sinner. Despite his name, he'd never caused me any trouble, so to have him yelling at anyone shocked me. The other part that didn't shock me was who he was yelling at. I blinked to be sure I was seeing things correctly, but the scene didn't change. Standing there with her hands on her hips was Tessa and beside her was Sylvia.

Sheila was working tonight. I watched her trying to get them to settle down, but they weren't listening. Or at least the two women weren't. Savage was trying to extricate himself by the looks of him, but the women weren't letting him. Sylvia and Tessa were facing off with each other and he was in the middle. I took a moment to see if I could figure out what was happening.

"I'm done. I don't want either of you to play with

me tonight. Jesus Christ, what's gotten into you two? All I did was ask Sylvia if she was interested and you came at us like a crazy person, Tessa. Screw it," Sinner said loudly. He scowled and shook his head. I'd heard enough. I stepped in.

"The three of you, come with me right now," I snapped. No way was I airing this where everyone could see and hear us.

"Thank God, Master M. I didn't do anything," Sylvia whined. She tried to latch onto my arm, but I shook her off. Tessa gave me petulant glances, and Sinner looked like he was ready to pull out his hair.

He gave me a weary look. "Sure thing, Mikhail. I'm sorry for this."

I could tell the ladies weren't happy about coming with me, but I didn't give a damn. As I turned around, Reuben came through the crowd with two of the security guys. "I need your office," I told him. He nodded.

It was a quiet group who followed him and I to his office. My security guys hung with us until we got there, then I dismissed them. We could handle them. Inside Reuben's office, I pointed to the seats.

"Sit," I ordered. Again, Sinner gave me no problems but Tessa flounced over to take hers, and Sylvia was trying to talk to me. I refused to interact until she did as I said. Finally, after they were all seated, I leaned against Reub's desk while he leaned against the wall next to the door.

"Alright, I want to know what the hell that fiasco was about. You know I don't allow shit like that here. Sinner, tell me what happened."

"Why him? Why don't you ask me?" Tessa whined.

"Because he was the only one who acted like he had any sense. You'll get your turn. Let him talk," I growled at her. After her shit and what happened with Tajah, she was already on thin ice with me.

"I'm sorry, Mikhail. I had no damn idea this would happen. All I did was ask Sylvia if she would be open to doing a scene with me tonight. She didn't even get a chance to answer me, when out of nowhere Tessa came barreling into the mix and she said I should pick her. That she had more experience at doing them. I informed her that may be so, but I wasn't into her kind of things tonight. It set her off, and she started arguing and trying to get Sylvia to say no and me to change my mind."

Not liking what I was hearing, I turned to Sylvia next. She hadn't said a word, and I didn't know how much of this she was truly in trouble for. "Sylvia, what do you have to say? Is what Sinner said true?"

She hesitated then nodded. "Yes, it's true. He did ask me exactly what he told you. I was about to tell him I couldn't when she came tearing into us. She wouldn't listen to either of us. It was like she was bound and determined to have him play with her. I don't want any trouble, Master M."

"You're not in trouble. I just want to know what caused this. Okay, Tessa, what do you have to say for yourself? It sounds like you were out of line."

She crossed her arms over her chest and gave me a pissed look. "Why is it all of a sudden I'm shit around here? I've been coming here for four years. She's been here a year. I've never had anyone not prefer me. As soon as I'm no longer your sub, everyone starts treating me like crap. When I was, they couldn't wait for me to either stop being yours, or to take on another play partner. I was only trying to explain to Sinner why I would make a much better playmate than her. There's a lot she won't do."

"Yes, you've been here four years, and that means you know better! God, no one has to choose you over someone else. It's all about free choice and consent, Tessa. As for how people treated you when we played together and since, maybe they don't like your attitude. You're acting like I dumped you then turned others against you. I never said a word about our time together in front of anyone, but I am now. It was never anything other than play as I explained to you. We mutually parted ways. Your desire to be my sub again is declined. You know why. Acting up with the other Doms and subs to cause trouble and drama won't be tolerated. This is your only warning. Do something again and your membership will be revoked. Understood?"

"That's not fair!" she shouted in outrage.

I was about to tell her the warning was now an official goodbye when I felt my phone vibrate. I took it out to check. I prayed it wasn't something else wrong. Luckily, I saw it was Tajah. I couldn't help but smile. Reuben, who'd been silent until then came over to me.

"You go see what Tajah wants. I'll finish up with this bunch. Sorry I didn't get to them and handle it before you had to. I was caught in the back with one of the staff having an issue."

"Anything I need to know?"

"Nothing urgent. I'll tell you later. Go. I'll make sure Tessa goes home for the rest of the night and that the other two are alright."

"You sure?"

He nodded. I looked at our patrons. Sinner looked ready to leave. Tessa was fuming and Sylvia kept giving me beseeching looks. "Reuben is gonna finish taking care of this. Sinner, Sylvia, I'm sorry you got pulled into this. Tessa, I meant what I said. Now, excuse me, I'm needed upstairs."

Sinner and Sylvia murmured their goodbyes, and Tessa hissed. I heard her mutter, "She's calling and he goes running."

I chose to ignore her. She was out the door soon. I could see the writing on the wall. Whatever her problem was, it wasn't one I would allow her to continue to play out here. Maybe I should just oust her, but I liked to give most people a chance. I'd give her the same. I didn't waste time sending a text to let my woman know I was coming back up to her.

# Tajah: Chapter 17

I sat back and smiled. I was almost there. Just a couple more chapters and the epilogue and my first book in my kink series would be done. I was feeling pretty proud of it. Now all I had to do was share it and see what others thought.

Cady was always good about reading them and giving me feedback, as well as catching typos and things. She'd read what I had so far and told me she really loved it, so that was one in the yes column. I thought about asking Carver, but I didn't see him being interested in reading romances, even if he did know about the lifestyle. I knew who I would love to read it, but I was hesitant to ask, even if it was part of our original deal. What if he hated it and thought it was rubbish? On the other hand, he was an expert and could catch anything I'd messed up. Which would hurt more? Him saying it was awful or me messing it up terribly and offending readers who lived the life?

I was debating it when arms came around me and a kiss landed on the back of my neck. I shivered. I loved his touch no matter what it was. I hadn't heard the door chime. I must've been deep in my head, which happened when I wrote.

"How's it going, babe?"

"It's going rather fast actually. What're you doing back so early? Is everything alright? No more Tessa acting up like last week?"

He let go and moved around to sit on the edge of my desk. "It's all quiet, thank God. Tessa hasn't been back since that night. Maybe she took the hint and won't. One more screw up and she's done. I can't believe she did that with Sinner and Sylvia. The staff know if she shows up, to keep an eye on her. She's being ridiculous," he grumbled.

I smiled and put my hand on his thigh to rub it. "I can understand why she's doing it."

He gave me a surprised look. "You can?"

"Yeah, she's upset she made a mistake in walking away from you. She realized she messed up and thought she could waltz back in and you'd start back up with her. You might've thought it was casual, but she obviously didn't. I think she wanted you to make her your permanent sub and girlfriend. Maybe she agreed to the breakup, thinking it would make you miss her and take that step when she came back. You said she was with other men after you two ended it. Did you ever think that was to make you jealous? If I was her and lost you, I wouldn't be happy. Which is why I can't help but wonder if she's the one calling in the complaints. I know Outlaw said he can't find proof it's her or Duncan, but then who else would have reason to do it?"

"If she thought that, it's her own delusion. It would never have been more. And you have nothing to worry about because I'll never let you go. You're stuck with me."

I smiled at him. "Well, it's a good thing I feel the same way. If you're done working, what do you wanna do?"

"I am and you know what I'd love to do, but first there's something else."

"What?"

"Why did you gloss over how the book is coming along? You never really talk about it other than to ask questions for your research. Do you let anyone read your books before you publish them or is that a no-no? I was hoping I'd get to read it."

"Are you sure you're not a mind reader? I was thinking about that very thing right before you came in. Cady usually reads them and my mom. I have a few people who're what we call beta readers who see it right before it publishes and they give me feedback and catch errors and stuff. I was nervous to see if Cady would like this one or not. She says she does so far. Mom always likes them and assures me it's not just because I'm her daughter. There's no way I'd ask Carver. He wouldn't read a romance if his life depended on it."

"And what about me? Do you think I won't read it because of the genre?"

"I don't really know actually. And even if you were willing, I'm nervous I've totally screwed up the whole thing. If you hate it and tell me it's a disaster, it'll hurt, but publishing it and having readers hate it, especially those who know about the life, would be worse. It makes me sick to my stomach to think about it."

He stood then leaned over to pull me to my feet. His arms came around me and he hugged me tight. "Dove, there's no way it's a disaster. None of your other books are. As for the content, as many notes and questions you've asked, I highly doubt you blew it and readers will hate it. If you want, I'd love to read it. I'll give you honest feedback, but if anything needs to be rewritten, I'm more than happy to help you do it."

"How do you know my other books aren't awful?"

"I've been reading them, of course. You think I'm not gonna support my woman? I have to say, I really love them and I'm not saying that because you're mine. I can't wait to see what this series has. The others are hot as hell, yet they have suspense, murder, and torture. If all romance books are like yours, I should've been reading them a long time ago."

I grabbed the back of his neck, so I could lower his head far enough to reach his mouth. I nipped at his bottom lip then licked it. He groaned, which opened his mouth a tiny bit. I took the opening and thrust my tongue inside. He growled, and it became a match to see who could control the kiss. We were both hungrily kissing each other.

When we parted to take a couple of deep breaths, I winked at him. "Well, you convinced me. I'll let you read it."

"Why don't you grab whatever you have for me to read it on and we'll go to the bedroom? I think we might find some things to expand on or even act out.

You know, purely for research and realism purposes," he replied with a smirk.

I couldn't hold back my shriek then a giggle. He let go long enough for me to save what I wrote and grab my tablet. It would be easier for him to read the document on it. He didn't waste time sweeping me along with him.

☙☙☙

It was official. I would never write another book without letting Mikhail read it and help me with the scenes, no matter whether it was a kink book or not. When he began to read it out loud and his growly voice read the male parts, I shivered. The man could make it as a narrator. He put the right spin on the words and made them come to life. I guess there was no end to his talents.

It took a while for him to finish it since we kept getting distracted but in the end, he finished it off a couple of days later. He'd given me great suggestions. Much to my excitement, he didn't say it was awful. In fact he praised how I'd done it. His feedback gave me the push to see if Mom wanted to read it. I would send it as soon as I was done writing it. It would still be a few months before I published it, so the betas wouldn't read it yet, but I liked to get it as polished as possible when I was writing it.

The weekend had been a busy one not only because of our reading adventures but the club. I'd spent part of Saturday and Sunday evening with Mikhail. I was still determined to learn as much as I could so I could support him. Thankfully, there were no big issues. Now it was Monday and I was back to working on the book. I wanted to finish it this week if I could.

In anticipation of doing that, Mikhail suggested we have a dinner party at his place the Saturday after next. He was going to invite a few of his people and he wanted me to see if Carver, Cady, and anyone else I was close to would come. He even hinted he thought I should see if my mom would. I wasn't sure if he was ready to meet her. I loved my mom, but she was a quirky person. I warned him, but all he did was laugh and tell me he could handle her.

It was his insistence that had me sitting at my desk biting my thumb nail as I placed my call. I'd already asked Cady and Carver. They both said yes. Other than them and my mom, I wasn't really that close to other people. I was more of a loner, but being with Mikhail was opening me up more.

"Hello, my darling. How're you?" Mom's breezy greeting came through the phone. I couldn't hold back the smile it put on my face. She was a little crazy but I did love her.

"Hi, Mom, I'm great. We haven't talked in a while. I have a lot to catch you up on. First though, how have your trips been? Still having fun traveling with your friends?"

Mom liked to travel and do cruises and other trips. She did it because she and Dad had always planned to travel once he retired but it never happened. I told her to do it. No need for her to sit at home missing him. It took her a couple of years to start but she loved it once she did. She'd found a core group of people she became good friends with who went on most of them with her. She was only sixty, so she potentially had a lot of years to live. I wanted her to enjoy them.

"It's always fun. I've been meaning to call you. There's something I wanted to talk to you about." Her tone got serious. I tensed up.

"Is something wrong?"

"No, nothing's wrong, but you remember Gideon, don't you?"

Gideon was one of the men in her friend group. "Yes, of course I do. Is he alright?" I asked worriedly.

"He's good. Well, I, uhm..." was her response.

Hearing her at a loss for words, I was suddenly sure I knew what she wanted to tell me. I knew she loved my dad and had mourned his loss for a long time. However, she deserved to be happy and loved. If she found someone who could give her that, then I would be happy for her. Just like I hoped she'd be the same for me when I told her about Mikhail.

"Mom, just spit it out."

"Fine, Gideon and I are dating. He asked me to be his lady friend a couple of weeks ago. Am I terrible for doing it? I loved your father so much, but I got lonely. I miss companionship and cuddling. I miss sex."

"Whoa, none of the sex talk," I teased her. We didn't have an issue talking about it unlike most moms and daughters.

She laughed. “Really, my romance author daughter doesn’t want to talk about sex. I don’t believe it.”

“You’re right, I don’t mind, although I should be grossed out. I know you loved Dad and I think if you found something with Gideon then you should go for it. What did my brothers say?” as if I had to ask.

She sighed. “You know how they are. I swear I don’t know how such sticks in the mud prudes are my kids. They both said I was disgusting for hooking up with another man. I should respect your dad’s memory and the idea of me wanting sex is gross. They said I was terrible. I told them until they got the sticks out of their asses, I didn’t want to talk to them. I’m done with them. I hated what they did to you when you and Sam divorced, and I had hoped they’d grow up, but it’s not happening. At this point, I doubt it ever will.”

“It’s their loss, Mom. You do whatever makes you happy. I know they won’t ever accept me and I don’t care. They especially won’t accept me now.”

“Oh, really, what did you do, naughty girl?” she asked excitedly.

“Remember I told you I wanted to write a new series about the kink lifestyle and I asked Carver to help me get into a club so I could do research?”

“Yes, and you had to pester him to get him to agree. So how was it? Did you get the information you needed? When is the first book out? Oh God, I wanna read it.”

"Mom, calm down. Yes, I got to do the research and I'm working on the book right now. I promise to send it as soon as I finish. It's because of all that and what happened afterward that I'm calling. I wanted to know if you would come to a dinner party the Saturday after next in Nashville. You're more than welcome to bring Gideon. It's a small, intimate one of just friends."

"Of course, I'll come! Where? Your apartment is too small for a party, honey."

"I'll send you the address. It's actually at the House of Lustz, in the owner's apartment, which is more than big enough for a party."

There was a moment or two of silence as what I had said sunk in and then she came back at me, like I knew she would. I was having fun prolonging the torture a bit. "Tajah, why in the world would you be having a party at the owner's apartment?"

"Well, it might be because he's my boyfriend."

Her shriek almost deafened me. I heard her yelling hallelujah and thanking God. I let her settle before I said anything else. "Mom, are you still with me?"

"My heart is pounding. Tell me everything! How did this happen? He's the owner? What's his name? Does he do any of the stuff people do in his club? What does he look like? How is he in bed?"

"Stop! Oh my God, you're too much. Listen. His name is Mikhail Ivanova, and yes, he owns the House of Lustz. I met him after Carver helped me join. He wasn't here initially when I did, so I didn't meet him until a few weeks later. We had a little misunderstanding about what I was trying to accomplish there and planned to write. He kicked me out at first, but then he changed his mind. When he asked me to come back, he made it a stipulation he be the one to answer my questions and show me what the club and the lifestyle entailed. It went from there. The answer to your question, does he do the stuff people do at the club, the answer is a lot of it." I paused to take a breath.

"I have to see him. Do you have a picture?"

"I do."

"Send it right now," she demanded.

Knowing she wouldn't let it go, I quickly found one I'd taken the other day when we were relaxing in the apartment and sent it to her. I knew when she saw it because she gasped. "Oh Tajah, he's gorgeous. His eyes are piercing. I see tattoos on his arms. Please tell me he's great in bed. You so need and deserve that."

"Mom, he's beyond great in bed. The things he makes me feel are incredible. I still can't believe he feels about me the way I do about him. He's amazing."

"And why shouldn't he feel the same? You're wonderful. You love him, don't you?"

"I do and he says he loves me, too. I know it's crazy fast and all, but I have never felt like this, not even when I thought I loved Sam. He's never been married. He's forty-five and says he knows what he wants and it's me and a life together, which includes kids."

She squealed again. "Oh there's no doubt I'm coming to dinner. It might kill me to wait until then. I'll see if Gideon wants to come. Do I need to bring anything? How many people are coming?"

"I'm not sure how many he's inviting. I asked you, Cady, and Carver. His best friend Reuben, who's his assistant manager, will be here I know. And one of his security guys, Hoss. They're close to him. No need to bring anything. He's having it catered so we can all relax and enjoy it. It starts at seven but you can come earlier if you like."

"Oh I will. I have to check him out to be sure he's good enough for my daughter. Tell him to get ready."

This led to us laughing about the few dates I had growing up and how my dad used to scare the crap out of the guys with his threats and Mom with her unfiltered mouth. It was a wonder I ever had more dates. We chatted for a while longer then I told her I had to get back to work. As I hung up, I heard a chuckle from behind me. I whipped around to find Mikhail standing there.

"How long have you been there?"

"Oh, since your mom asked you about how I was in bed. I couldn't resist. Are you mad at me?"

I blushed even though with what we did together, this should be the least thing to make me do it. I gave him a stern look, but then I lost it and laughed. "No, I'm not mad. As you could tell, Mom thinks you're hot. Just be ready. She'll grill you when she comes, and you'll probably want to break up with me when she gets done."

He shook his head and came over to me. He gave me a come-hither look which I immediately complied with. He picked me up, so I had no choice but to wrap my arms and legs around him. He stared deeply into my eyes. "Dove, there's nothing and no one in this world who can scare me away from you. Your mom could be Attila the Hun and I would still gladly handle her. She sounds fun and sweet. Who's Gideon?"

"He was one of her travel buddies who my mom is now dating. She was nervous to tell me, but I'm happy for her. She's been so lonely without Dad. I wish my brothers would be more supportive of it. They gave her a hard time, so she's not talking to them."

"Babe, one day you'll have to introduce me to your asshole brothers so I can set them straight. Believe me, I'd like to have them see the light even if it's while they're looking up from the flat of their backs after I lay them out. How can they be raised by the same parents as you were?"

"Honey, I love you want to do that, but they're not worth scuffing your knuckles on. I have no clue how we're related. I know Mom didn't cheat on Dad. She swears they're not adopted. They look too much like Dad to be switched in the hospital, so the only possibility is they got dropped on their heads a lot."

He snorted. "Yeah, bounced like a basketball you mean. I came over to see how you're doing. I have a couple more hours of work to do in the office. Do you need anything?"

I snuggled against him. "I'm good. I called and did my invites to our dinner, and I was planning to get back to writing. Thank you for asking. Is there anything I can get you?"

"A kiss would be great. I need it to survive," he whispered.

I gladly gave him one. Of course, it turned me on and I wanted to say the hell with working but we had to be adults. There would be time for sex later. He growled in protest when I stopped, but after a few more little pecks and explaining I'd make it up to him later, he let me down and went back to his main office. I happily sat down. I had been hit with inspiration. I knew exactly what I wanted to write next.

# Tajah: Chapter 18

The next two weeks flew by. We'd both stayed super busy with work and preparing for our dinner party. I wanted everything to be perfect. Since Mikhail insisted it be catered and the cleaning lady, Sandra, was to take care of making sure the apartment was spotless, it left me to work on the decorations. I loved to have different themes for the table. In the fall, I decked out my table with all the autumn colors and flowers. At Christmas, I'd change it up again. I had ones for most of the major holidays and all four seasons. Since we were still a month away from official fall, I stuck with summer.

I found a gorgeous table runner which was dark blue and white striped with small bouquets of bright flowers scattered on it. Along with it I found white cloth napkins with bright lemons on them. They went with the centerpiece idea, which was a large square vase with fresh lemon slices surrounding all sides and in the middle was lovely fresh blue and white hydrangeas. The plates were a mix of white and sky blue. Mikhail had lovely crystal goblets, flutes, and wine glasses, which would round it out perfectly. He smiled when I told him what I wanted to do. He didn't voice a single objection. In fact, he told me to buy whatever I wanted. That was right before he handed me his credit card. Recalling that moment, I had to grin.

*"Dove, you do whatever you want. If you want to change out all the furniture then do it, but don't drive yourself crazy. No matter what, they'll love it."*

*"I just want to make the table and decor shine. I won't get rid of your furniture."*

*"You have free rein. Here's my card. Spend what you need," he held out a black credit card.*

*I stared at it then at him. I didn't take it. Instead, I shook my head. "Babe, no, I don't need you to pay for it. This is all on me. I can cover it. I only wanted to be sure you were okay with it and to see if you had any ideas of your own that you wanted me to incorporate. It's not just my friends and family coming."*

*"I know it's not but you aren't spending a dime of your money. Are you planning to get rid of those things when we're done with the party?"*

*"No, of course not."*

*"Do you think we'll use them again in the future?"*

*"Yes, there's a lot I can do with them and combine them with other stuff. Why? What does that have to do with anything?"*

*"It means they're for our home, our table, our lives. This is as much your home as it is mine now. Maybe I should've told you this earlier, but I've been trying not to scare you by going too fast."*

*"Huh?"*

*"You stay here with me every night. Most of your clothes and other personal stuff are here. Other than to get your mail and check on the place, you don't go to your apartment. I want you to give up your place and move in with me permanently. Anything you want to change out and replace with your stuff, do it. The rest we can get rid of or put in storage. There's no damn way I can sleep without you. I want you in every part of my life and vice versa. With that said, all those things you plan to get for the dinner party will become part of our home. I want to be the one to buy stuff like that."*

*I was stunned to hear him say all of it. It was true I was staying here all the time and if I was honest, I didn't miss my apartment a bit. Sure there were some things I liked and would want to take to a new home, but my apartment had always been just a place to sleep and work. It was decent to live there, but I wasn't in love with it, not like I would be with an actual house.*

*His apartment was much bigger and despite being above the club, it had a better home-like feel to it. It wasn't as nice as a house would be, but that was a topic for the future. Maybe one day he'd be willing to have a home away from the club, However, I didn't expect him to pay for everything. I made a decent living with my writing now that I'd become established.*

*"Misha, I don't expect you to pay for everything. I love the fact you want me to move in with you and yes, it's fast but I want to do it. However, I'll pay my share for our home and the rest. I make enough money to do it. If you want me to live with you, I need to know what my half of the mortgage is, utilities, etcetera. Buying these things for*

*the party is my first contribution to our home."*

*He shook his head. "Baby, there's no mortgage. The club, the whole building is paid for. As for utilities, not happening. As your man, I need to take care of you. Your money can be used for fun stuff you want to do or gifts for your friends and family. Anything else, I'll pay for."*

*"So you'll pay for my car, insurance, cell phone and stuff? If I want to get new furniture, you'll pay."*

*"Exactly," he said with a smile.*

*"No, not exactly. I don't need to be kept, Misha! I'll be a full partner or nothing. I don't know what kind of woman you're used to, but it's not one like me."*

We'd gone back and forth arguing. He didn't see it as keeping me. He saw it as caring for me. I had to work to get him to see it from my point of view. In the end, he'd reluctantly agreed to go half with me on the decor. There was no way I could get him to let me do it all. I knew we'd have more battles over this in the future, but eventually I thought he'd get to the point of seeing it my way and I'd work to meet him in the middle. The one thing we did agree on was me moving in. I told him we had time but my man wasn't patient I found out.

The next day he came to me with the name of a moving company which would be able to pack my stuff and move it and several dates they could do it, that were over the next few weeks. All he needed was for me to decide what to bring to his place and what to put in storage. He had one of those storage units already for things he kept. I knew not to fight him so I agreed and promised to go to the apartment and put labels on what

I wanted stored so they'd know when the time came.

I did get him to let us get through the dinner first before I'd go to label the furniture and have them come pack it up. The end of next week was the day I agreed to do it. Thankfully, my writing had been going well, and I finished up the first book and Cady was reading the last part. I'd wait until she was done before letting Mom read it. Not only was my work humming along, but so was his. The club was sailing along great. There had been no more surprise visits from inspectors due to complaints called into various regulatory agencies. I hoped this meant whoever had been doing it was done. We still wished we knew who but we might never figure out who or why.

Even though it was Saturday night, Reuben and Hoss were able to take the night off to join us. Hoss traded a day with one of the other guys, Tuck, to be here. Reuben made sure the most experienced floor managers were on duty. Hopefully, neither he nor Mikhail would get any calls. I was anxious to see how Mom, Gideon, Cady, and Carver got along with Mikhail. Carver knew him but not on a personal level. Cady had met him briefly the day we went shopping. She would be eager to question him, I knew. Mom would have questions too. I prayed he was prepared. I tried to warn him but he waved me away saying he could handle anything they asked or did.

As for me, I was anxious about the other two guests he informed me he invited once they said yes. In order not to overwhelm me, he stuck to only four people as well. In addition to Hoss and Reuben, he invited his cousin Matvey and his wife. To say the least, I was very nervous to meet a member of his family and to have it be the head of the Russian mob scared me spitless. He assured me I had nothing to worry about. Matvey would be here as family, not the *Pakhan* of the Bratva. Plus, as the head of the family on his dad's side, it would go a long way with the others if he was the first to meet me and give me his stamp of approval. When I almost hyperventilated at the thought of him disapproving of me, he promised me Matvey would love me. I prayed he was right. I begged him not to let me disappear, which made him laugh at me, the bastard.

After days of worry, the time had come to see if tonight would end as a success or a total disaster. Sheila called up a couple of minutes ago to tell us my guests were here. Reuben was downstairs and told her to tell us he'd show them up. I wondered if Hoss was with him.

"It's gonna be great. Breath," Mikhail told me softly.

I took a deep breath as the door beeped then swung open. I saw Mom and Gideon first and right behind them was Cady and Carver. Bringing up the rear was Reuben. Mom let out a loud squeal when she saw me and ran to me. I opened my arms knowing what she wanted. She was a hugger and kisser. She hugged me tightly, as she gave me a kiss on each cheek. Gideon was behind her with an indulgent smile on his face. He knew how she was. I gave her a kiss back.

"Hello, Mom, it's good to see you."

"Oh honey, it's been too long. We can't go this long again. I need my baby girl. You look so good. Let me look at you," she babbled as she stepped back to look me up and down. When she got done, I held out a hand to Gideon.

"Hello Gideon, I'm so glad you could come. Are you ready to keep her under control?" I teased him.

He came forward and gave me a kiss on the cheek. "Sweetheart, no one can control her. I'm just along for the ride and to soak up her sunshine."

"Good answer," I told him with a wink.

By then, Mom was studying Mikhail. I hurried to make introductions. "Mom, Gideon, this is Mikhail Ivanova. He owns the club and he's my boyfriend. Misha, honey, this is my mom, Tamara, and her boyfriend, Gideon."

Not being shy, Mom moved over to him and gave him a kiss on each cheek and a hug. I saw the flash of surprise on his face, but he returned them with a smile. When she moved back, he held out his hand to Gideon so they could shake. "It's a pleasure to finally meet both of you. I've heard a lot about you. Welcome to our home. Please, make yourself comfortable. We're waiting on a couple more people. They should be here any minute."

"Our home? Is there something you forgot to tell me?" Mom asked excitedly.

"Mom, let me greet Cady and Carver then you can start the inquisition." I told her. She was practically vibrating with excitement.

"Oh fine, make me suffer," she pretended to pout. This made Cady laugh. Carver just rolled his eyes and gave her an indulgent look. They'd known her for too many years not to know how she was. Gideon looked at her like she was amazing. I'd always suspected he liked her more than as a friend.

Hugging my two friends, I passed them off to Mikhail. He shook Carver's hand and gave Cady a hug. She sent me a surprised look. Reuben shut the door and we went to sit in the living room. Once we were seated, Mikhail made sure they knew Reuben's name and who he was.

"I made introductions downstairs. I told them if it wasn't for me, you wouldn't be able to find your own pants," Reuben joked.

"Ha, ha, yeah, sure. The truth is, if I didn't take pity on him and give him a job, he'd be living in someone's basement," Mikhail fired back.

"Oh my Tajah, if this is the example of the men around here, whew," Mom said as she fanned herself.

"Mom," I warned.

"Don't *Mom* me. It's true and I have eyes. I'm not dead, ya know? Okay, back to my earlier question. Our home?"

Mikhail took my hand and smiled at me. I was opening my mouth to answer her when there was a knock at the door.

"That must be our other guests. Excuse me a moment," Mikhail told them as he got to his feet.

I was suddenly too weak in the legs to get up.

He gave me an encouraging look before he went to answer it. I watched him go. When he swung open the door, my eyes landed on an older gentleman. He had an imposing presence even without saying anything. Looking at him, I would've known he was related to Mikhail without being told. He had the same general features. Beside him was an attractive older woman. She was smiling at Mikhail. Behind them I saw the towering figure of Hoss.

Matvey's booming voice made me jump as he called out, "*Kusen*, it's about time we got together." He had a slight Russian accent unlike Mikhail, although he spoke Russian flawlessly. He'd talked to me in it one day when I asked if he did know the language. Matvey held out his arms. Mikhail stepped into them. They slapped each other hard on the back.

"Matvey, welcome. Now, move so I can give Victoria a proper welcome. You always try to keep her all to yourself," Mikhail teased as he playfully pushed his cousin aside so he could hug Matvey's wife. She smiled even wider as she gave him a kiss on the cheek.

"Of course, I do. You don't let men near a treasure like her. I would hope you know that for yourself now. Hurry up. I want to meet your *lyubimoy*."

As Mikhail moved back to let them inside, I caught a glimpse of men in suits in the hallway. I'd forgotten about them. He'd told me Matvey traveled with bodyguards. They went to enter before their boss, but Matvey waved them off.

"There's no need for that here. Misha would never

let anyone in his home who would harm us. Stay here. Try to stay out of trouble."

"Yes, *Pakhan*," the one on the left said. I could tell they weren't thrilled, but they did as commanded.

"*Pahkan*? Is that Russian? What was that other word he said?" Mom asked in what she thought was a whisper. It wasn't. Four sets of eyes landed on us as the door was closed.

"Yes, it's Russian. *Lyubimoy* means beloved. The other simply means boss. Misha, please make the introductions," his cousin told him.

"I will if you give me a second. So impatient. Victoria, after all these years you still haven't cured him of that?"

I tried not to snicker, but I couldn't help it. Look who was calling someone impatient. My man raised his brow at me as he stalked over and eased me to my feet. Hoss gave me a wink behind his back. I nervously met Matvey's gaze. He was studying me intently. I couldn't tell whether he approved of what he saw or not. His wife was more open. She at least had a tiny smile on her face.

"Tajah, this is my cousin Matvey and his wife, the saint Victoria. Cousin, this is my Tajah and yes, she is my beloved, so I know exactly what you mean. I assume Hoss introduced himself already. These are Tajah's friends, Carver, and Cady. They're siblings. You've met Reuben before. Reuben is my assistant manager and best friend, Victoria. And this is Tajah's mom, Tamara, and her boyfriend, Gideon."

I let out a tiny squeak because Matvey abruptly took the hand I held out and pulled me into his chest. He hugged me then kissed my cheeks. As he stepped back he smiled. "She's *krasivye*, beautiful. It's a pleasure to meet the woman who brought Misha to his knees. Thank you for inviting us. Later, you and I need to talk. I have so many things to tell you about him."

His eyes warmed as he spoke, which made me feel a tad more at ease. "Welcome and thank you for coming, and I'd love to hear all the stories he doesn't want me to know. It's a pleasure to meet you as well, Mrs. Ivanova," I said to his wife.

"Please, we're family now, call me Victoria. He's just Matvey. We're both thrilled to meet you." She gave me a hug and kiss. With the ice broken, we brought them over to join the others. It took a few minutes to get everyone settled with drinks. Dinner was due to arrive shortly.

"Matvey, you and your wife got here just in time. We were asking Mikhail what he meant by welcome to our home," Mom didn't hesitate to tell them. I groaned.

"What? I want to know if I have more to celebrate or not. That is assuming he's the sort to take care of my daughter and treat her like she's a queen. If not, then we'll be having a talk," was Mom's reply to my groan.

"Tamara, you have nothing to worry about. Tajah is my queen, and I plan to show her that for the rest of her life. I haven't waited this many years to find her to risk losing her. I said our home because she's agreed to move in here with me. In fact, it'll be next weekend. I hope I can prove to you before you leave tonight that she couldn't be in better hands."

I swear I saw her melt at his words. The whole time he spoke, he had his arm around me. I saw his cousins smiling. Carver and Gideon appeared to be taking it all in. Reuben and Hoss were grinning. Cady was the only one who seemed to be studying him. I knew she'd be a tougher one to convince than even Mom. She'd been there when Sam had devastated me, however, I didn't expect her to do it immediately or so obviously.

"Talk is cheap. How do we know you won't change your mind or turn into an utter asshole like her ex? I'm warning you, if you do, I'll find a way to make your life hell," she said suddenly.

"Cady!" I hissed at her. This wasn't the time or place for her to be doing this.

"Don't Cady me. I won't let you get hurt like that again. Sam fooled us. Those other two were jerks. What's to say Mikhail isn't the same? I mean, look at him. He owns this place, and he's used to having whoever he wants whenever he wants. What happens when he gets bored?"

I flushed in embarrassment. For the first time ever, I wanted to smack my best friend.

"Cady, enough," Carver barked at her.

"I won't shut up. I—" she was cut off by Hoss of all people.

"Tiny, I don't know who this Sam was or those

other men you spoke of, but I know Mikhail. He's a straight shooter, and he would never declare himself to Tajah or ask her to move in, if he wasn't positive of his feelings for her, and he didn't want to spend their lives together. I understand wanting to get to know him for yourself, but this isn't the time or place to do this. Tonight is supposed to be a relaxing night for everyone to meet."

"Don't call me Tiny! You don't know me. Of course, you'd defend your boss. You don't want him to fire you," she snapped back. I was shocked at her behavior. I knew she was protective, but this was more than that. Her lashing out like this wasn't her norm.

Hoss laughed at her. "Tiny, I don't need this job. I do it because I enjoy it. I don't say what I don't mean either. Sounds like someone needs an ass spanking," he told her with a smirk.

"In your dreams," she snarled as she came to her feet. She headed for the door. I jumped up and went after her. I grabbed her arm before she could open it.

"What is your problem? I can't believe you're acting like this! Mikhail has done nothing to deserve you being ugly toward him, or for you to act like this."

"He's a man. They're all users. They take what they want and then leave you hurt and alone. Don't come to me when he breaks your heart wanting a shoulder to cry on because I'll just tell you I told you so." As her words struck me I saw tears in her eyes. Shit, I was right. There was something wrong, and it had nothing to do with Mikhail and me.

"Cady, don't go. Tell me what's wrong," I urged her softly.

"I need to go."

She didn't give me a chance to say more before she yanked the door open. The bodyguards on the other side came to attention. She scowled at them, then took off for the elevator. I wanted to go after her, but I wouldn't leave our other guests in the lurch. I'd call her tomorrow after we both calmed down. Closing the door, I felt a hard body behind me. I leaned back against Mikhail.

"Come on my Sweetest Dove, let's enjoy our night. You can call her tomorrow and find out what she was upset about."

"I'm so sorry. I've never seen her like that. Misha," I whispered to him.

"You have nothing to apologize for. I didn't take it personally. We'll figure it out. Let's go." He led me to the living room where the others were waiting for us.

It took a few minutes for the tension to ease. Carver suggested he leave, but we told him to stay. Luckily, by the time dinner was delivered we were talking more. Other than not having Cady here, the night went well. Victoria and Mom raved about how beautiful the table was. I knew the guys couldn't care less, but we women got it. I was way more relaxed with Matvey by the time the evening ended. His wife was sweet, and she and Mom seemed to hit it off. Mom had grilled Mikhail, but nicely and he had no problem answering her numerous questions. Gideon was quiet, but that was him.

Hoss and Reuben kept us laughing. Carver eventually joined in. By the time everyone left, I had promised Matvey and Victoria I would make Mikhail bring me to the next family gathering. Mom demanded we have lunch next week. Carver whispered he'd talk to his sister and see if he could find out what her issue was. All in all, it could've been worse. When the last person left, I was sagging with fatigue.

"Let me give you a nice hot bath and then we can go to bed."

"Sounds heavenly," I told him as he led me to our room. I'd worry tomorrow.

# Mikhail: Chapter 19

I knew Tajah needed to let go. The past couple of weeks since the dinner party had been stressful as hell for her. On top of moving in with me, she and Cady still weren't truly talking. She tried more than once to talk to her, but for some reason Cady was unwilling to tell her what set her off that night. Instead, she was avoiding her calls and texts. I could understand Cady being concerned that her friend would be hurt again like Sam had hurt her, but when Tajah told me what she said at the door about men, it made me even more convinced it had only a little to do with me, and more to do with something in her life.

I offered to speak to her, but Dove told me they'd hash it out, eventually. They'd been friends since grade school. There was no way she could see their friendship ending over something like this. It was the fixer in me, who wanted to make it right for her. She told me she loved me for wanting to do it, but women usually only wanted a man to listen to them, not fix stuff for them. I took note of that for future reference, but I wasn't sure how I could turn instinct off.

Her mom, on the other hand, seemed to like me and was excited about us. Tajah's lunch date with her had gone really well, and she was smiling when she came home afterward. As for my side of the dinner party, there were no issues with Hoss or Reuben with Tajah. They already adored her. Matvey and Victoria rang me the next day to tell me how much they liked her and her mom. They were eager to have the rest of the family meet her. They also asked if we'd figured out her friend's problem. I had to tell them no, but they'd work it out. Carver had come to me a couple days later to apologize for Cady's behavior. I made sure he knew he had nothing to apologize for. Cady was an adult. Her actions were hers alone, and I wouldn't hold it against him.

Hoss on the other hand wanted to go find her and spank her ass. I knew he didn't just want to do it as my friend. He was into impact play, and I saw his interest in her, even when she was acting like a bitch. He was imagining himself taming her no doubt. If he went after her, I'd wish him luck because he'd need it. She wouldn't be an easy one to tame if it was even possible.

With all this in mind, I knew it was time to surprise my dove. We'd been sharing more and more of ourselves, but I hadn't told her every single thing about me yet. I'd been waiting for the right time, and tonight was the perfect time to show her more. Reuben would be here to take care of the club, so we could get away. I'd worked on getting everything ready for our couple of days away for the past few days. It would take us over an hour to get to our destination. When I told her to pack a bag with enough clothes for three days, she asked where we were headed, but I told her it was a surprise. Excitement kept building inside of me.

I'd packed clothes and other things I thought we'd need and had them already in the car. It was all I could do to concentrate on finishing up the last few things I needed to do before we left. The very last would be a quick walk through of the club to check with Reuben, and then we'd be off. I wanted to get there before nightfall.

It was around three in the afternoon when I finished off the last email to my accountant. Shutting down my computer, I headed downstairs to say goodbye to Reuben. Tajah was in the apartment waiting on me. She'd spent the day doing research on her next book. We'd checked in with each other throughout the day. It was the new norm for us. When I got to the club, I lucked out and found him on the first floor. He was at the bar talking to the bartender.

He grinned when he saw me. He walked over and slapped me on the shoulder. "Are you ready to go?"

"Hell, yeah. I can't wait to get her out there. I hope she'll like what I have in store."

"I have no doubt she will. You guys have fun, and don't worry about this place. I've got it under control."

"I know you do."

"Get out of here. You don't want to delay your special plans."

"That's for damn sure. See you Saturday. Or who knows, if it goes well, we might not be back until Sunday."

He laughed and wiggled his eyebrows at me. I laughed. Not wanting to delay another second, I rushed upstairs to get her. Ten minutes later we were on the road. She kept trying to get out of me where we were headed.

"Misha, tell me."

"Nope, you'll just have to be patient. I can tell you it's in Tennessee."

"Oh, well that clears it up. Have I told you I don't like surprises?"

"No, and too bad if you don't because I love to give them to you. Just relax and enjoy the scenery."

It didn't go as quickly as I hoped. We hit the beginning of rush hour traffic out of Nashville to outlying towns, so it was closer to an hour and a half before we got close to our destination. It was southwest of Nashville. The area was an unincorporated section of Maury County called Culleoka. It was a rural setting, where most properties were several acres and the houses were in all different designs and sizes. There were no communities of the same houses everywhere. They were unique, which was one of the things which attracted me to them.

The final long dirt road I drove down was surrounded by woods on both sides. She was looking around with interest. "Misha, where are we?"

"You haven't been to Culleoka before?"

"No, I don't think so. It's so pretty out here, though. Look at the trees. They're almost ready to start changing to fall colors. Are we visiting someone?"

"Five more minutes and you'll see," I promised

her.

A couple of miles further and the road changed from a gravel dirt road into a long, paved driveway. I glanced over to see her reaction when she saw our final destination. Her eyes were sparkling as she scanned the house. She looked over at me. "You have to tell me now. Who lives here? Why didn't you tell me we were visiting someone? Is it more family?"

"I didn't tell you because we're not visiting anyone. It's just us."

"You mean you rented this for the weekend? I can't believe it. It's so gorgeous and peaceful out here," she said excitedly.

"No, I didn't rent it. This is my house."

She gaped at me in surprise. "You own this? Wait, if you have a house, why do you live in town? How long have you had this place?"

"I've had it for five years. When it came on the market, I couldn't pass it up. I love the country, and the only reason I don't live out here is because it's only me. I didn't see the need to drive back and forth every day. The apartment above the club sufficed for most days, and I came here when I needed to get away for a night or a couple of days. However, if you like it, then I'd love for us to move out here."

"Wait, you want us to move here? But I just moved to the apartment."

"I know, and we don't have to move if you prefer living in town. We can keep this as our retreat, but one day, I'd like us to move, even if we build a new house out here or find another property somewhere. I can't see raising kids above the club. I want them to be able to go outside to run and play," I told her as I opened the garage door and drove inside.

When she didn't say anything, I hurried to reassure her. "I don't expect an answer right now. Just let me show you the place and spend the next couple of days here with me. See what you think and then give it some thought. We have plenty of time to decide. I've been saving this. Will you let me show you the house and why I love it?"

"Of course, you can. I admit, I'm kinda stunned, but I'm willing to consider it. I agree with giving kids space to play, and I do enjoy the country, so lead the way. I want to see everything." I heard what I hoped was a note of excitement in her voice.

I wanted to say thank you when I heard she wasn't pissed at me. Maybe I should've kept all the talk about moving here for another time, but I was excited to have her love it as much as I did. Not bothering with the bags right then, I got out and opened her door. Unlocking the inner door between the garage and the house, I led her inside. The house wasn't huge. It was just a bit more than twenty-three hundred square feet. It had three large bedrooms and two and a half bathrooms.

Since it had only ever been me out here, the master was the only bedroom furnished, along with the living room and kitchen. The breakfast nook had a small table for four. I'd never shared this place with anyone but her. It was like my special room at the apartment. I'd bought it with the vague hope that one day I'd have someone special enough to bring here, but I never felt right doing it until her.

We took our time going from room to room. I was pleased with all her comments. She appeared to love it. It had an expansive yard surrounded by thick woods on three sides. I didn't say anything, but I could picture a play set and other things for the kids in the back, along with a fenced-in pool. I had twenty acres in total. It was more than enough privacy, which I craved. When I was done showing her around, I left her to gaze out the back windows in the living room while I got our bags.

Coming back to join her when I was done, I gave her a kiss. It was almost six o'clock in the evening, and the sun would be setting in a couple of hours. Even though it was September, the weather was hot, which was perfect for my plans later. First though, I needed to make sure we had energy. I went to the kitchen and opened the fridge.

"Honey, what're you doing?" she asked as she joined me.

"I'm getting out the stuff for dinner."

"Tell me what you need me to do."

"Nothing. Just sit there, look beautiful and talk to me. Tonight is my night to cook. We're having steak and baked potatoes along with grilled asparagus."

"Yum, sounds great, but I can help."

I shook my head and walked her over to one of the

stools at the island. I pulled it out and pressed her down on it. Going back to the fridge, I fixed her a glass of her favorite tea and myself a beer.

Time flew by as I worked and we talked. No matter what we were doing, even the simplest things like this, I enjoyed them with her. I never got bored with our conversations and it wasn't all me talking. We equally shared about ourselves, growing up and our work. When it was close to time for everything to be done, I set the table and lit the candles before turning off the lights. Before seating and serving her, I poured us both a glass of wine. I knew what she liked, and thankfully our tastes were similar. I didn't drink wine all the time, but when I did, I usually went for a red one.

We took our time, and I was happy with how the food turned out. I wasn't a gourmet chef, but I could handle steak and potatoes without messing them up. She ate hungrily and so did I. She was complimentary and cleaned her plate. Dinner wouldn't be complete without dessert. Making dessert was beyond me unfortunately, so I ended up buying a gourmet cheesecake. I knew it was one of her favorites. Once it was eaten and we couldn't eat another bite, we rested a few minutes before we cleaned up together, since she refused to let me do it alone. Taking a seat in the living room after we were finished, I cuddled her close. With one hunger sated, it was time to think about sating another.

It wasn't long before talking petered off and we started kissing. Any time we kissed, my hunger for her grew fast. It wasn't long before our desires grew into needing more than just our mouths connected.

I'd been half hard the whole way here and throughout dinner. Now, I was fully engorged, and becoming more and more frantic to be inside of her. I'd had her this morning, but it felt like it had been days. She drew back making me growl in protest. The heat in her gaze pleased the hell outta me.

"Misha, let's go to the bedroom," she moaned, as she ran her fingers through my hair.

"No."

"No? Why not?" she asked in surprise.

"I don't want to go to the bedroom. I want to let my primal loose."

Pleasure showed on her face. "So you want to stay down here. I'm fine with that," she said as she moved, and then straddled my lap.

"Not here. Out there," I told her as I pointed outside.

Her eyes widened. "Out in the yard?"

"No, out in the woods. Your dragon needs to chase his Dove. I need you to resist me. My beast needs his mate," I growled, before nipping her neck with my teeth.

She gave a full body shiver and moaned as her head fell back. I licked up her neck to her ear. She ground her core down on my throbbing erection. As a primal, it had been years since I'd been out in the woods, not since my introduction to my kinky nature in fact.

"Will you play with me, my love? Will you let my

beast have his prey?" I whispered.

"God yes, I'd love to. How do you want to do this?" she moaned brokenly.

"There's no one around for miles. I want you to go outside and strip for me but keep your shoes on. I don't want you to hurt your feet. I'll give you a head start. Hide wherever you want. Further in the woods there's an old barn. It's safe just in case you want to hide there."

"Can I have a few minutes to prepare first?"

"Absolutely."

"Stay here," she said, before giving me a quick kiss, then she got up and headed to the bedroom.

I sat there wondering what preparations she was making. I rubbed my hand over my bulge. I could feel myself leaking precum into my underwear. I wanted to get out of my clothing. I didn't know how long it was before she came back because I was lost in my fantasies about what I was going to do to her. She had braided her hair. She knew I would likely take it out as soon as I caught her. She'd changed out of her skirt and top into a pair of shorts and a tank. On her feet was a pair of simple canvas shoes. As she passed me, she licked her lips.

I lunged for her, but she danced out of reach and giggled as she ran for the back door. It was all I could do to control myself and not chase her right then. To keep myself from doing it, I went to the bedroom and stripped off my clothes. I wasn't worried about my feet, so I took everything off. Before heading out after her, I turned down the bed, set up flameless candles around the bedroom, and laid out some fun things for us to enjoy later. Having her once tonight wouldn't be nearly enough. Knowing I wanted to take my time when I caught her, I gripped my cock and stroked it. I had to take the edge off. Coming too soon was the last thing I wanted to do. The chase would only ramp up my excitement.

I pictured her naked and what she'd look like in the woods. My desire increased more. I was dripping for her as it was, but those images made me even hornier. I stood staring at the toys and imagined using them on her. It only took me a couple of minutes to feel the tingle in my balls growing, then they began to draw up tight. A few more hard strokes had me grunting as my cum shot out on my stomach. I groaned as squirt after squirt relieved some of the pressure in my balls. After shooting my load, I had to sit for a few minutes to regain my senses. When I thought I could walk, I wiped my seed off with a washcloth. I'd waited long enough. It was time to go find my Dove and mate with her. By the time I was done with her tonight, she'd have no doubts I was beyond hungry for her.

Rushing to the back door, I flung it open and took off. I wanted to howl at the joy racing through me. It was like instincts took over my mind and body. The warm air caressed my body. There was a breeze blowing gently, but enough to stir the leaves. I saw clouds rolling in. The forecast said no rain, but it appeared they might have gotten it wrong. No matter, as long as it didn't turn into a terrible storm, it would only enhance our play. The sun had set, but it was still light out. There was to be a full moon tonight. Another reason I picked these days. No way did I want her running in pitch black woods. I didn't want her to get hurt.

Since the yard was pretty open and flat other than some trees scattered around, it only took a cursory look to determine she'd headed into the woods like I wanted. The woods would take much longer to search, but I doubted being her first time in it, she'd stray too far from the paths inside it. The barn was about a half mile in there.

Elation for the hunt was rising in me. I took my time searching behind the larger trees along the paths. There were some deadfalls, which would make great hiding places, too. I thoroughly checked them all. Even as eager as I was, I didn't want it to end too soon.

As I searched, I called out, "Dove, I'm coming for you. You'd better hide."

After checking out another section, I drew close to the barn. I yelled again, making sure she could hear the growl in my voice. "When I catch you, I'm eating that pussy until you scream, then I'm gonna fuck you so good and fill you full of my seed. You'll be dripping for days when I get done with you."

I paused to listen to see if I heard anything. Nothing. Damn, did she go further into the woods? I went to the barn and opened the door. Inside was dark as hell. Lucky for me. I kept a battery-operated camping lamp out there. I found it on the wall and turned it on. The inside had bales of hay and some farm equipment I hadn't bothered to get rid of in it. Overhead was a hay loft. I decided to start at the top and work my way down. Climbing the wooden ladder, I reached the loft. It was empty, so all it took was a quick scan and I knew she wasn't there.

Climbing back down, I went to the nearest pile of hay bales. I was coming back around from searching behind them and was going toward a hay bailer when I saw a flash of movement and heard a rustling sound. As the light from the lamp hit the object moving, I saw her. I growled deeply, which made her squeal as she ran to the door. My inner animal raised his head, and the hunt was on. I chased after her.

She was running hard and weaving in and out of trees. I caught her looking over her shoulder. Even in the dim light, I could see elation mixed with a bit of fear and desire. She was loving it, and we hadn't even gotten to the good parts yet.

"Run little Dove, but you won't get away. This dragon is having you in every way."

She cried out as she ducked around a deadfall. I increased my speed. It was time to catch her and see how much of a fight she put up. As I sped up, I felt a drop of water hit me. Looking up, a few more hit my face. Shit, it was raining.

I made sure to growl, grunt, howl, and even roar as I gave chase even harder. I was gaining on her, and I could tell she was trying to find a place to hide, but she was too late. I ran faster and was soon right behind her. She shrieked when she saw me. She was busy looking back at me and didn't see the small branch on the ground in front of her. As she tripped on it and fell, I reached out and wrapped her in my arms, preventing her from hitting the ground and hurting herself. She screamed as I did.

I lifted her off the ground. She was struggling to get loose but I had her arms pinned. Her legs though were free, and she kicked like a mule. I widen my stance to get my legs out of her way. Despite that, she still scored a couple of times and they hurt. I nipped the back of her neck with my teeth. She threw back her head to catch me in the face, but I dodged it.

"Let go," she yelled. My Dove got into the role perfectly.

"No, you're mine now. I can and will do anything I want with you."

"What do you want, damn you?"

"I want to eat your pussy until you scream and come in my mouth. Then I want to sink my cock into your tight, hot pussy and fuck you until we both come. Hell, I even want that tight asshole of yours. I want my seed in every hole. And when you beg me to stop, I'll give you more. I want to consume you," I told her.

Talking about it and having her struggle in my arms had me dripping. My cock was so damn hard it hurt. I pressed it hard into her back. She whimpered before she answered me.

"If that's what you want, then you'll have to make me give it to you. I'll fight. I only want the strongest dragon as my mate," she hissed.

Fuck, she'd been studying on the side. She'd never said this to me before, but God did it turn me on even more.

"Then fight, Dove."

Next thing I knew, her nails bit into my forearms and she scratched them hard. Hard enough to almost draw blood. I hissed. Then she pinched me harder. I laughed.

"You'll have to do better than that, my love."

"Oh, I will," she said right before she bowed her body away from mine, then slammed it back. She caught my cock between us. Thankfully, it was lying against my stomach, but it still hurt like hell, especially when she pinched my balls. I couldn't help but cry out, and my arms automatically loosened to let go, so I could cup myself. That's what the little witch wanted. She wiggled like a slippery eel, and next thing I knew she was out of my arms and running again.

I had to catch my breath and let the pain recede a moment or two, before I took off after her. I let out a roar. She squealed and tried to run faster, but I had been holding back before. Not now. I chased her hard. She didn't get far before I caught her. I pinned her to a tree with her facing away from me. I knew the bark was biting into her skin. She whimpered. I bit her shoulder then licked it.

Pressing into her, I wedged my cock between her ass cheeks and rubbed it hard up and down her slick folds. Fuck, she was so wet. The rain was coming down harder, too. My hands gripped her tits and I squeezed them. "I should shove my cock in you right now. I bet you'd take it all wouldn't you?"

"No, I don't want it," she yelled. She was trying to press away from the tree, but I held her fast.

Moving my hips, I pressed the head to her tight asshole. She froze. We'd played with fingers and even small toys, but I hadn't truly fucked her ass. We'd been building up to it. I'd never just take her like that, but I would threaten her.

"What if I take this ass?"

She shuddered. I pushed slightly, but not enough to breach her. I waited to hear her use her safe words. I hadn't done this to her before. I hoped it wasn't going too far. And that she knew I would never actually do it. "Remember your words," I whispered.

She didn't utter either of them. Instead, she wiggled against me. I groaned at the sensation. I closed my eyes for a second. She caught me off guard when I did. I jerked as her teeth bit into my arm. Despite the pain, I held on and swung her around, taking her to the ground. I eased back, so she could try to get away. My excitement was so goddamn high I was ready to burst. I planned to play longer, but she had me on the edge.

She flipped onto her back, and then somehow rolled me so she was on top. She went on the attack. She scratched and bit, but in between, she licked and sucked, too. Not wanting her to have the upper hand, I rolled her under me again, and quickly slid down to pry her thighs apart. I didn't wait to attack her soaked pussy with my mouth and fingers. She screamed and tugged on my hair, but I didn't stop.

I ate her like a hungry animal with his first meal in weeks. She beat on my upper back and shoulders, but I kept going. The taste of her and her scent drove me even wilder. I need her to come, so I could fuck her. The rain hitting my back only added to the sensory overload. Thankfully, it was warm rain.

Sucking her clit then nibbling on it as I finger fucked her and licked all over her folds made her cream even more. After a few minutes of that, I could tell she was ready to blow, so I bit down on her clit and growled as I thrashed it with the tip of my tongue. She screamed long and loud as she came shaking. She flooded my mouth with her sweetness, and I gladly lapped up every bit of it.

I let her stop shaking, barely, before I was up and I turned her over onto her stomach. She whimpered. Mud coated her back. You might think it was a turn off, but it wasn't. Grabbing her hips, I jerked her to her knees. I ran my hands up her sides and over her back. It was slick from the rain and mud. I massaged the rain and mud over her skin. I leaned over her back, blanketing her.

I kneeled on one knee, while the other leg was bent with my foot on the ground. I raked my teeth down the side of her throat and told her hoarsely, "You lose. Submit. Give me my pussy. Let your mate mount you."

She didn't give it to me immediately. She made me wait for her answer, ramping up my urge more. Finally, after what felt like forever she nodded. "I'm yours, Dragon. Take me. Fill me with your seed."

I didn't say a word before I thrust my cock into her in one hard stroke. She cried out and threw back her head. I used my hands on her hips to move her back and forth on my cock. Jesus, she was tighter than I remembered. She was hugging me like a fucking glove. She was so warm and wet. My fingers were biting into her hips. I hoped I wouldn't leave too many bruises. I tried to ease up.

"Harder," came her broken plea when I did.

I gave her what she wanted. The sound of our skin slapping together all wet and my balls hitting her folds was heaven. I couldn't stop my grunts and growls. She was whimpering and moaning, as she slammed back to meet my thrusts. It was hard, raw, and almost brutal, but at the same time it was amazing and fucking unreal. Never had I felt this or been this wild for anyone.

Wanting to change position, I reached up and grabbed her braid. I used it to pull her head back, which bowed her back, then it had her lifting toward me. Once her back was flush to my chest, I moved her so she rode me while I sat back on my heels. Holding her hair in one fist, I wrapped the other around her throat and tightened it just enough to make it slightly harder for her to breathe. I knew she liked it because she grew wetter.

"That's it. Come for me, Dove. Your dragon needs you to milk his cock. I need to come. Harder," I panted.

She sped up riding me and I felt my balls tightening and the tingles were rushing up from my feet. "Touch yourself," I ordered.

She did as I asked, and it only took a few strokes over her engorged clit to make her detonate. She sobbed and screamed my name as she came. She squeezed me so tightly, I thought for a moment she was gonna cut my cock in half. I made it two more strokes then I came. You'd think after jacking off in the house, I wouldn't have much of a load, but I did. I grunted and roared as I pumped her full. As I did, the need to have her pregnant hit me again. This was it. She was stopping the birth control so I could breed her. I didn't care what I had to do to convince her.

As we came down from our incredible highs, we slumped to the ground. I rolled off her, so I wouldn't hurt her. She crawled on top of me, curled up like a kitten, and laid her head on my chest. "That was incredible, Misha. Oh God, we'll never top that," she whispered.

"Challenge accepted, my love," I told her as I chuckled. She moaned.

# Tajah: Chapter 20

Mikhail helped me back to the house eventually, after we recovered enough to move. That whole experience had been mind-blowing. We had to do it again and soon. I was worried about the mess we'd drag into the house from the rain and mud, but he told me not to worry. Thankfully, the house was mostly hardwood and tile flooring. The only rugs were the area one in the living room and one in the master bedroom, which we avoided stepping on. Right before we got to the bedroom, he ordered me to close my eyes. I was too mellow to fight him or ask why. He swept me up in his arms, then took me to the bathroom. He sat down on the edge of the large soaking tub and held me on his lap as he started the water running in it.

As it filled, he placed tender kisses all over my face and mouth. "I love you so damn much, Tajah. I don't want you to ever doubt that or truly fear me."

I straightened to look at him closer. "Misha, I know you do and I don't doubt it. I don't fear you either. What's wrong?"

"I know things got a bit wild out there. I hope you know I would've never taken your ass like I insinuated. If you never want that, I won't push it. I only said it to up the fight."

"I know that and it did do that for sure, but I have to admit, after the playing we've done, I'm curious. I just don't know if I can handle something the size of you. It'll hurt."

"I won't lie and say it won't, but like what we've already done. The pain does turn to pleasure, or it does for most, so I've heard. Like I said, we don't have to ever do it. I just wanted to be sure you knew I wouldn't hurt you like that."

"Baby, I know you won't." I gave him a long tender kiss.

By the time we parted, the tub was full. He shut it off then stood and carried me to the shower. I was confused for a moment, then I realized he meant to rinse off the mud in there and then we'd soak in the tub. It didn't take long to get the water hot then we got under the spray. It felt good to get the mud off. He made sure to thoroughly rinse me then himself. Once he was satisfied, he shut it off and then carried me to the tub. I knew better than to tell him I could walk. He was in aftercare mode.

The hot water felt amazing as we sank into it. I groaned as I lay back against his chest. He had my shower gel, a loofah, along with my shampoo and conditioner. He'd taken out my braid in the shower, so he could rinse out the mud. He tenderly washed then conditioned my hair before wringing it out and securing it in a messy bun on top of my head. From there he washed me down to my toes. When he washed between my legs, I couldn't help but get turned on. He fondled and teased me.

"You're being naughty. If you keep that up, I'll be attacking you," I warned him.

He laughed. "That's the idea. Surely you don't think I'm done with you yet. Oh no, I have more in store for you, Dove. Rest, you're gonna need it."

My nipples peaked into hard nubs. Not wanting him to feel unloved. When he was done with me, I insisted on washing him just like he had me. I was slowly getting him to accept I had as much need to care for him as he did for me. I got the impression his past lovers had only taken. That wasn't how I was made.

By the time we were both clean, we were thoroughly aroused again. I felt his hard cock pressing into my lower back. My nipples were still hard and my pussy slick. "I think it's time to get out of here," I told him. His smirk told me he knew what I wanted. Just to be sure, as he dried me off, I made sure to stroke his cock several times.

"Fuck, I wanted to take my time, but you're pushing it," he muttered.

"Good. Come to bed and I'll push it more."

He led me into the bedroom and over to bed. I saw what he'd wanted to hide from me when we entered. There were candles scattered all around, which gave the room such a romantic glow. It was dark now, so it really showed off the work he'd done. There were things on the nightstand, but he had me to the bed too fast to see them all. Whatever they were, I was excited. I pushed him down first, then I crawled on it and between his legs. He widened them automatically for me.

His cock was standing tall, and the head gleamed with precum. I grasped the base and lowered my head to swirl my tongue around it. I hummed at his taste as he groaned. I lifted up and teased him. "More? Or should I stop?"

His growl made me chuckle, as he grabbed my bun and forced my head down. I gladly opened wide and took him after a cursory bit of resistance. I wanted him to fuck my face. It excited the hell out of me when he did it. I loved to see him lose control and take me anyway he wanted, like a beast. The more my eyes watered as I took him deeper and I gagged, the wetter I became. The bite of his fingers on my scalp and his guttural words made it even worse.

"Suck it. That's it. You love my cock don't you? Be a good girl and do it."

I tried to nod as I hummed in agreement.

"Fuck, I'm close already. Either move or you're swallowing," he warned me.

I stayed where I was and massaged his tight sac. I was eager for the taste of his cum, which was salty and slightly sweet to me. It only took him a minute or two to orgasm. He shouted my name as he gave me his cum, which I swallowed just as eagerly as he ate my pussy earlier. I was so turned on, I couldn't stop from touching myself. I rubbed my clit hard then up and down my folds. I was so into it and sucking him dry, that I didn't notice that he had seen what I was doing. Suddenly, I was pulled off him and tossed on my back. As I yelped in surprise, he crouched over me. His eyes were burning.

"That's my job. Hands off. You wanna come, I'll make you come."

I nodded up at him. I figured I was about to get eaten again, which I didn't mind at all, only I was wrong. Instead, he stood up and went to the nightstand. I raised up on my elbows and my eyes widened when I saw what he had. I'd never seen it before. He came back to me and held it up. It looked like a dildo only it wasn't shaped exactly like any I'd seen or used. It was black, bumpy, and rough all over.

He smirked at me as he asked, "Do you know what this is?"

"No."

"This is a dragon's cock. You say I'm your dragon, so I think it's only fair you get to feel what it's like to be fucked by one. This is as close as I can get you to that."

I moaned as I imagined what it would feel like. The rough texture would feel so good inside me. "Yes, God, yes, please," I pleaded.

He chuckled darkly, then I watched him put some lube on it. "Just in case. I don't want it to hurt you, only to make you wild. Now spread those legs and let me see you," he ordered.

He didn't need to tell me twice. I did it, then lay there with my heart pounding. He didn't give it to me though. Instead he lowered his head and licked me. I whimpered. He kept going so I went with it. I was in the zone and starting to climb toward an orgasm in no time. It was while I was there and had my eyes closed, that he made his move. I felt a hard probe at my entrance, then he was sinking it into me in a slow constant push.

The rough texture did things to my pussy I'd never felt before. I cried out as it rubbed over my G-spot. As soon as he had it all inside me, he pulled it back and thrust again. This time he did it faster and just a bit harder. I moaned. Opening my eyes, I had to watch him.

His eyes were glued to my pussy as he fucked me. The desire on his face was apparent. "Fuck Tajah, watching your pretty pussy take this makes me wish it was mine. God, I want to fuck you with mine. Son of a bitch, you're close aren't you?"

"Yes," I moaned, swiveling my hips, and thrusting back to meet his next stroke.

"Yeah, ride that dragon cock. Come for me," he muttered.

I did and in no time I was coming in a gush. I came so hard I felt faint and my throat hurt from screaming. If I thought once I was done he'd stop, I found out quickly I was wrong. He kept going and turned me into a mindless nymphomaniac. As I came again minutes later, I knew I needed him, not a toy, no matter how wonderful it was, and I knew exactly how I wanted him. Grabbing his hand to stop his thrusts, I told him, "I need you."

He grinned as he stroked his hard again cock. "Gladly," he said as he removed the dildo. I whimpered at the loss. However, before he could thrust himself inside me, I stopped him.

"I want you to take my ass, Misha. Do what you wanted to do out in the woods. Fuck my ass with your big cock." I was still slightly apprehensive, but my desire was greater.

He froze and gave me an incredulous look. "Baby, you're excited, I know but no, not that, not now."

"Yes, I'm excited and I want you to do it. I wanna know. Please, try it. God, I'm burning up. Please fuck me. Imagine how tight it is. I bet you'll blow so hard," I taunted him.

His expression was already half wild. I knew it wouldn't take much to push him over the edge and into his beast mood. The growl he let out told me he was there, so I pushed a tad more. "Master Misha, please fuck my tight virgin ass."

I could barely understand him as he growled, "Are you sure?"

"Yes!" I screamed.

I was tugging on my nipples hard and biting my lip. I felt crazy. The next thing I knew, I was yanked to the edge of the bed, then flipped onto my belly. I heard the snap of the lube lid and then a few seconds later slick fingers ran around my hole and then pressed inside. I sighed and relaxed. We'd done this enough I knew what to do. He coated me inside thoroughly then pulled out. I looked over my shoulder to find him applying more all over his cock. I lifted my ass and wiggled it. He roared as he fell on me.

Despite how crazed he seemed, he didn't just ram it inside. He pressed the head to my opening then slowly pushed. He took his time despite how avidly I knew he wanted me. It burned and hurt much worse than his fingers or the small toys we'd used before, but along with pain and burning, there was underlying pleasure, so I didn't ask him to stop. Not to say I didn't hiss or moan several times. Each time I did, he'd ask the same thing and I'd reply the same.

"Are you okay? Keep going? I can stop."

"Yes, I'm okay. Please don't stop."

He would groan then press deeper. When he finally got all the way inside, he paused and let me adjust. The pain eased after a minute or so. The first couple of strokes were still more painful than not when he started back up but then as he kept going, it turned to more and more bliss. As it did, I began to push back to meet his strokes. Eventually I told him, "Harder. I need it harder."

"Goddamn, you're so damn tight. Jesus Christ," he uttered hoarsely, before he gave me more. The burning and pain was morphing into something I wanted more of.

"Mmm, that's it. Rut that ass and fill me up with your cum, Master Misha," I whimpered.

That snapped his last restraint, and he began to pound my ass as he grunted and growled. A wave of deep bliss started in my toes, and then ran up my whole body until it centered in my core, and I came screaming and crying. I clamped down on him and he swore.

"Motherfucker!" He shouted, then he came and pumped his seed deep in my ass. He jerked for a long time before he stopped. By the time he did, I was limp. I could barely keep my eyes open. As I slipped off, he pulled out and kissed me.

"You're so fucking incredible. Thank you," he whispered. All I could do was smile.

☘☘☘

I couldn't breathe. I coughed to clear my throat but it got worse. I tried again, and that's when it registered. I smelled smoke, and it was clogging my airway. I struggled to wake up. As I got closer to consciousness, I panicked. The house was on fire! I rolled over and felt for Mikhail. My hand landed on his chest. He wasn't moving. I shook him hard.

"Misha!" I tried to yell. It came out hoarse. I tried again. "Misha, wake up!"

I sighed in relief when I felt him jerk. Suddenly, he was sitting up coughing. "What the fuck?" he rasped out.

His hands reached over and grabbed me. I was hauled off the bed and into his arms. He frantically pulled shorts and a top from my bag. As I struggled to get them on, he pulled on shorts then helped me. It was getting harder to breathe and see. When I was dressed, I tried to tell him I could walk, but I couldn't seem to talk. I felt so weak, and my head was spinning. Somehow, I don't know how, he got me to the other side of the house. This took us closer to the flames and smoke, but also closer to the doors to the outside. I couldn't even see a foot in front of us. Oh my God, we were gonna die!

I knew I was crying, but I couldn't stop. I wasn't ready to die. There was so much I still wanted to do. And I'd just found the love of my life. He sat me down on my feet and then I heard a crash and breaking glass. The flames grew higher. I was lifted again, and abruptly I was out in the cool, clean air. I sucked it in despite it making me cough harder. I did it over and over. Mikhail got me off the back deck and to the yard. We both fell to our knees and hacked and sputtered. I don't know how long we kneeled there before we began to look around us.

The house was half engulfed in orange flames. His beautiful house was being destroyed. In the distance, I thought I heard sirens, but that surely wasn't possible. The nearest neighbor was miles away, and it was the middle of the night. They would be in bed. I was staring at the house when I heard him swear.

"Motherfucker," he growled, and then he was up and running. I stumbled to my feet and went after him. He was way faster than me, but as we ran, I saw what looked like a figure running ahead of him. Mikhail was a determined man. Somehow he ran faster and soon he was on top of the person taking them to the ground. I heard a shriek and I froze in confusion. It sounded like a woman, not a man who had cried out. I scrambled the remaining distance and came up beside him. He was struggling with someone.

"Stop it or I'll break your fucking neck," he snarled. The person froze. Only a fool would think he was kidding.

As he eased back, the moon allowed me to see the person he was holding down. I stood there stunned. I couldn't believe my eyes. Lying there, staring up at us with a look of hate on her face, was Laura from the club. Mikhail's employee. What the hell?

"What the hell did you do? Why?" he shouted at her.

"Hey, is everyone out?" a man's voice asked from behind us. Mikhail whipped his head around to look at him.

"Who're you?"

"I'm your neighbor, Preston, from down the road. I was coming home from a night out with friends, and I saw the glow of the flames in the sky. I called the fire department. I'm sorry I didn't get here sooner. Are any of you hurt? Why are you sitting on that woman?"

"We're fine, no thanks to her. She set the damn fire. I caught her running. Goddamn it, Laura, why?"

"You know her?" Preston asked in amazement.

"Yeah, she works for me, or she did. What the hell are you doing here?" He asked her, but she remained silent.

The sirens were getting closer. I came to stand next to Mikhail. "Laura, why would you do this?" I asked.

She gave me what could only be described as a hate-filled look. Her lip curled up and she spewed bile at me. "You stole him, whore! It's all your fault. He was supposed to be mine. You ruined everything. Why couldn't you just leave? They should've done their job and shut down the club so you'd go. He would've forgotten about you, but you did something to him. I'm the woman for him. I waited and waited. Tessa gave him up. I love him. I should be in his home, not you. I hate you. Die bitch!" She screamed. I stumbled back.

Her crazy thoughts made an odd sense. From what she said, I knew we'd found who was calling in the complaints about the club. Although, her other logic on Mikhail wanting her if I was gone made no sense. If she wanted him, why light the house on fire with him in it? And how did she know about it? According to him at dinner, no one had been here other than Reuben when he bought it.

"You set the house on fire with him in it! How can you say you love him if you'd do that? And how did you know about this place?" I shouted at her.

She was back to fighting, and it was obvious she wanted to get to me. He pressed her hard to the ground. Preston was standing there taking it all in.

"I do love him, but if I can't have him, no one can. I heard him tell Reuben he was going away with you. That it was someplace special. I followed you. How could you do that to me? I saw you in the woods." The last part she aimed at him.

I felt sick to my stomach at the thought of her watching our private, intimate moments in the woods. It wasn't because someone had seen us, it was because it was her and due to her obvious obsession with him. I had to turn so I could throw up.

"Tajah, baby, sit down. Are you okay?"

All I could do was nod. The sirens sounded right outside the house. Preston took off toward the front. I hoped he was going to tell them we were over here, but who knew? Images of the two of us in the woods kept filtering through my head. I had no idea how long it was before a couple of sheriff deputies came up to us. They were frowning. I vaguely noticed firefighters working on the fire, but it was a total loss. I don't know why they were even bothering.

"Sir, your neighbor said this woman started the fire. Tell us what happened, but first you need to let go of her."

"I'll let go once you secure her. Yes, she set it. I think she's crazy. We woke up to smoke and flames." he explained. I let him tell them the whole story as I sat there in a daze, shivering.

I didn't tune back in until a warm blanket was wrapped around me. I glanced up to find Mikhail crouching beside me with a concerned expression on his face. I looked past him to find Laura was no longer there and neither were the cops. Where did she go? I tried to scramble to my feet, but he wouldn't let me.

"Where is she?" I asked in a panic.

"Shh, everything is alright. She's in the cop car. They arrested her. Dove, you're scaring me. You totally checked out on me. Let the paramedics check you out." I let him direct me to them, and they listened to my lungs and put some oxygen on me. He seemed to be doing better than me. I couldn't seem to shake the altered sensations I was feeling.

Despite Mikhail insisting I needed to go to the hospital, they didn't feel I needed to. "But she's not acting right, and she vomited not long ago," he protested.

I grabbed his hand. He was beginning to get loud. "Honey, I'm fine. It was just a shock. I don't need to see a doctor. They need to check you over."

"I'm fine."

"Maybe but I won't feel better unless I know you're okay. Please."

He gave in when he heard that. It was a quick assessment before they declared him good to go. Just as they gave us both medical clearances, the sheriff who did the talking earlier came back over to us.

"I hate to add to your already crappy night, but we're gonna need both of you to come to the station and make an official statement. Ms. Phillips will be processed there. You can ride in the other squad car. I assume you need to call someone. If you want, you can use my phone." he handed his cell to Mikhail.

"Thank you Sheriff Noble, I appreciate it. We'll come with you as soon as I make my call. Babe, do you want to call your mom?"

"No, she'll freak out if I do, especially in the middle of the night. I'll call her later. Who're you calling?"

"I think it should be Reub. He can get us some clothes from the apartment and bring some other stuff. Plus, he probably hasn't gone to bed for the night. It's only," he glanced at the phone, "two-thirty in the morning. If you're sure about your mom, let me call him."

I nodded. He punched in the number then hit the call button. After he did, he drew me against him and rubbed soothingly up and down my arm. I was kinda feeling numb at the moment. I listened as he filled Reuben in on what happened and what we needed. I could clearly hear Reub swearing without being on speaker. The call lasted about five minutes. Mikhail hung up after he was assured Reuben would be at the sheriff's station in Columbia as soon as possible. It was still about an hour drive from Lustz to Columbia. After he hung up, he placed a second call.

"Otto, it's Mikhail Ivanova. Sorry for calling so late, but I believe I have a need for you. I need you to meet me at the Maury County Sheriff's office in Columbia. One of my employees committed arson on my home in Culleoka, while me and my girlfriend were sleeping inside. She's been arrested, but I want legal representation there to make sure they don't let her out. I think she's crazy to be honest. I'll explain everything when you get there."

He listened for a couple of minutes, nodding as he did. Finally, he spoke again. "We're both fine, thank God, but the house is a total loss, and she did it because of my girlfriend. Luckily for us, a neighbor called the fire department and my woman woke up in time to wake me and we got out. I appreciate it. See you then." This time when he hung up he handed it back to Sheriff Noble, who'd stayed there unabashedly listening.

"Let's head there if you're ready," Noble said kindly.

I didn't know of a reason to hang around. Holding me close, Mikhail took me toward the front of the house where the cars were. When we got close to them, I heard muffled screaming and thumping sounds. I looked around and that's when I saw Laura in the back of a squad car. She was glaring at me and screaming as she was kicking the door from the inside. The other sheriff went over and jerked the door open and said something to her. She ignored him as she tried to get out despite the fact she had her arms cuffed behind her. I could hear what she was saying then.

"I'll kill you, bitch! He'll be mine. You wait and see."

The sheriff had to push her back in and slam the door fast. Mihail hurried me to the other one, and we got in the back. It made me nervous to be sitting back there with the wire separating us from the sheriff when he got in. So this was what a criminal saw, I mused. I stared out the window at the darkness, as we were driven to the station. I was exhausted, and it looked like this night was far from over.

I wasn't wrong. It was hours later after tons of questions, plus the blur of meeting the lawyer, Otto Devine, and having Reuben show up with our things and his reaction to all of it. By the time we left with Reuben, who took us home, the sun was up and I could barely keep my eyes open. I dropped off to sleep as he sped toward Nashville and the two of them talked softly. Mikhail sat in the backseat, so he could hold me. It was like he couldn't stand to let go of me. I clung to him. I'd almost lost him. I held him tighter. He kissed my forehead. "I've got you," he whispered softly. I sighed and closed my eyes.

# Mikhail: Epilogue- One Month Later

It had been a helluva month for us since the fire. However, despite it, most of it hadn't been terrible. Sure, the part where we lost the house due to a crazy woman was bad. It wasn't until she was fully questioned by the police, then evaluated by a court-appointed psychiatrist, that the extent of Laura's delusions and obsession were discovered.

She had truly started it as a way to get rid of her competition. In her mind, she'd failed to lure me away from Tajah, and since she hadn't, she would rather I be dead than with someone other than her. Apparently, she'd been obsessed with me for a long time, but never cracked or whatever, until I broke it off with Tessa and didn't end up with her.

The night of the fire, she'd followed us from Lustz and spied on us. She waited until she was sure we were deeply asleep, then started the fire at the front of the house, using gasoline she had in her trunk. She'd gone as far as to block the back door so it couldn't be opened. That's why I had to use a stool to smash out the glass in the French doors, then kick out the wooden framing when it wouldn't open for me. Every time I thought of how close I came to losing Tajah, I would get nauseous.

Laura had been the one making the complaints and we were right to be suspicious of the second one who came, the electrical guy. He knew she was the one to file the complaint. He was a guy who lived in her apartment complex, who was interested in her. She used him to get information by acting like her boss, me, was shady. A little flirting on her part, and he'd been more than happy to "help" her. He had no idea she was crazy and wanted me. He'd been appalled when confronted with evidence of it. I doubted he'd ever let a woman use him like that again.

We finally settled the matter based on Otto's suggestion. If she pled guilty due to insanity, she would avoid prison for arson and attempted murder charges, but she'd have to spend an extensive amount of time in a locked psychiatric facility receiving treatment. They were estimating she could be there for years. As long as she didn't get out and come after us or anyone else again, we were satisfied. She was sick and needed help. Prison wouldn't give her that. The remaining staff at Lustz were recovering from finding out what one of their peers did. They were still amazed none of them knew she was unbalanced. We'd hired a replacement for Laura who I thought would work out well.

An additional bright spot in my opinion and Tajah's was Tessa. She was no longer around Lustz to cause issues for anyone, let alone us. After her tantrum with Sinner and Sylvia, she stayed away for a few weeks, then canceled her membership. I heard through the gossips who knew about not only my club but the others that she'd been going to one of the lesser clubs. I wished her and them well. I only hoped she knew what she was doing.

Our friends and family were appalled when they heard what happened. Tamara had been hysterical, and it took a couple of weeks to get her to stop calling Tajah several times a day to check on us. Matvey offered to have Laura taken care of, but I passed up on the offer. He agreed to not do it as long as Tajah and I came to his birthday party next month. We happily agreed. I informed him he didn't need to use that to get us to come. He laughed.

Cady had sorta come around when she heard what happened. At least she was back to talking to Tajah, and she and I had more than a few talks and she had been to our apartment a few times. She apologized for reacting the way she did, and I accepted it. However, she still wasn't confessing what had set her off that night. Tajah was convinced she would tell her. I wasn't sure. Although, it might be gotten out of her by Hoss. He'd taken an interest in her and it didn't appear to be waning, despite her ignoring and rebuffing his attempts. I was enjoying watching him and her spar. I'd never seen him act like this around a woman, ever. I couldn't wait to see how it turned out.

On the really positive side of things, with the destruction of the house, it left the property a clean slate once I had the burned remains removed. We'd talked about what I brought up to her that evening before the fire, about my desire to move there with her. I was worried she'd be against it after the fire, but she surprised me. She grew excited at the prospect, and we were in the process of having a new house designed.

Once it was finished, which wouldn't be too long, we'd get our builder going on it. I'd asked Tank, Payne's club brother who oversaw the club's construction company, AW Construction, if they would be willing to do it. I knew they tried to stick close to home, but I knew they did quality work and I trusted them. He assured me he could make it happen.

I sighed in relief as I crawled into bed with my dove. Being able to go to bed with her every night and to wake up to her every morning made me wish I'd met her years ago. We could've been together for ages. Although she assured me it happened when it was meant to. If we had met years ago, who knows if we would've both been ready for each other. I was convinced that I would never settle down back then, and she'd been raw from her ex-husband's betrayal, so maybe she was right.

I smiled when she gave me a sweet smile and laid her head on my chest. Her hand came up to rest on my stomach. My greatest joy this past month shined up at me. On her left ring finger was the engagement ring I gave her a week ago. After surviving what we did, I didn't want to wait any longer than I had to before making her my wife. Luckily, she said yes, so I didn't have to get down on my knees and beg. I would've done it, too. I picked up her hand and kissed the ring.

"You're still celebrating popping the question and me saying yes, aren't you?" she asked in an amused tone.

"Damn right I am. Do you know how humiliating it would've been to go down on my knees and have you say no and have to tell everyone," I teased her.

"I would've never done that! Stop it. You know I love you, and you've made me so happy I can't think straight. You asking me was the beautiful part. I see it as a gift. And since you did something so wonderful for me, I want to do something I hope is equally as wonderful for you. Well, for both of us. Really." She gave me an expectant look.

"Babe, you're marrying me by next year. We're building our dream home soon. Our lives are pretty damn perfect in my opinion. What could you give me that would make it better?"

She reached under her pillow and came out with something in her hand. It took a couple of moments for it to register what she held. When it did, I sat up and grabbed it away from her. I was afraid to ask, but I did anyway.

"Are you meaning what I think you're meaning?"

"If you're thinking yesterday was the last day of that packet of birth control pills, and I didn't renew it, then yes, I mean it. So Master Misha, what would you say to us practicing so we can be sure when the time is right, you can give me our first baby? Unless you've changed your mind."

My answer was a deep rumbling growl before I pounced on her. As she giggled, I kissed up her neck to her mouth. When I reached it, I paused long enough to tell her. "Your dragon is ready to play, my Dove. Prepare yourself. You'll be pregnant before the month is out."

As soon as I said it, I sealed my mouth to hers and

kissed her hungrily. I knew how we'd be spending most of our down time. She'd better get as many naps as she could.

**The End Until House of Lustz**
**Book 2: Hoss's Limits**

Printed in Great Britain
by Amazon

43176526R00215